"1 ...ur... ...ated by
the re........table and apparently tireless Stephen Jones, skillfully offers
us a particularly fine sampling of this sort of thing in the form of a
kind of two-pronged attack which combines a first-rate anthology of
short stories featuring the fearless activities of some of the most heroic
and renowned psychic sleuths who ever encountered and dispatched
the most horrid (it is impossible to avoid superlatives and still keep
the appropriate mood when one's discussing this fictional arena)
supernatural menaces ever faced, and what amounts to a brand-new
book by that dashing master of perilous pastiche, Kim Newman."
Gahan Wilson, REALMS OF FANTASY

"Dark Detectives is more than a themed collection with a spot-on non-
fiction piece to kick off with. It is a mixture of reprints and original
stories, and they have been arranged (more or less) chronologically . . .
The whole point of Dark Detectives is homage. And Stephen Jones has
managed to get the balance right."
INTERZONE

"The stellar collection includes contributions from Neil Gaiman, William
Hope Hodgson, Basil Copper and Clive Barker, as well as a riveting
eight-part novella created by Kim Newman especially for this volume."
PUBLISHERS WEEKLY

"Once again, master-editor Stephen Jones uses his phenomenal
knowledge of the field and inventive intelligence to select classics both
old and new . . . In addition to the fine content, Randy Broecker's
perfectly atmospheric interior illustrations make this
publication bliss for any book-lover."
HORRORONLINE

DARK
DETECTIVES

AN ANTHOLOGY OF
SUPERNATURAL MYSTERIES

Edited by STEPHEN JONES

Illustrated by RANDY BROECKER

TITAN BOOKS

Dark Detectives: An Anthology of Supernatural Mysteries
Print edition ISBN: 9781783291281
E-book edition ISBN: 9781783291298

Published by Titan Books
A division of Titan Publishing Group Ltd
144 Southwark Street, London SE1 0UP

First Titan Books edition: March 2015

2 4 6 8 10 9 7 5 3 1

For

MR. MYCROFT AND MR. MORAN
who published my kind of detective fiction.

Falkirk Council	
Askews & Holts	2015
AF	£8.99

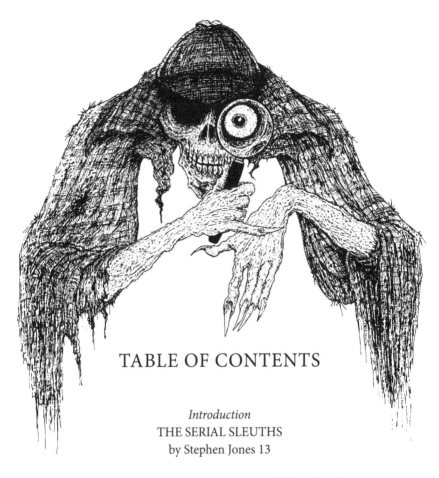

TABLE OF CONTENTS

ILLVSTRATION

Introduction

THE SERIAL SLEUTHS

PSYCHIC DETECTIVES. PHANTOM Fighters. Ghostbusters. Call them what you will; for more than 170 years these fictional sleuths have been investigating the strange, the bizarre and the horrific while protecting the world from the forces of darkness and evil.

It is generally accepted that the modern detective story began with Edgar Allan Poe's 'The Murders in the Rue Morgue' (1841), in which the author introduced French detective C. Auguste Dupin, who solves a grotesque murder through logical deduction. Poe returned to the character twice more, in 'The Mystery of Marie Rogêt' (1842) and 'The Purloined Letter' (1844).

Michael Harrison continued the character's exploits in a series of seven stories in *Ellery Queen's Mystery Magazine* in the 1960s. These were eventually collected by August Derleth through his Mycroft & Moran imprint as *The Exploits of Chavalier Dupin* (1968). An expanded edition that included a further five tales appeared in Britain as *Murder in the Rue Royale* in 1972.

George Egon Hatvary used Dupin to investigate the death of his creator in the 1997 novel *The Murder of Edgar Allan Poe*, while a search for the detective himself was the basis of Matthew Pearl's *The Poe Shadow* (2006).

The character was also featured in the first two issues of Alan Moore's acclaimed comic book series *The League of Extraordinary*

Gentlemen (1999). In 2013 he was revived by author Reggie Oliver to track down a serial killer at the Paris Exhibition in 'The Green Hour' (in *Psycho-Mania!*), and such contributors as Mike Carey, Joe R. Lansdale, Lisa Tuttle and Stephen Volk for the anthology *Beyond Rue Morgue: Further Tales of Edgar Allan Poe's 1st Detective*, edited by Paul Kane and Charles Prepolec.

Although there is no cast known for the 1914 short film version of *Murders in the Rue Morgue*, and the character does not appear in the 1932, 1954 or 1971 adaptations, George C. Scott played the wily detective in a 1986 TV movie. Edward Woodward portrayed Dupin in a 1968 BBC version of the story, as did Daniel Gélin in a 1973 French TV adaptation.

In the early 1940s, Universal Pictures may have briefly considered a series of films featuring Patric Knowles as detective Dr. Paul Dupin, but only *The Mystery of Marie Roget* (aka *Phantom of Paris*, 1942) was ever made. Joseph Cotten starred as a character named Dupin, but turned out to be someone else entirely, in the 1951 movie *The Man with a Cloak*, based on a story by John Dickson Carr.

It was C. Auguste Dupin's analytical mind that most influenced Arthur Conan Doyle when he created Sherlock Holmes for 'A Study in Scarlet', first published in *Beeton's Christmas Annual of 1887*. However, when Dr. John Watson compares Holmes to Dupin in that debut story, the Great Detective flatly dismisses Poe's character as "a very inferior fellow".

Within four years the Holmes stories had become incredibly popular as a result of their serialisation in *The Strand* magazine, and the eccentric consulting detective and his loyal friend and colleague Dr. Watson not only had brushes with the supernatural in the classic novel *The Hound of the Baskervilles* (1901–1902) and such later stories as 'The Adventure of the Creeping Man' (1923) and 'The Adventure of the Sussex Vampire' (1924), but Doyle also created a celebrated formula from which most subsequent psychic sleuths (and their assistants) would be moulded.

On screen, Holmes has of course been portrayed by numerous actors over the years, and many liberties have been taken with the stories, especially when it comes to implications of horror and the supernatural. Some of the more notable instances include *The Hound of the Baskervilles* (1939) and *The Scarlet Claw* (1944), both with Basil Rathbone; Hammer Films' *The Hound of the Baskervilles* (1959) with Peter Cushing; *A Study in Terror* (1965) with John Neville; *The Last Vampyre* (1993) with Jeremy Brett, and *The Case of the Whitechapel Vampire* (2002), with Matt Frewer, to name only a few.

One of the earliest short stories featuring a supernatural sleuth appeared in the Christmas 1866 issue of the *London Journal*: 'The Ghost Detective' was written by Mark Lemon, the founder and first editor of the satirical magazine *Punch*. J. Sheridan Le Fanu created the German "physician of the mind" Dr. Martin Hesselius, an expert on psychic or physical affliction, to introduce the stories in *In a Glass Darkly* (1872), while M.P. Shiel's decadent Russian investigator uses logic to solve crimes without leaving his Gothic castle in *Prince Zaleski* (1895).

The exploits of ghost-hunter Mr. John Bell, the Master of Mysteries, first appeared in *Cassell's Family Magazine* during 1897 before being collected the following year in *A Master of Mysteries* by L.T. Meade and Robert Eustace. Although mother and son Kate and Hesketh Prichard began writing their series of stories about Flaxman Low in 1896, they didn't see print in *Pearsons Magazine* until two years later, and then under the byline "E. and H. Heron". "Flaxman Low" was supposedly an alias for a leading psychologist of the day who investigated genuine cases of the supernatural. Twelve stories were published in *Pearsons* between 1898 and 1899, including 'The Story of Baelbrow', in which the occult investigator battles a living mummy. Collected in 1899 simply as *Ghosts*, these dozen stories were reissued by The Ghost Story Press in 1993 as *Flaxman Low, Psychic Detective* and Ash-Tree Press in 2003 as *The Experiences of Flaxman Low*.

Between 1830 and 1837, Blackwood's *Edinburgh Magazine* published a series entitled 'Passages from the Diary of a Late Physician', in which the anonymous doctor-narrator sometimes encounters physical and psychological maladies that border on the bizarre. When the publisher was forced to go to court to protect his copyright, the uncredited author of this successful series was revealed as Samuel Warren.

Arthur Machen's Dyson first delved into the supernatural in

'The Innermost Light' (1894), before the character turned up in the 1895 story cycle *The Three Impostors* and again in 'The Shining Pyramid' (1925). Although best remembered for *The King in Yellow* (1895), Robert W. Chambers also created Westrel Keen, who uses scientific principals to locate missing persons, for a series of stories that appeared in *The Idler* in 1906. They were collected under their generic title the same year as *The Tracer of Lost Persons*.

In 1908 Algernon Blackwood's collection *John Silence* was published and, due to an extensive advertising campaign mounted by the publisher, quickly became a bestseller. Blackwood based the case files of Dr. Silence, Physician Extraordinary, on his own experiences travelling through Europe at the beginning of the 20th century.

These were usually chronicled by Silence's associate Mr. Hubbard, and among the best-known tales are 'Ancient Sorceries', 'A Psychical Invasion' and the werewolf story, 'The Camp of the Dog'. Despite the book's phenomenal success, Blackwood only published one other John Silence story—'A Victim of Higher Space' appeared in the December 1914 edition of *The Occult Review*, but had been written earlier and omitted from the book because the author didn't think it was strong enough.

'Ancient Sorceries' was adapted in 1962 for an episode of the now lost Associated-Rediffusion Television series *Tales of Mystery*, featuring John Laurie as host Algernon Blackwood.

With 'The Gateway of the Monster' in *The Idler* (January, 1910), William Hope Hodgson introduced readers to Thomas Carnacki, who uses a combination of science and sorcery to overcome the supernatural. The character went on to appear in a further eight stories, including one—'The Hog' (*Weird Tales*, January 1947)—which, it has been speculated, might actually have been written or at least extensively revised by August Derleth. On TV, Donald Pleasence portrayed the character in a 1971 adaptation of 'The Horse of the Invisible'.

Along the same lines as John Silence, Australian Max Rittenberg's Dr. Xavier Wycherley, Mental Healer, is another psychic psychologist. A total of eighteen stories were published, beginning with 'The Man Who Lived Again' in the February 1911 edition of

London Magazine, and a selection was subsequently collected as *The Mind-Reader* (1913).

Twelve stories by British-born pulp writer Victor Rousseau (Avigdor Rousseau Emanuel) about Greek-born "soul specialist" Dr. Phileas Immanuel originally appeared in *Holland's Magazine* between 1913–14, and were finally collected in *The Tracer of Egos* (2007).

Clearly modelled after Sherlock Holmes, Aylmer Vance is a clairvoyant detective with consulting rooms in London's Piccadilly and a trusty literary assistant and acolyte named Dexter. Created by Alice and Claude Askew, eight stories appeared in *The Weekly Tale-Teller* in 1914 and were later collected in *Aylmer Vance: Ghost-Seer* (1998).

Six stories by Harold Begbie featuring "dreamland" investigator Andrew Latter appeared in the *London Magazine* in 1904 and were subsequently collected in *The Amazing Dreams of Andrew Latter* (2002). Slightly more interesting is antique dealer Moris Klaw, the Dream Detective, created by Sax Rohmer (Arthur Sarsfield Ward), whose most famous character—the insidious Oriental mastermind Fu Manchu—is opposed by his own Holmes and Watson team of Sir Denis Nayland Smith and Dr. Petrie.

Moris Klaw solves the cases he is consulted on by sleeping at the scene of the crime and absorbing the psychic vibrations. The first story appeared in 1913, but they were not collected in book form—as *The Dream Detective*—until seven years later. A similar talent was employed by Herman Landon's Godfrey Usher, who is consulted by the police and tunes into the vibrations at the scene of the crime in a series of stories that appeared in *Detective Story Magazine* in 1918.

During this period, psychic detectives proliferated in the cheaper weekly and monthly periodicals. These included Bertram Atkey's Mesmer Milann, Moray Dalton's Cosmo Thaw, Rose Champion de Crespigny's Norton Vyse: Psychic, Douglas Newton's Dr. Dyn in *Cassell's Magazine* and Paul Toft in *Pearson's Magazine*, and Vincent Cornier's Barnabas Hildreth, who was possibly an immortal priest of Ancient Egypt.

Probably the first female psychic sleuth was Sheila Crerar, created by Ella Scrymsour, who encountered ghosts and werewolves in a series of stories in *The Blue Magazine* in 1920. Uel (Samuel) Key's Professor Arnold Rhymer is a "specialist in spooks" who becomes involved in attempts by Germany to use psychic powers against Britain during the First World War. Five stories were collected in *The Broken Fang* (1920). Prominent ghost-hunter Elliott O'Donnell recreated his own real-life experiences in a series of stories featuring Damon Vance that appeared in *The Novel Magazine* in 1922.

Like Algernon Blackwood, Dion Fortune (Violet Mary Firth) was also a member of the Hermetic Order of the Golden Dawn, one of many new mystical movements that emerged in late Victorian times, and she later founded her own Society of the Inner Light. Using her experiences as a medium and her knowledge of occult lore as background, Fortune created psychologist Dr. Taverner, who runs a nursing home and investigates the supernatural with the aid of his associate and biographer, Dr. Rhodes. Fortune strongly implied that her hero was based on a real person, most likely MacGregor Mathers, one of the founders of the Golden Dawn. Some of these stories first appeared in *Royal Magazine* and were later collected in *The Secrets of Dr. Taverner*, published in 1926.

In 1925 Seabury Quinn created Jules de Grandin, a French detective living in New Jersey, who solves fantastic cases with the help of the county doctor, Samuel Trowbridge. Quinn, the editor of a magazine for undertakers, had been struggling for a new fiction idea and Farnsworth Wright, the editor of *Weird Tales*, had suggested he make the dapper detective the lead character in a series of stories. The first, 'The Horror on the Links', was published in the October 1925 issue of *Weird Tales*, and over the next twenty-six years Quinn wrote ninety-three stories about de Grandin and Trowbridge, with many of these tales voted into first place by the readers of the pulp magazine. The author subsequently selected and revised ten of the most popular adventures for the 1966 Mycroft & Moran collection, *The Phantom-Fighter*.

Victor Rousseau created Dr. Martinus for rival pulp *Ghost Stories*, introducing psychic researcher Martinus, a Dutchman living in New York, and his assistant Eugene Branscombe in 'Child or Demon— Which?' in the October 1926 issue. Concurrently with this series, Rousseau was also chronicling the exploits of Dr. Brodsky, Surgeon of Souls, in *Weird Tales*. Over at *Strange Tales*, adventure writer Gordon MacCreagh published two stories about Dr. Muncing—

Exorcist and his confrontation with a nasty demon. More jovial was Henry A. Hering's Mr. Psyche, of Psyche & Co.—Ghosts and Spectre Purveyors, Archipelago Street, Soho, who appeared in the first of a series of stories in the *Windsor* magazine in 1927.

A.M. (Alfred McLelland) Burrage's ten stories of occult detective Francis Chard and his assistant Torrance ran in consecutive issues of *Blue Magazine* from February 1927. These were collected in *The Occult Files of Francis Chard: Some Ghost Stories* (1996), along with two earlier stories featuring Derek Scarpe, "the man who made haunted houses his hobby", which originally appeared in the June and July 1920 issues of *Novel Magazine*.

After Conan Doyle published his last Sherlock Holmes story in 1927, young Wisconsin writer August Derleth wrote to the author asking if he could continue the series. When his request was rejected, Derleth went ahead anyway and created Solar Pons, whose Watson was Dr. Lyndon Parker. The characters were first introduced in 'The Adventure of the Black Narcissus' in *Dragnet* (February, 1929), and Derleth completed sixty-eight stories about Pons before his death in 1971. The series was subsequently continued by Basil Copper, and the Mycroft & Moran imprint was revived in 1998 to publish Derleth's *The Final Adventures of Solar Pons*, an original collection comprising a novel and six early stories.

Gregory George Gordon was a former policeman turned detective known as Gees, who appeared in a series of novels written by British author Jack Mann (E. Charles Vivian). After his non-supernatural debut in *Gees' First Case* (1936), the character encountered werewolves, ancient sorcerers and even an Egyptian cat goddess, before becoming involved with a witch in the final novel, *Her Ways Are Death* (1940).

Throughout the 1930s, many pulp characters—such as Maxwell Grant's The Shadow, Grant Stockbridge's The Spider, Kenneth Robeson's Doc Savage, Zorro's Doctor Death and Paul Ernst's Dr. Satan—combined the attributes of the psychic detective with that of the comic-book superhero or villain. Gordon Hillman's globe-trotting tales of Cranshawe were more traditional and appeared throughout the decade in *Ghost Stories*. However, the public started to lose interest in stories about the supernatural during the real-life horrors of World War II, and many pulp titles began to fold.

One of the last strongholds of this type of fiction was *Weird Tales*, and a new three-part serial began in the January 1938 issue that introduced occult investigator Judge Keith Hilary Pursuivant. 'The Hairy Ones Shall Dance' was written by Manly Wade Wellman under the pen name "Gans T. Field", and the author chronicled Pursuivant's adventures in three more tales, concluding with 'The Half-Haunted' (*Weird Tales*, September 1941), in which the character is amusingly consulted by Seabury Quinn's Jules de Grandin and Dr. Trowbridge.

Wellman used another pseudonym, "Hampton Wells", for 'Vigil', a story in the December 1939 issue of *Strange Tales* that marked the only adventure of supernatural savant Professor Nathan Enderby and his Chinese servant, Quong. Far more enduring was Wellman's John Thunstone, a New York playboy and student of the occult who battles evil with his silver sword cane. He made his debut in 'The Third Cry of Legba' (*Weird Tales*, November 1943) and appeared in fourteen more stories in the magazine up until 1951. Wellman returned to the character in the 1980s with another story and a couple of novels.

Back in Britain, Dennis Wheatley created Neils Orsen, "the world's greatest psychic investigator", for four stories that were published in the collection *Gunmen, Gallants and Ghosts* (1943). This character was modelled after real-life occultist Henry Dewhirst, who supposedly accurately predicted Wheatley's success as a novelist before the writer's career had even started. Meanwhile, Margery Lawrence's *Number Seven Queer Street* (1945) established the address of psychic Dr. Miles Pennoyer, whose cases are recorded by his young friend and psychic sensitive, solicitor Jerome Latimer.

The 1950s were not particularly kind to the psychic sleuths. Norman Parcell was forced to self-publish his collection *Costello, Psychic Investigator* (1954) under the pen name "John Nicholson". At least Manly Wade Wellman continued to keep the genre alive with his tales of John the Balladeer, who travels the Carolina mountains and battles the forces of evil with his silver-stringed guitar. Originally published in *The Magazine of Fantasy and Science Fiction*, John's adventures were finally collected in the Arkham House volume *Who Fears the Devil?* (1963).

Edward D. Hoch introduced his possibly immortal investigator Simon Ark in the story 'Village of the Dead' (*Famous Detective Stories*, February 1955). After that Hoch published nearly forty stories featuring Ark, a 2,000-year-old Coptic priest who had been cursed at Christ's crucifixion, many of them collected in *The Judges of Hades and Other Simon Ark Stories* (1971), *City of Brass and Other Simon Ark Stories* (1971) and *The Quests of Simon Ark* (1984).

John Rackham's Egyptologist Dr. K.N. Wilson made his first appearance in the December 1960 issue of the British magazine *Science Fantasy*. Three more stories followed over the next two years. Ron Goulart introduced bungling Victorian detective Dr. Plumrose with the eponymously titled story 'Plumrose' in the June 1963 *Fantastic* Stories. Two further stories appeared the same year before the author turned his attentions to his comic scientific sleuth Max Kearny.

A welcome return to form came with Joseph Payne Brennan's Lucius Leffing, a contemporary investigator who lives in a house surrounded by Victorian trappings in New Haven, Connecticut. Brennan himself is Leffing's associate and chronicler, and the two first team up to solve the mystery of 'The Haunted Housewife' in the Winter 1962 issue of the author's own small press magazine, *Macabre*. Over the next fifteen years the Leffing stories appeared in *Mike Shayne's Mystery Magazine* and *Alfred Hitchcock's Mystery Magazine* and were collected in *The Casebook of Lucius Leffing* (1972) and *The Chronicles of Lucius Leffing* (1977). Publisher Donald M. Grant collaborated with Brennan to write *Act of Providence* (1979), a short Leffing novel set during the First World Fantasy Convention, and a collection of further stories, *The Adventures of Lucius Leffing*, appeared in 1990, the year of Brennan's death.

Randall Garrett's Lord Darcy is usually involved in more magical mysteries. Set in an alternate-world England, Darcy is Investigator-in-Chief for the Court of Good King John, assisted by forensic sorcerer Sean O Lochlainn. The Lord Darcy series comprises the novel *Too Many Magicians* (1967) and two collections, *Murder and Magic* (1979) and *Lord Darcy Investigates* (1981). Following Garrett's death in 1987, Michael Kurland (who had previously published a pair of enjoyable Sherlock Holmes pastiches) extended the series with two further adventures, *Ten Little Wizards* (1988) and *A Study in Sorcery* (1989).

While developing his own version of H.P. Lovecraft's famed Cthulhu Mythos, Brian Lumley introduced occult detective Titus Crow in 'An Item of Supporting Evidence' in the Summer 1970 issue of *The Arkham Collector*. This story along with several more featuring Crow appeared in the author's first collection, *The Caller of the Black* (1971), since when the character has been featured in a number of other tales and a series of successful novels.

Frank Lauria's aptly titled novel *Doctor Orient* (1970) introduced readers to Dr. Owen Orient, a physician and psychic adept who has evolved beyond other men. This master of telepathic powers and initiate of dark mysteries returned in *Raga Six* (1972), *Lady Sativa* (1973) and *Baron Orgaz* (1974). A belated coda to the series was *The Seth Papers* (1979), in which Orient is pursued by various nations and a neo-fascist cult seeking to exploit his occult gifts.

Describing himself as "the world's only practising psychic detective", Francis St. Clare was the creation of Ronald Chetwynd-Hayes. This consulting detective and his sexy assistant Frederica Masters first appeared in 'Someone is Dead' (in *The Elemental*, 1974), since when they have been featured in more than half-a-dozen further stories and the 1993 novel *The Psychic Detective*.

Screenwriter/director Nicholas Meyer's Sherlock Holmes pastiche *The Seven PerCent Solution* (1974) became a bestseller and was adapted by the author for the movies two years later. He has continued the "posthumous memoirs" of the Great Detective in *The West-End Horror* (1976) and *The Canary Trainer* (1993), the latter involving Gaston Leroux's famed Phantom of the Paris Opera House. The following year both characters clashed again, this time in Sam Siciliano's *The Angel of the Opera*.

Also published in 1994, Sir Arthur Conan Doyle and famed magician and escapologist Harry Houdini (Enrich Weiss) team up to solve a series of bizarre murders based on various short stories by Edgar Allan Poe in William Hjortsberg's *Nevermore*.

Houdini himself was the hero of 'Imprisoned with the Pharaohs', battling subterranean monstrosities beneath the Egyptian pyramids in the May–June 1924 issue of *Weird Tales*, although the story was in fact ghostwritten for the showman by H.P. Lovecraft. Lovecraft and Houdini have themselves been teamed up, alongside other famous names, in such books as *Pulptime* by Peter H. Cannon (1984) and *The Arcanum* by Thomas Wheeler (2004).

Based on a then-unpublished novel by Jeff Rice, the 1971 TV movie *The Night Stalker* introduced audiences to Darren McGavin's investigative Chicago journalist, Carl Kolchak, who uncovers a world of the supernatural that no one will believe. When first broadcast, it was the highest-rated TV movie ever in America and led to a sequel, once again scripted by Richard Matheson, entitled *The Night Strangler* (1972). A single season of *Kolchak: The Night Stalker* followed on ABC-TV (1974–75), and Rice's novels of the two TV movies were published in 1973 and 1974, respectively.

An acknowledged inspiration for *The X-Files* (1993–2002), *The Night Stalker* was unsuccessfully revived as a short-lived TV series in 2005 with Irish actor Stuart Townsend miscast as Kolchak, and since 2003 Moonstone Books has been publishing a series of comic books, anthologies and new novels by C.J. Henderson based on the character.

During the 1970s, Manly Wade Wellman returned to the psychic investigator genre with a number of tales about mountain man Lee Cobbett, a friend of Judge Pursuivant. These appeared in *Witchcraft & Sorcery* 9 (1973), *Whispers* (June 1975) and the *World Fantasy Convention 1983* souvenir book, and both characters turned up in 'Chastel' in *The Year's Best Horror Stories Series VII* (1979). Hal Stryker, a young wanderer interested in the occult, was another of Wellman's mountain man heroes. He appeared in a trio of stories published in *The Magazine of Fantasy & Science Fiction* (March 1978), *Whispers* (October 1978) and *New Terrors 1* (1980).

A more modern variation on the theme is F. Paul Wilson's Repairman Jack, who made his début in the novel *The Tomb* (1981). A self-made outcast who exists within the gaps of modern society, Jack has no official identity, no social security number and pays no taxes. He hires himself out for cash to "fix" situations that have no legal remedy. Further novelettes and short stories have appeared in various anthologies, and Jack has been featured in a string of popular novels, including a youthful version of the character aimed at young adults.

Guy N. Smith's Mark Sabat is an ex-priest, SAS-trained killer and exorcist whose mission is to hunt down and destroy his mortal enemy, his brother, who has chosen the Left Hand Path of Evil. The character was introduced in the novel *Sabat 1: The Graveyard Vultures* (1982), and his exploits continued in *2: The Blood Merchants* (1982), *3: Cannibal Cult* (1982) and *4: The Druid Connection* (1983). The first Sabat short story, 'Vampire Village', appeared in *Fantasy Tales* #1 (1988) and *The Sabat Omnibus* was published in 1996.

The July 1982 issue of the Italian weird fantasy magazine *Kadath* was a special Occult Detectives edition that not only included a new John Thunstone story by Manly Wade Wellman and a new Titus Crow novella by Brian Lumley, but it also featured the début of two new series to the canon of psychic sleuths: Brian Mooney's 'The Affair at Durmamnay Hall' marked the first appearance of Reuben Calloway and his assistant, Catholic priest Roderick Shea, while Mike Chinn's 'The Death-Wish Mandate' introduced readers to near-immortal aviator Damian Paladin and his business partner Leigh Oswin. Mooney's Calloway and Shea went on to appear in such anthologies as *Shadows Over Innsmouth* (1994) and *The Anthology of Fantasy & the Supernatural* (1994), while two further Paladin stories appeared in *Winter Chills* 2 (1987) and *Fantasy Tales* #11 (1987) before all three were revised and included, along with three original tales, in the chapbook *The Paladin Mandates* (1998).

When his family is kidnapped by supernatural forces, family man Dan Brady transforms himself into an avenging enemy of the occult in the novel *Nighthunter 1: The Stalking* (1983), written by Robert Holdstock under the pen name "Robert Faulcon". Brady continued his quest to track down his wife and children and defeat the dark forces that had taken them in *2: The Talisman* (1983), *3: The Ghost Dance* (1983), *4: The Shrine* (1984), *5: The Hexing* (1984) and *6: The Labyrinth* (1987).

Created by Australian author Rick Kennett, motorcycle-riding Ernie Pine investigated a haunted village in 'The Roads of Donnington' (in *The 20th Fontana Book of Great Ghost Stories*, 1984) and his further encounters with the supernatural are chronicled in the chapbook *The Reluctant Ghost-Hunter* (1991). Kennett also discovered that both A.F. Kidd and himself had been independently writing new stories about William Hope Hodgson's Carnacki. These three individual stories, plus one collaboration, were eventually collected in a 1992 Ghost Story Society chapbook and expanded by a further eight tales ten years later into *No. 472 Cheyne Walk: Carnacki, the Untold Stories*.

Carnacki teamed up with the second Doctor and his two companions in Andrew Cartmel's novella, *Doctor Who: Foreign Devils* (2002). Meanwhile, Hodgson's ghost-finder also came to the aid of Sherlock Holmes, who is suffering from amnesia, in *The Shadow of Reichenbach Falls* (2008) by John R. King (J. Robert King), and the pair teamed up again in Guy Adams' 2012 novel *Sherlock Holmes: The Breath of God*.

The two detectives also investigated the occult together in Barbara Hambley's short story 'The Adventure of the Antiquarian's Niece' in *Shadows Over Baker Street* (2003) and A.F. Kidd's 'The Grantchester Grimoire' in *Gaslight Grimoire: Fantastic Tales of Sherlock Holmes* (2008), and Carnacki was revealed to be one of the members of an earlier League in Alan Moore's 2007 graphic novel *The League of Extraordinary Gentlemen: Black Dossier*.

Best known for his possession novel *The Manitou* (1975) and its various sequels featuring demon-busting rogue psychic Harry Erskine, in 1997 British author Graham Masterton published *Rook*, about the eponymous remedial high school teacher who can see ghosts and investigates supernatural cases. It was followed by *Tooth and Claw* (1997), *The Terror* (1998), *Snowman* (1999), *Swimmer* (2001), *Darkroom* (2003), *Demon's Door* (2011) and *Garden of Evil* (2013), in which Rook helps his students overcome a variety of evil entities.

Mark Valentine's Ralph Tyler investigates the occult for excitement. He first teams up with the narrator in 'The Grave of Ani' (*Dark Dreams #1*, 1984) and further tales appeared in a number of small-press journals. In 1987 a short collection of two Tyler tales was published under the title *14 Bellchamber Tower*, and *Herald of the Hidden and Other Stories* (2013) collected ten stories (three previously unpublished).

Valentine also created The Connoisseur, a collector of the *outré* and bizarre, who made his début in the 1990 issue of *Dark Dreams*. The author went on to write more than twenty further tales about the aesthetical detective, which have been collected by Tartarus Press in *In Violet Veils* (1999), *Masques and Citadels* (2003) and, in collaboration with John Howard, *The Collected Connoisseur* (2010).

Harry D'Amour is the creation of bestselling fantasist Clive Barker. A down-at-heel investigator in the classic Raymond Chandler mould, D'Amour first appeared in 'The Last Illusion' in *Clive Barker's Books of Blood Volume 6* (1985) and 'The Lost Souls' in the Christmas 1986 issue of *Time Out*. He was subsequently featured in the novels *The Great and Secret Show* (1989) and *Everville* (1994), before becoming the hero of Barker's 1995 movie *Lord of Illusions*, as portrayed by Scott Bakula. The character has also played a major role in the Boom! Studios comic series *Hellraiser* (2011) featuring the demonic Pinhead, and the two characters are due to be reunited Barker's long-awaited novel *The Scarlet Gospels*.

Working-class sorcerer, occult detective and sometimes con man, John Constantine was created by Alan Moore, Steve Bissette and John Totleben for DC Comics' *The Saga of the Swamp Thing #37* in June 1985. The cynical Londoner went on to appear in his own comics, *Hellblazer* (1988–2013) and *Constantine* (2013–), and he has been portrayed by Keanu Reeves in an eponymous 2005 movie and Matt Ryan in a 2014 TV series.

Comics writer Neil Gaiman has featured Constantine in editions of *The Sandman* and *The Books of Magic*, while John Shirley has written three *Hellblazer* novelisations, including a tie-in to the film.

Along the same lines, Max Payne was a character created in 2001 for an action-packed video game, inspired by Norse mythology. Following the murder of his family, the former NYPD Detective uncovers a government conspiracy while battling, amongst other opponents, a self-styled messenger of Hell. Mark Wahlberg played the character in a 2008 movie loosely based on the game.

James Herbert was another bestseller who, in his 1988 novel *Haunted*, decided to try his own hand at the psychic detective genre. What makes Herbert's David Ash different is that he is renowned for his dismissal of all things supernatural, until three nights of terror in a reputedly haunted house force him to re-evaluate his beliefs. *Haunted* was filmed in 1995 by director Lewis Gilbert with Aidan Quinn as Ash, and the character reappeared in

Herbert's novels *The Ghosts of Sleath* (1994) and *Ash* (2013).

Penelope Pettiweather, Northwest Ghost Hunter, is another rare female psychic sleuth created by Jessica Amanda Salmonson in the collection *Harmless Ghosts* (1990). The author subsequently revived her letter-writing investigator for one half of *The Mysterious Doom and Other Ghostly Tales of the Pacific Northwest* (1992). *Absences: Charlie Goode's Ghosts* (1991) was a chapbook that collected five stories about Steve Rasnic Tem's eponymous antique collector and amateur archaeologist, who has an affinity for the occult. The character has since appeared in stories in *All Hallows* #2 (1990) and *Fantasy Macabre* #14 (1992).

Kim Newman first introduced readers to Charles Beauregard, an adventurer in the service of the Diogenes Club, in his alternate-world novella 'Red Reign' (in *The Mammoth Book of Vampires*, 1992), which he expanded into the novel *Anno Dracula* the same year. Since then, the influence of secret agent Beauregard and the mysterious cabal he works for has spread to various sequels and spin-offs, and served as a unifying nucleus for many of the author's short stories and subsequent novels.

Parapsychologist Ryerson Biergarten was introduced by T.M. Wright in his 1992 novel *Goodlow's Ghosts*. *Sleepeasy* (1994) was a sequel that resurrected a deceased character from the earlier book, while Biergarten himself was back, this time on the trail of a serial killer, in *The Ascending* (1994).

In Mark Frost's *The List of 7* (1993), a young Dr. Arthur Doyle teams up with mysterious special agent Jack Sparks (possibly the model for Sherlock Holmes) to confront the supernatural schemes of a secret cabal. The two protagonists were reunited in *The 6 Messiahs* (1995), set ten years after the original.

New Orleans FBI agent Aloysius Xingu L. Pendergast and NYPD detective Lt. Vincent D'Agosta first appeared as supporting characters in Douglas Preston and Lincoln Child's debut novel *Relic* (1995), about a mythical monster loose in the New York Museum of Natural History. They both returned in the sequel, *Reliquary* (1997), and have continued to appear in a number of other bestsellers from the writing team. Although the 1997 movie *The Relic* omitted the pivotal character of Pendergast, Tom Sizemore played D'Agosta.

Marty Burns was once famous. Then he became just another fallen star in Hollywood, working as a low-rent private eye, until the search for a missing hooker in Jay Russell's *Celestial Dogs* (1996) involved him in a centuries-old conflict with Japanese demons. Since then, Russell has continued Marty's exploits in the novels *Burning Bright* (1997) and *Greed & Stuff* (2001), the novella *Apocalypse Now, Voyager* (2005), and a number of short stories.

A Wine of Angels (1998) was the first novel to feature Phil Rickman's "Deliverance Consultant for the Diocese of Hereford" Merrily Watkins, who investigates supernatural mysteries. So far the author has written eleven further novels about the Anglican priest, her pagan daughter Jane and damaged musician Lol Robinson.

John Connolly's Charlie Parker, a former NYPD detective hunting the killer of his wife and young daughter, made his first appearance in the author's debut novel, *Every Dead Thing* (1999). Since then he has also been featured in eleven increasingly macabre mysteries.

The start of the 21st century saw an explosion of occult investigators in fiction, mostly fuelled by the rise of the bestselling "paranormal romance" genre. These included P.N. Elrod's vampire private detective Jack Fleming, Tanya Huff's undead Henry Fitzroy, and Jim Butcher's Chicago wizard-for-hire Harry Dresden.

The Occult Detective (2005) contains seven stories about psychic detective Sidney Taine by Robert Weinberg, while *Visions* (2009) is a collection of twelve fantasy and horror stories by Richard A. Lupoff, four featuring the author's psychic detective Abraham ben Zaccheus.

Paul Kane's *Dalton Quayle Rides Out* (2007) contains two humorous tales of the eponymous psychic investigator and his good friend, Dr. Humphrey Pemberton. *The Adventures of Dalton Quayle* appeared four years later and collected seven stories.

With the occult adventure *Sherlock Holmes: Revenant* (2011), Canadian-based Scottish author William Meikle continued the exploits of Sir Arthur Conan Doyle's Great Detective in a pastiche novel that was authorised by the Doyle Estate. He followed it with *Sherlock Holmes: The Quality of Mercy and Other Stories* (2013), containing ten short stories and 'A Prologue' by "John Hamish Watson, M.D.".

Meikle's *Carnacki: Heaven and Hell* (2011) was a collection of ten original stories based on the character originally created by William Hope Hodgson, who didn't even rate a credit in the book.

Of course, there have also been previous anthologies of psychic detective stories. Although it is surprising that August Derleth never compiled one for his Mycroft & Moran imprint, Michel Parry's *The Supernatural Solution* (1976) reprinted nine stories about detectives and ghosts by J. Sheridan Le Fanu, E. and H. Heron, William Hope Hodgson, L.T. Meade and Robert Eustace, Dion Fortune, Arthur Machen, Seabury Quinn, Manly Wade Wellman and Dennis Wheatley. Parry also collected six reprints (half of them from his earlier book) by Hodgson, Eustace, E. and H. Heron and Sir Arthur Conan Doyle for the slim 1985 volume *Ghostbreakers*.

A more satisfying compilation was *Supernatural Sleuths* (1986) from veteran editor Peter Haining, which reprinted twelve stories by Mark Lemon, Algernon Blackwood, Sax Rohmer, Henry A. Hering, Gordon MacCreagh, Gordon Hillman, Margery Lawrence, Joseph Payne Brennan and those old standbys Conan Doyle, E. and H. Heron and Wheatley.

Despite appropriating Haining's title, *Supernatural Sleuths* (1996) edited by Charles G. Waugh and Martin H. Greenberg cast its net for reprint stories wider, including among its fourteen selections tales by William F. Nolan, Ron Goulart, August Derleth and Mack Reynolds, Robert Weinberg and Larry Niven, along with such familiar names as Wellman, Hodgson and Quinn.

Gaslight Grimoire: Fantastic Tales of Sherlock Holmes (2008), edited by J.R. Campbell and Charles Prepolec, contains eleven original stories by Barbara Hambley, Barbara Roden, Chris Roberson, Kim Newman and others. It was followed by *Gaslight Grotesque: Nightmare Tales of Sherlock Holmes* (2009) and *Gaslight Arcanum: Uncanny Tales of Sherlock Holmes* (2011). Justin Gustainis edited *Those Who Fight Monsters: Tales of Occult Detectives* (2011) which features fourteen "urban fantasy" stories by, amongst others, Carrie Vaughn, Tanya Huff, Lilith Saintcrow, Simon R. Green and T.A. Pratt.

In many ways, this present volume can be viewed as a companion-piece to my *Shadows Over Innsmouth* trilogy (1994–2013) and the anthology *The Mammoth Book of Dracula* (1997). As with those other books, it contains a combination of new and reprint fiction and is assembled along a loosely constructed chronology (stretching from Ancient Egyptian times through to the 21st century). I would therefore advise that, for maximum enjoyment, you read this book from beginning to end, and do not dip in and out of the stories. This is especially true of Kim Newman's multi-part short novel, which was written especially for this volume.

So now it is time to meet some of the greatest fictional detectives (and their faithful amanuenses) who have ever confronted the bizarre and the unusual. Already the forces of darkness are abroad and occult powers are gathering. In the everlasting battle between Good and Evil, these investigators of the unusual set out to solve ancient mysteries and unravel modern hauntings with the aid of their unique powers of deduction and the occasional silver bullet.

Once again, for the supernatural sleuths, the game is afoot . . .

Stephen Jones
London, England

IN EGYPT'S LAND
by KIM NEWMAN

After Dracula *(1897), The* Jewel of the Seven Stars *(1903) is Bram Stoker's best and best-known book. It chronicles the gradual possession of Margaret Trelawny by Tera, an ancient Egyptian queen of evil, whose mummified remains have been brought back to their London home by Margaret's archaeologist father.*

Although it never attained the popularity of the author's earlier novel, The Jewel of the Seven Stars *was first adapted as "Curse of the Mummy" in 1970 for the television series* Mystery and Imagination. *It has subsequently been filmed several times— by Hammer as* Blood from the Mummy's Tomb *(1971), as The* Awakening *(1980) starring Charlton Heston and, most recently, as* Bram Stoker's Legend of the Mummy *(1997) with Lou Gossett, Jr.*

For his story cycle in this volume, Kim Newman has borrowed bits from Stoker's book—notably the jewel itself, and the character of Abel Trelawny—much as he co-opted the author's vampire Count for his Anno Dracula *series.*

Pai-net'em is a real historical figure, a Pharaoh's scribe and councillor whose mummy was discovered in 1881. Most biblical scholars, and Yul Brynner in The Ten Commandments *(1956), assume that the Pharaoh of Exodus was Rameses II. However, Newman has arbitrarily chosen Meneptah III on the grounds that he was even more unpleasant than Rameses and therefore the sort of person to oppress the Israelites and deserve the curses. Egyptian history doesn't bother to mention the plagues at all, or the Israelites much.*

ALL THEBES, ALL *Egypt*, was filled with the stench. Pai-net'em had bound up his head with linen, bandaging nose and mouth as if wrapping himself for interment. The stench got through, filling his nostrils and throat, curling his tongue.

His eyes were swollen almost shut by weeping boils. Insects clumped around his bloody tears, regathering every time he wiped them away. Eggs laid in the gum around his eyes hatched hourly. Newborn flies chewed with tiny teeth.

Progress through the city was slow. The roads were filled with the dead, animals and men. Darkness was relieved only by the spreading fires. Most of the people were too concerned with private griefs to lend their hands to fighting the flames.

Truly, this was the time of calamities.

A priest, a man of science, Pharaoh's closest advisor, he was brought as low as a leper. He could not hold in his mind all that had happened in the last month. Looking at the mottled swellings and punctures on his body, he could not tell the marks of sickness from insect bites, even from the scars left by hailstones.

The Gods must hate Egypt, to let this happen.

Pai-net'em could not number the dead of his household. His grief had been spent on lesser catastrophes, sickening cattle and rioting slaves. Now, with brother and son struck down, his wife dead by her own hand, servants' corpses strewn like stones about his estates, he had no more grief, no more feeling, in him.

A stream of blood trickled past Pharaoh's Palace. Tiny frogs hopped in the reddened water. A living carpet—millions of locusts, flies and gnats—covered the streets, slowly reducing the fallen to skeletons. Insects assaulted the feet of those like Pai-net'em who waded perversely about, fixed like stars on their own courses.

The guards lay dead at their posts, wavering masks of flies on their faces. Pai-net'em passed through the open doors. Even here, inside Pharaoh's house, insects swarmed and gnawed. With the crops and the cattle blasted, many more would die of famine even after the darkness abated.

Lightning was striking all through the city.

Pai-net'em found Pharaoh in his morning room, hunched on his day-bed, face as swollen and distorted as the lowest slave's. The great were not spared; indeed, Pharaoh seemed to suffer more than his subjects, for he had far more to lose. If all who lived under him were obliterated, his name would pass from memory.

The old Pharaoh had done much to preserve his name, built many temples, left many writings. This younger man, so addicted to luxury that he neglected public works, had taken to having his name inscribed on tablets over those of his predecessors. It was a desperate act, a cry against the advance of oblivion.

"Pai-net'em," Pharaoh said, mouth twisting, tongue swollen. "What has brought these curses upon Egypt?"

Pai-net'em found he did not have the strength to rise from his kneeling position.

"The Israelites claim responsibility, sire."

"The Israelites? The conquered people?"

"Yes. They say their God has visited his wrath upon Egypt."

Pharaoh's eyes widened.

"Why?"

"They are a sorcerous people. But their claims are fatuous. They have but one God, a child beside our Gods."

"This is not the work of the Gods."

Pai-net'em agreed with Pharaoh.

"We both know what is at the bottom of this."

"You have it here, sire?" Pai-net'em asked.

Pharaoh got off his day-bed, flies falling from his robes. Blood streaked his legs. His chest was sunken, his skin rubbed raw or bloated with sickness.

Pai-net'em stood, coughing fluid into his mouth-linen.

Pharaoh opened a wooden box. The darkness of the morning room was assaulted by red light. Pai-net'em remembered the first time he had seen the glow. Then, Pharaoh had been slim and swift and powerful. And he had been secure in his own health, his position.

Bravely, Pharaoh took the object out of the box. It seemed as if he had dipped his hand into fire and pulled out a solid lump of flame.

Pai-net'em got closer and looked at the jewel. A ruby as big as a man's fist. Inside glinted seven points of red light, in the shape of the seven stars of the night sky. It had fallen into the Nile, from the stars themselves, and turned the river to blood. It was not a jewel, given in tribute to Pharaoh. It was a curse, spat from above at Egypt. It was the source of all miseries, of the insects and the lightning, of the darkness and the death.

"Such a beautiful thing," Pharaoh mused, "to contain such curses."

Pai-net'em saw the beauty, yet the jewel was hideous, crawling with invisible filth.

He shook his head, thinking with bitter humour of the Israelites' claim. This was beyond the Gods of any people. This was death made into an object. It could not be destroyed—that had been tried, with chisels and fire—only passed on, to the unwitting.

"Take it," Pharaoh said, tossing the jewel to Pai-net'em.

He caught the thing, feeling its horrid pulse.

"Take it far from here."

Pai-net'em bowed his head.

He would die in the execution of this task. But he had no other purpose. His name would be remembered for this sacrifice. As long as Egypt endured, so would Pai-net'em.

Outside the Palace, he held the jewel to his chest, cupping it with his hand. He thought himself the calm centre of a storm. All around, insects and death whirled in bloody darkness. Evils flowed from the stone, but he was shielded from them. It was as if he were inside it rather than it inside his fist.

Everything was tinted red, as if he were looking through the ruby. His limbs were heavy and he felt trapped.

He started to run, away from the Palace.

A burning began in his chest, where the jewel was clutched, as if a blob of molten metal had struck him and was eating its way towards his heart.

He let his hand fall, but the jewel was stuck to his torso, sinking in. Agony filled his chest, and he tore the linen from his face, screaming.

But he still ran, wading through the streams of frogs and locusts. The weakness of his legs was washed away. He no longer felt anything.

He knew he was dying, but that the jewel kept his body from falling. He shrank inside himself, withdrawing into the ruby, suspended among the Seven Stars. This was not death as he knew it, a calm passage into a dignified afterlife where his family and servants awaited, but a change of perception. He would remain in the world, but be apart from it. As he had served Pharaoh, so would he now serve the Seven Stars.

From the heart of the red night, he looked down on the devastation that was the Land of Egypt.

And could not weep.

Sister Fidelma

OUR LADY OF DEATH
by PETER TREMAYNE

Sister Fidelma is around twenty-seven years old. Born in Cashel in the 7th century, she is the youngest daughter of Failbe Fland, the king, who died the year after she was born.

Fidelma is a member of the Celtic Church. She is not only a religieuse but a dálaigh or advocate of the Brehon courts of ancient Ireland, where she studied her law under the Brehon (Judge) Morann of Tara. She is qualified to the level of anruth, one degree below the highest qualification the ecclesiastical and secular schools and universities in Ireland can bestow. All her actions and judgments are made according to the Brehon laws. Her main territory is the kingdom of Munster, of which her brother Colgú is king at Cashel.

Ireland's answer to Brother Cadfael made her debut in the short story 'Hemlock at Vespers' in Midwinter Mysteries 3 *(1993). Other stories have subsequently appeared in such anthologies as* The Mammoth Book of Historical Whodunnits *(1993),* Great Irish Detective Stories *(1993),* Constable New Crimes 2 *(1993),* Midwinter Mysteries 4 *(1994),* The Mammoth Book of Historical Detectives *(1995),* Midwinter Mysteries 5 *(1995),* Murder at the Races *(1995),* Classical Whodunnits *(1996),* Murder Most Irish *(1996) plus various issues of* Ellery Queen Mystery Magazine.

Peter Tremayne's first Sister Fidelma novel, Absolution by

Murder, *was published in 1994. It has since been followed by twenty-five further titles, the most recent being* The Devil's Seal *(2014) and* The Second Death *(2015).*

THE AWESOME MOANING of the wind blended chillingly with the howling of wolves. They were nearby, these fearsome night hunters. Sister Fidelma knew it but could not see them because of the cold, driving snow against her face. It came at her; clouds of whirling, ice-cold, tiny pellicles. It obliterated the landscape and she could scarcely see beyond her arm's length in front of her.

Had it not been for the urgency of reaching Cashel, the seat of the kings of Mumha, she would not have been attempting the journey northwards through these great, forbidding peaks of Sléibhte an Comeraigh. She bent forward in the saddle of her horse, which only her rank as a *dálaigh* of the law courts of the five kings of Ireland entitled her to have. A simple religieuse would not be able to lay claim to such a means of transportation. But then Fidelma was no ordinary religieuse. She was a daughter of a former king of Cashel, an advocate of the law of the *Fénechus* and qualified to the level of *anruth*, one degree below the highest qualification in Ireland.

The wind drove the snow continuously against her. It plastered the rebellious strands of red hair that spilled from her *cubhal*, her woollen headdress, against her pale forehead. She wished the wind's direction would change, even for a moment or two, for it would have been more comfortable to have the wind at her back. But the wind was constantly raging from the north.

The threatening howl of the wolves seemed close. Was it her imagination or had it been gradually getting closer as she rode the isolated mountain track? She shivered and once more wished that she had stopped for the night at the last *bruidhen* or hostel in order to await more clement weather. But the snowstorm had set in and it would be several days before conditions improved. Sooner or later she would have to tackle the journey. The message from her brother Colgú had said her presence was needed urgently for their mother lay dying. Only that fact brought Fidelma traversing the forbidding tracks through the snow-bound mountains in such intemperate conditions.

Her face was frozen and so were her hands as she confronted the fierce wind-driven snow. In spite of her heavy woollen cloak, she found her teeth chattering. A dark shape loomed abruptly out of the snow nearby. Her heart caught in her mouth as her horse shied and skittered on the trail for a moment. Then she was able to relax and steady the nervous beast with a sigh of relief as the regal shape of a great stag stared momentarily at her from a distance of a few yards before recklessly turning and bounding away into the cover of the white curtain that blocked out the landscape.

Continuing on, she had reached what she felt must be the crest of a rise and found the wind so fierce here that it threatened to sweep her from her horse. Even the beast put its head down to the ground and seemed to stagger at the icy onslaught. Masses of loose powdery snow drifted this way and that in the howling and shrieking of the tempest.

Fidelma blinked at the indistinct blur of the landscape beyond.

She felt sure she had seen a light. Or was it her imagination? She blinked again and urged her horse onwards, straining to keep her eyes focussed on the point where she thought she had seen it. She automatically pulled her woollen cloak higher up around her neck.

Yes! She had seen it. A light, surely!

She halted her horse and slipped off, making sure she had the reins looped securely around her arm. The snow came up to her knees, making walking almost impossible but she could not urge her mount through the drifting snow without making sure it was safe enough first. After a moment or two she had come to a wooden pole. She peered upwards. Barely discernible in the flurries above her head, hung a dancing storm lantern.

She stared around in surprise. The swirling snow revealed nothing. But she was sure that the lantern was the traditional sign of a *bruidhen*, an inn, for it was the law that all inns had to keep a lantern burning to indicate their presence at night or in severe weather conditions.

She gazed back at the pole with its lantern, and chose a direction, moving awkwardly forward in the deep, clinging snow. Suddenly the wind momentarily dropped and she caught sight of the large dark shadow of a building. Then the blizzard resumed its course and she staggered head down in its direction. More by good luck than any other form of guidance, she came to a horse's hitching rail and tethered her beast there, before feeling her way along the cold stone walls towards the door.

There was a sign fixed on the door but she could not decipher it. She saw, to her curiosity, a ring of herbs hanging from the door almost obliterated in their coating of snow.

She found the iron handle, twisted it and pushed. The door remained shut. She frowned in annoyance. It was the law that a *brughfer*, an innkeeper, had to keep the door of his inn open at all times, day and night and in all weathers. She tried again.

The wind was easing a little now and its petulant crying had died away to a soft whispering moan.

Irritated, Fidelma raised a clenched fist and hammered at the door.

Did she hear a cry of alarm or was it simply the wailing wind?

There was no other answer.

She hammered more angrily this time.

Then she did hear a noise. A footstep and then a harsh male cry.

"God and his saints stand between us and all that is evil! Begone foul spirit!"

Fidelma was thunderstruck for a moment. Then she thrust out her jaw.

"Open, innkeeper; open to a *dálaigh* of the courts; open to a sister of the abbey of Kildare! In the name of charity, open to a refugee from the storm!"

There was a moment's silence. Then she thought she heard voices raised in argument. She hammered again.

There came the sound of bolts being drawn and the door swung inwards. A blast of warm air enveloped Fidelma and she pushed hurriedly into the room beyond, shaking the snow from her woollen cloak.

"What manner of hostel is this that ignores the laws of the Brehons?" she demanded, turning to the figure that was now closing the wooden door behind her.

The man was tall and thin. A gaunt, pallid figure of middle-age, his temples greying. He was poorly attired and his height was offset by a permanent stoop. But it was not that which caused Fidelma's eyes to widen a fraction. It was the horror on the man's face; not a momentary expression of horror but a graven expression that was set deep and permanently into his cadaverous features. Tragedy and grief stalked across the lines of his face.

"I have a horse tethered outside. The poor beast will freeze to death if not attended," Fidelma snapped, when the man did not answer her question but simply stood staring at her.

"Who are you?" demanded a shrill woman's voice behind her.

Fidelma swung round. The woman who stood there had once been handsome, now age was causing her features to run with surplus flesh, and lines marked her face. Her eyes stared, black and apparently without pupils, at Fidelma. She had the expression that here was a woman who, at some awesome moment in her life, the pulsating blood of life had frozen and never regained its regular ebb and flow. What surprised her more was that the woman held before her a tall ornate crucifix. She held it as if it were some protective icon against the terror that afflicted her.

She and the man were well-matched.

"Speak! What manner of person are you?"

Fidelma sniffed in annoyance.

"If you are the keepers of this inn, all you should know is that I am a weary traveller in these mountains, driven to seek refuge from the blizzard."

The woman was not cowed by her haughty tone.

"It is not all we need to know," she corrected just as firmly. "Tell us whether you mean us harm or not."

Fidelma was surprised.

"I came here to shelter from the storm, that is all. I am Fidelma of Kildare," replied the religieuse in annoyance. "Moreover, I am a *dálaigh* of the courts, qualified to the level of *anruth* and sister to Colgú, *tánaiste* of this kingdom."

The grandiloquence of her reply was an indication of the annoyance Fidelma felt for normally she was not one given to stating more than was ever necessary. She had never felt the need to mention that her brother, Colgú, was heir apparent to the kingdom of Cashel before. However, she felt that she needed to stir these people out of their curious mood.

As she spoke she swung off her woollen cloak displaying her habit and she noticed that the woman's eyes fell upon the ornately worked crucifix which hung from her neck. Did she see some expression of reassurance in those cold expressionless eyes?

The woman put down her cross and gave a bob of her head.

"Forgive us, sister. I am Monchae, wife to Belach, the innkeeper."

Belach seemed to be hesitating at the door.

"Shall I see to the horse?" he asked hesitantly.

"Unless you want it to freeze to death," snapped Fidelma making her way to a large open fire in which sods of turf were singing as they caused a warmth to envelope the room. From the corner of her eyes she saw Belach hesitate a moment longer and then, swinging a cloak around his shoulders, he took from behind the door a sword and went out into the blizzard.

Fidelma was astonished. She had never seen a hosteller take a sword to assist him in putting a horse to stable before.

Monchae was pushing the iron handle on which hung a cauldron across the glowing turf fire.

"What place is this?" demanded Fidelma as she chose a chair to stretch out in front of the warmth of the fire. The room was low beamed and comfortable but devoid of decorations apart from a tall statuette of the Madonna and Child, executed in some form of painted plaster, a gaudy, alabaster figurine. It dominated as the centre display at the end of a large table where, presumably, guests dined.

"This is Brugh-na-Bhelach. You have just come off the shoulder of the mountain known as Fionn's seat. The River Tua is but a mile to the north of here. We do not have many travellers this way in winter. Which direction are you heeding?"

"North to Cashel," replied Fidelma.

Monchae ladled a cup of steaming liquid from the cauldron over the fire and handed it to her. Although the liquid must have been warming the vessel, Fidelma could not feel it as she cupped her frozen hands around it and let the steaming vapour assail her nostrils. It smelled good. She sipped slowly at it, her sense of taste confirming what her sense of smell had told her.

She glanced up at the woman.

"Tell me, Monchae, why was the door of this hostel barred? Why did I have to beg to be admitted? Do you and your husband, Belach, know the law of hostel-keepers?"

Monchae pressed her lips together.

"Will you report us to the *bóaire* of the territory?"

The *bóaire* was the local magistrate.

"I am more concerned at hearing your reasons," replied Fidelma. "Someone might have perished from the cold before you and your husband, Belach, opened your door."

The woman looked agitated, chewing her lips as if she would draw blood from it.

The door opened abruptly, with a wild gust of cold air, sending snow flakes swirling across the room and a stream of icy air enveloping them.

Belach stood poised a moment in its frame, a ghastly look upon his pale features and then with a sound which resembled a soft moan, he entered and barred the door behind him. He still carried the sword as a weapon.

Fidelma watched him throw the bolts with curiosity.

Monchae stood, both hands raised to her cheeks.

Belach turned from the door and his lips were trembling.

"I heard it!" he muttered, his eyes darting from his wife to Fidelma, as though he did not want her to hear. "I heard it!"

"Oh Mary, mother of God, save us!" cried the woman swaying as if she would faint.

"What does this mean?" Fidelma demanded as sternly as she could.

Belach turned pleading to her.

"I was in the barn, bedding down your horse, sister, and I heard it."

"But what?" cried Fidelma, trying to keep her patience.

"The spirit of Mugrán," wailed Monchae suddenly, giving way to a fit of sobbing. "Save us, sister. For the pity of Christ! Save us!"

Fidelma rose and went to the woman, taking her gently but firmly by the arm and leading her to the fire. She could see that her husband, Belach, was too nervous to attend to the wants of his wife and so she went to a jug, assessed its contents as *corma*, a spirit distilled from barley, and poured a little into a cup. She handed it to the woman and told her to drink.

"Now what is all this about? I cannot help you unless you tell me."

Monchae looked at Belach, as if seeking permission, and he nodded slowly in response.

"Tell her from the beginning," he muttered.

Fidelma smiled encouragingly at the woman.

"A good place to start," she joked lightly. But there was no humorous response on the features of the innkeeper's wife.

Fidelma seated herself before Monchae and faced her expectantly.

Monchae paused a moment and then began to speak, hesitantly at first and then more quickly as she gained confidence in the story.

"I was a young girl when I came to this place. I came as a young bride to the *brughfer*, the innkeeper, who was then a man named Mugrán. You see," she added hurriedly, "Belach is my second husband."

She paused but when Fidelma made no comment, she went on.

"Mugrán was a good man. But often given to wild fantasies. He was a good man for the music, an excellent piper. Often he entertained here in this very room and people would come far and wide to hear him. But he was a restless soul. I found that I was doing all the work of running the inn while he pursued his dreams. Mugrán's younger brother, Cano, used to help me but he was much influenced by his brother.

"Six years ago our local chieftain lit the *croistara*, the fiery cross, and sent his rider from village to village, raising the clans to send a band of fighting men to fight Guaire of Connacht in the service of Cathal Cú cen máthair of Cashel. Mugrán one morning announced he and young Cano were leaving to join that band of warriors. When I protested, he said that I should not fear for my security. He had placed in the inn an inheritance which would keep me from want. If anything happened to him then I would not be lacking for anything. With that, he and Cano just rose and left."

Even now her voice was full of indignation.

"Time passed. Seasons came and went and I struggled to keep the inn going. Then, when the snows of winter were clearing, a messenger came to me who said a great battle had been fought on the shores of Loch Derg and my man had been slain in it. They brought me his shattered pipes as token and his bloodstained tunic. Cano, it seemed, had been killed at his side, and they brought me a bloodstained cloak as proof."

She paused and sniffed.

"It is no use saying that I grieved for him. Not for my man, Mugrán. We had hardly been together for he was always searching out new, wild schemes to occupy his fancy. I could no more have tethered his heart than I could train the inn's cat to come and go at my will. Still, the inn was now mine and mine by right as well as inheritance for had I not worked to keep it while he pursued his fantasies? After the news came, and the *bóaire* confirmed that the inn was mine since my man was dead by the shores of the far-off loch, I continued to work to run the inn. But life was hard, it was a struggle. Visitors along these isolated tracks are few and come seldom."

"But what of the inheritance Mugrán had left in the inn that would keep you from want?" asked Fidelma intrigued and caught up in the story.

The woman gave a harsh bark of laughter.

"I searched and searched and found nothing. It was just one of Mugrán's dreams again. One of his silly fantasies. He probably said it to keep me from complaining when he left."

"Then what?" Fidelma pressed, when she paused.

"A year passed and I met Belach." She nodded to her husband. "Belach and I loved one another from the start. Ah, not the love of a dog for the sheep, you understand, but the love of a salmon for the stream. We married and have worked together since. And I insisted that we renamed this inn Brugh-na-Bhelach. Life has been difficult to us, but we have worked and made a living here."

Belach had moved forward and caught Monchae's hand in his. The symbolism assured Fidelma that Monchae and Belach were still in love after the years that they had shared together.

"We've had five years of happiness," Belach told Fidelma. "And if the evil spirits claim us now, they will not steal those five years from us."

"Evil spirits?" frowned Fidelma.

"Seven days ago it started," Monchae said heavily. "I was out feeding the pigs when I thought I heard the sounds of music from high up on the mountain. I listened. Sure enough, I heard the sound of pipe music, high up in the air. I felt suddenly cold for it was a tune, as I well remember, that Mugrán was fond of playing.

"I came into the inn and sought out Belach. But he had not heard the music. We went out and listened but could hear nothing more than the gathering winds across the mountains that betokened the storms to come.

"The next day, at the noon hour, I heard a thud on the door of the inn. Thinking it a traveller who could not lift the latch. I opened the door. There was no one there`. . . or so I thought until I glanced down. At the foot of the door was . . ." Monchae genuflected hastily. "At the foot of the door was a dead raven. There was no sign of how it met its death. It seemed to have flown into the door and killed itself."

Fidelma sat back with pursed lips.

She could see which way the story was going. The sound of music, a dead raven lying at the door. These were all the portents of death among the rural folk of the five kingdoms. She found herself shivering slightly in spite of her rational faith.

"We have heard the music several times since," interrupted Belach for the first time. "I have heard it."

"And whereabouts does this music comes from?"

Belach spread one hand, as if gesturing towards the mountains outside.

"High up, high up in the air. All around us."

"It is the lamentation of the dead," moaned Monchae. "There is a curse on us."

Fidelma sniffed.

"There is no curse unless God wills it."

"Help us, sister," whispered Monchae. "I fear it is Mugrán come to claim our souls, a vengeance for my love for Belach and not for him."

Fidelma gazed in quiet amusement at the woman.

"How did you reckon this?"

"Because I have heard him. I have heard his voice, moaning to me from the Otherworld, crying to me. 'I am alone! I am alone!' he called. 'Join me, Monchae!' Ah, how many times have I heard that ghostly wail?"

Fidelma saw that the woman was serious.

"You heard this? When and where?"

"It was three days ago in the barn. I was tending the goats that we have there, milking them to prepare cheese when I heard the whisper of Mugrán's voice. I swear it was his voice. It sounded all around me."

"Did you search?" Fidelma asked.

"Search? For a spirit?" Monchae sounded shocked. "I ran into the inn and took up my crucifix."

"I searched," intervened Belach more rationally. "I searched, for, like you, sister, I look for answers in this world before I seek out the Otherworld. But there was no one in the barn, nor the inn, who could have made that sound. But, like you, sister, I continued to have my doubts. I took our ass and rode down into the valley to the *bóthan* of Dallán, the chieftain who had been with Mugrán on the shores of Loch Derg. He took oath that Mugrán was dead these last six years and that he had personally seen the body. What could I do further?"

Fidelma nodded slowly.

"So only you, Monchae, have heard Mugrán's voice?"

"No!" Belach interrupted again and surprised her. "By the apostles of Patrick, I have heard the voice as well."

"And what did this voice say?"

"It said—'Beware, Belach. You walk in a dead man's shoes without the blessing of his spirit.' That is what it said."

"And where did you hear this?"

"Like Monchae, I heard the voice speak to me within the barn."

"Very well. You have seen a dead raven, heard pipe music from far off and heard a voice which you think is that of the spirit of Mugrán. There can still be a logical explanation for such phenomena."

"Explanation?" Monchae's voice was harsh. "Then explain this to me, sister. Last night, I heard the music again. It awoke me. The snow storm had died down and the sky was clear with the moon shining down, reflecting on the snow making it as bright as day. I heard the music playing again.

"I took my courage in my hands and went to the window and unfixed the shutter. There is a tiny knoll no more than one hundred yards away, a small snowy knoll. There was a figure of a man standing upon it, and in his hands were a set of pipes on which he was playing a lament. Then he paused and looked straight at me. 'I am alone, Monchae!' he called. 'Soon I will come for you. For you and Belach.' He turned and . . ."

She gave a sudden sob and collapsed into Belach's embrace.

Fidelma gazed thoughtfully at her.

"Was this figure corporeal? Was it of flesh and blood?"

Monchae raised her fearful gaze to Fidelma.

"That is just it. The body shimmered."

"Shimmered?"

"It had a strange luminescence about it, as if it shone with some spectral fire. It was clearly a demon from the Otherworld."

Fidelma turned to Belach.

"And did you see this vision?" she asked half expecting him to confirm it.

"No. I heard Monchae scream in terror, it was her scream which awoke me. When she told me what had passed, I went out into the night to the knoll. I had hoped that I would find tracks there. Signs that a human being had stood there. But there were none."

"No signs of the snow being disturbed?" pressed Fidelma.

"There were no human tracks, I tell you," Belach said irritable. "The snow was smooth. But there was one thing . . ."

"Tell me."

"The snow seemed to shine with a curious luminosity, sparkling in an uncanny light."

"But you saw no footprints nor signs of anyone?"

"No."

The woman was sobbing now.

"It is true, it is true, sister. The ghost of Mugrán will soon come for us. Our remaining time on earth is short."

Fidelma sat back and closed her eyes a moment in deep thought.

"Only the Living God can decide what is your allotted span of life," she said in almost absentminded reproof. Monchae and Belach stood watching her in uncertainty as Fidelma stretched before the fire. "Well," she said, at last, "while I am here, I shall need a meal and a bed for the night."

Belach inclined his head.

"That you may have, sister, and most welcome. But if you will say a prayer to Our Lady . . .? Let this haunting cease. She needs not the deaths of Monchae and myself to prove that she is the blessed mother of Christ."

Fidelma sniffed in irritation.

"I would not readily blame the ills of the world on the Holy Family," she said stiffly. But, seeing their frightened faces, she relented in her theology. "I will say a prayer to Our Lady. Now bring me some food."

Something awoke Fidelma. She lay with her heart beating fast, her body tense. The sound had seemed part of her dream. The dropping of a heavy object. Now she lay trying to identify it. The storm had apparently abated, since she had fallen asleep in the small chamber to which Monchae had shown her after her meal. There was a silence beyond the shuttered windows. An eerie stillness. She did not make a further move but lay, listening intently.

There came to her ears a creaking sound. The inn was full of the creaks and moans of its aging timbers. Perhaps it had been a dream? She was about to turn over when she heard a noise. She frowned, not being able to identify it. Ah, there it was again. A soft thump.

She eased herself out of her warm bed, shivering in the cold night. It must be well after midnight. Reaching for her heavy robe, she draped it over her shoulders and moved stealthily towards the door, opening it as quietly as she could and pausing to listen.

The sound had come from downstairs.

She knew that she was alone in the inn with Monchae and Belach and they had retired when she had, their room being at the top of the stairs. She glanced towards it and saw the door firmly shut.

She walked with quiet padding feet, imitating the soft walk of a cat, along the wooden boards to the head of the stairs and peered down into the darkness.

The sound made her freeze a moment. It was a curious sound, like something soft but weighty being dragged over the bare boards.

She paused staring down the well of the stairs, into the main room of the inn where the eerie red glow of the dying embers of the fire cast a red, shadowy glow. Shadows chased one another in the gloom. Fidelma bit her lip and shivered. She wished that she had a candle to light her way. Slowly, she began to descend the stairs.

She was halfway down when her bare foot came into contact with a board that was loose. It gave forth a heavy creak which sounded like a thunderclap in the night.

Fidelma froze.

A split second later she could a scuffling noise in the darkness of the room below and then she was hastening down the rest of the stairs into the gloom-shrouded room.

"If anyone is here, identify yourself in the name of Christ!" she called, making her voice as stern as she could and trying to ignore the wild beating of her heart.

There was a distant thud and then silence.

She peered around the deserted room of the inn, eyes darting here and there as the red shadows danced across the walls. She could see nothing.

Then . . . there was a sound behind her.

She whirled round.

Belach stood with ghastly face on the bottom stair. His wife, Monchae, stood, peering fearfully over his shoulder.

"You heard it, too?" he whispered nervously.

"I heard it," confirmed Fidelma.

"God look down on us," sighed the man.

Fidelma made an impatient gesture.

"Light a candle, Belach, and we will search this place."

The innkeeper shrugged.

"There is no purpose, sister. We have heard such noises before and made a search. Nothing is ever found."

"Indeed," echoed his wife, "why search for temporal signs from a spectre?"

Fidelma set her jaw grimly.

"Why would a spectre make noises?" she replied. "Only something with a corporeal existence makes a noise. Now give me a light."

Reluctantly, Belach lit a lamp. The innkeeper and his wife stood by the bottom of the stair as Fidelma began a careful search of the inn. She had barely begun when Monchae gave a sudden shriek and fell forward onto the floor.

Fidelma hurried quickly to her side. Belach was patting her hands in a feeble attempt to revive her senses.

"She's fainted," muttered the man unnecessarily.

"Get some water," instructed Fidelma and when the water had been splashed against the woman's forehead and some of it nursed between her lips, Monchae blinked and opened her eyes.

"What was it?" snapped Fidelma. "What made you faint?"

Monchae stared at her a moment or two, her face pale, her teeth chattering. "The pipes!" she stammered. "The pipes!"

"I heard no pipes," Fidelma replied.

"No. Mugrán's pipes . . . on the table!"

Leaving Belach to help Monchae to her feet, Fidelma turned, holding her candle high, and beheld a set of pipes laying on the table. There was nothing remarkable about them. Fidelma had seen many of better quality and workmanship.

"What are you telling me?" she asked, as Monchae was led forward by Belach, still trembling.

"These are Mugrán's pipes. The pipes he took away with him to war. It must be true. His ghost has returned. Oh, saints protect us!"

She clung desperately to her husband.

Fidelma reached forward to examine the pipes.

They seemed entirely of this world. They were of the variety called *cetharchóire*, meaning fourtuned, with a chanter, two shorter reeddrones and a long drone. A simple pipe to be found in almost any household in Ireland. She pressed her lips tightly, realising that when they had all retired for the night there had been no sign of any pipes on the table.

"How are you sure that these are the pipes of Murgán?" she asked.

"I know them!" The woman was vehement. "How do you know what garment belongs to you, or what knife? You know its weave, its stains, it markings . . ."

She began to sob hysterically.

Fidelma ordered Belach to take the woman back to her bed.

"Have a care, sister," the man muttered, as he led his wife away. "We are surely dealing with evil powers here."

Fidelma smiled thinly.

"I am a representative of a greater power, Belach. Everything that happens can only occur under His will."

After they had gone, she stood staring at the pipes for a while and finally gave up the conundrum with a sigh. She left them on the table and climbed the stairs back to her own bed, thankful it was still warm for she realised, for the first time, that her feet and legs were freezing. The night was truly chill.

She lay for a while thinking about the mystery which she had found here in this desolate mountain spot and wondering if there was some supernatural solution to it. Fidelma acknowledged that there were powers of darkness. Indeed, one would be a fool to believe in God and to refuse to believe in the Devil. If there was good, then there was, undoubtedly, evil. But, in her experience, evil tended to be a human condition.

She had fallen asleep. It could not have been for long. It was still dark when she started awake.

It took a moment or two for her to realise what it was which had aroused her for the second time that night.

Far off she could hear pipes playing. It was a sweet, gentle sound. The sound of the sleep-producing *súantraige*, the beautiful, sorrowing lullaby.

"*Codail re suanán saine . . .*"

"Sleep with pleasant slumber . . ."

Fidelma knew the tune well for many a time had she been lulled into drowsiness as a child by its sweet melody.

She sat up abruptly and swung out of bed. The music was real. It was outside the inn. She went to the shuttered window and cautiously eased it open a crack.

Outside the snow lay like a crisp white carpet across the surrounding hills and mountains. The sky was still shrouded with heavy grey-white snow clouds. Even so, the nightscape was light, in spite of the fact that the moon was only a soft glow hung with ice crystals that produced a halo around its orb. One could see for miles. The atmosphere was icy chill and still. Vapour from her breath made bursts of short-lived clouds in the air before her.

It was then that her heart began to hammer as if a mad drummer was beating a warning to wake the dead.

She stood stock-still.

About a hundred yards from the inn was a small round knoll. On the knoll stood the figure of a lonely piper and he was playing the sweet lullaby that woke her. But the thing that caused her to feel dizzy with awe and apprehension was that the figure shimmered as if a curious light emanated from him, sparkling like little stars against the brightness of the reflecting snow.

She stood still watching. Then the melody trailed off and the figure turned its head in the direction of the inn. It gave vent to an awesome, pitiful cry.

"I am alone! I am alone, Monchae! Why did you desert me? I am alone! I will come for you soon!"

Perhaps it was the cry that stirred Fidelma into action.

She turned and grabbed her leather shoes and seized her cloak, and she was hurrying down the stairs into the gloomy interior of the main room of the inn. She heard Belach's cry on the stair behind her.

"Don't go out, sister! It is evil! It is the shade of Mugrán!"

She paid no heed. She threw open the bolts of the door and went plunging into the icy stillness of the night. She ran through the deep snows, feeling its coldness against her bare legs, up towards the knoll. But long before she reached it, she realised that the figure had disappeared.

She reached the knoll and paused. There was no one in sight. The nocturnal piper had vanished. She drew her cloak closer around her shoulders and shivered. But it was the night chill rather than the idea of the spectre that caused her to tremble.

Catching her breath against the icy air, she looked down. There were no footprints. But the snow, on careful inspection, had not laid in pristine condition across the knoll. Its surface was rough, ruffled as if a wind had blown across it. It was then she noticed the curious reflective quality of it, here and there. She bent forward and scooped a handful of snow in her palm and examined it. It seemed to twinkle and reflect as she held it.

Fidelma gave a long, deep sigh. She turned and retraced her steps back to the inn.

Belach was waiting anxiously by the door. She noticed that he now held the sword in his hand.

She grinned mischievously.

"If it were a spirit, that would be of little assistance," she observed dryly.

Belach said nothing, but he locked and bolted the door behind Fidelma as she came into the room. He replaced the sword without comment as she went to the fire to warm herself after her exertion into the night.

Monchae was standing on the bottom step, her arms folded across her breast, moaning a little.

Fidelma went in search of the jug of *corma* and poured out some of the spirit. She swallowed some and then took a wooden cup to Monchae and told her to drink it.

"You heard it? You saw it?" The wife of the innkeeper wailed.

Fidelma nodded.

Belach bit his lip.

"It is the ghost of Mugrán. We are doomed."

"Nonsense!" snapped Fidelma.

"Then explain that!" replied Belach, pointing to the table.

There was nothing on the table. It was then Fidelma realised what was missing. She had left the pipes on the table when she had returned to bed. "It is two hours or so until sunrise," Fidelma said slowly. "I want you two to return to bed. There is something here which I must deal with. Whatever occurs, I do not wish either of you to stir from your room unless I specifically call you."

Belach stared at her with white, taut features.

"You mean that you will do battle with this evil force?"

Fidelma smiled thinly. "That is what I mean," she said emphatically.

Reluctantly, Belach helped Monchae back up the stairs, leaving Fidelma standing in the darkness. She stood still thinking for a while. She had an instinct that whatever was happening in this troubled isolated inn, it was building up towards its climax. Perhaps that climax would come before sunrise. There was no logic to the idea but Fidelma had long come to the belief that one should not ignore one's instincts.

She turned and made her way towards a darkened alcove at the far end of the room in which only a deep wooden bench was situated. She tightened her cloak against the chill, seated herself and prepared to wait. Wait for what, she did not know. But she believed that she would not have to wait for long before some other manifestation occurred.

It was a short time before she heard the sounds of the pipe once more.

The sweet, melodious lullaby was gone. The pipes were now wild keening. It was the hair-raising lament of the *goltraige*, full of pain, sorrow and longing.

Fidelma held her head to one side.

The music was no longer outside the old inn but seeming to echo from within, seeping up under the floorboards, through the walls and down from the rafters.

She shivered but made no move to go in search of the sound, praying all the while that neither Monchae nor Belach would disobey her instructions and leave their room.

She waited until the tune came to an end.

There was a silence in the old building.

Then she heard the sound, the sound she had heard on her first waking. It was a soft, dragging sound. Her body tensed as she bent forward in the alcove, her eyes narrowed as she tried to focus into the darkness.

A figure seemed to be rising from the floor, upwards, slowly upwards on the far side of the room. Fidelma held her breath.

The figure, reaching its full height, appeared to be clutching a set of pipes beneath its arms. It moved towards the table in a curious limping gait.

Fidelma noticed that now and again, as the light of the glowing embers in the hearth caught it, the figure's cloak sparkled and danced with a myriad pinpricks of fire.

Fidelma rose to here feet.

"The charade is over!" she cried harshly.

The figure dropped the pipes and wheeled around, seeking to identify the speaker. Then it seemed to catch its breath.

"Is that you, Monchae?" came a sibilant, mocking whisper.

Then, before Fidelma could prepare herself, the figure seemed to fly across the room at her. She caught sight of light flashing on an upraised blade and instinct made her react by grasping at the descending arm with both hands, twisting her body to take the weight of the impact.

The figure grunted angrily as the surprise of the attack failed.

The collision of their bodies threw Fidelma back into the alcove, slamming her against the wooden seat. She grunted in pain. The figure had shaken her grip loose and once more the knife hand was descending.

"You should have fled while you had the chance, Monchae," came the masculine growl. "I had no wish to harm you or the old man. I just wanted to get you out of this inn. Now, you must die!"

Fidelma sprang aside once more, feverishly searching for some weapon, some means of defence.

Her flaying hand caught against something. She dimly recognised it as the alabaster figure of the Madonna and Child. Automatically, her fingers closed on it and she swung it up like a club. She struck the figure at where she thought the side of the head would be.

She was surprised at the shock of the impact. The alabaster seemed to shatter into pieces, as she would have expected from a plaster statuette, but its impact seemed firm and weighty, causing a vibration in her hand and arm. The sound was like a sickening smack of flesh meeting a hard substance.

The figure grunted, a curious sound as the air was sharply expelled from his lungs. Then he dropped to the floor. She heard the sound of metal ringing on the floor planks as the knife dropped and bounced.

Fidelma stood for a moment or two, shoulders heaving as she sought to recover her breath and control her pounding emotions.

Slowly she walked to the foot of the stairs and called up in a firm voice.

"You can come down now. I have laid your ghost!"

She turned, stumbling a little in the darkness, until she found a candle and lit it. Then she went back to the figure of her erstwhile assailant. He lay on his side, hands outstretched. He was a young man. She gave a soft intake of breath when she saw the ugly wound on his temple. She reached forward and felt for a pulse. There was none.

She looked round curiously. The impact of a plaster statuette could not have caused such a death-blow.

Fragments and powdered plaster were scattered in a large area. But there, lying in the debris was a long cylindrical tube of sacking. It was no more than a foot high and perhaps one inch in diameter. Fidelma bent and picked it up. It was heavy. She sighed and replaced it where she had found it.

Monchae and Belach were creeping down the stairs now.

"Belach, have you a lantern?" asked Fidelma, as she stood up.

"Yes. What is it?" demanded the innkeeper.

"Light it, if you please. I think we have solved your haunting."

As she spoke she turned and walked across the floor to the spot where she had seen the figure rise, as if from the floor. There was a trapdoor and beneath it some steps which led into a tunnel.

Belach had lit the lamp.

"What has happened?" he demanded.

"Your ghost was simply a man," Fidelma explained.

Monchae let out a moan.

"You mean it is Mugrán? He was not killed at Loch Derg?"

Fidelma perched herself on the edge of the table and shook her head. She stooped to pick up the pipes where the figure had dropped them onto the table.

"No; it was someone who looked and sounded a little like Mugrán as you knew him. Take a look at his face, Monchae. I think you will recognise Cano, Mugrán's young brother."

A gasp of astonishment from the woman confirmed Fidelma's identification.

"But why, what . . .?"

"A sad but simple tale. Cano was not killed as reported at Loch Derg. He was probably badly wounded and returned to this land with a limp. I presume that he did not have a limp when he went away?"

"He did not," Monchae confirmed.

"Mugrán was dead. He took Mugrán's pipes. Why he took so long to get back here, we shall never know. Perhaps he did not need money until now, or perhaps the idea never occurred to him . . ."

"I don't understand," Monchae said, collapsing into a chair by the table.

"Cano remembered that Mugrán had some money. A lot of money he had saved. Mugrán told you that if he lost his life, then there was money in the inn and you would never want for anything. Isn't that right?"

Monchae made an affirmative gesture.

"But as I told you, it was just Mugrán's fantasy. We searched the inn everywhere and could find no sign of any money. Anyway, my man, Belach, and I are content with things as they are."

Fidelma smiled softly.

"Perhaps it was when Cano realised that you had not found his brother's hoard that he made up his mind to find it himself."

"But it isn't here," protested Belach, coming to the support of his wife.

"But it *was*," insisted Fidelma. "Cano knew it. But he didn't know where. He needed time to search. How could he get you away from the inn sufficiently long to search? That was when he conceived a convoluted idea to drive you out by pretending to be the ghost of his brother. He had his brother's pipes and could play the same tunes as his brother had played. His appearance and his voice made him pass for the person you once knew, Monchae, but, of course, only at a distance with muffled voice. He began to haunt you."

"What of the shimmering affect?" demanded Belach. "How could he produce such an affect?"

"I have seen a yellow claylike substance that gives off that curious luminosity," Fidelma assured them. "It can be scooped from the walls of the caves west of here. It is called *mearnáil*, a phosphorus, a substance that glows in the gloom. If you examine Cano's cloak you will see that he has smeared it in this yellowing clay."

"But he left no footprints," protested Belach. "He left no footprints in the snow."

"But he did leave some tell tale sign," Fidelma pointed out. "You see, he took the branch of a bush and, as he walked backwards away from the knoll, he swept away his footprints. But while it does disguise the footprints, one can still see the ruffled surface of the snow where the bush has swept over its top layer. It is an old trick, taught to warriors, to hide their tracks from their enemies."

"But surely he could not survive in the cold outside all these nights?" Monchae said. It was the sort of aspect which would strike a woman's precise and practical logic.

"He did not. He slept in the inn, or at least in the stable. Once or twice tried to search the inn while you lay asleep. Hence the bumps and sounds that sometimes awakened you. But he knew, however, that he could only search properly if he could move you out."

"He was here with us in the inn?" Belach was aghast.

Fidelma nodded to the open trapdoor in the floor.

"It seemed that he knew more of the secret passages of the inn than either of you. After all, Cano was brought up in this inn."

There was a silence.

Monchae gave a low sigh.

"All that and there was no treasure. Poor Cano. He was not really evil. Did you have to kill him, sister?"

Fidelma compressed her lips for a moment.

"Everything is in God's hands," she said in resignation. "In my struggle, I seized the statuette of Our Lady and struck out at Cano. It caught him on the table and fragmented."

"But it was only alabaster. It would not have killed him, surely?"

"It was what was inside that killed him. The very thing that he was looking for. It lies there on the floor."

"What is it?" whispered Monchae, when Belach reached down to pick up the cylindrical object in sackcloth.

"It is a roll of coins. It is Mugrán's treasure. It acted as a bar of metal to the head of Cano and killed him. Our Lady had been protecting the treasure all these years and, in the final analysis, Our Lady meted out death to him that was not rightful heir to that treasure."

Fidelma suddenly saw the light creeping in through the shutters of the inn.

"And now day is breaking. I need to break my fast and be on my way to Cashel. I'll leave a note for your *boáire* explaining matters. But I have urgent business in Cashel. If he wants me, I shall be there."

Monchae stood regarding the shattered pieces of the statuette.

"I will have a new statuette of Our Lady made," she said softly.

"You can afford it now," replied Fidelma solemnly.

Charles Beauregard
SEVEN STARS EPISODE ONE

THE MUMMY'S HEART
BY KIM NEWMAN

The Diogenes Club is situated behind a discreet door in London's Pall Mall, on the fringes of Whitehall. Through its unexceptional foyer pass the city's most unsociable and unclubbable men. The greatest collection of eccentrics, misanthropes, grotesques and unconfined lunatics outside the House of Lords is to be found on its membership lists.

Ostensibly for the convenience of that species of individual who yearns to live in monied isolation from his fellows, this unassuming establishment is actually much more. A soundproofed suite on the top floor is set aside for the use of the club's Ruling Cabal of five persons, each connected, mostly in minor official capacities, with Her Majesty's Government.

Charles Beauregard is at the disposal of the Diogenes Club, and when he is called upon, it invariably results in a voyage to some far corner of the world and involves confidential matters affecting the interests of Great Britain. Although Beauregard considers himself something between a diplomat and a courier, he has at times been required to be an explorer, a burglar, an impostor and a civil servant. The invisible business of government has afforded him a varied and intriguing career.

Sometimes the business of the Diogenes Club is known in the outside world as the Great Game. Charles Beauregard was first introduced in Kim Newman's acclaimed novella 'Red Reign' in The Mammoth Book of Vampires *(1992), which the author expanded into the award-winning novel* Anno Dracula *the same year. Since then Beauregard, along with Irish journalist turned vampire Katharine Reed, have appeared in the sequels* The Bloody Red Baron *(1995) and* Dracula Cha Cha Cha *(1999), although these novels are set on an alternate timeline to the one of Seven Stars. Kate Reed, who is also the protagonist of Newman's 'Coppola's Dracula' (*The Mammoth Book of Dracula, *1997), 'The Gypsies in the Wood' (*The Fair Folk, *2005), 'Aquarius' (the Titan Books edition of* Anno Dracula: Dracula Cha Cha Cha, *2012) and 'Grand Guignol' (*Horrorology: The Lexicon of Fear, *2015), was created by Bram Stoker, but never written up by him.*

*The Diogenes Club was also invented by Conan Doyle—Sherlock Holmes' brother Mycroft is a member—in his story 'The Greek Interpreter' (*The Strand, *September 1893), but it was co-writer/ director Billy Wilder who established its status as an intelligence agency in his 1970 movie,* The Private Life of Sherlock Holmes. *Newman's* The Secret Files of the Diogenes Club *(2007) collected seven stories featuring members of the club, along with a couple of useful appendices for American readers. It was followed by* The Mysteries of the Diogenes Club *in 2010, containing four novellas and the 'Seven Stars' sequence.*

IT WAS THE size of a human heart. Charles Beauregard let his hand hover over it, fingers outstretched. He shut one eye but could not quite blot out the jewel.

"Aren't rubies generally smaller than this?" he asked.

Professor Trelawny shrugged. "So I believe. I'm an Egyptologist, not a geologist. Strictly, a ruby is a pure transparent red corundum, though the term is loosely applied to merely red gemstones, like certain varieties of spinel and garnet. In rock-tapping circles, there's an argument that this isn't a ruby proper. Corunda, as you know— sapphire, emery and so on—are second only in hardness to diamond. The Seven Stars is at least as hard as diamond."

Trelawny tapped the Seven Stars with a knuckle, touching it with a diamond ring. He did not try to scratch the priceless artefact. Presumably for fear of breaking his ring.

"So it's a red diamond?" Beauregard assumed.

Trelawny's huge eyebrows wriggled. "If such exists, it may well be. Or mighthap a gemstone unknown to modern science. A variety perhaps once familiar to the Pharaonic Kings, lost to obscurity and now rediscovered, for the glory of our own dear Queen."

Ever since the cloth was unfolded and the jewel disclosed, Beauregard had felt an urge to touch the stone. But he kept his fingers away. Though it was absurd, he had the impression the jewel would be hot as fire, as if just coughed from a volcano.

"Why is it called the Seven Stars?"

Trelawny smiled, weathered face crinkling.

"Turn up the gaslight, would you?"

Beauregard obliged. The flame grew with a serpent's hiss, casting more light. The basements of the British Museum were divided into dozens of storerooms, offices and laboratories. Trelawny's lair, a surprisingly uncluttered space, was currently devoted to the study of the Jewel of Seven Stars.

Trelawny pulled on a white cotton glove and lifted the stone. He had to stretch his thumb and little finger to get a secure grip.

"Look *through* the jewel, at the flame."

Beauregard stepped around the table. Trelawny held the gemstone like a lens. In the red depths, seven fires burned. Beauregard shifted position and the fires vanished. He moved back, and they shone again. Seven pinpoints of light, in a familiar pattern.

"Ursa Major," he commented.

Trelawny set the jewel down again.

"The Great Bear, Charlemagne's Wain, the good old Plough. Also known, I understand, as the *Septentrionnes*, the Seven Ploughing Oxen, and, to the Hindoo, the Seven *Rishis* or Holy Ancient Sages. Or, as our American cousins would have it, the Big Dipper. What in Hades do you think a dipper is, by the way?"

"A ladle. Do you take an interest in astronomy, Professor?"

Trelawny laughed and indicated the jewel.

"I take an interest in this. The rest of it I got from an encyclopedia."

"Is it a natural effect?"

"If not, Ancient Egyptian jewellers were possessed of secrets lost to memory. Which is, incidentally, not an entirely unlikely hypothesis. We still don't really know how they managed to build pyramids. I incline, however, to consider the stars a natural, or supernatural, phenomenon."

"Supernatural?"

Trelawny's eyebrows waved again.

"There's a curse, you see."

"Of course there is."

Without the light behind it, the jewel seemed a dead lump, a giant blood clot. There was certainly blood in its history.

"I can't take curses too seriously," Trelawny announced. "Every ancient site has been at least thrice-accursed. If you consider its collection of maleficent objects from unhallowed graves, you'd have to deem the British Museum the most curse-plagued spot in the Empire. But hundreds of visitors traipse around upstairs every day without suffering ill-effects. Unless, of course, they've first stopped at the pie stall in Great Russell Street."

Beauregard thought the professor might be whistling in the dark.

"And yet," he mused, "this little item has its secrets."

"I assure you, Professor, I should not be here if those secrets were not taken very seriously by eminent persons."

"So I understand."

Trelawny was an open man, not at all the stuffy professor. He had spent more years in deserts and digs than classrooms and storerooms. Beauregard had liked him at first sight. However, the professor was wary of him.

Beauregard must seem mysterious: not a policeman or a diplomat, yet given charge of this delicate matter. When called upon to explain his position, he was supposed to describe himself as a servant of the Queen and not mention the Diogenes Club, the adjunct of the Crown to which he was attached.

"Since the Seven Stars was discovered . . ."

"In the Valley of the Sorcerer, two years ago," Trelawny footnoted.

"Nine men have died. In connection with this stone."

Trelawny shrugged. Beauregard knew most of the dead had been the professor's colleagues.

"Nothing mysterious in that, Beauregard. The jewel is of enormous academic interest but also great value. The traditional tomb-robbers believe Egyptologists are, so to speak, poaching on their preserve. To us, these remnants of the past are miraculous glimpses of lost history, but generations of *fellahin* have seen the tombs of the long-dead as a field of potatoes, to be dug up and sold."

Beauregard's gaze kept returning to the jewel. It was one of those objects that had the power of fascination. Even without the light behind it, there was a fire there.

"It was found, I understand, *inside* a mummy?"

Trelawny nodded. "Not common practice, but not unknown. The mummy was that of Pai-net'em, of the household of Meneptah II. From the fragmentary records, it seems Pharaoh relied on him much as our own dear Queen relies on Lord Salisbury. An influential advisor. Meneptah, a wastrel, left the duller administrative chores to men like old Pai-net'em."

"Was he the sorcerer for which the valley was named?"

"Almost certainly not. Pai-net'em was squeezed in among many tombs. His place of interment is modest, especially considering his importance. By rights, he should have been buried in the Theban version of Westminster Abbey. At first, we believed the mummy to be one of Pai-net'em's servants but evidence—not least, the Seven Stars—later revealed the body as the man himself."

"The jewel?"

"We shipped the mummy here for examination. When Sir Joseph Whemple and I supervised the unwrapping, it was as if fire exploded from its chest. A trick of the light, but startling. It's a unique find. The Cairo Museum of Antiquities started hemming and hawing and asking for *their* mummy back, oh and the the jewel of course. Lord Cromer convinced the *khedive* the most apt course of action would be to make a gift of the Seven Stars to the Queen, in honour of her Jubilee."

"Sir Joseph was subsequently murdered?"

Trelawny nodded.

"Some devil cut his throat. In his office. Four doors down the corridor. With a dull knife. It was as if his neck were clawed open."

"But the jewel was safe?"

"*In* a safe, actually. We have vaults for items of especial value."

Beauregard had seen the police reports. Half the Egyptian scholars in London had been ungently interrogated, suspected of membership of some fanatic cult. No arrests had been made.

The death of Sir Joseph brought the Seven Stars to the notice of the Diogenes Club. Mycroft Holmes, of the Ruling Cabal, had clipped the report from the *Times* and predicted the affair would be forwarded to his department of service.

"Has the mummy been returned to Cairo?"

Beauregard was relying on a favourite tactic, asking a question to which he knew the answer. Mycroft taught that facts themselves were often less significant than the way facts were presented by individuals.

"Now there's a question," Trelawny said, brow crinkled. "Whoever killed Sir Joseph stole the mummy. It was a light enough carcass. Still, not an easy item to get past our stout night watchmen. And of little worth in monetary terms. Mummies are ten a penny. Most were robbed of their funerary ornaments thousands of years ago. If the jewel hadn't been *inside* Pai-net'em, the robbers would have had it along with the rest of his grave goods."

"Certain occult practitioners have use for the ancient dead," Beauregard commented.

"Good Lord, what for?"

"Charms and potions and totems and such. Ingredients in arcane rituals."

Trelawny said nothing. At Oxford, he had been a member of an occult society, the Order of the Ram.

" 'Eye of mummy, toe of dog', that sort of thing," Beauregard prompted.

Finally, Trelawny snorted.

"Some dunderheads do take an interest in that sort of rot," he admitted. "In my student days, I ran into a pack of them myself. The sons of the clods I knew probably still pay through the nose for crumbled horse manure passed off as the ashes of the mages of Atlantis. Pai-net'em's poor bones might fetch something on that singular market. I trust the police are pursuing that avenue of inquiry."

"So do I."

Beauregard looked back at the Seven Stars.

"I shall not entirely be sorry to see the jewel go to the Tower," Trelawny said. "The death of Sir Joseph rattled me, I don't mind telling you. The scientist in me says I should cling to the stone until its mysteries are exhausted. But the cautious man tells me to let the next fellow worry about it."

"And I'm the next fellow?"

Trelawny smiled, sadly. He dropped a cloth on the Seven Stars.

"From Meneptah to Pai-net'em," the professor said. "And now from Abel Trelawny to Queen Victoria. From pharaoh to sovereign in just three thousand years. Perhaps that'll be the end of it. For my part, I certainly hope so."

Beauregard made his way upstairs. Late in the afternoon, the crowds were thinning. He touched his hat-brim to Jenks, the Diogenes man who wore the uniform of an attendant and had been working here, keeping an eye out, ever since the murder of Sir Joseph.

The Hall of Egyptian Antiquities, always popular, was almost empty. A noseless giant head dominated the room, eyes eerily impassive. Beauregard wanted to take a look at some mummies, to get an idea of what was missing.

Under glass was the bandage-wrapped corpse of a young girl.

He thought of his late wife, Pamela. She was buried in the hill country of India, a world away. Would she find herself on display millennia hence, a typical specimen of the 19th Century Anno Domini?

He felt an instant of connection. With the girl.

The plaque said she was unknown, but the daughter of wealth. *Ushabti* mannikins were found in her grave, to be her servants in the afterlife. Her bindings were an intricate herringbone. Her nose still had definition under ancient cloth.

Beauregard had a sense that he was a moment in history, a pause in a story which had begun long before him and would continue well past his death. People came and went, but some things remained, eternal.

He thought of the Seven Stars, undisturbed for three thousand years. And who knew how old the jewel was when buried inside Pai-net'em?

A chill crept up his spine. He felt eyes upon his back, but the only reflection in the glass of the display case was that of the blind stone head.

He turned, and saw a woman with a pale face and smoked glasses. Almost a girl, fair and fragile. He thought for a moment she might be blind too, but she was watching him.

He almost said something, then, very swiftly, she was gone.

In another life . . .

He looked at the mummy again, wondering why he was so stirred inside.

He bade Jenks a good day and left the museum.

Pall Mall was half-decorated. London was disappearing under cheerful swathes of patriotic bunting in honour of the Queen's Diamond Jubilee. Her sixty years on the throne had seen unimaginable changes in Britain and her Empire. The Queen had weathered constitutional crises, setting an example in conduct that many of her subjects, from her own children down, could not match.

He had taken an open cab from the British Museum, enjoying the early June evening. The Jubilee, not yet fully upon the city, encouraged an opening-up. People wore sashes and ribbons in celebration of a Queen who ruled through love, not the fear Meneptah and his like had wielded like a lash.

In years of service, he had seen the Empire at its best and worst. He hated the pettiness and cruelty that existed as much in this city as in the farthest outpost, but admired fiercely the aspirations to decency and honour embodied in Victoria's great heart. To him, the Union Jack was not the trademark of some gigantic financial concern or the territorial stink of a bristling bulldog but a banner which meant the innocent were protected and the helpless defended.

He entered the lobby of the Diogenes Club and was discreetly admitted to the chamber of the Ruling Cabal. Mycroft Holmes, the huge spider at the centre of the nation's intelligence web, sat in his custom-made leather armchair, plump fingers pyramided, brows knit in thought. He did not greet Beauregard for a full minute, as he finished some mental calculation.

"Beauregard," he said. "This is a delicate business."

Beauregard agreed.

"You've seen the bauble?"

"It's considerably more than that, Mycroft. A ruby as big as my fist."

"It's not a ruby."

"I fail to see how the geology is germane to the affair."

"One should consider a jewel from all angles, the better to appreciate its many facets. This is a jewel like no other."

"I couldn't agree more."

"It won't attract as much attention as the *Koh-i-noor* or the Moonstone or the Eye of the Little Yellow God. But it's the more remarkable."

"It's washed in blood."

"All great gems are."

"This one looks like it."

"Tell me, Beauregard, what of the points of light?"

"The Seven Stars. Exactly in the configuration of Ursa Major. That's an uncanny feature. As if the stone were a star map."

"Stent, the Astronomer Royal, has suggested the Seven Stars fell to Earth as a meteor. Maybe it is a message from those stars."

Beauregard shuddered again. He didn't like to think of a red streak nearing the Earth, millennia ago.

"It's a strange thing," he admitted.

"And what of the murder of Sir Joseph Whemple and the theft of the mummy?"

Beauregard considered the little he had learned.

"Trelawny went out of his way to pooh-pooh a suggestion that the mummy might have been stolen for use in magical rituals. Yet he was, admittedly as a youth, involved in such rites himself. It's my consideration that he suspects as much, but does not dare propose the theory strongly lest his past be looked into too closely."

Mycroft's fat face crumpled in mild irritation. "We know much about Abel Trelawny and the Society of the Ram. Have you heard of Declan Mountmain?"

"The Fenian?"

"Not strictly. We came close to gaoling him for that dynamite business at Lord's but he slipped through the net, found subordinates to take the blame."

Beauregard remembered the atrocity. It was a wonder no one had been killed.

"Mountmain is a crank," declared Mycroft, "but a dangerous one. Most advocates of Irish Home Rule distance themselves from him. The Fenian Brotherhood regard him as a loose cannon of the worst sort. He wrote a pamphlet which was suppressed as obscene, alleging prominent cabinet ministers and churchmen constitute a cult devoted to the pagan worship of a goddess incarnated as our Queen. Apparently, we are given to snatching drabs from the alleys of the East End and ritually disembowelling them in a temple beneath Buckingham Palace."

Beauregard found the suggestion disgusting.

"Mountmain himself believes none of it. He is merely trying to project his own methods and manners on those he deems his foemen. He is an adept in occult sciences, and remains the Great Pooh-Bah of the Order of the Ram. His beliefs are a mixture of paganism and Satanism, with a little Hindoo or Ancient Egyptian tosh thrown in. He blathers about Atlantis and R'lyeh and the Plateau of Leng, and Elder Gods from the Stars. All very arcane and eldritch, no doubt."

"You believe this Mountmain to be behind the attempts on the Seven Stars?"

"I believe nothing that cannot be proven. Mountmain has an old connection with Trelawny. He is a collector of weird artifacts. He has a fortune at his disposal, augmented by funds extorted from supporters of his dubious political cause. He is by no means the only blackguard of his stripe—you've heard me remark that the mountaineer Aleister Crowley is a young man worth watching—but he is currently the worst of his shabby crowd."

"Should I make some discreet inquiries about Declan Mountmain?"

"If you think it worthwhile."

As usual with Mycroft, Beauregard felt he had been led through a maze to a foregone conclusion. It was the Great Man's knack to draw his own ideas out of other people.

"Very well. I think I know where to start."

A mere hundred yards from the Diogenes Club were the offices of the *Pall Mall Gazette*. He strolled casually, pondering the two sides to his immediate problem.

When Mycroft mentioned Declan Mountmain, he knew he would have to bring Katharine Reed into it. She was a reporter, the sole woman in regular employment at the *Gazette*, at least when she wasn't in jail for suffragette agitations. Kate knew as much about the Irish Home Rule movement as any man, probably because she was in it up to her spectacles. She also had a knack for finding out things about prominent personages that did them no credit. He was certain Kate would know about Mountmain.

The other side of the coin was that Kate was insatiably curious and as tenacious as a tick. Every time she was asked a question, she would ask one back. And trade answer for answer. With her disarming manner and steel-trap mind, she might latch on, and follow him to what she imagined was a story worth printing. The Diogenes Club prided itself on being the least-known arm of the British Government. Mycroft had a positive distaste for seeing the organisation's name, let alone his own, in the papers. Such things he left for his more famous, though less acute, brother.

Kate had been a friend of Pamela's. She shared with his late wife a trick of looking through Charles Beauregard as if he were a pane of glass. And he was about to recruit her for a confidential mission.

He thought, not for the first time, that he must be mad. He knew where Kate's cubby hole was, but would have been able to identify it anyway. By the shouting.

A large, well-dressed man, neck scarlet, was blustering.

"Come out from that desk and be thrashed!"

He recognised Henry Wilcox, the financial colossus.

He guessed at once that the *Gazette* must have carried some story under Kate's byline that revealed an irregularity on Wilcox's part.

"Shift yourself, coward," the colossus roared.

Wilcox was standing over a sturdy desk. He lashed it with a riding-crop. The desk shook.

Kate, Beauregard gathered, was underneath.

He wondered whether he should intervene, but thought better of it. Kate Reed didn't care for it if other people fought her battles for her, though she was herself practiced at pitching in to any brawl that came along.

Wilcox savagely whipped a typewriting apparatus.

The desk heaved upwards and a small woman exploded from her hiding-place.

"How dare you!" she shouted. "Henry Wilcox, you have a great deal to be ashamed of!"

The colossus, as imposing physically as he was financially, was given pause. Kate, red-haired and freckled and often hesitant in polite company, was in a fine fury. Up on her toes, she stuck her face close to Wilcox's and adjusted her thick spectacles.

"This piece which names me," he began.

"Do you deny the facts?"

"That's not the point," he snarled.

"I rather think it is. Maybe we should print a follow-up article. You want your side of it to be given. Well, Mr. Wilcox, now is your chance."

Kate set her chair upright and fed a sheet of paper into her typewriter.

"First of all, there's the question of the girl's age. What was your initial estimate?"

"I didn't come here to be insulted."

"Really? Where do you go to be insulted? I understand the house which employs your young associate offers many varieties of satisfaction."

"Your manner does not become your sex."

Kate Reed looked as if she was about to breathe fire.

"I suppose seeking Biblical knowledge of children is a noble and worthy occupation for the mighty male gender."

"That's libel."

"No, that's slander. It is only libel if we print it. And if it's proven untrue."

"She'd never furnish proof."

"Your soiled dove? How much would you wish to wager on that?"

Wilcox's entire face was red. Beauregard wondered if the colossus were not on the verge of a coronary. From what he gathered, the man was an utter swine.

Kate typed rapidly, fingers jabbing like little knives.

"Would you care to take the address of the *Gazette*'s solicitors with you? Your own can get in touch with them when this piece runs."

Wilcox muttered a word Beauregard had hoped never to hear in a lady's presence. Kate, unblushing, kept on typing.

The financial colossus put on his hat and withdrew, pushing impatiently past Beauregard.

"Stupid little tart," he said.

"The girl or me?" Kate shouted after him.

Beauregard replaced Wilcox in Kate's line of fire, standing by her desk. She looked up, smiled a little, and kept on typing.

"Charles, good day to you. What trouble am I in now?"

"You seem more than able to find enough on your own."

"That man buys children for unspeakable purposes. And yet he'll probably wind up with a knighthood."

"I doubt that."

"Others have before him," she broke off typing, and looked at him. "Oh, I see. Words in the right ears. A name crossed off a list. Closed ranks. Nothing in the open, you know, where it might upset the rabble. Just an understanding. Some things aren't done, you know. He has money all right, and the house, and the prospects. But he's not a *gentleman*. You can probably do it. I don't underestimate your shadowy influence. But getting him blackballed isn't the scope of my ambitions for the monstrous thug. I'd rather see him deballed."

Beauregard was shocked. Kate was habitually forward, but he'd never heard her voice such an extreme sentiment.

She softened, and rested her elbows on her desk. Her hair had come undone.

"I'm sorry. I shouldn't rail at you. It's not your fault."

Beauregard pulled the paper from the typewriter. Kate had been typing a nursery rhyme.

"Mr. Stead won't publish anything more about Wilcox," she admitted, referring to the editor. "He's a crusading soul, hot on exposing the 'maiden tribute of modern Babylon', but to be frank our solicitors aren't up to the level Wilcox can afford. Stead wants to stay in business."

Kate took the sheet of paper, crumpled it into a ball, and missed a wicker basket.

Beauregard wondered how best to broach the subject.

"What are your plans for the Jubilee?" he asked.

"Are you offering to escort me to that little ceremony at the Tower

I'm not supposed to know you're arranging? If you were, I'd suspect you were only luring me there so I could be clapped in irons and penned in the deepest dungeon."

"As a reporter, I thought you might be interested."

"She's a nice enough old girl, the Queen. But I don't think she ought to be ruling over my stretch of the world. Or quite a few other patches of red on the map. I was imagining I'd celebrate the Jubilee by cosily chaining myself to some nice railings and being spat on by patriotic crowds."

Beauregard couldn't miss the seam of self-doubt in Kate's calculated outrageousness.

"Can I depend on your discretion?"

She looked at him with comical pity.

"Of course I can't," he said, smiling. "However, needs must when the Devil drives. What do you know about Declan Mountmain?"

Anything comical was wiped from Kate's face.

"Charles, *don't*."

"I don't understand."

"Whatever involves Mountmain, don't pursue it. There are fools and blackguards and rogues and monsters. He's all of them. Beside Mountmain's sins, Henry Wilcox's are mere errors of judgement."

"His name has come up."

"I want nothing to do with it. Whatever it is."

"Then you won't want to be my guest at the Tower. To see the Jewel of Seven Stars."

"That's different. I accept that invitation. Thank you, kind sir."

She stood up and leaned over the desk to kiss his cheek.

"What shall I wear? Something green?"

He laughed. "Don't you dare."

She giggled.

The deepness of her feelings about Mountmain shadowed their gaiety. Uncomfortably, Beauregard suspected Mycroft had set him on the right road, and that he would not like where it was leading.

There were policemen in the courtyard of the British Museum. And a light burning behind one set of tall windows. Beauregard realised that the illuminated room was the Hall of Egyptian Antiquities.

He had been summoned from his house in Chelsea by a cryptic message. Before being shaken awake by his manservant, Bairstow, he had been dreaming an Egyptian dream, floating down the Nile on a barge, pursued by the hordes of the Mahdi—which had actually happened to him in this life—and of the Pharaoh of Exodus—which certainly hadn't.

In the Hall, caped constables stood over a sheeted form. A small, whiskered man in a bowler hat, fretted.

"Good morning, Lestrade."

"Is it?" the policeman asked. Dawn was pinking the windows. "Seems like the start of another long bloody day to me."

There was a lot of damage about. The case of the mummy he had looked at earlier was smashed in, broken shards of glass strewn over the Egyptian girl. Other exhibits were knocked over and scattered.

"I needn't tell you how unpleasant this is," Lestrade said, nodding to a constable, who lifted the sheet.

It was Jenks, throat torn away.

"We thought he was just a keeper," Lestrade said. "Then we found his papers, and it seems he was one of your mob."

"Indeed," Beauregard said, not committing.

"Doubtless poking around into the last business. The Whemple murder. Behind the backs of the hardworking police."

"Jenks was just watching over things. There's a crown jewel in the basement, you know."

"There was."

The phrase was like a hammer.

"The vault was broken into. Nothing subtle or clever. Looks like dynamite to me. The blast woke up every guard in the building. The ones who slept through this."

"The Jewel of Seven Stars is gone?"

"I should say so."

Beauregard looked at Jenks's wound.

"Is this what Whemple looked like?"

Lestrade nodded. "Ripped from ear to ear, with something serrated and not too sharp."

Beauregard had seen tiger-marks in India, crocodile attacks in

Egypt, lion maulings in the Transvaal, wolf victims in Siberia and the Canadian Northwoods.

"Could have been an animal," he said.

"We thought of that. With Whemple, there was nothing missing, if you get my drift. Ripped this way and that, but not chewed, torn off, or eaten. Animals don't do that. They always at least try to eat what they've killed."

For some reason, he thought of the woman in smoked glasses, who had been here when last he saw Jenks. In his memory, she had teeth like a dainty cannibal, filed to points.

"It's unusual."

"I don't like the unusual ones, sir. They always mean that poor old coppers like me get pushed aside and clever fellows like you or the chap from Baker Street are let loose on my patch. What I like is a murderer who gets drunk and takes a cudgel to his wife, then sits down blubbing until the police turn up. That's a proper murder. This is just fiendishness."

"Your murderer has made two bad mistakes tonight, Lestrade. In taking the Seven Stars, he has robbed the Queen. And in killing Jenks, he has aroused the ire of the Diogenes Club. I should not care to exchange places with him."

Declan Mountmain's London address was a Georgian mansion in Wimpole Street. Just the lair for a viper who wished to nestle close to the bosom of Empire.

Beauregard deemed it best to make a direct approach. It would be interesting, considering last night's business at the Museum, to gauge Mountmain's condition this morning. Were his ears ringing, as if he had been in the vicinity of an explosion in a confined space?

He knocked on Mountmain's sturdy front door, and waited on the step for the butler to open up.

"Mr. Mountmain isn't receiving visitors, sir," said the sharp-faced servant. "He has taken to his bed."

"He'll see me," Beauregard said, confidently.

The butler hesitated.

"Are you the doctor, sir? The *confidential* doctor?"

Beauregard looked up and down the street, as if suspecting he was being followed. As it happens, there was a suspiciously human-sized bundle in a doorway a dozen houses distant. This was not a district in which gentlemen of the road sleeping under the stars were much tolerated.

"Do you think you should mention such matters out on the street where anyone might hear you?" The butler was chastened, and—unless Beauregard wildly missed his guess—terrified.

The door was pulled open wide, and Beauregard allowed in. He tried to project from within the impression that he was a disgraced physician on a hush-hush mission of dark mercy. Such impersonations were surprisingly easy, especially if one didn't actually claim to be who one was pretending to be but merely let others make assumptions one did not contradict.

Mountmain's hallway was dark. The windows were still curtained. A line of wavering light under a door revealed that one of the rooms was occupied, and low voices could be made out. The butler did not lead Beauregard to that door, but to another, which he opened.

A single lamp burned, a dark lantern set upon a table. A man lay on a divan, a sheet thrown over him. He was groaning, and a black-red stain covered a full quarter of the sheet.

The butler turned up the lamp and Beauregard looked at the man. He was deathly pale beneath grime, teeth gritted, pellets of sweat on his forehead.

Beauregard lifted the sheet.

A gouge had been taken out of the man, ripping through his shirt, exposing ribs.

The wounded man gripped Beaureagard's arm.

"A priest," he said. "Get a priest."

"Come now, Bacon," boomed a voice. "Have you so easily turned apostate and reverted to the poor faith of your feeble fathers?"

Beauregard turned.

In the doorway stood the man he knew to be Declan Mountmain. Short and stout, with a high forehead growing higher as his black hair receded away from the point of his widow's peak, Mountmain was somehow an impressive presence. He wore a Norfolk jacket and riding boots, unmistakably blooded. Not the sort of outfit for lounging around the house before breakfast, but ideal wear for an after-midnight adventure in larceny and murder.

Bacon's wound was irresistibly reminiscent of the fatal injuries suffered by Jenks and Whemple.

"Who might you be, sir?" Mountmain asked. "And what business have you poking around in young Bacon's open wound? You're no damned doctor, that's certain."

Beauregard handed over his card. "I wished to consult you in your capacity as an expert on occult matters."

Mountmain looked at the card, cocked a quizzical eyebrow, then landed a slap across the face of his butler, slamming him against the wall.

"You're a worthless fool," he told his servant.

"This man needs medical attention," Beauregard said. "And, by his admission, spiritual attention too."

Mountmain strode over.

Beauregard felt Bacon's grip strengthen as Mountmain neared. Then it was suddenly limp.

"No, he needs funerary attention," Mountmain said.

Bacon's dead hand fell. There was blood on Beauregard's sleeve.

"Very tragic," Mountmain said, deliberate despite his rage. "A carriage accident."

According to Mycroft, people who volunteer explanations as yet unasked for are certain to be lying. Beauregard realised Mountmain's contempt for others was such that he did not even take the trouble to concoct a believable story.

Mountmain's jacket was dusty and odiferous. He recognised the Guy Fawkes Night smell that lingers after a dynamite blast.

"There will now be tedious complications as a result of my charitable taking in of this stranger. I should be grateful if you quit this house so I can make the proper, ruinously costly, arrangements."

Beauregard looked at the dead man's face. It was still stamped with fear.

"If I can be of assistance," he ventured, "I shall report the matter to the police. I am in a small way officially connected."

Mountmain looked up at Beauregard, calculating.

"That will not be necessary."

"The young man's name was, what did you say, Bacon?"

"He blurted it as he was carried into the house."

Mountmain spread his arms and looked down at his blood- and dirt-smeared clothes. He did not say so outright, but implied he was in this condition because he had hauled an injured passerby off the street. Now his rage was cooling, he showed something of the canniness Beauregard expected of such a dangerous man.

"The business upon which I called . . ."

"I can't be expected to think of that," Mountmain said. "There's a corpse ruining the furniture. Put your concerns in writing and send them to my secretary. Now, if you will be so kind as to leave . . ."

Mountmain's door slammed behind Beauregard. He stood outside the house, mind swarming around the problem.

He glanced at the doorway where the vagrant had been earlier but it was unoccupied. He half-thought the bundle might have been Kate, pursuing a story. She was certainly not above disguising herself as an urchin.

A man had died in his presence.

No matter how often it happened, it was shocking. Death struck deep in him, reaching that portion of his heart he thought buried with Pamela. All death took him back to the hill country, to his wife bathed in blood and their stillborn son. Then, he had wept and raged and had to be restrained from taking a sabre to the drunken doctor. Now, it was his duty to show nothing, to pretend he felt as little as Mountmain evidently did. Death was at worst a rude inconvenience.

He concentrated. His hands did not shake. He walked away from the house with even steps. An observer would not think he was about business of great moment.

Mountmain and Bacon, and who knows how many confederates, had been at the Museum last night, and had certainly set the charges that blew the safe. The man had a habit of meddling with dynamite. He must be after the Seven Stars, though it was not yet clear whether Mountmain's interest in the stone was down to its monetary value, its political import, or an as yet unknown occult significance.

He paused casually and took a cigar from his case. He stepped into the shelter of a doorway to light the cigar, turning and hunching a little to keep the match-flame out of the wind. He paused to let the flame grow the length of the match, and lit up the doorway. A scrap of rag wound around the boot-scraper, some grey stuff brittle with dust.

He puffed on his fine cigar and picked up the rag, as if he had dropped it when taking his matches from his pocket. It almost crumbled in his hands and he carefully folded it into his silver cigar case.

A hansom cab trundled by, looking for custom. Beauregard hailed it.

Trelawny was in shock at the loss of the Seven Stars. His room was turned upside down, and the corridor outside blackened by the blast. Beauregard had the impression Mountmain had overdone the dynamite. Lestrade's men were still pottering around.

"Ever since the Valley of the Sorcerer, it's been like this," Trelawny said. "Blood and shot and death. In Egypt, you expect that sort of thing. But not here, in London, in the British Museum."

"Do you know a man named Mountmain?"

"Declan Mountmain? The worst sort of occult busybody. Half-baked theories and disgusting personal habits."

"Were you not close to him at Oxford? In the Order of the Ram?"

Trelawny was surprised to have that brought up. "I wouldn't say 'close'. I took a passing interest in such concerns. It's impossible to get far in Egyptology without trying to understand occult practices. Mountmain and I quarrelled without relief and I broke with him long ago. To him, it's all about *power*, not knowledge."

"I believe that last night Mountmain stole the Seven Stars."

Trelawny sat down, astonished.

"He has many low associations. He would know the cutters and fences who could deal with such booty."

Trelawny shook his head.

"If it's Mountmain, it's not for the money. I believe I mentioned that the Seven Stars was as hard as diamond. Actually, it is far harder. I doubt if it could be broken into smaller stones for disposal. It would probably be a blessing if that were possible, though the process might well merely disperse the ill fortune throughout the world."

"If not the money . . .?"

"The magic, Beauregard. Mountmain believes in such things. For him, they seem to work. At Oxford, he had a fearful row with one of the professors and cast an enchantment on the fellow. It was a terrible thing to see."

"He sickened and died?"

"Eventually. First, he lost his position, his standing, his reputation. He was found guilty of unholy acts, and claimed that voices compelled him."

"The Seven Stars?"

". . . would be of incalculable use to Mountmain. There are references in certain books, the sort we keep under lock and key and don't allow in the index. Though lost since the time of Meneptah, there are references to the Jewel of Seven Stars. It has a shadowy reputation."

"Mountmain would know this?"

"Of course."

"He would wish to employ the stone in some species of ritual?"

"Indubitably."

"To what end?"

Trelawny shook his head.

"Something on a cyclopean scale, Beauregard. According to the *Al Azif* of the mad Arab Al-Hazred, the last time the jewel was the focus of occult power was in the thick of the Plagues of Egypt."

Beauregard took out his cigar case.

"What do you make of this?"

Trelawny looked at the scrap of cloth.

"Is this part of the debris?"

Beauregard said nothing.

"I'd heard one of the mummies upstairs was damaged. This looks like a funerary binding. It's certainly ancient. I say, you shouldn't just have picked it up as a souvenir."

Beauregard took the rag back and folded it again.

"I think I'll hang on to it for the moment."

Kate hadn't got all of the story out of him, but he had doled her a few of the less arcane facts.

They were in Covent Garden, at a café. The awning was draped with flags. A portrait of the Queen hung proudly in prime position.

"You believe Mountmain has this gem? In his town house? And he has a dead man on the premises?"

Beauregard sipped his tea and nodded.

"If Ireland and dynamite are involved, such niceties as due process and search warrants usually go out the window. So why hasn't Lestrade descended on the scene with a dozen flatfeet and torn the house apart?"

"It's not quite that simple."

"Yes it is, Charles. And you know it."

"I don't mind telling you, I didn't much care for your countryman."

Kate almost laughed.

"'My countryman'. I suppose you wouldn't mind at all if I habitually referred to Blackbeard, Charley Peace, Jonathan Wild and Burke and Hare as 'your countrymen.'"

"I'm sorry. And Burke and Hare were Irish."

"I believe in Home Rule for the people of Ireland, and Egypt and India come to that. Mountmain's interest in the country of his birth involves replacing the muddled and unjust rule of England with the monstrous and tyrannical rule of Declan Mountmain. Have you read any of his pamphlets? He claims descent from the Mage-Kings of Erin, whomsoever they might be. If he ever has a Diamond Jubilee, it will be celebrated by ripping out the beating hearts of Wicklow virgins. Distasteful as all this Union Jackery might be, Vicky doesn't insist her ministers cut throats at the Palace. At least, not since Palmerston."

"You wouldn't happen to have been passing Mountmain's town house this morning, in the borrowed clothes of a tramp?"

Kate's eyes went wide.

"Wherever did you get that idea?"

"Something glimpsed out of the corner of my eye."

"What are you going to do about your blessed jewel?"

Beauregard considered the matter.

"I rather thought I might try to steal it back."

Kate smiled, eyes crinkling behind spectacles. She was much more appealing than generally reckoned, he thought. A face made beautiful by character (and wit) wore far better than one made beautiful by nature (and paint).

"Now that's a lovely notion. Charles, I always admire you most in your all too infrequent excursions into larceny. Do not even consider embarking on such a venture without me."

"Kate, you know that's absolutely impossible."

"Then why did you mention it? You know me too well to think I'd just flutter my handkerchief and let you bravely go about your business while I fret the night away in fear of your life. Make no mistake, Charles, that young fellow you saw wasn't the first corpse to be found in the immediate vicinity of Declan Mountmain."

He could give in now, or he could argue the afternoon away and give in around teatime. Or he could give in now, and tell Kate that the burglary was set for tomorrow night then make the attempt this evening.

"By the way," she said. "If you're thinking of telling me you don't intend to do your housebreaking later than this very night, I shall not believe you."

"Very well, Kate. You may come with me. But you will not come into the house itself. You shall wait outside, to alert me to any danger. By whistling."

"We'll discuss the specifics when we come to them."

"No, now. Kate, promise."

Her nose twitched and she looked everywhere but at him.

"I promise," Kate said. "I'll be the whistler."

He raised his cup and she clinked hers against it.

"To larceny," she said, "and the ruin of rogues of all nations."

After arranging with Kate to meet later, Beauregard took a cab back to Chelsea. He wished to call on one of his near neighbours in Cheyne Walk. The occult wasn't his field of expertise, and he wanted a little more knowledge before venturing into Mountmain's lair.

Mr. Thomas Carnacki, the celebrated "ghost-finder", admitted Beauregard to his comfortable sitting room.

"I'm sorry to interrupt."

Carnacki had been entertaining an actorly looking man. He waved aside the apology.

"Machen and I were just yarning. You know his work, of course."

Beauregard was unfamiliar with the author.

"I am pleased to meet you, Mr. Beauregard," said Machen,

offering a bony hand to be shaken. There was a little Welsh in his accent, thinned by London.

"I've come to make inquiries on a matter relating to your speciality."

"Machen might help, as well," Carnacki said.

The dapper little man offered Beauregard brandy, which he declined. He wanted to keep his head clear for the rest of the night's business.

"Have you heard of the Jewel of Seven Stars?"

Carnacki and Machen said nothing, in the distinctive manner of people reluctant to venture onto shivering sands.

"I see that you have. I assume you know of its recent discovery, inside a mummy."

"I had doubted its authenticity," Machen said. "It's a fabled object."

"Professor Trelawny is convinced that it is the genuine gem," Beauregard said to Machen. "It is certainly as old as the mummy. Three thousand years."

"That merely means that it's an old fake. Made in imitation of an item that probably never existed."

"There's a curse, of course," said Carnacki.

"Of course," Beauregard agreed.

"One might say, the curse of curses."

"Trelawny mentioned the Plagues of Egypt."

"Frogs, locusts, boils, blood, gnats, and so forth," Machen chanted.

"There's been blood."

"I hardly think we need to fear the Plagues of Egypt. Pharaoh, after all, held the Israelites in bondage. All are free in our Empire."

Carnacki swilled his brandy, beaming. To him, this was a parlour game. He prided himself on never being rattled.

"It is a mistake to take Exodus, as it were, as gospel," Machen commented. "Egyptian records make little of the tribes of Israel. And the plagues are almost totally expunged. Of course, the Egyptians believed that to forget a thing or a person was to revoke their very existence. To blot the plagues from the histories would mean they could be averted, as it were, in retrospect."

Beauregard wondered if Mountmain might not see himself as Ireland's Moses. He decided to drop the name.

"Do you know Declan Mountmain?"

As vehement as Kate's reaction to the name had been, Carnacki's and Machen's were more extreme. The ghost-finder spat a mouthful of brandy back into his glass, and Machen's thin lips pressed together in disgust and rage.

"He's one of your occult fellows, isn't he?" Beauregard prompted, disingenuously.

"Mountmain wants to bring things back," Machen said. "Old things. Things best left in the beyond."

"Is he after the Seven Stars?" Carnacki asked. Beauregard had forgotten the little man had the instincts of a detective. "They'd make a deuced combination."

He distracted himself for the cab journey by running through the plagues of Egypt, in order. First, the waters of the Nile turned to blood. Second, hordes of frogs. Third, the dust became swarms of gnats. Fourth, an infestation of flies. Fifth, the cattle struck dead. Sixth, an epidemic of boils. Seventh, lightning and hail struck the crops and livestock. Eighth, locusts. Ninth, darkness covered the land for three days. And tenth, the death of all the firstborn throughout the country.

In Exodus, the story reads strangely. It's all down to the Lord and Pharaoh. The suggestion seems to be that the Lord visits the plagues on Egypt but influences Pharaoh to ignore them, "hardening his heart" against letting the tribes of Israel go free. Beauregard remembered officers in India who were like that, alternately inflicting hideous punishments and encouraging the offenders to defy them, as an excuse for continuing with the punishment.

On the whole, it wasn't the sort of behaviour one expected from a proper God. One of Mountmain's eldritch and arcane Old Ones, perhaps.

Carnacki seemed to suggest that the Israelites didn't really come into it. The point was the plagues.

The effect of all ten must have been devastation on a vast scale. In the aftermath, with no crops or cattle, most people maddened by disease or bereavement, the chaos would take generations to pass away.

If he had been Pharaoh, Beauregard would have felt he had a legitimate complaint that disproportionate sentence had been inflicted.

He had the cab drop him off in Cavendish Square.

Kate turned up on a bicycle. She wore britches and a tweed-cap. He thought better of asking her if she were disguised as a youth.

They walked up Wimpole Street.

"Where do you think Mountmain has the jewel?" she asked.

"I don't expect to find it. I just want to get the lie of the land. Consider this an exploratory expedition. Later, Lestrade and his stout fellows can go through the place and recover the swag."

"You make a poor cracksman."

"I should hope so, Kate."

"Is that the address? It doesn't look all that foreboding."

Mountmain's house was dark. Beauregard did not make the mistake of assuming it therefore empty or the household abed. He had the impression that the Irish Mage conducted much of his business away from the windows. The room in which Bacon had died was windowless.

"Do you favour the first or the second storey for your illicit entry, Charles?"

"Neither. I hope to go in through the basement."

Iron, spear-topped railings stood in front of the house. The steps to the front door rose above a row of windows at ground level. He assumed these led to the kitchens or the wine cellars.

"Have you noticed the device on the arch-stone above the door?"

Beauregard looked up. Inset into the stone were what looked like polished nail-heads.

"Ursa Major," he said.

The glints were in the form of the constellation. He looked up at the cloudless sky. Despite the warm glow of gaslight, the stars in the heavens shone.

"This all leads back to the Great Bear," Kate said. "To the stars."

"I'm going. Remember, if there's trouble, whistle. If I don't come out, alert Lestrade."

"And the Diogenes Club?"

He was uncomfortable hearing the name on her tongue.

"Them too."

"One more thing," she insisted.

He looked at her. She kissed him, standing on tiptoes to peck at his lips.

"For luck," she said.

He felt a great warmth for Kate Reed. She was a kindly soul. He squeezed her shoulder and scooted across the street, deftly vaulting the railings.

The first window he tried was fastened. He took out his penknife and scraped away old putty. A pane came away entire, and he set it to one side. The black curtain wafted inwards with the rush of night air.

He slid himself through the curtain, setting his rubber soles down on a flagstone floor about six feet below the level of the window. Glass crunched beneath his boots.

The room was dark. He stood still as a statue, continuing to hear the crunch as if it were a volley of shots. His breath was even and his heartbeat regular. He was used to this sort of night-creeping, but it did not do to get too cocky.

Had someone dropped something?

He chanced a match and found himself in a storeroom. It was as cold as a larder, but the jars and vials on the shelves lining the walls did not suggest domestic arts. Free-floating eyeballs peered at him.

If he had tried the next window along, he would have found it broken. Some mischance, or a less professional cracksman, had smashed it in.

A tiny scrap hung from a spar of glass still in the frame. It was a fragment of cloth, similar to the stuff he still had in his cigar case. He thought of a man-shaped huddle, and shuddered. The match burned his fingers. He shook it out and dropped it.

The after-trail of flame wiggled on the surface of his eyes. He had a fix on the door, and took a grip of the handle. He had a lock-pick in case he found himself shut in. He pulled, and the door moved more easily than he expected. He felt the jamb and realised the door had been locked, but forced. The lock itself was torn out of the wood, but the metal tongue was still out, fixed.

He stepped into a passageway. His eyes were used to the dark. He proceeded down the passage, trying doors. All were broken in, locks smashed.

He took out his revolver.

Someone had invaded this house before him.

The rooms were all like the one he had been in, stores for arcane items. He recognised certain occult implements. One room, a windowless hole, was given over to ancient books, and had been torn apart. Priceless volumes were strewn on the floor, leaking pages like flesh from a wound.

Upstairs, there was a thunderous knocking at the door.

It couldn't be Kate. She would have whistled.

Light leaked down. The gas in the hallway had been turned up. There were footsteps, and offensive shouts.

Mountmain answered his own door. He had probably discharged the butler.

Beauregard couldn't resist a smile.

The light showed a set of double doors, of some metal, at the end of the passageway. They had been abused and wrenched around the locks.

"What the Devil do you want?" Mountmain roared.

"The Seven Stars," boomed a familiar voice.

"What are they? And who are you?"

"You know that as well as I do, Declan. I haven't changed so much since Oxford."

It was Trelawny.

"Get out of the house, or I shall summon the police."

"Very well," Trelawny called Mountmain's bluff.

"Seven Stars, you say?"

"And the mummy! Where's Pai-net'em?"

A tiny hand took Beauregard's sleeve and tugged.

His heart spasmed and he turned, raising his revolver and aiming directly at a startled face.

Kate whistled, almost soundlessly.

He did not waste words in protest. She had disobeyed him and come into the house. She must have seen Trelawny barge in.

Mountmain and Trelawny continued their argument. It sounded as if blows would soon be exchanged. Mountmain was unlikely to hear them moving about beneath his feet.

He nodded to Kate, and proceeded to the double doors.

After a breath, he pushed the doors open.

The room was large, and dimly lit by Aladdin-style lamps. Kate gasped at the obscenity of the bas-reliefs that covered the walls and the altar. Fishy chimerae and alarmed nymphs coupled with joyless frenzy.

Beauregard was surprised to see the Jewel of Seven Stars laying in the open, on the altar. It held the lamp-lights, and its stars burned.

Kate gasped at her first sight of the jewel.

Another item of stolen property lay on the floor, stretched out facedown before the altar. Its bandages were unravelled around its ankles and arms, and it was broken into a scarecrow pose, crucified rather than curled up at rest.

The mummy of Pai-net'em. Kate stepped over the mummy and looked at the Seven Stars. Her fingers fluttered near it, tips reddened by the stone's inner glow.

"It's a beauty," she said.

Beauregard had not bargained for something as easy as this.

"Should we just take it and leave?" Kate asked.

Beauregard hesitated.

"Come on, it's one in the eye for Mountmain."

She took a hold of the jewel, and screamed.

A spindly arm had shot out, and a sinewy hand grabbed her leg, pulling her down.

It couldn't be the mummy. It was someone wrapped in mouldering bandages, a grotesque guardian for the jewel.

At the scream, Mountmain and Trelawny stopped arguing.

The mummy man rose up, loose-limbed and faceless, and threw Kate away. Her cap fell on the floor, and her hair tumbled loose. The jewel cast a bloody light across the mummy's sunken chest.

Living eyes looked out of the dead mask.

Beauregard caught Kate and hugged her. He kept the mummy man covered with his revolver.

Mountmain charged into the room and was struck dumb by what he saw.

"What in the name of Gla'aki!"

Underneath ancient linen, a lipless mouth smiled.

Trelawny was at Mountmain's shoulder. He barged past the

Irishman and towered over the mummy man.

"Stay back, Professor," Beauregard warned.

Trelawny reached for the Seven Stars. The mummy launched a claw-fingered hand at the professor's throat, and ripped it away. A rain of gore fell onto the jewel and seemed to be absorbed.

Trelawny fell to his knees, still trying to draw air into his lungs through his ruptured throat. He pitched forward, dead. The mummy hung his head, almost in tribute.

Beauregard put three shots into the monster's chest, about where his heart should have been. He saw dusty divots raised in the cloth-wrapped flesh. It staggered but did not fall.

Mountmain was backing away from the altar.

"Interfering fool," he snarled at Beauregard. "Are you content now?"

"What is that?" Beauregard indicated the mummy.

"What do you think? It's Pai-net'em, wanting his jewel back. It's all he's ever wanted."

The mummy stood over the altar.

Beauregard saw he had been wrong. It couldn't be a man dressed up. The legs were too thin, like shrouded bones. This was an ancient, dried thing, somehow animate, still imbued with soul.

"He's the saving of your rotten world," Mountmain said. "But he'll rip you apart. My design may not be accomplished, but you'll get no joy from my thwarting. Mr. Beauregard, and whoever you might be young sir, I bid you goodbye."

The Irish Mage stepped back through the doors and slammed them shut.

They were trapped with Pai-net'em.

"Young sir!" Kate sneered. "The cheek of the man."

The mummy had killed Whemple, Jenks, Bacon and Trelawny. And others. All who stood between it and the Jewel of Seven Stars. Now Mountmain thought it would kill Beauregard and Kate.

The mummy bobbed a little, like a limber puppet. Flesh gobbets still clung to its claw-hand. It hovered by the altar, where the jewel was fixed.

Beauregard was prepared to throw himself to Pai-net'em, to protect Kate. He did not think he could come out best in a wrestling match. And clearly his revolver was useless against this dead-alive thing from an ancient grave. Had he lain for three thousand years, seven sparks inside the jewel to keep him warm?

Through the thin bandage, Beauregard saw Pai-net'em's snarl.

"Take it," Beauregard said, indicating the jewel. "It was robbed from you. On behalf of my queen, I return it to you, with honour."

Did Pai-net'em listen? Could he understand?

The mummy snatched up the jewel and held it to his breast. The Seven Stars sank in and the hole closed over. A red glow seemed to throb in Pai-net'em's chest. He slumped, dormant.

Kate let out a breath, and clung to Beauregard.

He kissed her hair.

By dawn, Declan Mountmain was in custody, apprehended at Victoria Station attempting to board the boat train. With two corpses (three, counting the mummy) in his house, he would be detained for some time. The Seven Stars, Beauregard had decided, should remain where it was. It did not strike him as a fitting addition to Her Majesty's collection and he had taken on himself to relinquish it for the nation. He had an idea Victoria would approve.

Kate, who had to keep out of the way while Lestrade was poking around, sat on the front steps, waiting for him.

"The house is full of stolen property," he told her. "Manuscripts from university libraries, impedimenta from museums. There are even body parts, too repulsive to mention, which seem not to be of ancient origin."

"I told you Declan Mountmain was a bad 'un."

"He'll trouble us no longer."

Kate looked at him oddly.

"I wouldn't be so sure of that, Charles. We can't exactly stand up in court and honestly tell the tale, can we?"

Kate scratched her ankle, where the mummy had grasped.

"I'd love to write it up, just to see Stead's face as he spiked the story."

She stood up, linked arms, and walked away from Mountmain's house. It was the Day of the Jubilee. Flags were unfurled and streets were filling, as London began its great celebration.

"I shall not get to go to the Tower," Kate said. "And I had a dress picked out."

"It's always possible you'll end up in the Tower."

She punched his arm.

"Get away with you, Charles."

"I'm afraid the best I can offer is a trip to the British Museum, to see Pai-net'em returned to his sarcophagus. I doubt he'll go on exhibition. My recommendation is that he be misfiled and lost in the depths of the collection."

Kate was thoughtful.

"Nothing's solved, Charles. The Seven Stars remains a mystery. We're not closing the book, but leaving the story to be taken up by the as-yet unborn. Is that not always how it is?"

Carnacki

THE HORSE OF THE INVISIBLE
by WILLIAM HOPE HODGSON

Thomas Carnacki uses a combination of contemporary science and occult wisdom in his battles with the supernatural. Along with such modern equipment as a flash-camera, he draws upon the knowledge contained in a 14th-century Sigsand Manuscript and utilises the Saaamaaa Ritual to protect himself and others against the forces of evil. All his cases are related as after-dinner stories told to the narrator and other acquaintances invited to Carnacki's house in Chelsea's Cheyne Walk. At the end of each narrative, the detective abruptly dismisses his guests and sends them out into the night to ponder upon what they have just heard.

Probably inspired by the incredible success of Algernon Blackwood's collection of stories, John Silence *(1908), William Hope Hodgson's (1877–1918) first Carnacki story, 'The Gateway of the Monster', appeared in the January 1910 edition of* The Idler. *It was followed by four more tales in the magazine and another in* The New Magazine, *before all six were collected in* Carnacki The Ghost-Finder *(1913). When the book was published by August Derleth's Mycroft & Moran imprint in 1947, three more stories were added. These included 'The Haunted Jarvee', which had previously appeared in the March 1929 issue of* The Premier Magazine, *plus 'The Find' and 'The Hog', although there has been much speculation over the years that the latter two were in fact written by Derleth himself.*

Since then, Carnacki's exploits have been chronicled by, amongst others, Rick Kennett, A.F. Kidd, Andrew Cartmel, Barbara Hambley, Alan Moore, John R. King, William Meikle and Guy Adams.

The following story was effectively dramatised on television in 1975 as an episode of The Rivals of Sherlock Holmes, *starring Donald Pleasence as Carnacki.*

I HAD THAT afternoon received an invitation from Carnacki. When I reached his place I found him sitting alone. As I came into the room he rose with a perceptibly stiff movement and extended his left hand. His face seemed to be badly scarred and bruised and his right hand was bandaged. He shook hands and offered me his paper, which I refused. Then he passed me a handful of photographs and returned to his reading.

Now, that is just Carnacki. Not a word had come from him and not a question from me. He would tell us all about it later. I spent about half an hour looking at the photographs which were chiefly "snaps" (some by flashlight) of an extraordinarily pretty girl; though in some of the photographs it was wonderful that her prettiness was so evident for so frightened and startled was her expression that it was difficult not to believe that she had been photographed in the presence of some imminent and overwhelming danger.

The bulk of the photographs were of interiors of different rooms and passages and in every one the girl might be seen, either full length in the distance or closer, with perhaps little more than a hand or arm or portion of the head or dress included in the photograph. All of these had evidently been taken with some definite aim that did not have for its first purpose the picturing of the girl, but obviously of her surroundings and they made me very curious, as you can imagine.

Near the bottom of the pile, however, I came upon something *definitely* extraordinary. It was a photograph of the girl standing abrupt and clear in the great blaze of a flashlight, as was plain to be seen. Her face was turned a little upward as if she had been frightened suddenly by some noise. Directly above her, as though half-formed and coming down out of the shadows, was the shape of a single, enormous hoof.

I examined this photograph for a long time without understanding it more than that it had probably to do with some queer case in which Carnacki was interested.

When Jessop, Arkright and Taylor came in Carnacki quietly held out his hand for the photographs which I returned in the same spirit and afterwards we all went in to dinner. When we had spent a quiet hour at the table we pulled our chairs round and made ourselves snug and Carnacki began:—

"I've been North," he said, speaking slowly and painfully between puffs at his pipe. "Up to Hisgins of East Lancashire. It has been a pretty strange business all round, as I fancy you chaps will think, when I have finished. I knew before I went, something about the 'horse story,' as I have heard it called; but I never thought of it coming my way, somehow. Also I know *now* that I never considered it seriously—in spite of my rule always to keep an open mind. Funny creatures, we humans!

"Well, I got a wire asking for an appointment, which of course told me that there was some trouble. On the date I fixed old Captain Hisgins himself came up to see me. He told me a great many new details about the horse story; though naturally I had always known the main points and understood that if the first child were a girl, that girl would be haunted by the Horse during her courtship.

"It is, as you can see already, an extraordinary story and though I have always known about it, I have never thought it to be anything more than an old-time legend, as I have already hinted. You see, for seven generations the Hisgins family have had men children for their firstborn and even the Hisgins themselves have long considered the tale to be little more than a myth.

"To come to the present, the eldest child of the reigning family is a girl and she has been often teased and warned in jest by her friends and relations that she is the first girl to be the eldest for seven generations and that she would have to keep her men friends at arm's length or go into a nunnery if she hoped to escape the haunting. And this, I think, shows us how thoroughly the tale had grown to be considered as nothing worthy of the least serious thought. Don't you think so?

"Two months ago Miss Hisgins became engaged to Beaumont,

a young Naval Officer, and on the evening of the very day of the engagement, before it was even formally announced, a most extraordinary thing happened which resulted in Captain Hisgins making the appointment and my ultimately going down to their place to look into the thing.

"From the old family records and papers that were entrusted to me I found that there could be no possible doubt that prior to something like a 150 years ago there were some very extraordinary and disagreeable coincidences to put the thing in the least emotional way. In the whole of the two centuries prior to that date there were five firstborn girls out of a total of seven generations of the family. Each of these girls grew up to Maidenhood and each became engaged, and each one died during the period of engagement, two by suicide, one by falling from a window, one from a 'broken-heart' (presumably heart-failure, owing to sudden shock through fright). The fifth girl was killed one evening in the park round the house; but just how, there seemed to be no exact knowledge; only that there was an impression that she had been kicked by a horse. She was dead when found.

"Now, you see, all of these deaths might be attributed in a way—even the suicides—to natural causes, I mean as distinct from supernatural. You see? Yet, in every case the Maidens had undoubtedly suffered some extraordinary and terrifying experiences during their various courtships; for in all of the records there was mention either of the neighing of an unseen horse or of the sounds of an invisible horse galloping, as well as many other peculiar and quite inexplicable manifestations. You begin to understand now, I think, just how extraordinary a business it was that I was asked to look into.

"I gathered from one account that the haunting of the girls was so constant and horrible that two of the girls' lovers fairly ran away from their ladyloves. And I think it was this, more than anything else that made me feel that there had been something more in it than a mere succession of uncomfortable coincidences.

"I got hold of these facts before I had been many hours in the house and after this I went pretty carefully into the details of the thing that happened on the night of Miss Hisgins' engagement to

Beaumont. It seems that as the two of them were going through the big lower corridor, just after dusk and before the lamps had been lighted, there had been a sudden, horrible neighing in the corridor, close to them. Immediately afterward Beaumont received a tremendous blow or kick which broke his right forearm. Then the rest of the family and the servants came running to know what was wrong. Lights were brought and the corridor and, afterwards the whole house searched, but nothing unusual was found.

"You can imagine the excitement in the house and the half incredulous, half believing talk about the old legend. Then, later, in the middle of the night the old Captain was waked by the sound of a great horse galloping round and round the house.

"Several times after this both Beaumont and the girl said that they had heard the sounds of hoofs near to them after dusk in several of the rooms and corridors.

"Three nights later Beaumont was waked by a strange neighing in the nighttime seeming to come from the direction of his sweetheart's bedroom. He ran hurriedly for her father and the two of them raced to her room. They found her awake and ill with sheer terror, having been awakened by the neighing, seemingly close to her bed.

"The night before I arrived, there had been a fresh happening and they were all in a frightfully nervy state, as you can imagine.

"I spent most of the first day, as I have hinted, in getting hold of details; but after dinner I slacked off and played billiards all the evening with Beaumont and Miss Hisgins. We stopped about ten o'clock and had coffee and I got Beaumont to give me full particulars about the thing that had happened the evening before.

"He and Miss Hisgins had been sitting quietly in her aunt's boudoir whilst the old lady chaperoned them, behind a book. It was growing dusk and the lamp was at her end of the table. The rest of the house was not yet lit as the evening had come earlier than usual.

"Well, it seems that the door into the hall was open and suddenly the girl said:—'S'ush! what's that?'

"They both listened and then Beaumont heard it—the sound of a horse outside of the front door.

"'Your father?' he suggested, but she reminded him that her father was not riding.

"Of course they were both ready to feel queer, as you can suppose, but Beaumont made an effort to shake this off and went into the hall to see whether anyone was at the entrance. It was pretty dark in the hall and he could see the glass panels of the inner draught-door, clear-cut in the darkness of the hall. He walked over to the glass and looked through into the drive beyond, but there was nothing in sight.

"He felt nervous and puzzled and opened the inner door and went out on to the carriage-circle. Almost directly afterward the great hall door swung to with a crash behind him. He told me that he had a sudden awful feeling of having been trapped in some way—that is how he put it. He whirled round and gripped the door-handle, but something seemed to be holding it with a vast grip on the other side. Then, before he could be fixed in his mind that this was so, he was able to turn the handle and open the door.

"He paused a moment in the doorway and peered into the hall, for he had hardly steadied his mind sufficiently to know whether he was really frightened or not. Then he heard his sweetheart blow him a kiss out of the greyness of the big, unlit hall and he knew that she had followed him from the boudoir. He blew her a kiss back and stepped inside the doorway, meaning to go to her. And then, suddenly, in a flash of sickening knowledge he knew that it was not his sweetheart who had blown him that kiss. He knew that something was trying to tempt him alone into the darkness and that the girl had never left the boudoir. He jumped back and in the same instant of time he heard the kiss again, nearer to him. He called out at the top of his voice:—'Mary, stay in the boudoir. Don't move out of the boudoir until I come to you.' He heard her call something in reply from the boudoir and then he had struck a clump of a dozen or so matches and was holding them above his head and looking round the hall. There was no one in it, but even as the matches burned out there came the sounds of a great horse galloping down the empty drive.

"Now you see, both he and the girl had heard the sounds of the horse galloping; but when I questioned more closely I found that the aunt had heard nothing, though it is true she is a bit deaf, and she was further back in the room. Of course, both he and Miss Hisgins had been in an extremely nervous state and ready to hear anything. The door might have been slammed by a sudden puff of wind owing to some inner door being opened; and as for the grip on the handle, that may have been nothing more than the sneck catching.

"With regard to the kisses and the sounds of the horse galloping, I pointed out that these might have seemed ordinary enough sounds, if they had been only cool enough to reason. As I told him and as he knew, the sounds of a horse galloping carry a long way on the wind so that what he had heard might have been nothing more than a horse being ridden some distance away. And as for the kiss, plenty of quiet noises—the rustle of a paper or a leaf—have a somewhat similar sound, especially if one is in an over-strung condition and imagining things.

"I finished preaching this little sermon on commonsense, versus hysteria as we put out the lights and left the billiard room. But neither Beaumont nor Miss Hisgins would agree that there had been any fancy on their parts.

"We had come out of the billiard room by this time and were going along the passage and I was still doing my best to make both of them see the ordinary, commonplace possibilities of the happening, when what killed my pig, as the saying goes, was the sound of a hoof in the dark billiard room we had just left.

"I felt the 'creep' come on me in a flash, up my spine and over the back of my head. Miss Hisgins whooped like a child with the whooping-cough and ran up the passage, giving little gasping screams. Beaumont, however, ripped round on his heels and jumped back a couple of yards. I gave back too, a bit, as you can understand.

"'There it is,' he said in a low, breathless voice. 'Perhaps you'll believe now.'

"'There's certainly something,' I whispered, never taking my gaze off the closed door of the billiard room.

"'H'sh!' he muttered. 'There it is again.'

"There was a sound like a great horse pacing round and round the billiard room with slow, deliberate steps. A horrible cold fright took me so that it seemed impossible to take a full breath, you know the feeling, and then I saw we must have been walking backwards for we found ourselves suddenly at the opening of the long passage.

"We stopped there and listened. The sounds went on steadily with a horrible sort of deliberateness, as if the brute were taking a sort of malicious gusto in walking about all over the room which we had just occupied. Do you understand just what I mean?

"Then there was a pause and a long time of absolute quiet except for an excited whispering from some of the people down in the big hall. The sound came plainly up the wide stairway. I fancy they were gathered round Miss Hisgins, with some notion of protecting her.

"I should think Beaumont and I stood there, at the end of the passage, for about five minutes, listening for any noise in the billiard room. Then I realised what a horrible funk I was in and I said to him:—'I'm going to see what's there.'

"'So 'm I,' he answered. He was pretty white, but he had heaps of pluck. I told him to wait one instant and I made a dash into my bedroom and got my camera and flashlight. I slipped my revolver into my right-hand pocket and a knuckle-duster over my left fist, where it was ready and yet would not stop me from being able to work my flashlight.

"Then I ran back to Beaumont. He held out his hand to show me that he had his pistol and I nodded, but whispered to him not to be too quick to shoot, as there might be some silly practical-joking at work, after all. He had got a lamp from a bracket in the upper hall which he was holding in the crook of his damaged arm, so that we had a good light. Then we went down the passage towards the billiard room and you can imagine that we were a pretty nervous couple.

"All this time there had been a sound, but abruptly when we were within perhaps a couple of yards of the door we heard the sudden clumping of a hoof on the solid parquet-floor of the billiard room. In the instant afterward it seemed to me that the whole place shook beneath the ponderous hoof-falls of some huge thing, coming towards the door. Both Beaumont and I gave back a pace or two, and then realised and hung on to our courage, as you might say, and waited. The great tread came right up to the door and then stopped and there was an instant of absolute silence, except that so far as I was concerned, the pulsing in my throat and temples almost deafened me.

"I daresay we waited quite half a minute and then came the further restless clumping of a great hoof. Immediately afterward the sounds came right on as if some invisible thing passed through the closed door and the ponderous tread was upon us. We jumped, each of us, to our side of the passage and I know that I spread myself stiff against the wall. The clungk clunck, clungk clunck, of the great hoof-falls passed right between us and slowly and with deadly deliberateness, down the passage. I heard them through a haze of blood-beats in my ears and temples and my body extraordinarily rigid and pringling and I was horribly breathless. I stood for a little time like this, my head turned so that I could see up the passage. I was conscious only that there was a hideous danger abroad. Do you understand?

"And then, suddenly, my pluck came back to me. I was aware that the noise of the hoof-beats sounded near the other end of the passage. I twisted quickly and got my camera to bear and snapped off the flashlight. Immediately afterward, Beaumont let fly a storm of shots down the passage and began to run, shouting:—'It's after Mary. Run! Run!'

"He rushed down the passage and I after him. We came out on to the main landing and heard the sound of a hoof on the stairs and after that, nothing. And from thence onward, nothing.

"Down below us in the big hall I could see a number of the household round Miss Hisgins, who seemed to have fainted and there were several of the servants clumped together a little way off, staring up at the main landing and no one saying a single word. And about some twenty steps up the stairs was the old Captain Hisgins with a drawn sword in his hand where he had halted, just below the last hoof-sound. I think I never saw anything finer than the old man standing there between his daughter and that infernal thing.

"I daresay you can understand the queer feeling of horror I had at passing that place on the stairs where the sounds had ceased. It was as if the monster were still standing there, invisible. And the peculiar thing was that we never heard another sound of the hoof, either up or down the stairs.

"After they had taken Miss Hisgins to her room I sent word that I should follow, so soon as they were ready for me. And presently, when a message came to tell me that I could come any time, I asked her father to give me a hand with my instrument-box and between us we carried it into the girl's bedroom. I had the bed pulled well out into the middle of the room, after which I erected the electric pentacle round the bed.

"Then I directed that lamps should be placed round the room, but that on no account must any light be made within the pentacle; neither must anyone pass in or out. The girl's mother I had placed within the pentacle and directed that her maid should sit without, ready to carry any message so as to make sure that Mrs. Hisgins did not have to leave the pentacle. I suggested also that the girl's father should stay the night in the room and that he had better be armed.

"When I left the bedroom I found Beaumont waiting outside the door in a miserable state of anxiety. I told him what I had done and explained to him that Miss Hisgins was probably perfectly safe within the 'protection'; but that in addition to her father remaining the night in the room, I intended to stand guard at the door. I told him that I should like him to keep me company, for I knew that he could never sleep, feeling as he did, and I should not be sorry to have a companion. Also, I wanted to have him under my own observation, for there was no doubt but that he was actually in greater danger in some ways than the girl. At least, that was my opinion and is still, as I think you will agree later.

"I asked him whether he would object to my drawing a pentacle round him for the night and got him to agree, but I saw that he did not know whether to be superstitious about it or to regard it more as a piece of foolish mumming; but he took it seriously enough when I gave him some particulars about the Black Veil case, when young Aster died. You remember, he said it was a piece of silly superstition and stayed outside. Poor devil!

"The night passed quietly enough until a little while before dawn when we both heard the sounds of a great horse galloping round and round the house, just as old Captain Hisgins had described it. You can imagine how queer it made me feel and directly afterward, I heard someone stir within the bedroom. I knocked at the door, for I was uneasy and the Captain came. I asked whether everything was right; to which he replied yes, and immediately asked me whether I had heard the sounds of the galloping, so that I knew he had heard them also. I suggested that it might be well to leave the bedroom door open a little until the dawn came in, as there was certainly something abroad. This was done and he went back into the room, to be near his wife and daughter.

"I had better say here that I was doubtful whether there was any value in the 'Defence' about Miss Hisgins, for what I term the 'personal-sounds' of the manifestation were so extraordinarily material that I was inclined to parallel the case with that one of Harford's where the hand of the child kept materialising within the pentacle and patting the floor. As you will remember, that was a hideous business.

"Yet, as it chanced, nothing further happened and so soon as daylight had fully come we all went off to bed.

"Beaumont knocked me up about midday and I went down and made breakfast into lunch. Miss Hisgins was there and seemed in very fair spirits, considering. She told me that I had made her feel almost safe for the first time for days. She told me also that her cousin, Harry Parsket, was coming down from London and she knew that he would do anything to help fight the ghost. And after that she and Beaumont went out into the grounds to have a little time together.

"I had a walk in the grounds myself and went round the house, but saw no traces of hoof-marks and after that I spent the rest of the day making an examination of the house, but found nothing.

"I made an end of my search before dark and went to my room to dress for dinner. When I got down the cousin had just arrived and I found him one of the nicest men I have met for a long time. A chap with a tremendous amount of pluck and the particular kind of man I like to have with me in a bad case like the one I was on.

"I could see that what puzzled him most was our belief in the genuineness of the haunting and I found myself almost wanting something to happen, just to show him how true it was. As it chanced, something did happen, with a vengeance.

"Beaumont and Miss Hisgins had gone out for a stroll just before the dusk and Captain Hisgins asked me to come into his study for a short chat whilst Parsket went upstairs with his traps, for he had no man with him.

"I had a long conversation with the old Captain in which I pointed out that the 'haunting' had evidently no particular connection with the house, but only with the girl herself and that the sooner she was married, the better, as it would give Beaumont a right to be with her at all times and further than this, it might be that the manifestations would cease if the marriage were actually performed.

"The old man nodded agreement to this, especially to the first part and reminded me that three of the girls who were said have been 'haunted' had been sent away from home and met their deaths whilst away. And then in the midst of our talk there came a pretty frightening interruption, for all at once the old butler rushed into the room, most extraordinarily pale:—

"'Miss Mary, Sir! Miss Mary, Sir!' he gasped. 'She's screaming . . . out in the Park, Sir! And they say they can hear the Horse—'

"The Captain made one dive for a rack of arms and snatched down his old sword and ran out, drawing it as he ran. I dashed out and up the stairs, snatched my camera-flashlight and a heavy revolver, gave one yell at Parsket's door:—'The Horse!' and was down and into the grounds.

"Away in the darkness there was a confused shouting and I caught the sounds of shooting, out among the scattered trees. And then, from a patch of blackness to my left, there burst suddenly an infernal gobbling sort of neighing. Instantly I whipped round and snapped off the flashlight. The great light blazed out momentarily, showing me the leaves of a big tree close at hand, quivering in the night breeze, but I saw nothing else and then the tenfold blackness came down upon me and I heard Parsket shouting a little way back to know whether I had seen anything.

"The next instant he was beside me and I felt safer for his company, for there was some incredible thing near to us and I was momentarily blind because of the brightness of the flashlight. 'What was it? What was it?' he kept repeating in an excited voice. And all the time I was staring into the darkness and answering, mechanically, 'I don't know. I don't know.'

"There was a burst of shouting somewhere ahead and then a shot. We ran towards the sounds, yelling to the people not to shoot for in the darkness and panic there was this danger also. Then there came two of the gamekeepers, racing hard up the drive with their lanterns and guns and immediately afterward a row of lights dancing towards us from the house, carried by some of the menservants.

"As the lights came up I saw that we had come close to Beaumont. He was standing over Miss Hisgins and he had his revolver in his hand. Then I saw his face and there was a great wound across his forehead. By him was the Captain, turning his naked sword this way and that, and peering into the darkness; a little behind him stood the old butler, a battleaxe from one of the arm-stands in the hall, in his hands. Yet there was nothing strange to be seen anywhere.

"We got the girl into the house and left her with her mother and Beaumont, whilst a groom rode for a doctor. And then the rest of us, with four other keepers, all armed with guns and carrying lanterns, searched round the home-park. But we found nothing.

"When we got back we found that the Doctor had been. He had bound up Beaumont's wound, which luckily was not deep, and ordered Miss Hisgins straight to bed. I went upstairs with the Captain and found Beaumont on guard outside of the girl's door. I asked him how he felt and then, so soon as the girl and her mother were ready for us, Captain Hisgins and I went into the bedroom and fixed the pentacle again round the bed. They had already got lamps about the room and after I had set the same order of watching as on the previous night, I joined Beaumont outside of the door.

"Parsket had come up while I had been in the bedroom and between us we got some idea from Beaumont as to what had happened out in the Park. It seems that they were coming home after their stroll from the direction of the West Lodge. It had got quite dark and suddenly Miss Hisgins said 'Hush!' and came to a standstill. He stopped and listened, but heard nothing for a little. Then he caught it—the sound of a horse, seemingly a long way off, galloping towards them over the grass. He told the girl that it was nothing and started to hurry her towards the house, but she was not deceived, of course. In less than a minute they heard it quite close to them in the darkness and they started running. Then Miss Hisgins caught her foot and fell. She began to scream and that is what the butler heard. As Beaumont lifted the girl he heard the hoofs come thudding right at him. He stood over her and fired all five chambers of his revolver right at the sounds. He told us that he was sure he saw something that looked like an enormous horse's head, right upon him in the light of the last flash of his pistol. Immediately afterwards he was struck a tremendous blow which knocked him down and then the Captain and the butler came running up, shouting. The rest, of course, we knew.

"About ten o'clock the butler brought us up a tray, for which I was very glad, as the night before I had got rather hungry. I warned Beaumont, however, to be very particular not to drink any spirits and I also made him give me his pipe and matches. At midnight I drew a pentacle round him and Parsket and I sat one on each side of him, but outside of the pentacle, for I had no fear that there would be any manifestation made against anyone except Beaumont or Miss Hisgins.

"After that we kept pretty quiet. The passage was lit by a big lamp at each end so that we had plenty of light and we were all armed, Beaumont and I with revolver and Parsket with a shotgun. In addition to my weapon I had my camera and flashlight.

"Now and again we talked in whispers and twice the Captain came out of the bedroom to have a word with us. About half past one we had all grown very silent and suddenly, about twenty minutes later, I held up my hand, silently; for there seemed to be a sound of galloping out in the night. I knocked on the bedroom door for the Captain to open it and when he came I whispered to him that we thought we heard the Horse. For some time we stayed, listening, and both Parsket and the Captain thought they heard it; but now I was not so sure, neither was Beaumont. Yet afterwards, I thought I heard it again.

"I told Captain Hisgins I thought he had better go back into the bedroom and leave the door a little open and this he did. But from that time onward we heard nothing and presently the dawn came in and we all went very thankfully to bed.

"When I was called at lunchtime I had a little surprise, for Captain Hisgins told me that they had held a family council and had decided to take my advice and have the marriage without a day's more delay than possible. Beaumont was already on his way to London to get a special License and they hoped to have the wedding next day.

"This pleased me, for it seemed the sanest thing to be done in the extraordinary circumstances and meanwhile I should continue my investigations; but until the marriage was accomplished, my chief thought was to keep Miss Hisgins near to me.

"After lunch I thought I would take a few experimental photographs of Miss Hisgins and her *surroundings*. Sometimes the camera sees things that would seem very strange to normal human eyesight.

"With this intention and partly to make an excuse to keep her in my company as much as possible, I asked Miss Hisgins to join me in my experiments. She seemed glad to do this and I spent several hours with her, wandering all over the house, from room to room and whenever the impulse came I took a flash light of her and the room or corridor in which we chanced to be at the moment.

"After we had gone right through the house in this fashion, I asked her whether she felt sufficiently brave to repeat the experiments in the cellars. She said, yes, and so I rooted out Captain Hisgins and Parsket, for I was not going to take her even into what you might call artificial darkness without help and companionship at hand.

"When we were ready we went down into the wine-cellar, Captain Hisgins carrying a shotgun and Parsket a specially prepared background and a lantern. I got the girl to stand in the middle of the cellar whilst Parsket and the Captain held out the background behind her. Then I fired all the flashlights and we went into the next cellar where we repeated the experiment.

"Then in the third cellar, a tremendous, pitch-dark place, something extraordinary and horrible manifested itself. I had stationed Miss Hisgins in the centre of the place, with her father and Parsket holding the background, as before. When all was ready and just as I pressed the trigger of the 'flash,' there came in the cellar that dreadful, boggling neighing that I had heard out in the Park. It seemed to come from somewhere above the girl and in the glare of the sudden light I saw that she was staring tensely upward, but at no visible thing. And then in the succeeding comparative darkness, I was shouting to the Captain and Parsket to run Miss Hisgins out into the daylight.

"This was done instantly and I shut and locked the door afterwards making the First and Eighth signs of the Saaamaaa Ritual opposite to each Post and connecting them across the threshold with a triple line.

"In the meanwhile Parsket and Captain Hisgins carried the girl to her mother and left her there, in a half-fainting condition; whilst I stayed on guard outside of the cellar door, feeling pretty horrible for I knew that there was some disgusting thing inside, and along with this feeling there was a sense of half-ashamedness rather miserable, you know, because I had exposed Miss Hisgins to the danger.

"I had got the Captain's shotgun and when he and Parsket came down again they were each carrying guns and lanterns. I could not possibly tell you the utter relief of spirit and body that came to me when I heard them coming, but just try to imagine what it was like, standing outside of that cellar. Can you?

"I remember noticing, just before I went to unlock the door, how white and ghastly Parsket looked and the old Captain was grey-looking and I wondered whether my face was like theirs. And this, you know, had its own distinct effect upon my nerves, for it seemed to bring the beastliness of the thing bash down on to me in a fresh way. I know it was only sheer willpower that carried me up to the door and made me turn the key.

"I paused one little moment and then with a nervy jerk sent the door wide open and held my lantern over my head. Parsket and the Captain came one on each side of me and held up their lanterns, but the place was absolutely empty. Of course, I did not trust to a casual look of this kind, but spent several hours with the help of the two others in sounding every square foot of the floor, ceiling and walls.

"Yet, in the end I had to admit that the place itself was absolutely normal and so we came away. But I sealed the door and outside, opposite each door-post I made the First and Last signs of the Saaamaaa Ritual, joining them as before, with a triple line. Can you imagine what it was like, searching that cellar?

"When we got upstairs I inquired very anxiously how Miss Hisgins was and the girl came out herself to tell me that she was all right and that I was not to trouble about her, or blame myself, as I told her I had been doing.

"I felt happier then and went off to dress for dinner and after that was done, Parsket and I took one of the bathrooms to develop the negatives that I had been taking. Yet none of the plates had anything to tell us until we came to the one that was taken in the cellar. Parsket was developing and I had taken a batch of the fixed plates out into the lamplight to examine them.

"I had just gone carefully through the lot when I heard a shout from Parsket and when I ran to him he was looking at a partly developed negative which he was holding up to the red lamp. It showed the girl plainly, looking upward as I had seen her; but the thing that astonished me was the shadow of an enormous hoof, right above her, as if it were coming down upon her out of the shadows. And you know, I had run her bang into that danger. That was the thought that was chief in my mind.

"As soon as the developing was complete I fixed the plate and examined it carefully in a good light. There was no doubt about it at all, the thing above Miss Hisgins was an enormous, shadowy hoof. Yet I was no nearer to coming to any definite knowledge and the only thing I could do was to warn Parsket to say nothing about it to the girl for it would only increase her fright, but I showed the thing to her father for I considered it right that he should know.

"That night we took the same precautions for Miss Hisgins' safety as on the two previous nights and Parsket kept me company; yet the dawn came in without anything unusual having happened and I went off to bed.

"When I got down to lunch I learnt that Beaumont had wired to say that he would be in soon after four; also that a message had been sent to the Rector. And it was generally plain that the ladies of the house were in a tremendous fluster.

"Beaumont's train was late and he did not get home until five, but even then the Rector had not put in an appearance and the butler came in to say that the coachman had returned without him as he had been called away unexpectedly. Twice more during the evening the carriage was sent down, but the clergyman had not returned and we had to delay the marriage until the next day.

"That night I arranged the 'Defence' round the girl's bed and the Captain and his wife sat up with her as before. Beaumont, as I expected, insisted on keeping watch with me and he seemed in a curiously frightened mood; not for himself, you know, but for Miss

Hisgins. He had a horrible feeling he told me, that there would be a final, dreadful attempt on his sweetheart that night.

"This, of course, I told him was nothing but nerves; yet really, it made me feel very anxious; for I have seen too much not to know that under such circumstances a premonitory *conviction* of impending danger is not necessarily to be put down entirely to nerves. In fact, Beaumont was so simply and earnestly convinced that the night would bring some extraordinary manifestation that I got Parsket to rig up a long cord from the wire of the butler's bell, to come along the passage handy.

"To the butler himself I gave directions not to undress and to give the same order to two of the footmen. If I rang he was to come instantly, with the footmen, carrying lanterns and the lanterns were to be kept ready lit all night. If for any reason the bell did not ring and I blew my whistle, he was to take that as a signal in the place of the bell.

"After I had arranged all these minor details I drew a pentacle about Beaumont and warned him very particularly to stay within it, whatever happened. And when this was done, there was nothing to do but wait and pray that the night would go as quietly as the night before.

"We scarcely talked at all and by about 1:00 a.m. we were all very tense and nervous so that at last Parsket got up and began to walk up and down the corridor, to steady himself a bit. Presently I slipped off my pumps and joined him and we walked up and down, whispering occasionally for something over an hour, until in turning I caught my foot in the bellcord and went down on my face; but without hurting myself or making a noise.

"When I got up Parsket nudged me.

" 'Did you notice that the bell never rang?' he whispered.

" 'Jove!' I said, 'you're right.'

" 'Wait a minute,' he answered. 'I'll bet it's only a kink somewhere in the cord.' He left his gun and slipped along the passage and taking the top lamp, tiptoed away into the house, carrying Beaumont's revolver ready in the right hand. He was a plucky chap, as I remember thinking then and again, later.

"Just then Beaumont motioned to me for absolute quiet. Directly afterwards I heard the thing for which he listened—the sound of a horse galloping, out in the night. I think that I may say I fairly shivered. The sound died away and left a horrible, desolate, eerie feeling in the air, you know. I put my hand out to the bellcord, hoping that Parsket had got it clear. Then I waited, glancing before and behind.

"Perhaps two minutes passed, full of what seemed like an almost unearthly quiet. And then, suddenly, down the corridor at the lighted end there sounded the clumping of a great hoof and instantly the lamp was thrown down with a tremendous crash and we were in the dark. I tugged hard on the cord and blew the whistle; then I raised my snapshot and fired the flashlight. The corridor blazed into brilliant light, but there was nothing and then the darkness fell like thunder. I heard the Captain at the bedroom-door and shouted to him to bring out a lamp, *quick*; but instead something started to kick the door and I heard the Captain shouting within the bedroom and then the screaming of the women. I had a sudden, horrible fear that the monster had got into the bedroom, but in the same instant from up the corridor there came abruptly the vile, gobbling neighing that we had heard in the park and the cellar. I blew the whistle again and groped blindly for the bellcord, shouting to Beaumont to stay in the pentacle, whatever happened. I yelled again to the Captain to bring out a lamp and there came a smashing sound against the bedroom door. Then I had my matches in my hand, to get some light before that incredible, unseen Monster was upon us.

"The match scraped on the box and flared up dully and in the same instant I heard a faint sound behind me. I whipped round in kind of mad terror and saw something in the light of the match—a monstrous horse-head, close to Beaumont.

"'Look out, Beaumont!' I shouted in a sort of scream. 'It's behind you!'

"The match went out abruptly and instantly there came the huge bang of Parsket's double-barrel (both barrels at once), fired evidently single-handed by Beaumont close to my ear, as it seemed. I caught a momentary glimpse of the great head in the flash and of an enormous hoof amid the belch of fire and smoke seeming to be descending upon Beaumont. In the same instant I fired three chambers of my revolver. There was the sound of a dull blow and then that horrible, gobbling neigh broke out close to me. I fired twice at the sound. Immediately afterward something struck me and I was knocked backwards. I got on to my knees and shouted for help at the top of my voice. I heard the women screaming behind the closed door of the bedroom and was dully aware that the door was being smashed from the inside, and directly afterwards I knew that Beaumont was struggling with some hideous thing near to me. For an instant I held back, stupidly, paralysed with funk and then, blindly and in a sort of rigid chill of gooseflesh I went to help him, shouting his name. I can tell you, I was nearly sick with the naked fear I had on me. There came a little, choking scream out of the darkness, and at that I jumped forward into the dark. I gripped a vast, furry ear. Then something struck me another great blow, knocking me sick. I hit back, weak and blind and gripped with my other hand at the incredible thing. Abruptly I was dimly aware of a tremendous crash behind me and a great burst of light. There were other lights in the passage and a noise of feet and shouting. My handgrips were torn from the thing they held; I shut my eyes stupidly and heard a loud yell above me and then a heavy blow, like a butcher chopping meat and then something fell upon me.

"I was helped to my knees by the Captain and the butler. On the floor lay an enormous horse-head out of which protruded a man's trunk and legs. On the wrists were fixed great hoofs. It was the monster. The Captain cut something with the sword that he held in his hand, stooped and lifted off the mask, for that is what it was. I saw the face then of the man who had worn it. It was Parsket. He had a bad wound across the forehead where the Captain's sword had bit through the mask. I looked bewilderedly from him to Beaumont, who was sitting up, leaning against the wall of the corridor. Then I stared at Parsket again.

" 'By Jove!' I said at last, and then I was quiet for I was so ashamed for the man. You can understand, can't you? And he was opening his eyes. And you know, I had grown so to like him.

"And then, you know, just as Parsket was getting back his wits and looking from one to the other of us and beginning to remember, there happened a strange and incredible thing. For from the end of the corridor there sounded, suddenly, the clumping of a great hoof. I looked that way and then instantly at Parsket and saw a horrible fear in his face and eyes. He wrenched himself round, weakly and stared in mad terror up the corridor to where the sound had been, and the rest of us started, in a frozen group. I remember vaguely, half sobs and whispers from Miss Hisgins' bedroom, all the while that I stared frightenedly up the corridor.

"The silence lasted several seconds and then, abruptly, there came again the clumping of the great hoof, away at the end of the corridor. And immediately afterward the clungk, clunk—clungk, clunk of mighty hoofs coming down the passage towards us.

"Even then, you know, most of us thought it was some mechanism of Parsket's still at work and we were in the queerest mixture of fright and doubt. I think everyone looked at Parsket. And suddenly the Captain shouted out:—

"'Stop this damned fooling at once. Haven't you done enough!'

"For my part, I was now frightened for I had a *sense* that there was something horrible and wrong. And then Parsket managed to gasp out:—

"'It's not me! My God! It's not me! My God! It's not me!'

"And then, you know, it seemed to come home to everyone in an instant that there was really some dreadful thing coming down the passage. There was a mad rush to get away and even old Captain Hisgins gave back with the butler and the footmen. Beaumont fainted outright, as I found afterwards, for he had been badly mauled. I just flattened back against the wall, kneeling as I was, too stupid and dazed even to run. And almost in the same instant the ponderous hoof-falls sounded close to me and seeming to shake the solid floor as they passed. Abruptly the great sounds ceased and I knew in a sort of sick fashion that the thing had halted opposite to the door of the girl's bedroom. And then I was aware that Parsket was standing rocking in the doorway with his arms spread across, so as to fill the doorway with his body. I saw with less bewilderment. Parsket was extraordinarily pale and the blood was running down his face from the wound in his forehead; and then I noticed that he seemed to be looking at something in the passage with a peculiar, desperate, fixed, incredible masterful gaze.

But there was really nothing to be seen. And suddenly the clungk, clunk—clungk, clunk recommenced and passed onward down the passage. In the same moment Parsket pitched forward out of the doorway on to his face.

"There were shouts from the huddle of men down the passage and the two footmen and the butler simply ran, carrying their lanterns; but the Captain went against the side-wall with his back and put the lamp he was carrying over his head. The dull tread of the Horse went past him and left him unharmed and I heard the monstrous hoof-falls going away and away through the quiet house and after that a dead silence.

"Then the Captain moved and came towards us, very slow and shaky and with an extraordinarily grey face.

"I crept towards Parsket and the Captain came to help me. We turned him over and, you know, I knew in a moment that he was dead; but you can imagine what a feeling it sent through me.

"I looked up at the Captain and suddenly he said:—

"'That—That—That—', and I know that he was trying to tell me that Parsket had stood between his daughter and whatever it was that had gone down the passage. I stood up and steadied him, though I was not very steady myself. And suddenly his face began to work and he went down on to his knees by Parsket and cried like some shaken child. Then the women came out of the doorway of the bedroom and I turned away and left him to them, whilst I went over to Beaumont.

"That is practically the whole story and the only thing that is left to me is to try to explain some of the puzzling parts, here and there.

"Perhaps you have seen that Parsket was in love with Miss Hisgins and this fact is the key to a good deal that was extraordinary. He was doubtless responsible for some portions of the 'haunting'; in fact I think for nearly everything, but you know, I can prove nothing and what I have to tell you is chiefly the result of deduction.

"In the first place, it is obvious that Parsket's intention was to frighten Beaumont away and when he found that he could not do this, I think he grew so desperate that he really intended to kill him. I hate to say this, but the facts force me to think so.

"I am quite certain that it was Parsket who broke Beaumont's arm.

He knew all the details of the so-called 'Horse Legend,' and got the idea to work upon the old story for his own end. He evidently had some method of slipping in and out of the house, probably through one of the many French windows, or possibly he had a key to one or two of the garden doors, and when he was supposed to be away, he was really coming down on the quiet and hiding somewhere in the neighborhood.

"The incident of the kiss in the dark hall I put down to sheer nervous imaginings on the part of Beaumont and Miss Hisgins, yet I must say that the sound of the horse outside of the front door is a little difficult to explain away. But I am still inclined to keep to my first idea on this point, that there was nothing really unnatural about it.

"The hoof-sounds in the billiard room and down the passage were done by Parsket from the floor below by pomping up against the panelled ceiling with a block of wood tied to one of the window-hooks. I proved this by an examination which showed the dents in the woodwork.

"The sounds of the horse galloping round the house were possibly made also by Parsket, who must have had a horse tied up in the plantation near by, unless indeed, he made the sounds himself, but I do not see how he could have gone fast enough to produce the illusion. In any case, I don't feel perfect certainty on this point. I failed to find any hoof marks, as you remember.

"The gobbling neighing in the park was a ventriloquial achievement on the part of Parsket and the attack out there on Beaumont was also by him, so that when I thought he was in his bedroom, he must have been outside all the time and joined me after I ran out of the front-door. This is almost probable, I mean that Parsket was the cause, for if it had been something more serious he would certainly have given up his foolishness, knowing that there was no longer any need for it. I cannot imagine how he escaped being shot, both then and in the last mad action of which I have just told you. He was enormously without fear of any kind for himself as you can see.

"The time when Parsket was with us, when we thought we heard the Horse galloping round the house, we must have been deceived.

No one was *very* sure, except of course, Parsket, who would naturally encourage the belief.

"The neighing in the cellar is where I consider there came the first suspicion into Parsket's mind that there was something more at work than his sham-haunting. The neighing was done by him in the same way that he did it in the park; but when I remember how ghastly he looked, I feel sure that the sounds must have had some infernal quality added to them which frightened the man himself. Yet, later, he would persuade himself that he had been getting fanciful. Of course, I must not forget that the effect upon Miss Hisgins must have made him feel pretty miserable.

"Then, about the clergyman being called away, we found afterwards that it was a bogus errand, or rather, call and it is apparent that Parsket was at the bottom of this, so as to get a few more hours in which to achieve his end and what that was, a very little imagination will show you; for he had found that Beaumont would not be frightened away. I hate to think this, but I'm bound to. Anyway, it is obvious that the man was temporarily a bit off his normal balance. Love's a queer disease!

"Then, there is no doubt at all but that Parsket left the cord to the butler's bell hitched somewhere so as to give him an excuse to slip away naturally to clear it. This also gave him the opportunity to remove one of the passage lamps. Then he had only to smash the other and the passage was in utter darkness for him to make the attempt on Beaumont.

"In the same way, it was he who locked the door of the bedroom and took the key (it was in his pocket). This prevented the Captain from bringing a light and coming to the rescue. But Captain Hisgins broke down the door with the heavy fender-curb and it was his smashing the door that sounded so confusing and frightening in the darkness of the passage.

"The photograph of the monstrous hoof above Miss Hisgins in the cellar is one of the things that I am less sure about. It might have been faked by Parsket, whilst I was out of the room, and this would have been easy enough, to anyone who knew how. But, you know, it does not look like a fake. Yet, there is as much evidence of probability that it was faked, as against; and the thing is too vague for an examination to help a definite decision so that I will express no opinion, one way or the other. It is certainly a horrible photograph.

"And now I come to that last, dreadful thing. There has been no further manifestation of anything abnormal, so that there is an extraordinary uncertainty in my conclusions. If we had not heard those last sounds and if Parsket had not shown that enormous sense of fear, the whole of this case could be explained in the way in which I have shown. And, in fact, as you have seen, I am of the opinion that almost all of it can be cleared up, but I see no way of going past the thing we heard at the last and the fear that Parsket showed.

"His death—no, that proves nothing. At the inquest it was described somewhat untechnically as due to heart-spasm. That is normal enough and leaves us quite in the dark as to whether he died because he stood between the girl and some incredible thing of monstrosity.

"The look on Parsket's face and the thing he called out when he heard the great hoof-sounds coming down the passage seem to show that he had the sudden realisation of what before then may have been nothing more than a horrible suspicion. And his fear and appreciation of some tremendous danger approaching was probably more keenly real even than mine. And then he did the one, fine, great thing!"

"And the cause?" I said. "What caused it?"

Carnacki shook his head.

"God knows," he answered, with a peculiar, sincere reverence. "If that thing was what it seemed to be one might suggest an explanation which would not offend one's reason, but which may be utterly wrong. Yet I have thought, though it would take a long lecture on Thought Induction to get you to appreciate my reasons, that Parsket had produced what I might term a kind of 'induced haunting,' a kind of induced simulation of his mental conceptions due to his desperate thoughts and broodings. It is impossible to make it clearer in a few words."

"But the old story!" I said. "Why may not there have been something in *that*?"

"There may have been something in it," said Carnacki. "But I do not think it had anything to do with *this*. I have not clearly thought

119

out my reasons, yet; but later I may be able to tell you why I think so."

"And the marriage? And the cellar—was there anything found there?" asked Taylor.

"Yes, the marriage was performed that day in spite of the tragedy," Carnacki told us. "It was the wisest thing to do—considering the things that I cannot explain. Yes, I had the floor of that big cellar up, for I had a feeling I might find something there to give me some light. But there was nothing.

"You know, the whole thing is tremendous and extraordinary. I shall never forget the look on Parsket's face. And afterwards the disgusting sounds of those great hoofs going away through the quiet house."

Carnacki stood up:—

"Out you go!" he said in friendly fashion, using the recognised formula.

And we went presently out into the quiet of the Embankment, and so to our homes.

Edwin Winthrop and Catriona Kaye
SEVEN STARS EPISODE TWO

THE MAGICIAN AND THE MATINEE IDOL
by KIM NEWMAN

Mustachioed ex-intelligence officer Edwin Winthrop and Catriona Kaye, the daughter of a West Country parson and an investigator into psychical research, are a partnership. Although not under the command of the Diogenes Club, they occasionally assist Edwin's mentor Charles Beauregard who, after years of service, now sits on the Ruling Cabal, highest echelon of the Secret Service.

Edwin and Catriona first appeared in Kim Newman's 1981 play My One Little Murder Can't Do Any Harm, *a 1920s country house whodunit. For the record, the author portrayed Winthrop, and Catriona was portrayed by Catriona O'Callaghan. They have a flashback to themselves, with the rest of the cast of the play, in Newman's novel* Jago *(1991), and Edwin is a leading character in* The Bloody Red Baron *(1995). He also rates a tiny mention in Jack Yeovil's* Demon Download *(1990) and appears in 'The Big Fish' (*Interzone #76, *October 1993), 'Angel Down, Sussex' (*Interzone #149, *November 1999), 'You Don't Have to be Mad. . .' (*White of the Moon, *1999), 'Clubland Heroes' (*The Secret Files of the Diogenes Club, *2007), 'Sorcerer Conjuror Wizard Witch' (*Mysteries of the Diogenes Club, *2010) and the Titan Books edition of* Anno Dracula: The Bloody Red Baron *(2012).*

As well as turning up in 'Angel Down, Sussex', 'Clubland Heroes', 'Sorcerer Conjuror Wizard Witch' and The Bloody Red Baron *with Edwin Winthrop, Catriona Kaye is also in 'The Pierce Arrow Stalled, and . . .' (*Famous Monsters, 1995*), 'Cold Snap' (*The Secret Files of the Diogenes Club*), An English Ghost Story (2013) and the forthcoming novel* The Secrets of Drearcliff Grange School.

Celebrated stage and screen actor John Barrymore (1882– 1942) was the brother of Ethel and Lionel Barrymore. A romantic matinée idol famous for his "Great Profile", he squandered his talents, and his career ultimately floundered in alcoholism and self-parody. At the peak of his powers he portrayed the titular detective in Sherlock Holmes *(1922), directed by Albert Parker for Goldwyn Pictures. Although a Hollywood production, extensive location shooting took place in London. Roland Young played Dr. Watson, with Austrian actor Gustav von Seyffertitz as a Caligari-like Moriarty, under which name the film was released in Britain.*

THE FEBRUARY CHILL made Catriona Kaye wish hemlines weren't being worn above the knee this season. Her bobbed hair, tucked under a cloche hat, left her slender neck bare, prompting her to wrap her fur collar tight around her throat.

Born with the century, now just twenty-two, she sometimes felt her obligation to follow the fashions of the times was a curse. Her father, a West Country parson, was always on at her about the scandalous way she dressed, not to mention her cacophonous American tastes in music. Edwin never chided, sometimes claiming in his lofty manner that she was a useful barometer: when she was up, so was the world; when she was down, calamity was in the offing.

Presently, she had much in common with the Grand Old Duke of York's Ten Thousand Men. She was neither up nor down. The wind blowing down Baker Street was winter, but the clarity of the air—no fog, no rain—was spring.

Things were about to change.

* * *

Two elderly matrons nearby had noticed the celebrity. They were frankly goggling, like children at the circus. Catriona thought them rather sweet about it.

The celebrity had just stepped out of a door which bore a famous, and famously hard-to-locate, address: 221B. He wore a fore-and-aft cap, and a checked ulster of Victorian cut. He turned to cast a hawk-like gaze at the distance, sharp profile distinct and distinctive, and raised a magnifying glass to his eye.

"Isn't that . . .?" began one of the matrons.

The object of their amazement was accompanied by a shorter, plumper, huffier man, in a bowler hat and moustache. He held a revolver.

"I do believe it is," the other matron agreed. "*John Barrymore!*"

The Great Profile turned full-face to the admiring dears, one eye hugely magnified by his glass, flashed a thin grin, and gallantly doffed his deerstalker. One matron swooned in the other's arms.

Catriona couldn't help but giggle.

A short man with a megaphone began shouting, chiding the matinee idol for "playing at the rear stalls".

"I'm afraid I shall never get the hang of this film business," Barrymore lamented.

Catriona understood the actor was mostly concerned with his impending *Hamlet*, and had little concentration left over for this photoplay of Mr. Conan Doyle's *Sherlock Holmes*, or rather Mr. William Gillette's celebrated stage drama. From what she'd seen of the "shooting", Barrymore's sleuth had quite a bit of the gloomy Dane about him and spent a great deal more time making goo-goo eyes at the heroine than plodding over the scene of the crime with Good Old Watson. Mycroft Holmes would be revolving—very slowly, and with great gravity—in his grave.

Edwin, her "whatever", affected to be interested in the intricacies of the camera, and spent his time interrogating the crew on tiny technical points. She knew that trick of his, to pretend one overwhelming enthusiasm in order to winkle out all manner of other unconnected information from those he was politely and unnoticeably interrogating.

Not for the first time, she felt a lot like Good Old Watson. She and Edwin were a partnership, but too many people—though not Edwin himself—thought of her as a decorative adjunct to the genius of a Great Man.

Admittedly, she wasn't expected to pen adulatory accounts of the exploits she shared with Edwin Winthrop. In most cases, the principles would certainly not care to find their confidential affairs written up in the popular press. The bally Baskervilles can hardly have been delighted to have the whole nation privy to their nasty squabbles, come to that. There were also, in some instances connected with Edwin's shadowy employers in the late War, questions of state secrecy to be considered.

Barrymore was annoying the director, a man named Parker, with his diffidence. When disinterested in his work, he tended to ignore his Prince's sound advice against "sawing the air". She noticed Roland Young, the cove playing Good Old Watson, was managing with extremely British tact not to be annoyed, in such a manner that his actual feelings were plain. Now that was real acting.

After two days of hanging about as the American film crew took location "shots", she was used to being mistaken for an actress or even one of the Great Profile's surplus mistresses. Remembering Edwin's advice, she took pains never to contradict or confirm assumptions.

As their occasional government commissions went, this was hardly momentous. Their business was usually with the living who are being bothered by the dead; in this case, they were here to protect the interests of the dead against slander. Edwin was doing an unofficial favour for the Diogenes Club, the institution which had found him official employment during the Great War and which still had occasional need to call on his services.

Mycroft Holmes, the consulting detective's less famous but more perspicacious brother, had once sat on the Ruling Cabal of the Diogenes Club, in the seat now occupied by the somewhat slimmer-hipped Mr. Charles Beauregard, to whom Edwin reported.

Last year, Edwin and Catriona had been involved by the Diogenes Club in a row involving a phantasmal samurai who wielded a very substantial sword in the Japanese Embassy, lopping off the heads of several uncomplaining staff members. The bloody business was eventually brought to a satisfactory conclusion, with human deviltry exposed and psychic shenanigans explained away. She was now the only girl she knew with a personal scroll of commendation from the Emperor of Japan in her dresser drawer.

This was far more routine. It came down to reputation. Though never under the command of the Diogenes Club, the Great Detective had once or twice assisted his brother with problems much as Edwin and Catriona now assisted Beauregard. It had been the cause of something of a rift between the Holmes Boyos that Good Old Watson and Mr. Doyle had written up a few of these bits of business, going so far as to mention the institution in print and giving some hint as to Mycroft Holmes's actual position in the British government.

That was all blown over now. But Beauregard, as much out of respect for the memory of his old chief, wanted the cloak of obscurity habitually worn by the Diogenes Club and all its operatives to fall heavy again.

"It will almost be a holiday," Beauregard had said. "Mingling with show-folk. Just make sure they stay away from the facts."

Parker was on at Barrymore again about his famous moustache. It was still not shaven off. Apparently, it would not show in "long shots", but would have to go for the "close-ups".

Catriona wondered whether Edwin's moustache was only coincidentally identical to the actor's. He professed to disdain fashion when he was making fun of her kimonos or shaven hackles, but he could be a touch dandyish in his own appearance.

"You'd be fastidious too," he would say, "if you'd spent four years in a uniform stiff with mud."

The War excused a lot.

Parker stormed away from the actors. Barrymore, treating the wide step of 221B as a stage, gave a bow for the gallery. The on-looking crowds applauded mightily. The director glared in frustration and muttered about cracking the whip when the company got back to the States.

"You, technical advisor," Parker addressed her. "What's wrong with that scene?"

"I don't like to mention it really," she said.

"It's what you're here for, isn't it? It's that blasted lip-fungus of John's."

"He could be in disguise," she said, trying to be generous.

Parker laughed bitterly.

"It's the address," she piped. "The front door would just have 221 on it. A and B and, for all we know C, would have doors on the landings."

Parker shook his head and stalked off.

"I am right," she told his back.

Though they lived—together! in sin! scandalously!—in the Somerset house Edwin had inherited from his disreputable father, they were more often found these modern days in their London *pied-à-terre*, a nice little flat in Bloomsbury which Catriona officially kept as a residence to allow her father to avoid a heart attack by believing she lived apart from Edwin. This evening, with Paul Whiteman's 'Whispering' on the gramophone, they discussed the day's work as they danced, occasionally dropping the odd inconvenient item of clothing.

"Old Beauregard has nothing to worry about, Cat," said Edwin, almost directly into her ear. "Along the chain that leads from Holmes to Watson to Doyle to Gillette to Barrymore, anything that might be taken as real or referring to reality has been stripped away."

"The Diogenes doesn't figure in the film scenario?"

One hand firmly in the small of her back, Edwin dipped her over, supporting her weight. She often felt on the point of losing her balance, but Edwin would pull her back just in time.

"No."

They kissed. The song ended. They occupied themselves upon the divan.

Afterwards, propped up among Turkish cushions, drawing on a cigarette through a long holder, kimono loose about her shoulders, she thought again about the errand.

"Surely, after all these years, no one actually cares about the dratted Bruce-Partington Plans any more."

Edwin laughed lazily. He was drifting towards a doze as she was becoming more awake. He claimed to be catching up on all the sleep missed through four years of shelling day and night.

"It's the principle, poppet. Secrecy. If everybody knew everything, there'd be mass panic."

She wondered about that.

"Darkness has become a habit for too many, Edwin."

"You shall cast light, Cat. You are a beacon."

He stroked her leg. She considered stabbing him with her lighted cigarette.

"Rotter," she snorted.

Edwin sat up, unconsciously passed his fingers over his (John Barrymore) moustache, and paid attention.

"Old secrets, dear," she said. "There are too many of them. And new ones piled on top."

"We only need dawdle about the kinema wallahs for a few more days," he said, taking her hand. "Then, I promise, we can find a nice ghost story, a bleeding nun with ghastly groans or a castle spectre with clanking chains. We shall explain it away with the shining light of science and rationality. Bit by bit, we shall banish the darkness from these isles."

She biffed him with a cushion.

Mostly, the darkness was subject to banishment when they applied themselves. But sometimes . . .

"What more do we need to know about this silly film?"

"Nothing, really. I telephoned Beauregard and passed on all that we've ferreted out. He particularly asked that we be present at the next 'location', to represent the nation's interests."

"The *nation's* interests?"

"Indeed. The Goldwyn Company has secured permission to take film in the private recesses of the national collection, in the basements of the British Museum—some confrontation between Holmesy and that mathematics professor of sorry memory—and we're to be there to see they don't break anything. They will be 'shooting' at night, after everyone has gone home."

She shook her head.

"I'm a serious person," she announced. "A scientific inquirer. My field, in which I am widely published and hailed even at my tender age, is psychical research. I do not mind, under certain circumstances, serving my country as a more-or-less secret agent. However, I draw the line at working as an unsalaried night watchman!"

He embraced her, and she knew she'd give in eventually.

"Haven't you ever wanted to find out what's *really* kept in all those vaults? We shall get to root about among artefacts and manuscripts forbidden to the public."

That was not fair. He knew she couldn't resist that temptation.

She kissed him, hungry again.

"You shall shine in the dark," he said.

The cellar was vast, a vaulted ceiling above a crate-filled trench. Though the tiled walls were cold to the touch, the cellar was remarkably free of damp. At one end, an uncrated Easter Island head, crown scraping the ceiling, surveyed the scene. The statue was as long-faced and beaky as the unprepossessing original currently impersonated by the classically handsome actor grappling centre stage with an ersatz Napoleon of Crime.

"This looks like an underground railway station," she commented.

"Exactly, Clever Cat," Edwin agreed. "Built as a stop for British Museum, but never finished. The company was bankrupted. Most of the line caved in, but the Museum has kept this as its deepest storeroom. Some things are too huge to stack in an ordinary basement."

"How silly," she said. "Plainly, the underground railway should be operated by a single company for the benefit of the nation, not by competing and inept rival factions who'll honeycomb under London until the whole city falls in."

He did not give her an argument.

Parker called "cut!", his megaphone-amplified voice booming through the cellar.

Barrymore—lip shorn at last, not entirely to the detriment of his looks—stood up, and a girl dashed in to reapply greasepaint to his cheeks. The site of his battle with Moriarty was now swarming with "crew", all intent on some tiny task.

A youth in knickerbockers assisted "Moriarty" to his feet. The Prof was impersonated by an authentically frightening-looking fellow with ragged hair, eyes like corpse-candle flames, and a thin-lipped sneer. An assistant director who, she realised, was slightly sweet on her, said Moriarty's impersonator was an Austrian by the aptly villainous name of Gustav von Seyffertitz. He had signed himself with the absurdly Yankee alias of "G. Butler Clonblough" during the late unpleasantness.

Barrymore could switch his Sherlock off and on like an electric lamp, melodramatic when the camera was cranking but larking outrageously between "takes". Von Seyffertitz, whom Barrymore liked because he made him look even more handsome by contrast, seemed always to be "on", and occupied himself by skulking villainously as the director shouted at Barrymore.

She nudged Edwin, and nodded at "Moriarty".

The actor was drifting out of the circle of artificial light, towards the pile of crates, as if drawn to worship at the chin of the Easter Island head.

"That's odd," Edwin commented.

"You're just jealous."

So far, they hadn't been able to take advantage of this opportunity to root about among forbidden treasures. The priceless and ancient artefacts were just backdrop, and heaven help anyone who strayed accidentally into the camera's line of sight. The director might well have the powers of instant trial and execution granted to battlefield commanders.

Von Seyffertitz was definitely looking for something. Through pince-nez, he peered at runic marks chalked on the crates, tutting to himself.

"Old Beauregard told us to be on our guard down here," Edwin said. "There was some bad business to do with the Museum in his day, round about the Jubilee. He's a bit cranky about it, if you ask me. Long and distinguished service and all that."

Ever since descending from street level, Catriona had felt a chill that was more than the cold. Beyond the fragile light, the shadows were deeper than they had any business to be.

"Mr. Beauregard is rarely mistaken," she reminded Edwin.

It was time for the antagonists to tussle again. Parker called the "crew" clear, and pulled Barrymore and von Seyffertitz together as if refereeing a boxing match. The Austrian seemed reluctant to leave off his poking-around for something as insignificant as doing his job.

"I'll bet that fellow gets fed up with being defeated," Edwin said. "I've seen him as the villain in a half-dozen flickers." Like her, Edwin was secretly devoted to the newest art. They attended the kinema far more than the theatre, and had an especial fondness for the serials made in Paris, *Fantômas* and *Judex*. When she had occasion to use an alias herself, Catriona often picked "Irma Vep", after the ambiguous villainess of *Les vampires*.

"I wonder if he is ever tempted to fight back properly, and best the hero. Just once."

She saw what Edwin meant. Moriarty was giving a strong account of himself for an elderly mathematics professor—in actuality, exactly the sort of person it is supremely easy to toss off a waterfall and Sherlock was taking all the knocks.

Von Seyffertitz weaved and punched like a far younger man, landing a few potential bruises on the famous face. Barrymore was in a bit of a sweat. Had the Professor forgotten the scenario? He *was* supposed to lose.

Von Seyffertitz got a wrestling hold on Barrymore and threw him to the floor. The director called "cut!" Concerned people descended in a swarm. The star was bleeding. Moriarty mouthed an insincere apology.

"My face, my face," wailed Barrymore, theatrical voice filling the cellar.

Edwin nodded that she should take a look.

She ventured near the actor, handkerchief out.

Blood trickled from both nostrils, replacing the shaven moustache with a red imitation.

"Is my dose broken?"

She staunched the flow of blood, and felt for give in Barrymore's nasal cartilage. She thought his valuable fizzog was not seriously damaged and told him so.

"Thank heavens," he declared, kissing her forehead, fulfilling the dreams of a million matinee-goers. She felt a sticky, unromantic discharge in her hair and discreetly scraped it off and onto a wall.

"I must save myself," the actor muttered. "This doesn't matter."

Barrymore was relieved beyond proportion. She realised he had been afraid for his long-awaited *Hamlet*.

"Bless you, child," he said. "For the merciful news. One cannot play the Prince with a patch of plaster in the middle of one's face.

To have lost that for this penny dreadful would have been too much to bear."

Actors were a rum lot.

Parker called an end to the night's "shoot". Until Barrymore's nose recovered, there was no point in going on. An assistant gleefully totted up how much this delay would cost.

"Tomorrow night, I want you to thrash that blasted Austrian within an inch of his ugly life!" demanded Parker.

"You have my word," Barrymore said, sounding better already.

The equipment was dismantled, and the company began to withdraw on the double.

Edwin touched her elbow and stepped into shadow, encouraging her to join him.

"Something's wrong," he said, trench-nerves-a-tingle.

She nodded. He was right. She felt it too.

The film lights were turned off, leaving deep darks and illusory afterimages. But there was another light, a reddish glow, almost infernal.

Was there a whiff of brimstone?

Equipment and persons were being crammed into a cage lift that was the most easy access to the surface.

The glow was coming from behind the Easter Island head. A shadow, like a man-sized stick insect, moved on the face of the head, clinging to the hatchet-nose.

"Look, Cat. You can see that the tunnel extends beyond that statue. It must be shored up and used as extra storage space."

The shadow detached itself from the nose and slipped around the head, briefly blotting the crimson glow, and disappeared into the tunnel.

"That was a man," Edwin said.

"Was it?" she ventured, unsure.

There was something in the way the shadow moved.

"Come on, Cat."

Edwin was after the shadow. She hesitated only a moment and followed him. He had produced a revolver from under his coat. This was no longer a holiday.

She wished she had dressed for this.

The film folk were busy leaving. Only a few remained, and they were intent on their business, noticing nothing. Edwin paused at the end of the platform and looked at the Easter Island head.

"I wonder how they got it down here?" he mused.

The face seemed to snarl at them.

Edwin led the way, climbing around the head by using the pendulous earlobe as a grip, and dropping to the cinder-strewn bed of the tunnel. She followed, fearing for the state of her silk stockings and white pumps.

In the tunnel, the glow was stronger. Definitely a red lamp somewhere, beyond the array of dilapidated crates. It was also much colder here. She shivered.

These crates were stacked more haphazardly. Some were broken, spilling straw onto the tunnel-bed. Some of the damage looked recent.

Edwin was attracted to a crate that lay open. Straw and African masks were strewn nearby, as if thrown out to make way for some new treasure. He lit a match and tutted. She stepped over to look in.

An elderly man, dressed in his unmentionables, was crammed into the crate, unconscious. She checked his breathing and pulse. Edwin lowered the match, to cast light on the man's face. It was von Seyffertitz, a chloroform burn around his mouth and nose.

"He's been here for a while," she said.

"Then who was playing the Prof?"

She shivered, not with the cold.

"I say," boomed a familiar voice, "who's there? What's going on?"

It was, of all people, John Barrymore.

"It's Miss Kaye, isn't it? The angel of nasal mercy. And you're the lucky fellow who knocks around with her."

"Edwin Winthrop," Edwin introduced himself.

"Are you sneaking off to, um, spoon?"

Edwin shook out the match too late. Barrymore had seen von Seyffertitz in the crate.

"Good God, a body!"

Edwin glumly lit another match.

"It's Gustav the Ghastly," Barrymore said.

"Someone has been impersonating him," Edwin admitted.

"I shouldn't wonder," Barrymore said. "He's easy to 'do'. I can look like him myself. A grotesque face is far easier to hide behind than a handsome one. When I played the uncanny Mr. Hyde . . ."

Edwin waved the actor quiet.

Barrymore became aware of the ruby light. He caught on at once that there was something strange about here.

Among the African masks was a white shock of hair. The wig "Moriarty" had worn. The pince-nez and a false nose were in with the mess.

Their quarry was so intent on his business that he didn't mind leaving a trail. That suggested an arrogance or confidence that was not comforting.

"Come on," said the matinee idol, striding forwards like a proper hero, "let's get to the bottom of this." Edwin took Catriona's arm, smoothing her gooseflesh, and held up the match as they walked towards the glow. When the match went out, there was enough light to see by. Somehow, that was more frightening than the dark.

A large brassbound trunk blocked almost the entire tunnel as if it were a dead end. But red light outlined it, revealing that there was a space beyond.

They crept up and pressed themselves to the wall, to look past the trunk.

It was hard to make sense of what they saw. An area had been cleared and a design marked on the cinder-floor in white powder or paint. At various points of the design stood Arabian Nights lamps, burning redly. Catriona could not at first discern the shape made by the lines and the lights. It was not the familiar magic circle, or a pentagram.

There were seven lamps, spread not quite in a line. She moved her head a little, and saw it.

"The plough," she whispered.

Edwin's grip on her arm momentarily strengthened.

"Clever Cat," he said, proud.

The lamps made up the Seven Stars. The constellation of Ursa Major.

An open case—not a wooden crate but a coffin-shaped metal container—was in the middle of the design. A point of red glinted within the case. She fancied she could see it even through the metal side.

And a thin figure stood over the case, arms spread wide, muttering in an unfamiliar language. The frock coat of Moriarty still hung from his shoulders, lifted by an otherwise-unfelt wind.

Some species of ritual was in progress. With every atom of sense in her body, Catriona felt this was Evil. She knew Edwin and Barrymore were as aware as she of this, and were struck quiet.

The man who had been Moriarty took a dagger from his inside pocket, and addressed the points of the constellation, tapping the tip of the dagger to his forehead and then pointing it at the individual starfires. Then, he let his loose sleeve fall back and swiftly carved a series of symbols into his left arm, raising lines of blood that dripped down into the crate. Switching hands, he as deftly repeated the carvings on his right arm, allowing a red rain to fall.

Barrymore squeezed into the space between the crate and the wall, drawn into the drama like a star pulled from the wings. Edwin let Catriona go and took hold of the actor's shoulder, holding him back. All three were now jammed into the small space.

She saw that a body lay in the case, a light burning in its chest. Blood sprinkled a papery face and arms.

The ritual-maker was not a young man. His face was as sunken as that of the actor he had impersonated, if not as that of the mummy he was incanting over. He was almost completely bald, and stringy in the arms and throat.

Barrymore got free of Edwin and stepped into the makeshift temple. The ritual-maker saw him and halted, dagger pointed now as a weapon rather than a magic tool.

"Back, play-actor," he said. "I've waited too many years to be interrupted now. This has to be done precisely, as I once learned to my cost. It's not easy to separate Pai-net'em from his treasure."

The ritual-maker spoke with an Irish accent.

Edwin and Catriona stood either side of Barrymore.

"Three interlopers," the ritual-maker sneered. A drop of his own blood sparked at the tip of his dagger. "You'll stay well back if you know what's good for you."

The light in the mummy's chest was pulsing.

"Twenty-five years a convict," the ritual-maker declared, "and months of waiting for a chance to come down here. This new wonder of the age, the cinematograph, was just stirring when I went into Princetown Jail. Now, it has opened doors, just as I am opening a door now, a door that will mean the ruination at last of England and all it stands for."

He was more than a madman.

"I know who you are," Edwin said, quietly. "Declan Mountmain."

The ritual-maker was shocked.

"So, I'm not forgotten after all. I had thought all the others long dead. Evidently, England remembers its foes. Who set you upon me?"

Edwin gave no answer, but Catriona thought to herself that this was no accident. Charles Beauregard and the Diogenes Club had foreseen something like this.

She had heard of Declan Mountmain. Some sort of magician from the last century. His reputation was not of the best.

"Your prison didn't kill me," Mountmain said. "And now, at last, I shall have my prize. The magicking is complete. Pai-net'em is bound. I may take the jewel. I'm glad of an audience, as a matter of fact. I might even let you live through the deluge to come, to tell the tale."

He knelt over the mummy and plunged the dagger into its chest. The corpse's eyes flew open and glared redly. But only the eyes moved, blazing with ancient frustration.

"Tied you proper, you Egyptian fool," Mountmain chuckled. "You'll walk no more."

The magician sawed at the mummy's chest, cutting around the glow like a butcher. He thrust his hand into the hole he had made and pulled out the source of the light.

Catriona could only gasp. She felt dizzy.

It was a huge jewel, burning with an inner light.

"With this, I shall bring down a cataclysm whose memory will last when the sun has turned cold."

Edwin raised his revolver and shot Mountmain.

The magician laughed. She *saw* the bullet strike him in the face, make a ripple as if in a reflection of a face on the surface of a pond, and disappear. The shot embedded itself in the brickwork of a wall a dozen feet behind Mountmain.

"The Jewel of Seven Stars has accepted me," the magician announced. "As it once accepted this dead thing."

Mountmain brought his boot heel down on the mummy's head, crushing it in its bandages. The eyes no longer moved.

"I am become the Destroyer of Empire!"

Mountmain's laughter filled the tunnel. His eyes shone, each reflecting the Seven Stars.

Whatever else the jewel had done for him, it had transformed him into the incarnation of the melodrama villain he had been impersonating. Mountmain was acting exactly like a Drury Lane dastard, threatening to evict the heroine's mother into the cold, cold snow unless she bent to his wicked will.

The jewel reached out to them.

Catriona felt its pull. She resisted the impulse to faint, as if she were turned into the feeble girl who would be tied to the railway tracks.

"O villainy!" Barrymore thundered. "Ho! Let the door be locked! Treachery, seek it out!"

Edwin fired another useless shot, this time at the jewel itself.

John Barrymore leaped upon Declan Mountmain.

The indecision of Hamlet was thrown aside, and he was Sherlock incarnate, incisive brain directing instant action.

She saw how surprised Mountmain was at this attack, how almost amused . . .

Barrymore's hands went to Mountmain's throat.

They grappled together, as if tottering on the brink of the Reichenbach. Mountmain fought back fiercely, as he had done when the camera was rolling. He clubbed Barrymore's head with the mighty jewel, causing flashes of bloody light to flood the tunnel.

Barrymore had Mountmain's dagger, and was gouging at the magician's wavering chest.

"The point envenomed too," Barrymore quoted. "Then, venom, to thy work."

The dagger seemed to affect Mountmain more than the bullet had.

Edwin was calculating the odds.

"The Seven Stars isn't for the taking," he said. "It has to be fought for. It has to be earned."

As usual, Catriona was annoyed that things were being kept from her. But she got the drift of the situation.

Barrymore and Mountmain fought like tigers. A lamp was knocked over, fire spreading along the white lines of the constellation. Shadows danced on the walls, and writhed on the contorted faces of the magician and the matinee idol.

"Here, thou incestuous, murd'rous, damnéd Dane, drink off this potion..."

"Pull down the stars," Catriona said.

Edwin understood at once.

Mountmain had drawn power from his design. It was a condition of the ritual. She kicked one of the lamps out of place, and it shattered against a far wall in a splash of burning oil. She did the same for another.

Edwin stamped on the burning lines, kicking the diagram to pieces.

Barrymore had Mountmain bent backwards over the case, pushing him down onto the mummy's bones. The jewel was trapped between them. There was blood on both men's faces.

Catriona kicked aside the last of the lamps.

Fire spread, but the constellation was gone.

Barrymore and Mountmain cried out together. It was as if needle-fingers scraped Catriona's bones. There was something inhuman in the shared scream.

Edwin held her.

Mountmain lay broken across the coffin-case, one of the mummy's arms around his chest. A last sigh escaped from him, with a whisp of smoke from his mouth.

Barrymore staggered to his feet, slowly. His shirt was torn open, and a great red wound showed on his chest.

"I am dead, Horatio," he declaimed.

"You that look pale and tremble at this chance,
That are but mutes or audience to this act,
Had I but time—as this fell sergeant Death
Is strict in his arrest—O, I could tell you—
But let it be Horatio, I am dead,
Thou liv'st. Report me and my cause aright
To the unsatisfied."

As he spoke, Barrymore's voice grew in strength. His wound pulsed, not with flowing red blood but flowing red light.

"It's *inside* him," Edwin breathed.

The flesh closed over the light, and the red was in the actor's eyes.

"O God, Horatio, what a wounded name,

Things standing thus unknown, shall live behind me!"

Then Barrymore stopped doing Hamlet, stopped doing Holmes. He stood still. His skin was smooth where his wound had been. Catriona thought she saw a faint light inside, as if his heart glowed. The jewel was gone.

Edwin picked up the dagger and looked at the stricken man.

Was he going to cut it out? As Mountmain had from the mummy. If so, would the jewel be his—with whatever that entailed—as it had been the mummy's?

Edwin thought it through and dropped the dagger.

Barrymore shook his head, as if he had just walked on stage without knowing his lines or his role.

The fires were burning out. Edwin arranged Mountmain in the coffin, tucking in his arms and legs, and put the lid on it, fitting it firmly into place.

Barrymore looked around with a "where am I?" expression.

"Let's get him out of this place," Catriona said.

Edwin agreed with her.

John Barrymore looked at the spectre, eyes bright with fear and love.

"Angels and ministers of grace defend us!

Be thou a spirit of health or goblin damned,

Bring with thee airs from heaven or blasts from hell,

Be thy intents wicked or charitable,

Thou com'st in such a questionable shape

That I will speak to thee . . ."

Catriona's hand closed on Edwin's. From their box, they could see the spots of sweat on the star's face. This was the opening night of Barrymore's greatest triumph. He seemed fairly to glow.

At last, she understood what the fuss was about. This was how her father must have felt when Irving gave his Dane. How the first audiences at the Globe Theatre must have felt.

The business under the British Museum was months gone, and they were an ocean away, in New York at the invitation of the star, his debt to them repaid with tickets to the opening of the century.

As the play went on, she wondered about the light in the actor's eyes, and thought about the jewel in his chest. He had been good before, but he was great now. Had the jewel anything to do with that? And was there a price to pay?

Then she was caught up in the drama, swept from her box back to Elsinore, when ghosts walked and vengeance warped the heart and soul.

Solar Pons

THE ADVENTURE OF THE CRAWLING HORROR
by BASIL COPPER

Solar Pons (whose name literally means "Bridge of Light") is the second most famous consulting detective in London. Whether slouched in the armchair at his apartments at No. 7B Praed Street, his thin fingers tented before him and his keen eyes fixed on the door, or following a clue along the mist-shrouded cobblestones of London's alleyways, Pons puffs thoughtfully on his pipe and uses his deductive reasoning to solve many strange cases, aided by his chronicler Dr. Lyndon Parker. Other familiar characters include landlady Mrs. Johnson, Inspector Jamison of Scotland Yard and Pons' brother Bancroft.

In the late 1920s, August Derleth (1909–1971)—then a young student at the University of Wisconsin—was extremely interested in classic British detective fiction. He wrote to Sir Arthur Conan Doyle in England asking if the author intended to publish any more Sherlock Holmes stories. When Conan Doyle replied that he did not, Derleth wrote back asking if he could write his own Holmes tales. Conan Doyle replied with an emphatic "No!" and so Derleth sat down to write his own Sherlock Holmes pastiches.

Solar Pons made his debut in 1929 and remained the author's favourite detective creation. Derleth wrote one or two Pons tales a year, reportedly devoting endless hours of research and authentication of details to the London milieu his characters inhabited. Derleth completed sixty-eight stories, which were collected in "In Re: Sherlock Holmes": The Adventures of Solar Pons *(1945),* The Memoirs of Solar Pons *(1951),* Three Problems for Solar Pons *(1952),* The Return of Solar Pons *(1958),* The Reminiscences of Solar Pons *(1961),* The Casebook of Solar Pons *(1965),* A Praed Street Dossier *(1968),* The Adventures of the Unique Dickensians *(1968),* The Chronicles of Solar Pons *(1973) and* The Final Adventures of Solar Pons *(1998), plus the novel* Mr. Fairlie's Final Journey *(1968), all originally published under the author's Mycroft & Moran imprint.*

In the late 1970s, Basil Copper (1924-2013) was asked to revise the entire Pontine Canon by James Turner, Derleth's successor at Arkham House. He spent two years on the task, correcting more than three thousand factual and procedural errors in Derleth's original texts, and the massive two-volume slipcased edition of The Solar Pons Omnibus *finally appeared in 1982.*

In the meantime, Copper was invited to continue the exploits of Pons in six further collections: The Dossier of Solar Pons, The Further Adventures of Solar Pons, The Exploits of Solar Pons, The Reminiscences of Solar Pons, The Secret Files of Solar Pons *and* Some Uncollected Cases of Solar Pons.

*Four of these—*The Dossier of Solar Pons *(1979),* The Further Adventures of Solar Pons *(1979),* The Secret Files of Solar Pons *(1979) and* The Uncollected Cases of Solar Pons *(1980)— were originally published in much altered paperback editions by Pinnacle Books, which the author disowned. Equally disappointing for Copper were two volumes produced in 1987 by Academy Chicago Publishers,* The Exploits of Solar Pons *and* The Further Adventures of Solar Pons.

At least Fedogan & Bremer issued The Exploits of Solar Pons *(1993) and* The Recollections of Solar Pons *(1995) in the author's preferred texts, corrected and restored, with illustrations by Stefanie K. Hawks. These were followed by the novel* Solar Pons versus The Devil's Claw *(2004) and the revised collection* Solar Pons: The Final Cases *(2005) from Sarob Press. Forthcoming is* The Complete Solar Pons *from PS Publishing.*

I

"THERE ARE SOME things, my dear Parker, into which it is better not to inquire too closely. They are far more poignant than words can express."

"Eigh, Pons?"

It was a bitterly cold January day; still, with a touch of ice in the air. I had finished my rounds early, it was just dusk and I was reading the newspaper in front of a glowing fire in our quarters at 7B Praed Street awaiting tea, while my friend Solar Pons busied himself with a gazetteer at a small table near the window. He turned his lean, feral face toward me and smiled faintly.

"I see from the headlines there that you had been reading of the Bulgar atrocities. From the expression on your face I surmise that the massacres in that quarter have moved you deeply."

"Indeed, Pons," I rejoined. "It recalled to my mind my own experiences in the field."

Solar Pons nodded and pushed back his chair from the table. He held out his thin hands to the fire and rubbed them briskly together.

"It is a sad commentary on mankind's foibles, Parker, that different countries cannot learn to live together. There is crime enough, poverty enough and disease enough without nations massacring one another over the finer points of doctrinaire religion or the pink and black shadings on a map."

I put down the paper and looked at Pons approvingly.

"At least you do a good deal to help the world, Pons, by bringing criminal miscreants to justice."

Solar Pons' eyes twinkled as he crossed over to take his favorite armchair at the other side of the fireplace.

"I do my humble best, Parker. But it is good of you to say so, all the same."

He broke off as a measured tread sounded on the stairs.

"Here is the excellent Mrs. Johnson. By the sound of it she is heavily laden. As you are the nearest to the door be so good as to open it for her."

I hastened to do as he requested, admitting the smiling figure of our motherly landlady. As she bustled about setting the table, I resumed my seat, appreciative of the appetising odour rising from the covered dishes.

"As you have a client coming at eight o'clock, Mr. Pons, I took the liberty of preparing high tea. I hope you have no objection, Dr. Parker?"

I glanced at Pons.

"Certainly not, Mrs. Johnson. If you wish, Pons, I can vacate the sitting room if you have private business . . ." Solar Pons smiled, his eyes on Mrs. Johnson. "I wouldn't dream of it, my dear fellow. I think it is a matter which might interest you. It promises some interesting features."

He tented his fingers before him.

"Perhaps you would be good enough to show my visitor up immediately on arrival, Mrs. Johnson. From the tone of the letter I have received he—or she—is of a retiring nature and wishes the visit to be as discreet as possible."

"Very good, Mr. Pons."

Mrs. Johnson finished laying the table and stood regarding us with a concerned expression.

"I hope you will set to at once, gentlemen, or the food will be spoiled."

Solar Pons chuckled, rising from his chair.

"Have no fear, Mrs. Johnson. We shall certainly do justice to it."

The meal, as Mrs. Johnson had indicated, was appetising indeed and my companion and I had soon disposed of the welsh rarebit with which the repast began and rapidly made inroads into the grilled kidneys and bacon with which it continued. I put down my knife and fork with satisfaction and poured myself a second cup of tea. I stared across at Pons.

"You have received a letter about this matter, then, Pons?"

Solar Pons nodded. He raised his head from the gazetteer he had been studying at the side of his plate.

"From Grimstone Manor in Kent, Parker. It does not seem to be marked on the map or indicated in this volume. It is my guess that it will turn out to be a remote area of the county on the marshes near Gravesend. Or failing that, somewhere in the Romney Marsh district."

"You expect to go there, Pons?"

"It is highly likely," replied Solar Pons casually. "From the tone of my client's letter it sounds a bizarre affair indeed."

He reached out for the pile of bread and butter Mrs. Johnson had left on the platter and liberally spread a slice with strawberry jam from the stoneware pot.

"It is as well to know something of the ground and the salient features of interest before one takes to the field. Though it seems as though I shall gain precious little out of it financially."

I stared at Pons interrogatively, aware of an ironic twinkle in his eye.

"I had never noticed that money was a decisive factor in your cases, Pons."

My companion chuckled.

"And neither is it, Parker. Except that my prospective client is either Silas Grimstone, the notorious miser and recluse . . ."

He drew a soiled and discoloured envelope from his pocket with an expression of disgust and pulled from it an even more disreputable-looking enclosure. He frowned at the signature.

". . . Or Miss Sylvia Grimstone, his equally miserly niece. From what I hear the couple live together with her acting as housekeeper. They are as rich as almost anyone you care to name, yet each outdoes the other in scrimping and saving. It is something of a contest between them."

He smiled again as he passed the crumpled letter to me.

"Which is the reason for my remarks. The letter, so far as I can make out, is merely signed S. Grimstone. But whichever of the unlovely pair wish to engage me as client you may bet your boots that my fee will be minimal."

I withdrew my eyes from the cramped writing to regard Pons.

"Why are you taking the case, then?"

Solar Pons shook his head, resting his hands on the table before him.

"I have already indicated, Parker, that the matter seems to present outstanding points of interest. I would not miss it if I decided to remit my fee altogether."

He shifted at the table and reached out for the bread and butter again.

"Pray read the letter aloud to me if you would be so good."

I started as best I could, stumbling and halting over the abominably written and much blotted text. The missive was headed Grimstone Manor, Grimstone Marsh, Kent and bore the date of the previous day.

I glanced at the envelope and realised the reason for Pons' sardonic attitude. He smiled thinly.

"Exactly, Parker. Mr. Grimstone or his niece affixed a used postage stamp to the envelope, presumably after steaming it off something else."

"Good heavens, Pons," I exclaimed. "It is disgraceful!"

"Is it not, Parker," he said with a light laugh. "The Post Office thought so too, because they levied a surcharge of three-pence on the envelope and I have had to reimburse Mrs. Johnson."

"Your recompense is likely to be small indeed, Pons," I said, turning back to the letter.

"As usual, you have got to the heart of the matter, Parker," said Solar Pons drily. He poured a final cup of tea and sat back at the table with a satisfied expression.

"But you have not yet read the letter."

"It presents some difficulties, Pons."

I smoothed out the crumpled paper and after some hesitant starts and re-readings finally deciphered the extraordinary message.

Dear Mr. Pons,

Must consult you at once in a matter of most dreadful urgency. This crawling horror from the marsh cannot be tolerated a moment longer. Please make yourself available when I shall explain everything. If I hear nothing to the contrary I propose to call upon you at eight o'clock on Wednesday evening, in absolute discretion.

Yours,
S. Grimstone.

I looked across at Pons.

"Extraordinary."

"Is it not, Parker. What do you make of the crawling horror?"

I shook my head.

"You are sure the Grimstones are not eccentric. Perhaps even a little mentally deranged?"

Solar Pons smiled grimly.

"Not from what I have heard of his activities in the City. But you are the medical man. I will leave you to judge of their sanity." I picked up the paper again, conscious of the rough edges.

"Hullo, Pons, something has been torn off here. Another small mystery, perhaps?"

Solar Pons shook his head, little glinting lights of humour in his eyes.

"Ordinarily, I would agree with you, my dear fellow. In this instance the answer is elementary."

I stared at him, my puzzlement self-evident.

"The Grimstones' habitual meanness, Parker. They have merely torn their disgraceful old sheet of notepaper in half, in order that they may use the remainder for something else."

I was so taken aback that I almost dropped the letter.

"Good heavens, Pons," I mumbled. "Apart from the mystery, your clients promise a study in comparative psychology in themselves."

"Do they not, Parker."

Solar Pons rose from the table and crossed over to his favourite chair by the fire. He glanced at the clock in the corner and I saw that it was almost a quarter to seven. He tamped tobacco in his pipe and waited politely until I had finished. The measured tread of Mrs. Johnson was soon heard on the stairs and in a few minutes our estimable landlady had expertly cleared the table and had spread a clean cloth upon it.

"I hope that was satisfactory, gentlemen."

"You have excelled yourself, Mrs. Johnson," said Solar Pons gravely.

Our landlady's face assumed a faint pink texture.

"If there is anything further, Mr. Pons?"

"Nothing, thank you, Mrs. Johnson. On second thoughts, if you would just leave the front door on the latch my client will let himself up."

"Very good, Mr. Pons."

She closed the door softly behind her and presently her footsteps died away down the stairs.

"An excellent soul, Parker," Solar Pons observed.

"Indeed Pons," I replied. "I don't know what we should do without her."

My companion nodded. He leaned over for a spill and lit it from a glowing coal on the hearth. He sat back in the chair, contentedly ejecting a stream of aromatic blue smoke from the bowl, dreamily watching the lazy spirals ascend to the ceiling. It was one of the most pleasant periods of the day and I did not break the reverie into which we had fallen but quietly resumed my own fireside chair and my interrupted reading of *The Times*.

II

It was a quarter to eight when we were interrupted by the distant slamming of the front door and an agitated tattoo of feet on the drugget of the staircase.

The man who first timidly knocked at our door and then entered the sitting-room was a most astonishing sight. Pons had risen from his chair and even his iron reserve was visibly breached as I saw the slight trembling of the stem of the pipe in his mouth.

The old gentleman who stood blinking and peering about him, first at Pons and then at me, was dressed in a long overcoat of some bottle-green material and of an ancient cut. When he had been in the room some minutes I realised that the coat was old indeed, for the green was not the colour but mildew and a miasma, heavy and polluting, hung about him, bringing the atmosphere of an old-clothes shop into our cosy chambers at 7B.

"Mr. Pons? Mr. Solar Pons?" he said in a high, piping falsetto, his trembling right hand extended to my companion.

"The same, Mr. Grimstone," said my companion, gingerly taking the shrivelled claw so proffered.

"Will you not be seated, sir?"

"Thank you, thank you."

The old man looked at me with fierce suspicion, until Pons made the introduction.

"My valued friend and colleague, Dr. Lyndon Parker."

"Proud to make your acquaintance, sir."

Our visitor bowed frostily and I half rose from my chair but was glad that he did not offer to shake hands with me. Even from where I was sitting I could smell the dank, malodourous stench which emanated from his clothing. At first I suspected that Grimstone suffered from paralysis agitans but after a short interval I concluded that nothing but common fright was responsible for the twitching eyes, nervous tics and sudden starts he exhibited in our company. He shied away and made as though to quit the room at any sudden and unexpected noise and once, when a motor-vehicle backfired in the street below our windows, I thought that he would have fled to the door. I had never seen a man with such a look of fear on him.

For the rest he wore a mildewed hat that must once have answered to the name of homburg and when he removed it in our presence, his long white flowing locks hung about his brows like hoary weeds overflowing from some untended garden. His black and white striped shirt, greasy and dirty, was held in place with two rusty safety pins and he was devoid of either collar or tie. He opened his overcoat with the heat of the fire and I could see a musty suit of the same shade as his outer garment beneath.

His shoes were worn and out at heel and I was astonished, even given our visitor's general appearance, to see that instead of laces his shoes were held to his feet by lengths of knotted string. Grimstone was probably nearer seventy than sixty and his face was lined, with deep furrows running from the corners of his eyes to his nostrils. His eyes were a pale green and the most cunning I had ever seen in my varied experience as a medical practitioner.

His nose was thin and raw red which I put down to the wind and the current cold weather and his mouth had a cadaverous and lopsided look. I found out later that this resulted from his wearing a set of secondhand dentures which did not fit him properly. As Pons had so properly observed, few men had ever existed with such miserly habits. His rimless pince-nez had evidently been garnered from the same source as the dentures; some dingy secondhand shop, for I was certain that they did not suit his eyesight, for he squinted ferociously over the top of them from time to time.

Altogether, he was one of the most remarkable specimens I ever beheld and the more I saw of him the more my initial impression of unpleasantness and shiftiness were reinforced. But Solar Pons seemed oblivious of all this and smiled at him pleasantly enough through his pipe-smoke, as he sat back in his easy-chair and favoured me with a subtle droop of his right eyelid.

"Well, Mr. Grimstone," he said at length. "Just how can I serve you?"

The old man looked at him suspiciously.

"You got my letter, Mr. Pons?"

"Indeed," said my companion. "In fact there was some difficulty in the matter. Some trifling oversight in the matter of the stamp. There was a surcharge of three-pence that my landlady had to pay."

I was astonished at Pons' words but even more so at our client's response. Far from being offended he drew himself up frostily and his eyes positively twinkled as he looked at Pons with something like admiration.

"A minor problem, my dear sir," he snapped. "No doubt covered by the overcharges on my bill."

He wagged his grubby forefinger at Pons.

"I have never yet met anyone who failed to overcharge me."

Solar Pons looked at him imperturbably, his penetrating eyes shot with humour through the pipe-smoke.

"In that case had you better not consult someone else in your problem?" he said mildly.

Grimstone jerked in his chair as though stung by some venomous insect. His voice rose to a high, strangled squawk.

"After having come all this way up from Kent, Mr. Pons? With the scandalously expensive fares imposed by the railways . . .?"

There was dismay as well as anger in the tones and Solar Pons glanced at me with an open smile.

"I have touched upon your Achilles heel, it would appear, Mr. Grimstone. Pray lay your problem before me without further ado."

Grimstone fixed Pons with glittering eyes.

"Ah, then you have decided to take the case, Mr. Pons?"

My companion shook his head slowly.

"I have not said so. If it presents points of interest I may agree to do so."

Our visitor actually rocked to and fro in his chair as though with anguish.

"And if you do not?" he snapped. "The railway fare, Mr. Pons! The fare! I shall write to my Member of Parliament."

Solar Pons chuckled easily, sending a lazy plume of smoke up toward the ceiling.

"I am not quite sure whether you are referring to the iniquitously high cost of railway travel, Mr. Grimstone, or to my conduct. But in either event your M.P. will be no more pleased at having to pay a surcharge on his letter than I was."

Grimstone was off on another tack. He crossed his bony legs and smirked.

"Ah, then we are at one, Mr. Pons," he mumbled, as though my companion had agreed with him. "I must have your help in this monstrous persecution to which I am being subjected. When could you come down? We do not exactly keep open house but we could accommodate you in some corner of the Manor."

"I should first prefer to hear something of the business which brings you here, Mr. Grimstone. Your letter was nothing if not sensational in its implications."

Grimstone drew down the corner of his mouth as though Pons had said something distasteful and momentarily lapsed into silence. For a second or two I glimpsed such fear on his face as I have seldom seen on a human being. It was obvious to me that Pons had also seen it and that Grimstone's newly assumed businesslike manner was a mere façade, which might crack at any moment.

Solar Pons paused a little to allow our visitor to recover himself, looking not unsympathetically at our strange caller through the aromatic clouds of tobacco-smoke.

"You spoke of a crawling horror, Mr. Grimstone?" he said at length. "Can you amplify that somewhat enigmatic statement?"

Grimstone shook his head, waving it from side to side so agitatedly that it looked as though he had palsy.

"I can, Mr. Pons," he said in a dead voice. "It is something that haunts me; something that I can never forget."

"You had better start at the beginning, my dear sir," said Solar Pons softly. "Take your time and tell the story in your own words."

Our client sat puffing his cheeks in and out for a few moments, looking with cunning eyes first at me and then at my companion. I must say that my distaste for him and his malodorous clothing was growing by the minute, but Solar Pons stared imperturbably in front of him and continued ejecting sweet-scented smoke from his pipe until our bizarre visitor should be ready to continue.

He began abruptly, without preamble, with the look upon him of a man who has suddenly made up his mind to take the plunge only because of dire necessity at his elbow.

"You probably know about me, Mr. Pons. My activities have not passed unnoticed in the City. I have amassed a certain amount of money, it is true, but I am a poor man in comparison with many I could name; and my expenses have been heavy—*extremely* heavy."

He paused as though expecting Pons to agree with him and receiving no reaction continued in a disappointed tone.

"I live quite frugally as befits my station, Mr. Pons, in an old manor house on the marshes near Gravesend. My niece, Miss Sylvia Grimstone, lives with me and keeps house and we do tolerably well. I am not much in the City these days and keep in touch by telephone. My health has not been too good these last few years and I have had to ease up a little."

Solar Pons ejected a cloud of blue smoke into the air of our sitting-room.

"What staff have you at the Manor, Mr. Grimstone?"

Our visitor looked startled.

"Staff, Mr. Pons?"

He smirked.

"Good gracious me, I cannot run to that. My niece sees to all our wants. In return she receives bed and board and a yearly stipend."

His voice dropped on the last words as though the stipend were a matter of great regret to him. Pons could not forbear an amused glance across at me.

"We lived an uneventful life until a few months ago, Mr. Pons, when these terrible things happened."

"What terrible things, Mr. Grimstone? You have told me little as yet. Pray be most precise as to circumstance and detail."

Solar Pons tented his thin fingers before him and fixed our visitor with a steady glance.

"As I have indicated, Mr. Pons, we live an isolated and sheltered life there on the Marsh. The Manor has been in our family for centuries and descended to me from my brother. Its isolation suited me and the property, which is a curious one, is actually on an island in the Marsh and approached by a causeway."

Solar Pons glanced at Grimstone, his eyes penetrating beneath his half-lowered lids.

"The Marsh is dangerous?"

"Oh, yes indeed, Mr. Pons. In some places it is actual swamp, though sheep and cattle graze on it here and there. Sometimes it claims an unwary beast and some areas are reputed to be literally bottomless."

"I see. But you know it well?"

"Certainly, Mr. Pons. I spent some time there with relatives when a child. But the Manor itself and the area immediately surrounding it is safe enough, and the causeway which links it with the firmer ground runs direct to a good secondary road."

Solar Pons nodded.

"It is as well to get the background details firmly in one's mind, Mr. Grimstone. I find it a great aid to the ratiocinative processes. Eh, Parker?"

"Certainly, Pons."

Our client nodded, his mean little eyes gleaming.

"Well, Mr. Pons, Grimstone Manor may seem a somewhat strange and out of the way place to a stranger, but it suits me and my niece."

He shifted in his chair and once again I caught the unpleasant smell of mould and old clothing.

"It was October, Mr. Pons. A cold, windy day, but toward sunset the wind dropped and a thin mist began to rise. I had been in to our local village of Stavely, some miles from Allhallows, and was walking back along the marsh road, which is, as you may imagine, elevated some way above its surroundings. It is a wild, bleak, lonely place even in summer and you can imagine what it must be like at dusk on a bitter autumn day."

Our client cleared his throat with a harsh rasping sound before going on with his narrative.

"I had got quite close to my own dwelling, thank God, when my attention was arrested by a singular noise. It was a low, unpleasant sound, like somebody clearing his throat. A pony and trap had passed me some minutes before, going toward Stavely, but I was completely alone in that bare landscape, Mr. Pons, and I can tell you that I was considerably startled. But I moved on, as I was only a few hundred yards from the entrance to Grimstone Manor causeway. Fortunate that I did so."

Pons' eyes were shining.

"Why so, Mr. Grimstone?"

"Because otherwise I would not be here talking to you now, Mr. Pons," the old man replied.

"I heard the strange noise a few moments later, and turned just short of the causeway. Mr. Pons, I had never seen anything like it. There was only the afterglow lingering in the sky and the harsh cry of some bird. I might have been upon the moon for all the human help at hand."

Our client swallowed heavily and his eyes were dark with fear.

"Mr. Pons, as true as I sit here, a corpse-figure was dragging itself from the edge of the marsh, all burning and writhing with bluish fire!"

III

The silence which followed was broken by a sound like a pistol-shot. It was made by Solar Pons slapping his right thigh with the flat of his hand.

"Capital, Mr. Grimstone! What then?"

"Why, Mr. Pons, I took to my heels, of course," said Silas Grimstone with commendable frankness, casting a resentful look at Pons.

"But the thing which pursued me had devilish cunning. It seemed to make its way across the marsh in a series of hops, as though to cut me off."

"It did not follow on the causeway, then?"

Solar Pons sat with his pipe wreathing smoke in his hand, completely absorbed in our visitor's narrative. Grimstone shook his head.

"It was trying to prevent me from getting to my house, Mr. Pons. I have never been so frightened in my life. At first it seemed to gain but when I looked back there was nothing but a bluish fire bobbing about some distance behind me. It was almost completely dark by this time and I had never been so glad to see the lights of the Manor, I can tell you."

"I can well imagine," said Solar Pons drily. "This figure made no sound?"

"No, Mr. Pons. Not that I heard. When I gained the safety of the courtyard in front of the house, I looked briefly back and saw a faint blue glow disappearing in the haze of the marsh."

"A terrifying experience, Mr. Grimstone," I put in.

"There is more to follow?" Solar Pons added crisply.

The old man nodded sombrely.

"Unfortunately, Mr. Pons. I did not tell my niece of the affair at first, as I did not wish to unduly alarm her. She is highly strung and it would be difficult to get someone to attend to my wants if she decided to leave."

"Indeed," said Solar Pons gravely.

"I thought at first, Mr. Pons, that I had been the victim of some sort of hallucination. The next time I went into Stavely, which was not until a fortnight later, I took the pony and trap and made sure I returned in daylight. I dismounted when I came to the spot near the causeway where I had seen the figure, but, of course, there was nothing to be seen."

Solar Pons replaced the pipe in his mouth and puffed thoughtfully.

"Why do you say, 'of course,' Mr. Grimstone?"

"Well, I had hoped that there would be some quite ordinary explanation such as marsh lights, or some strange but natural phenomenon to account for the apparition. But there was nothing to support such a theory."

"So you believe it to be a ghost?"

"I do not know what to believe, Mr. Pons."

"It was a human figure, though?"

"Undoubtedly, Mr. Pons. Though I could see no detail, just the blue phosphorescent fire."

"Pray continue."

"Well, Mr. Pons, nothing further happened for some weeks and I had hoped that was the end of the matter. I had been out in the opposite direction, to look at a property in which I had some interest, and was unmindful of the time. I had the pony and trap and was coming along the same road but from the southerly direction. It was again almost dusk when for the second time I had the same terrifying experience. Once more this ghastly figure rose from the edge of the marsh. The pony took fright and I had so much to do to control him and what with my work at the reins I quite forgot my terror and when we at last rattled across the causeway and I had a moment to take stock there was no sign of the figure."

"You still told your niece nothing?"

Grimstone shook his head.

"There seemed no point, Mr. Pons. That was November. The next thing that happened was quite near Christmas. It was coming closer to the house all the time, Mr. Pons."

"Pray be more explicit, Mr. Grimstone."

"Well, I had been ill with a cold, and had to curtail my business activities. I had not been to London for over a month and it wanted but ten days to Christmas. Again, it was dusk and I was sitting in a ground-floor room near the window, well wrapped up, my feet toward the fire. The sunset was dying out across the marsh. My niece was preparing tea in the kitchen and I was musing ruminatively as one does at such times. Imagine my horror, Mr. Pons, when I suddenly saw this bluish light hopping across the yard outside the house. It came on with quick strides and as I sat half paralysed this hideous face made of bluish fire was thrust against the window."

Our client licked his lips, he was so visibly moved by the recollection, and I felt a momentary flash of pity for him.

"Hmm. A nasty experience, Mr. Grimstone."

Solar Pons pulled reflectively at the lobe of his right ear.

"What did you do?"

"I gave a great cry, Mr. Pons. I jumped up at once but the thing had made off. It went in a strange, zig-zagging motion and the last I saw it was disappearing in the sunset haze toward the marsh. A coal had fallen from the fire about then and was threatening to burn the carpet. My niece came rushing in at my outburst but I gave the fallen coal as my excuse and the matter passed over. She made much of my paleness and agitation but I told her I felt ill again and went back to bed after tea. That was the third appearance of the apparition, Mr. Pons."

"There has been a fourth, then?"

Silas Grimstone nodded, his lined face lightened but not softened by the flickering firelight of our sitting-room.

"Before you come to that, Mr. Grimstone, I have one or two further questions. What do you think this thing is?"

The old man stubbornly shook his head.

"That is for you to tell me, Mr. Pons," he snapped, with a return to his old manner. "It would appear to be supernatural in origin but why it should choose to haunt me, I have no idea."

"I see."

Solar Pons was silent for a moment, his brooding eyes gazing into the heart of the fire.

"Tell me, Mr. Grimstone, are there any dwellings on the marsh itself from which this creature could have come?"

"You mean a domestic animal, Mr. Pons? That is hardly possible."

"I did not ask that, Mr. Grimstone."

The old man winced at the asperity in my companion's voice. "The marshes are a strange place, Mr. Pons. They extend for miles over that part of England. Between, there are agricultural areas, firm ground and rich fields. Then you will find a wild expanse of marsh, with here and there islands of solid farmland, which may be reached on foot by the bold. I understand there are some small-holdings on such pockets."

"I see. Tell me, Mr. Grimstone, have any persons been lost in the marsh? Sucked under or drowned, I mean?"

Silas Grimstone stared at Solar Pons with shadowed eyes.

"Many such, Mr. Pons, from time immemorial. In more recent times, the occasional sheep or cattle. I do not know of any other fatality, offhand."

"Why did you not inform the police of this figure which had chased you?"

"Police!"

There was a wealth of disgust in our client's voice. "That would be worse than useless, Mr. Pons. I did not want them tramping about my property. And what could I tell them? That I had seen a ghost?

157

They would have merely laughed. They do not deal in ghosts."

"Neither do I," said Pons.

"Mr. Grimstone has a point, Pons," I interjected.

My companion looked at me thoughtfully.

"Perhaps, Parker, perhaps," he said absently.

He turned back to Grimstone.

"What was this latest incident?"

"Only two nights ago, Mr. Pons. That was what prompted me to come to you. It has become unbearable."

"This apparition appears only at dusk, Mr. Grimstone?"

"Why, yes, Mr. Pons. I have called it a crawling horror and I speak truly."

"That is important, Parker. Pray continue."

"Well, Mr. Pons, my niece was present on this occasion, thank God."

Solar Pons' lean face was alive with interest.

"Excellent, Mr. Grimstone. That is of the utmost importance also."

Our client shot Solar Pons another resentful glance.

"No, Mr. Pons, I am not mad as you might have suspected. This apparition is visible to others than myself."

Solar Pons nodded.

"I am glad to hear it, Mr. Grimstone. But you may disabuse yourself of the supposition you have formed. It was never in my mind for one moment that your sanity was in question. Your financial reputation alone would have ruled that out."

The old man smiled grimly.

"You have only to see this thing to realise that something dreadful is at the back of it. To resume. Two evenings ago my niece complained of feeling jaded and cooped up in the house. She suggested a walk before dark. I was a little startled at the request but acquiesced, as she certainly does not get much change of air or exercise, other than her household duties. So we struck out along the main road and then took a well-marked path that loops across the marsh."

The old man paused and looked at my companion sharply, as though to assure himself that he was still listening.

"Sylvia is interested in wild flowers, nature and nonsense of that sort and I usually indulge her in such fancies though such things interest me not at all. We had gone about half a mile across the marsh, Mr. Pons, and it was a very lonely spot indeed and I was thinking of suggesting that we went back. The light was beginning to fade from the sky and though my niece's presence reassured me, I still had the incidents at dusk at the back of my mind.

"She had gone on ahead a little way to look at something and I was temporarily alone. Suddenly, I became aware of a faint noise. I turned quickly and judge of my horror, Mr. Pons, when I saw this same ghastly blue phosphorescent figure rising from the haze at the edge of the marsh. I stood rooted to the spot at the sight and then my sudden cry brought my niece running to my side."

"Just a moment, Mr. Grimstone. Where was your niece exactly when this happened?"

"As I have said, Mr. Pons, some distance away."

"Was she visible to you or not?"

Old Grimstone was evidently puzzled.

"As a matter of act, she was hidden by a fringe of bushes, Mr. Pons. Does it matter?"

"It might be of the greatest significance, Mr. Grimstone. Please go on."

"Well, Mr. Pons, my niece shrieked with fright on beholding this thing, as you might imagine. It made a sort of writhing motion and then disappeared into the marsh with incredible rapidity. We lost no time in regaining the high road and got back to the Manor without seeing it again, thank God."

"You made no attempt to follow?"

Grimstone looked at Pons as though he was out of his head. He shuddered.

"Not I, Mr. Pons."

"And once again, this phantom left no trace?"

Our visitor shook his head.

"We did not stop to look, Mr. Pons."

Solar Pons stroked his chin with thin fingers.

"A pity."

Grimstone cleared his throat with a harsh rasping noise.

"My niece and I sat up late that night discussing the matter. She suggested calling the police but for the reasons I have already enumerated I decided against. So I wrote to you yesterday and here

I am entreating you to come down to Kent as soon as you can, Mr. Pons. I am not a rich man, but . . ."

"Tut," interrupted Solar Pons. "The fee is never the decisive factor in my cases. I had decided long ago that the matter displayed features of great interest. I will come down tomorrow if that will be convenient. Can you get away, Parker?"

I glanced at Pons with enthusiasm.

"It will not be difficult, Pons. I have only to telephone my locum."

"I hope I shall not have to pay for Dr. Parker's presence," said old Grimstone in alarm.

Pons' features expressed wry amusement as I turned an astonished face toward our miserly client.

"Do not worry, Mr. Grimstone, I shall come at my own expense."

Grimstone gave a sigh of relief.

"The accommodation at the Manor is none of the best," he whined.

"We shall not strain your limited resources, Mr. Grimstone," said Pons blandly. "You have an inn in the village, no doubt? It should not be difficult to get bed and board in such a place at this time of the year."

"Dear me, no," said our client, considerably mollified.

"Then, if you would be good enough to reserve us two rooms we will be down tomorrow afternoon."

"Excellent, Mr. Pons. I will let them know at The Harrow."

Grimstone rose, wafting toward me once again the odour of stale, mildewed clothing. He glanced at the clock.

"Good heavens, is that the time? I am usually abed long before this. I have to rise early in the morning, and meet our local carrier in front of Charing Cross. He had to come to London today so I have travelled with him to save expense."

"I thought you said you came by train," observed Solar Pons with a wry smile. "You were complaining at the cost of rail fares, if I remember."

Grimstone turned toward the door in some confusion. "You must have been mistaken, Mr. Pons," he murmured.

"No doubt," said Pons dryly. "Until tomorrow, then."

"Until tomorrow. You can get a fast train, I believe."

"You may expect us at about four, Mr. Grimstone. Good evening."

IV

Solar Pons chuckled intermittently for several minutes after our visitor had left.

"Well, what do you make of him, Parker?"

"Of him or the case, Pons?"

"Both. He has not told me the half of it, I'll be bound."

I looked at my companion, startled.

"What on earth do you mean, Pons? You think this figure is a figment of his imagination?"

Solar Pons made an impatient clicking noise deep in his throat.

"Of course not, Parker. His niece saw the apparition in the marsh. No, this is a deep business. But I would like to have your views nevertheless."

"You flatter me, Pons."

"Do not underestimate yourself, Parker. Your observations, while not always apposite, do much to guide me in the right direction."

"I am glad to hear it," I said. "The man is a miserly curmudgeon, as you so rightly surmised. But as to this bizarre and sinister apparition, it is beyond me."

"Yet I am convinced that there is a purpose behind it, Parker, if we pursue it to its logical conclusion. That it is supernatural is as ridiculous as to suppose that Grimstone imagined it."

"Well, you are certainly right, Pons, as Miss Grimstone saw it too. But how do you explain the fact that the figure left no footprints?"

"Elementary, my dear Parker. Grimstone is not a trained observer, and the marshy ground would tend to eliminate tracks. The case presents a number of intriguing possibilities. Not least being the fact that Miss Grimstone was not in sight the last time this thing made its appearance. I commend that fact to you, my dear fellow."

And he said not a word further on the subject until we were en route the following morning. It was a bitterly cold day; colder if anything than the previous and both Pons and I were heavily muffled against the biting air. We left the train in bleak conditions at Gravesend, where we changed on to a small branch line.

There was a chill wind blowing from off the Thomas Estuary and as I glanced out of the carriage window at the cheerless acres of mud in which here and there clouds of seabirds blew like spray as they flocked round the hulk of some wrecked barge stranded in the ooze, I felt I had seldom seen a more depressing landscape.

But Solar Pons merely chuckled as he settled deeper into his raglan overcoat, rubbing his lean fingers briskly together as he shovelled aromatic blue smoke from his pipe.

"Capital, Parker," he remarked. "This is an admirable atmosphere in which Grimstone's crawling horror operates."

I glanced at him in some surprise.

"You astonish me, Pons. I thought you were not interested in nature as such."

"Atmosphere, Parker. I was talking of atmosphere," Pons reproved me. "There is a world of difference."

We had stopped momentarily at some wayside halt and now the door of the carriage was opened, bringing with it gusts of freezing air. A robust, bearded figure entered the carriage, apologising for the intrusion and we made way for him on the seats, removing our luggage to one side.

"Thank you, gentlemen," said the intruder in a strong, rough but not uncultured voice.

He was dressed in tweeds, with a thick check cap with earflaps and his heavy thigh-boots were liberally splashed with mud. He carried a pair of binoculars in a leather case slung by a strap round his neck and a stout canvas bag at his side had the flap partly open, disclosing plant specimens with ice still clinging to their roots.

His broad, strong face was red and burned with wind about the cheekbones and his deepset grey eyes looked at us both with interest.

"Inclement weather," I ventured.

He gave a hearty laugh.

"Oh, I think nothing of that, gentlemen. I am something of a naturalist and am used to collecting specimens and bird-watching about the marshes in all weathers. A country G.P. in places like this has few other diversions."

I looked at him with interest.

"So I should imagine. I am myself a doctor."

"Indeed?"

Our companion raised his eyebrows.

"Parker is the name," I went on. "This is my friend, Mr. Pons."

"Delighted to meet you! Dr. Strangeways, formerly of Leeds."

The big man half-rose from his seat and shook hands with us both.

"You must be very familiar with the marshes then, Doctor," said Solar Pons. "Perhaps you could tell us something about Grimstone. We are bound there."

The doctor smiled thinly.

"We shall see something of each other, then. My practice ranges wide but I live at Stavely nearby."

I nodded.

"We are staying at The Harrow there for a few days."

Dr. Strangeways looked at me with narrowed eyes.

"We are poorly served for inns hereabouts but it is the best in these parts."

He hesitated, looking from me to Pons and then back again.

"You will forgive me, doctor, but strangers are few and far between down here and Grimstone Marsh seems a strange destination for two gentlemen like yourselves."

I looked at Pons.

"We have some business with Mr. Silas Grimstone," he said shortly.

The doctor smiled sardonically.

"Well, then I wish you luck, Mr. Pons. He is one of my patients. My medical bill has not been paid this eighteen months, though he is as rich as Croesus."

"I am sorry to hear that," I said politely, looking from the bearded man opposite to the bleak prospect of marshland held in icy bondage by the weather, which was slowly passing the window.

"I have heard he is tightfisted," said Pons. "And I regret to learn he is so tardy with payment. I know you cannot violate medical confidence, but I should be glad to know if you have attended him in recent months."

Dr. Strangeways looked at my companion sharply. He shook his head.

"I have no objection to answering your question, Mr. Pons. Ethics do not come into it—rather business morality. I have not attended him for some eight months now. I was blunt and said I would not call again until my account was settled."

"A perfectly proper attitude, Dr. Strangeways," said Pons approvingly. He blew a stream of fragrant blue smoke from his pipe toward the carriage ceiling. He abruptly changed the subject.

"You get about the marshes a good deal, Doctor. You have no doubt seen some strange things in your time."

The doctor shrugged and settled himself back against the upholstery.

"It is a curious corner of the world down here, as you know," he admitted. "Which is probably one of the reasons why Dickens chose it for some of his most effective scenes in *Great Expectations*."

"Ah, yes," I put in. "When young Copperfield set out for his walk to Dover."

"You have got the wrong book," put in Pons reprovingly. "And he would have certainly gone a long way round."

Dr. Strangeways chuckled.

"Dr. Parker was no doubt having his little joke," he suggested.

"No doubt," said Pons disarmingly. "I have heard that the marshes harbour some strange creatures."

Dr. Strangeways fixed his grey eyes on the ceiling of the carriage, where swathes of grey-blue smoke clung, as though reluctant to leave the warmth of the compartment.

"Oh, there are plenty of old wives' tales," he said scoffingly. "There is supposed to be a Phantom Horseman. And every corner seems to have its complement of drowned smugglers from the eighteenth century."

"What about blue corpse-lights?" asked Solar Pons innocently, his hooded eyes fixed on the smoke-clouds.

The doctor stirred uncomfortably on his seat.

"You mean marsh-lights, the so-called will-o-the-wisps? One sometimes sees such natural phenomena from time to time. Certainly. The superstitious call them corpse-lights."

"What do they look like?"

The doctor shrugged.

"Marsh gas sometimes gives off a bluish light. More often a greenish-yellow."

"At dusk or daylight?"

Consternation spread over the doctor's bearded features.

"I have never heard of them in daylight," he said. "Naturally, they would be difficult to see. At dusk, of course. And at night. What is the purpose of these questions?"

"Idle curiosity," said Solar Pons, stretching himself in his corner by the window. "I have heard of someone who claimed to see a ghostly figure of bluish fire down on the marshes."

The doctor stared at Pons with incredulity. He cleared his throat.

"I have read such journalists' tales in the cheaper press," he admitted.

He laughed deep in his beard.

"I should be more included to put down such apparitions to D.T.'s. Such things are not unknown among my patients. I had a fellow in only last week who claimed to have seen some such thing. Old Tobias Jessel. He is far too frequently in the four-ale bar of The Harrow and I told him so."

He looked out of the window.

"Ah, this is as far as we go. It has been an agreeable journey, gentlemen, thanks to you. I am going to Stavely now and as I have my motor vehicle at the station allow me to offer you a lift."

Pons and I accepted with thanks and descending, found ourselves on the bare, windswept platform of one of the most bleak country railway stations I had ever beheld. There was only one staff member visible, a porter-cum-stationmaster and we three seemed to be the only passengers surrendering our tickets.

We hurried gratefully across the station forecourt and into the doctor's covered Morris and were soon bowling swiftly along the marsh road, the doctor driving with skill and obvious enjoyment. As we sped along the narrow road through the flat, monotonous countryside the dusk was creeping on apace and I could imagine the effect on old Silas Grimstone of seeing the spectral blue figure which pursued him amid this forbidding landscape. Now and again the doctor pointed out the features of the countryside, such as they were. Indeed, I felt they were but poor things, being a ruined windmill, an old martello tower and the crumbling remains of a wooden break water, to mention only the most notable.

Even Pons' normally sanguine nature seemed affected by the

dreariness of this area of mudflats and marsh with its cloudy scatterings of seabirds and it was with something like relief that we saw the gleam of light ahead and shortly after drove down the main street of a small village.

"Here you are, Mr. Pons," said Dr. Strangeways, drawing up in front of a cheerful-looking hostelry of medium size. With its brick walls and grey slate roof it was of no great charm but situated as we were it seemed most welcoming with the light shining from its windows and a mellow glow coming from the entrance porch.

We got down and Pons handed me my baggage while he sought his own. Strangeways jerked his thumb as he indicated a building almost opposite.

"There is my surgery, gentlemen. I am to be found there most evenings from six to eight if you need me. You must dine with me one night. My house is in a side street, not three hundred yards from where we are standing."

"That is most kind of you, doctor," I said, shaking hands.

Strangeways smiled deep in his beard. He pointed to the village street, which wound away in front of us.

"Grimstone Manor is about a mile from here, south along the marsh road yonder. The road is straight all the way and you cannot miss the causeway. I would run you there myself but I have to prepare for surgery and visit patients beforehand."

"We are in your debt already," said Solar Pons. "The walk will do us good, eh, Parker. And if we step it out we should be at the Manor before darkness falls. It is just a quarter past three."

We watched as the doctor drove off down the street with a salute on the horn. Then we turned into The Harrow. The landlord, a welcoming, jovial man of about forty, was expecting us and after we had registered, showed us to two plain but clean and comfortable rooms on the first floor.

"We serve dinner from eight o'clock onwards, gentlemen. Breakfast is from seven a.m. until nine."

"That will do admirably," Pons told him. "We expect to be out and about the marsh a great deal."

The landlord, whose name was Plackett, nodded.

"It is a quiet time of the year, sir, but we will do our best to make you comfortable. There is good walking hereabouts, if you don't mind the wind off the sea."

I had just time to wash my hands, tidy myself and unpack my few necessaries, before Pons was knocking at my door and shortly afterward we were walking out of Stavely, the wind in our faces, bound for Grimstone Manor.

V

It was, as old Grimstone had indicated, a lonely road and with darkness falling apace, a sombre one. Within a very few minutes the small hamlet of not more than five streets, had dropped away and to all intents and appearances we were alone in the illimitable landscape. Pons strode along in silence, his heavy coat drawn snugly about him, his pipe shovelling streamers of blue smoke behind him.

The road ran straight as an arrow across the marsh, ice glinting like steel in the irrigation ditches at either side. The sky was dark and lowering, though a little light from the dying sun stained the distant bar of the sea and turned the wetlands into scattered pools of blood. My thoughts were as melancholy as the lonely cries of the seabirds that fluttered dark-etched against the sunset and here and there the bones of some wrecked craft or a dark patch of mud stood out as a black silhouette.

The wind was gusting now and our footsteps echoed grittily behind us. There was not one human figure in all that space; not one vehicle in the long stretch of road that reached to the horizon in either direction. Pons abruptly broke the silence, stabbing with his pipe-stem to emphasise his points.

"Ideal is it not, Parker?"

I was startled.

"I do not know what you mean, Pons."

"Why, for purposes of elimination, of course. The landscape limits the phantom's activities."

He chuckled wryly. For some reason his attitude irritated me. I threw up my hands to emphasise the bleakness of the marsh all around us.

"I see nothing humorous in all this, Pons."

"You are quite right, Parker. It is a deadly serious affair whose purpose as yet eludes me. Yet the landscape is a vital factor. If this burning spectre which haunts old Silas Grimstone is a figure of flesh and blood, as I believe him to be, he is playing a deep and dangerous game. But the atmosphere, as I indicated on our journey down, plays a big part. While it may favour the menace which hangs over our client, it also acts in our favour."

I glanced sideways at the clear-minted, feral features of my companion.

"How do you mean, Pons?"

"The matter is self-evident, Parker. Let us take the points in this creature's credit-account. The marsh is vast and impenetrable to the stranger. Ergo, he knows it well. He can appear and disappear without trace. He materialised only at dusk so far; darkness and fog are also helpful for his purposes."

"I follow you so far, Pons."

Solar Pons chuckled again.

"But the marsh can also act against him. True, it masks his appearance and his movements, for any traces of his passage would be eliminated by the ooze. But the bog is just as dangerous for him, as for any other man. One false step and he is trapped as surely as any sheep or cow which wanders in. Mud may also leave traces of his passage. And his appearance is limited to the marsh. For if he ventures on to the high road or any other inhabited place, then we have him."

I looked at my companion in surprise.

"You almost sound as though you are pleased, Pons."

"Do I not, Parker."

Solar Pons rubbed his thin hands together as though to restore the circulation and glanced about the dying landscape with keen eyes.

"So we are looking for someone who has an intimate knowledge of the marshes; is strong and active. There is also one other important corollary . . . a secure place to hide."

He broke off and sniffed. With his nostrils flaring and his deep-set eyes probing the dusk he looked like nothing so much as a purebred hound hot on the scent.

"Dr. Strangeways might well fit that bill, Pons. He seems to know the marsh intimately."

Solar Pons looked at me sardonically.

"You have a point there, Parker. I had not overlooked the possibility. He seemed almost too friendly on the train. Ah! Here we are at our destination, if I am not much mistaken."

He pointed through the dusk to the left of the road, where stood the stout wooden fence and the causeway of which our client had spoken. A faint vapour was writhing from the ground and the solid earth dyke stretched away to a sort of island in the mist, at some considerable distance, where I could faintly discern the vague shadows of trees and the outline of buildings.

"I fancied I could smell the chimney smoke, Parker. But before we cross I will just have a look at the terrain here."

To my alarm Pons jumped agilely down the bank and was working up and down the margin of the reeds. He had his pocket torch out and now and again stooped toward the ground, examining the grasses and the muddy pools minutely. I stood on the road and kept my silence, knowing better than to interrupt him. He cast about him and broke off a heavy reed stem with a brittle snap.

He probed carefully at the surface of the marsh. Viscous mud parted, revealing the oily sheen of water in the last of the light. He cast the reed down and joined me on the bank. He pulled at the lobe of his left ear and looked thoughtfully across to where the final shafts of the dying day stained the depths of the marsh.

"A bad place, Parker," he said softly. "No wonder old Grimstone was frightened."

"It is unpleasant indeed, Pons," I asserted. "Did you discover anything?"

"Nothing of any great significance. Though the terrain here has strengthened the tentative theories I have formed."

And he led the way across a heavy timbered bridge that spanned a section of icebound water. Once on the dyke the dark seemed to encroach and the light was fast disappearing from the sky, the afterglow remaining. Even the birds were silent now and the only sounds were the faint trembling of the wind; our footsteps on the hard-packed mud of the causeway; and the pumping of my own heart.

We followed the heavy wooden handrail that bounded the causeway on either side, while now and again Pons flashed his torch to make sure of our bearings.

"What about this man Tobias Jessel, Pons?" I said as we neared the massive gates of Grimstone Manor. A thin curl of smoke rose from a single chimney in the multitude that jutted from the jumbled roofs of the ancient building.

"Ah, you have realised the significance of that factor, Parker?" said Pons with a thin smile. "I am glad to see that my training has not been wasted. Hullo! Silence, if you please."

He switched off his torch and grasped me by the arm. We halted in the shadow of some bushes and a few moments later I caught what his keen ears had already picked out; the thin, furtive shuffle of some moving figure ahead.

Pons worked his way forward quietly and I followed, placing my feet with some difficulty as there was so much heavy shrubbery about the Manor that it was almost totally dark now. There was a muffled exclamation and Pons' torch-beam flashed on, steadying up on the terrified face of old Silas Grimstone. He wore a heavy padded dressing gown over his indoor clothes and a sort of velvet skullcap which made him look like a second-hand dealer.

"Who's there?" he shouted in a quavering voice, screwing up his eyes against the torch-beam.

"Solar Pons and Dr. Parker," said my companion, stepping forward.

"Mr. Pons!" the old man stammered, relief in his voice. "I heard a noise and came to investigate."

"Very unwise, Mr. Grimstone," said Pons. "My advice is to stay indoors. If this apparition means you harm you are playing into its hands by wandering around alone at night like this."

"You are right, Mr. Pons," said Grimstone, putting a shrivelled claw on Solar Pons' arm and leading us forward through a large cobbled courtyard surrounded by substantial stone outbuildings. The Manor itself looked to be of Tudor construction, with plenty of exposed beams but even in the dim light coming from the windows I could see that it was in deplorable condition.

There was a large porch of oak beams, sagging and moss-hung

and our client led the way into the house without further ceremony. We found ourselves in a large, musty-smelling hall lit by only one oil lantern, hanging from a beam. The floor was composed of rose-coloured tiles. I had been prepared for a squalid and uncared-for interior but was surprised to see that things were fairly clean and tolerably tidy.

Silas Grimstone looked at me with a furtive smile, as though he read my thoughts.

"We keep most of the house locked up," he said, slamming the great door behind us and ramming home the bolt as if to emphasise his words. "My niece, whom you will meet in a moment, spends far too much time and money in maintaining the five rooms remaining open."

He turned his back and led the way forward into a large panelled chamber. Pons smiled faintly at me as we followed. The drawing room, or whatever Grimstone called it, had a great stone fireplace in which a tolerable fire burned; a few dim oils, portraits mostly, stared sombrely at us from the wainscot; and the heavy oak furniture made the apartment look more like the tap room of an inn.

Grimstone waved us into two uncomfortable wooden chairs by the fireside and went to sit in a padded armchair opposite. "This is the room in which you had such an unpleasant experience, Mr. Grimstone?"

"Yes, Mr. Pons."

Pons went forward and drew aside the faded red curtains from the window at Grimstone's back. He looked out into the darkness, his eyes brooding as though he could see across the bleak miles of marsh to the heart of the secret it contained. He examined the window and its surround carefully and then closed the curtains once more.

As he turned away there came the sound of footsteps from the hall outside and Grimstone's niece, Miss Sylvia Grimstone entered. She was a tall woman of about fifty years of age but, contrary to what I expected, not at all grim and forbidding. In fact she was quite smartly dressed and she bore a tray on which were silver tea things and plates of buttered scones.

I managed to conceal my consternation when the old man remarked, "You'll take tea with us, of course, Mr. Pons. Allow me to present my niece. Mr. Solar Pons, Dr. Lyndon Parker."

"I am delighted to meet you, gentlemen."

Miss Sylvia Grimstone had a square, strong face and her features were quite pleasant when she smiled, which she did briefly at the introductions.

Silas Grimstone smirked maliciously as I watched the preparations for tea and rubbed his blue-veined hands together.

"I do not stint myself in the matter of bodily comforts, Doctor. That would be foolish at my age, living here on the marsh as we do."

"Very wise," observed Solar Pons, taking a steaming cup Miss Grimstone handed him. "And most welcome in this weather."

His piercing eyes fixed Miss Grimstone thoughtfully as she set down teacups and a plate of buttered scones before her uncle.

"Tell me, Miss Grimstone. What do you make of this apparition which so startled you and Mr. Grimstone here?"

The woman turned a worried face toward us and then she looked rather defiantly toward the old man, it seemed to me.

"It was more than startling, Mr. Pons. It was terrifying. I have never been so frightened in my life."

"That is understandable," said Pons gently. "But I asked for your impressions."

There was a faint hesitation as the niece put down the silver teapot and seated herself in a carved wooden chair at the apex of a triangle formed by ourselves, Grimstone and herself.

"It was a human figure, in slightly old-fashioned clothing, Mr. Pons. It burned with a blue fire and appeared and disappeared with incredible rapidity."

"Was it a human figure or did it appear to you a supernatural phenomenon?"

Miss Grimstone shook her head.

"I do not know what to think."

"That is honest at any rate."

Pons turned back to Grimstone.

"I shall be in touch with you daily, Mr. Grimstone. In the meantime do not stir outside at night and bolt and bar your doors. You may reach me at the inn by telephone if you wish to communicate with me urgently."

"Very well, Mr. Pons. What will you be doing?"

"I shall not be idle, Mr. Grimstone. I propose to take a walk round the marshes in the morning and may drop by here. Incidentally, I met your family physician, Dr. Strangeways earlier today. In fact he gave us a lift to Stavely."

Silas Grimstone smiled sourly.

"He is my physician no longer, Mr. Pons. I found his services far from satisfactory."

Once again a somewhat disapproving look passed from niece to uncle.

"Nevertheless, Mr. Grimstone, it seems likely that he will be an invaluable witness to what goes on in the marsh. He tells me for instance that one of his patients has seen this fiery figure of yours."

Our client's features drained to a haggard yellow and then to white.

"Ah, then it is true," he muttered to himself.

"Is what true?" asked Pons sharply.

"This crawling horror, Mr. Pons," the old man croaked. "Perhaps even your powers may prove unequal to it."

Solar Pons smiled grimly.

"I do not know about that, Mr. Grimstone. But in any event Dr. Parker's pistol and a cartridge or two will test the veracity of your theory. And now, if you will excuse us, we have much to do. Come, Parker."

And with thanks for our refreshment, we quitted the room, leaving the oddly assorted couple sitting gazing into the fire as if they both saw spectral images dancing in the smouldering embers.

VI

It was a bitterly cold night and we were glad to regain The Harrow where cheerful fires blazed. Pons excused himself and I went to my room soon after and I did not again see him until I descended to dinner at about 7:30 p.m. This was served in a comfortable dining room with oak panelling and brass chandeliers with imitation candles adapted for electric light.

Normally I do not like this sort of thing but the effect that night, with a cheerful fire blazing in the great stone fireplace, and the surprisingly excellent dinner of roast beef served, almost put our mission on the marshes quite out of mind. Pons was at his best, drily analysing the vagaries and physical aspects of the elderly waiters until I felt I could see their entire life-histories conjured, as it were, from the air before us.

There were only a few people dining this evening and our waiter pointed out two fellow residents; an elderly gentleman in clerical garb dining alone in a comfortable nook near the fireplace; and a fresh-faced, broad-shouldered young man sitting by himself two tables away. He caught our eye and nodded in a most friendly manner.

Our waiter, in response to a query from Pons observed, "That is Mr. Norman Knight. A Colonial gentleman, I believe. He has been here some time and goes daily to business in Gravesend."

"Indeed," said Pons gravely.

He looked with twinkling eyes after the old fellow, who was wheeling a dessert trolley away down the room as though he would collapse and fall to the floor once its support were removed.

"Such old-fashioned employees are invaluable, Parker, for providing one with background information about people and places. Unfortunately they are a dying breed."

He looked round the dining room with sharp-eyed interest.

"I will wager that before the evening is over we will know a good deal more about Stavely and its surroundings than we did on arrival."

"No doubt, Pons," I remarked. "What are your plans?"

"The four-ale bar, Parker. A great levelling place where tongues loosened by wine—or in this instance beer—are inclined to wag a little too freely. Often great matters hinge on such small things. I remember that an indiscreet remark passed in the back parlour of a small public house near Tite Street enabled me to unravel The Great Cosmopolitan Scandal."

"I do not think I have heard of that case, Pons."

Solar Pons shook his head with a low laugh.

"There is no time this evening, Parker. It will have to await a slack period in my affairs before taking its place in your ubiquitous notebooks. Tonight we are on the track of the Crawling Horror of Grimstone Marsh."

Despite Pons' light tone and jesting face his last words sent a faint tingle of apprehension down my spine. I followed his glance over to the glassed-in partitions separating the bars from the dining room and saw that they appeared to be full.

"There seem to be a remarkable number of people, Pons."

"Does there not, Parker. It is often so in remote places. Folk come from far and wide to congregate together in the dark months of winter. I fancy our man may be among them."

"You mean Tobias Jessel?"

Solar Pons looked at me with approving eyes.

"Admirable, Parker! You are improving considerably. Dr. Strangeways' patient is the only other person, apart from Grimstone and his niece, who has seen this apparition."

"It may be that he can throw fresh light, in a quite literal sense, on the matter."

Solar Pon scribbled his signature on the pad the old waiter held out for him and after I had left something on the table for this loyal servitor, Pons and I took our coffee and liqueurs in the adjoining smoking room which was adjacent to the bars and commanded a good view of the humanity milling about in the dense atmosphere within.

After a few minutes Pons excused himself and when I rejoined him a short while afterwards, he was deep in conversation in the saloon bar with a bright-eyed old man whose red nose and broken-veined eyes bespoke long indulgence in liquor.

"Ah, there you are, Parker," said Solar Pons, turning as I came up through the bar, the confines of which were almost hidden through the haze of tobacco-smoke.

"I have taken the liberty of ordering for you." He pushed the schooner of sherry toward me and raised his own glass in salutation. "This is Mr. Tobias Jessel, who has an interesting story to tell. Pray fill up your glass again, Jessel."

"Thank you, sir," said the old man eagerly.

He had a fringe of white beard and his nautical-style peaked cap and thick blue clothing gave him the look of a seaman, though I understood from Pons that the man had never been farther than the marshes in his life. No doubt that was the impression he wished to give to visitors. When his drink had been brought in a pewter tankard bearing his own initials, he wiped his mouth with the back of his hand and smacked his lips appreciatively.

"Well, sir, people hereabouts are inclined to laugh at my stories, but they won't be inclined to do so much longer."

Solar Pons looked at him sharply.

"What makes you say that?"

The old man shook his head.

"There are strange things on the marshes, sir. Especially on these bleak winter nights. Spirits of those dead and gone."

Solar Pons studied our informant silently for a moment over the rim of his glass. The noise in the bar was deafening, everyone appearing to be conversing at the top of their voices. It looked as though the whole population of the marshes had gathered here this evening.

"I am more interested in recent doings than in the ghosts of the past, Jessel. Unless they have a bearing on the present."

The old man rested his tankard on the polished mahogany top of the counter and looked reflectively at the hurried runnings-about of the potman. He put a withered hand up to the side of his nose.

"Who's to tell, sir, whether the past does not have a bearing on the present? There are some—and they include me—who believe that they do; that our deeds on this earth, from cradle to grave, cast their shadow before."

Solar Pons' eyes twinkled and he cast a penetrating glance from Tobias Jessel to me.

"You are quite a philosopher, Jessel. Dr. Strangeways tells me you saw a weird apparition on the marsh recently."

"That I did, sir."

The old man lowered his voice to a hushed and confidential tone, though no one could have overheard us in our snug corner of the bar with all the hubbub going on.

"It was late at night. I had just left here and was walking back along the marsh road. My cottage is about two miles distant. It was a fine, moonlight night, but with a frost and a slight ground-mist coming up over the marshes. I had got almost opposite the causeway of Grimstone Manor when I heard a slight sound."

"What sort of sound?"

"Like a rustling in the reeds, sir."

"I see. Go on."

"Well, sir, I naturally turned. I'd had a bit to drink but I was soon sober, I can tell you. There was a ghastly blue figure, all wreathed in fire coming up at the edge of the marsh."

The old man's eyes were filled with fear and he again lowered his voice until I had a job to make his words out.

"Like one of those pictures of fiends burning in Hell, it was."

"Extremely apposite, Jessel," said Pons drily. "What was it doing?"

"It was my opinion it was making toward Grimstone Manor, sir. I naturally cried out, I was so startled with the sight. At almost the same moment the figure vanished."

"Vanished?"

"Vanished, sir. Just as though someone had pulled down a blind."

"Interesting, Parker."

"Indeed, Pons. An almost exactly parallel experience to that of Mr. Grimstone."

"I am glad you have seen the connection. Did you go toward the spot where you had seen the figure?"

A look of contempt passed across our informant's face.

"What do you take me for, sir? A fool?" he exclaimed indignantly. "I wouldn't have gone across that causeway for a thousand pounds, I can tell you. I took to my heels and didn't feel myself safe and secure until I was inside my cottage and had the door barred."

Solar Pons nodded and tamped fresh tobacco into his pipe. When it was drawing to his satisfaction he leaned forward and ordered a refill of Jessel's tankard. His penetrating eyes seemed to bore right into the old man.

"Now just pay attention, Jessel, as this is extremely important. When first you saw the figure was it down below the level of the road or up the embankment?"

A startled expression passed across the old man's features.

"Down below the steep bank, sir. I am sure of it."

Solar Pons nodded, his eyes glinting.

"And was there a wind that evening. Think carefully?"

The old man scratched his head and picked up his tankard with his unoccupied hand.

"Why, a bit of a wind had sprung up, sir. It was gusting and I noticed it was blowing the mist about at the edge of the marsh."

"Thank you, Jessel. You have been extremely helpful. Here is a guinea for your trouble."

Waving away the old man's thanks Solar Pons turned to me. His expression changed.

"Not a word of what we have just been discussing, Parker. Ah, Dr. Strangeways. It is good to see you. Will you not join us? The sherry is excellent."

"Thank you, Mr. Pons. I would prefer a whisky if it is all the same to you."

"By all means. Allow me to refill your own glass, Parker."

The doctor's bearded face looked chapped and red with cold and he clapped his hands together as he gazed round the crowded bar.

"How is my patient, Dr. Parker?"

I smiled.

"You mean old Mr. Grimstone? We have been out there earlier this evening. I mentioned the matter, but as you have already indicated, I fear it will be a long time before you collect your fees."

Strangeways smiled grimly.

"There are more ways than one of obtaining satisfaction," he said levelly. "He may need medical treatment urgently one of these days."

He chuckled throatily and reached out his hand for the glass Pons was proffering him. I raised my own and found a young man at my elbow. He blinked round at us.

"I am sorry to intrude, gentlemen. My name is Norman Knight. We are fellow guests, I believe."

"Oh, certainly, Mr. Knight. Do join us. May I get you something?"

"No thank you, Mr. Pons." The young man shook his head. "I still have the best part of a pint here. It was just that I understood you were a doctor. I do a good deal of walking hereabouts and I have had the misfortune to turn my ankle earlier tonight. I wondered if Dr. Strangeways might take a look at it."

Strangeways smiled benevolently at the fair-haired young man.

"Save your money, Mr. Knight. Unless there is a bone broken—

and I'll wager you would know it if there were—a cold compress left on all night will do the trick."

"Thank you, Dr. Strangeways."

Knight laughed, sipping at his tankard. He tried the weight on his right foot.

"No, I do not think there is anything broken. But it aches infernally and makes me limp."

"A towel soaked in cold water, then," said Dr. Strangeways crisply. "Bind it tightly round the ankle and leave it on all night. You will find it greatly improved by morning."

Strangeways put down his glass.

"And now my dinner is waiting in the dining room yonder, Mr. Pons, if you will excuse me."

Pons nodded and we watched as the huge form of the doctor threaded its way through the crowd.

"At least the medical profession in this country is not on the make," said young Knight carelessly, putting down his glass on the bar.

"You have been abroad much, then?" asked Solar Pons.

"Around the world a good deal, Mr. Pons," said the young man. "And now, if you will excuse me I will say goodnight also. I must put the good doctor's remedy into practice."

He shook hands pleasantly and walked over toward the street door which was more clear than the route taken by Strangeways. He was indeed limping heavily on his right foot.

"The sooner that young man gets into bed the better, Pons," I said. "He has most likely strained a ligament."

"I have no doubt your diagnosis is correct, Parker," said Pons.

I looked round in the smoky interior but could see nothing of Tobias Jessel. Solar Pons smiled.

"He left a good ten minutes ago, Parker. I fancy he had no desire for words with Dr. Strangeways again. Reading between the lines it must have been an interesting interview."

"Superstition versus scientific determinism, Pons," I said.

My companion looked at me approvingly.

"Or in layman's terms the truth as seen by Tobias Jessel against the doctor's diagnosis of D.T.'s."

"You may be right, Pons," I said cautiously. "You must admit the whole thing sounds fantastic. If we had not been consulted by Silas Grimstone and had the testimony of himself and his niece, in addition to that of Jessel, you would have dismissed it out of hand."

"Perhaps, Parker, perhaps," admitted Solar Pons smilingly. And he said not a word further on the subject between then and the time we retired to bed.

VII

I woke quite early from a refreshing sleep the following morning to find thick white mist lying damply at the window. I made a quick toilet and descended to the warmth and pleasant atmosphere of the hotel dining room. Early as I was, Pons was already at table. He looked fresh and alert and greeted me cordially.

"We have a good deal before us today, Parker, so I would advise a hearty breakfast."

He was already halfway through a substantial plate of bacon, kidney and eggs and I lost no time in joining him, my companion pouring the scalding coffee for me from the polished pewter pot. I caught a glimpse of young Knight seated a few tables away and there were several other people, in thick clothing, dotted about at various tables.

"There appears to be a curious influx of visitors, Pons," I said, surprise evident on my face.

Solar Pons chuckled.

"Does there not, Parker. A walking party, if you please, on the marshes at this time of year. I salute the hardihood of my compatriots."

"How is our friend's foot, Pons?" I remarked.

"Still troubling him a little, though it has much eased."

I reached out for the hot buttered toast brought by the old waiter who had served us the previous day and ordered another pot of coffee for the two of us.

"What are your plans for today, Pons?"

"I have a desire to see something of the marshes, Parker. There is nothing like penetrating to the heart of a mystery."

"That is all very well, Pons," said I, my mouth halffull of

buttered toast, "but did not the local people say they are extremely dangerous?"

"That is precisely the reason I wish to go," said Pons. "The sensible man takes wise precautions and I have already procured a large-scale Ordnance Survey map of the area, which our worthy landlord sells at the reception desk."

"I see, Pons. I hope you know what you are doing."

Solar Pons smiled enigmatically.

"I think I can read a map with some accuracy, Parker; and no doubt your excellent eyesight and your Army experience will provide admirable backing. You have your revolver, I take it?"

I looked at Pons in surprise.

"It is in my valise upstairs."

"I would suggest that you get it once breakfast is over, my dear fellow."

"You surely do not expect danger in daylight, Pons. So far as I understand this phantom does not appear except at night."

"The Bible says something about terror at noonday. I would feel a great deal easier when venturing into the marshes, if you were carrying it."

"I will certainly bring it, Pons."

"Excellent," said Solar Pons, his keen eyes raking the room and particularly the hearty groups of walkers at the adjoining tables. "I notice from the map that there is a solid path which leads into the heart of Grimstone Marsh from a point near old Grimstone's causeway. I would suggest we make that our objective this morning and perhaps call at the Manor later and see if we can solicit some lunch from our client."

My gloom at his words must have shown on my face for Pons chuckled again and added, "Come, Parker, it is not so bad. The Manor is on our way, after all, and we can always return here if need be."

"As you wish, Pons. I am at your disposal."

Solar Pons nodded.

"Finish your coffee then, and let us be off."

As we left the dining room we passed quite close to young Knight. He smiled pleasantly and made preparations for quitting his own table. I ascended to my room, dressed myself in some warm clothes suitable to our expedition and with the butt of my pistol making a comforting pressure against my shoulder muscles, descended to the hall of the hotel, where Pons was waiting.

Knight was making his own way back to his room again; he was still limping, though making light of the effort, and I noticed that Pons' glance rested on him sympathetically as he gained the head of the stairs. A few moments later we were out in the bitter air of the street and, the mist lifting a little, set off along the lonely road that led across the marsh in the direction of Grimstone Manor.

We walked in silence, each occupied with his own thoughts, our feet striking back echoes from the pallid blanket of vapour that edged the road. Once again I was struck with the exceptional melancholy of these cheerless wastes and even Pons seemed more than usually reflective, the streams of blue smoke from his pipe wreathing back over his shoulder.

We had gone about halfway to the causeway linking Silas Grimstone's manor house with the main road when we heard the sound of hooves on the highway in front of us and the faint murmur of men's voices. Pons put his hand on my arm and drew me to a halt, his lean, feral face expressing intense concentration.

"Hullo, Parker. Horse and cart. Five men by the sound of it."

Sure enough, two minutes later spectral figures materialised from the mist like negatives developing in the photographer's dish. A black horse, eyes wide and staring through the whiteness, drew a rough farm cart whose ironbound wheels made an unpleasant grating noise on the icy road. The men who confronted us were bareheaded and the stiff form beneath the rough tarpaulin on the cart instantly supplied the reason.

I glanced at Pons, noting that there were five men in the group, as he had already indicated. Heavy boots protruded from beneath the tarpaulin, encrusted with ice.

"Good morning, Mr. Pons! I am afraid this is a sad start to the day."

The massive, bearded form of Dr. Strangeways detached himself from the bareheaded villagers and came toward us.

"Indeed," said Solar Pons, moving over to stare downward at the sombre burden the cart contained. "A drowning?"

"A drowning, certainly," said Strangeways brusquely. "Though whether he went into the marsh intentionally is another matter. I would be glad of your opinion, Doctor."

He bent over the cart and drew back the canvas from the dead face. Ice glistened in among the stiffened fronds of hair and the face was so distorted and cyanosed that I had some difficulty in making out the visage of Tobias Jessel. Pons came to stand at my side and puffed unemotionally at his pipe.

"I fear your money was illspent, Pons," I said.

"Perhaps, Parker, perhaps," said my companion absently.

He fixed the doctor with a piercing eye.

"Just what did you mean by saying that Jessel may not have gone into the marsh intentionally, Doctor?"

The big doctor stamped his feet on the ground, an uneasy expression on his face.

"It is only what these people have been saying," he said defensively. "There has been some ill feeling in the past about this fellow's drunken habits. He was not short of enemies on the marsh."

"That is a serious charge, Doctor," said Solar Pons. "Let us just see what the indications are."

He pulled back the canvas further, revealing more detail of the old man's pathetic, stiffened form.

"There are some cuts on the hands, Pons," I said. "As though he had been defending himself."

"I have not overlooked them, Parker," said Solar Pons languidly.

He was busy with his magnifying lens while the four villagers in rough clothing stood awkwardly around the cart. They looked like nothing so much as mourners at a funeral.

"Where was he found?" Pons asked crisply.

"At the foot of a dyke younder, about half a mile back, sir," said one of the men, turning to point into the white mist in front of us. "Jethro Turner here was on his way to work. The mist happened to part and he saw the body in the ice at the edge of the marsh."

"That's right, sir," said the man referred to soberly. "There was nothing I could do for him, sir, so I set out for the village to rouse Dr. Strangeways here."

"You have done perfectly correctly, Turner."

Pons turned back to Strangeways.

"You have reported it to the Coroner, of course?"

Strangeways flushed and there was again a defensive look on his features.

"My surgery boy is on his way there now, Mr. Pons. There is little else we can do until I perform the post mortem."

"Of course not," said Pons. "I should be glad of a copy of your findings."

"I shall never forget the look on his face, sir," said the man Turner, inclining his lugubrious countenance toward us.

"Death is always a shock," said Strangeways roughly.

He jerked his head at the two of us.

"We must get on. A pleasant walk to you, gentlemen."

The man holding the horse's head urged the beast forward and the sad cortège moved on through the mist. Pons and I walked in silence for a while, my companion smoking furiously, his brows knotted.

"What do you make of it, Parker?" he said at length.

"It is an unpleasant business, Pons," I replied. "And things look black, particularly in view of this phantom of the marsh tale. Do you think Jessel could have seen something and been pushed in? His murder obviously took place when he was on his way home from the inn last night."

Solar Pons shook his head. "You have a point, Parker, but it is too early as yet to jump to conclusions. We must just reserve judgement."

"And there is the matter of the cuts on his hands, Pons. Supposing he were trying to ward off the blows of a knife?"

Solar Pons ejected a plume of fragrant smoke from between his strong teeth.

"Nevertheless, he drowned, Parker," he said enigmatically. "He was not stabbed to death. Ah, unless I am mistaken, here comes the first of the sun!"

Rays of light were beginning to penetrate the mist and in a quarter of an hour it started to disperse, revealing the flat and desolate landscape I had already come to detest. We were almost at the causeway of Grimstone Manor by now and Pons paused to consult his largescale map.

"The path should be about here, Parker," he said, leaving the road and leading me down toward the edge of the marsh.

"Be careful, Pons," I called, following him more gingerly.

He smiled briefly, glancing sharply about him as he led the way without hesitation among the tussocks as the mist cleared, though a faint haze still hung over the surface of the reeds.

"Just follow me closely, Parker. I fancy I shall not lead you astray."

"I am not so sure about that, Pons," I said wryly, as I followed him among the rustling reed-stems with some apprehension.

Pons ignored my remark as he was concentrating on the map, his sharp eyes stabbing about him. Undoubtedly he could read signs which were invisible to me but my confidence grew as we proceeded. Not once did my companion appear to put a foot wrong and within a few minutes the causeway and the roof of Grimstone Manor were completely out of sight.

"You will note, Parker," said Solar Pons, pausing briefly to re-light his pipe, "that the marsh proper is of a far deeper and greener texture than that of the path. And you will see, if you look yonder, that the reed-stems are encased in ice, proving that water covers them normally."

"You are right, Pons," I said, after careful observation. "I thought you had done something clever."

Solar Pons looked up from his map with a wry smile.

"The Master himself was not immune to such criticism. It is always a mistake to explain one's reasoning processes to the layman."

"You do me an injustice, Pons."

"Perhaps, Parker, perhaps. But I must confess there is an occasional sting in your otherwise innocuous remarks. You are improving considerably."

He took another glance at the map and then led the way unhesitatingly forward.

"If we keep our direction by the sun here, I do not think we shall go far wrong. But dusk or nightfall would be a different matter indeed."

"But what do you expect to find, Pons?"

"Evidence, Parker. Or at least some trace, however subtle, of human foot before us."

I followed cautiously in his tracks, pausing now and again to look round at our misty surroundings with a misgiving I could not suppress.

"I must say, Pons, I do not care for these marshes. They are bleak and inhospitable in the extreme."

"And yet people make their living here, Parker, and seem reasonably content to do so."

"Except for Strangeways."

Solar Pons turned and gave me a penetrating look from his piercing eyes.

"Ah, you have noticed that? A talented man dissatisfied with the sphere in which circumstances have placed him. At least, that is my reading."

"There is more to the doctor than appears on the surface, Pons."

"We shall see," he replied equably.

He led the way forward ever deeper into the marsh, our movements occasionally cloaked by thick undergrowth which grew on exposed humps of land which thrust themselves above the surrounding bog. A thin mist still hovered over the reeds but it was possible to see some way ahead and it was with considerable relief that I saw a large hummock of firmer ground and then the outlines of a dilapidated stone building. The harsh cries of birds occasionally broke the silence but apart from that and the faint noise our own footsteps made we might have been alone in the universe.

Pons folded the map and scrutinised it closely.

"Ah, this should be the place, Parker. A disused shepherd's hut and byre. Some of this land was once reclaimed from the marsh but as fast as gains were made, other areas were abandoned to their former state."

"You look as though you expect to find something here."

"Do I not. We have at least three points to aim for this morning and if we do not end up a little wiser my name is not Solar Pons."

We were off the path now and walking uphill toward the stone-built ruins. Seabirds cried harshly in the strengthening sunlight as we gained the island—for it was little more—that rose from the surrounding marshland.

A sudden explosion sent ducks whirring upward as we gained the edge of the ruins. I must confess my nerves were a little on edge for I had my hand on the butt of my revolver before Pons' warning glance brought me to myself. A burly, tweeded form lowered the shotgun as we came up. The man smiled affably.

"Good morning, gentlemen. Joshua Tebble at your service. Nothing like roast duck with your potatoes and green peas. There, Judy!"

The bright-eyed retriever went dashing into the marsh and emerged wetly a minute or two later carrying the bedraggled corpse of a plump duck in her mouth.

"An excellent meal, as you say, Mr. Tebble," I put in.

The tanned man looked at us shrewdly as he thrust the duck carelessly into the capacious canvas bag he carried slung over one shoulder.

"Staying in the neighbourhood, are you?"

"We are at the inn yonder for a few days," put in Solar Pons. "It seems an agreeable district."

"It's all right," said Tebble shortly. "Though if you were farming, like me, you would not say so. Difficult terrain for agriculture, gentlemen. Too much salt marsh hereabouts. And the land is inclined to flood at high tide in winter. Still, it's a living."

He ejected a cartridge from the breech of his shotgun.

"Shouldn't get wandering off the path, gentlemen. Highly dangerous on these marshes. Good day to you!"

And he was off, shouldering the shotgun and whistling to the dog to follow him. Solar Pons stood, smoke curling from the bowl of his pipe, a thin smile on his lips, as he followed Tebble's figure until it was lost in the haze.

"What do you make of him, Pons?"

"A bold fellow and an excellent shot by appearances."

"Do you think he is concerned with this business? It is highly suspicious finding him here by these ruins like this."

Solar Pons arched his eyebrows.

"I do not see why, Parker. You are here yourself."

"But only with you, Pons, on highly lawful business."

Solar Pons chuckled, pulling at the lobe of his left ear ruminatively.

"Mr. Tebble is hardly likely to know that, Parker. Now that we are here, let us just look about."

Having satisfied himself that we were now alone on the knoll, Pons produced his powerful pocket lens and went purposefully up and down the old ruins. It was indeed a tumbledown, Godforsaken spot and as the minutes passed and I watched his energetic, purposeful figure I marvelled once again at the patience and thoroughness with which he examined details of brickwork, earth flooring and broken reed-stems whose stories, so obvious to him, were literally a closed book to me.

There was an air of disappointment about him as he put the glass in its case with a snap.

"This is not the place, Parker."

He glanced up at the brightening sky.

"Well, I hardly thought we should hit the bull first shot. We must take another walk."

And without turning he walked energetically down the knoll and plunged forward into the marsh again.

VIII

Within some twenty minutes the landscape had again subtly changed; if anything, it had become even more bleak and sombre than that surrounding Grimstone Manor. Though the sun still shone, the slimy ooze ever deepened about us, as the warmth melted the ice which lingered in the hollows and a clammy vapour hovered thickly over the surface.

But Solar Pons was his old, energetic, purposeful self and led the way ever deeper into the heart of the bog with unerring precision, so that I was hard put to follow at times. Now and again he stopped to consult the map but was then swiftly off again like an animal upon some urgent scent. Just as I was about to become really worried, another knoll loomed up before us and there were the tumbled walls and remains of a really ancient building that looked, from its general outline, like a mediaeval abbey or monastery.

Solar Pons looked at me with warm approval.

"We are improving, Parker. It is not so very difficult to find one's way about, providing one reads the map accurately and uses one's commonsense."

"You have exceptional abilities, Pons," I murmured. "I would not care to chance my arm alone."

"Anyway, here we are at the Abbey," said Pons. "We have only one other objective this morning and you will no doubt be pleased to learn that we are casting about in a giant circle which should eventually bring us back somewhere within hailing distance of Grimstone Manor."

"I am glad to hear it, Pons," said I, setting foot on a solid earth path that led up toward the Abbey ruins. "I am becoming a little tired of marshland, birds and sheep."

Solar Pons smiled grimly, looking sharply about him. He uttered a low cry of annoyance as we came up closer to the ruins. There were people there; many people, dressed in thick clothes and with rucksacks.

"Good heavens, Pons!" I exclaimed. "These are the walkers; the people from the Inn."

"Are they not, Parker," said Pons ruefully. "Any evidence our phantom has left here will certainly be obliterated by now."

But whatever disappointment he felt he managed to conceal with his usual adroit manner and lounged up the path as though he had not a care in the world, exchanging friendly nods at the polite greetings of our fellow guests of the morning.

"The Cistercians were remarkable builders, Parker, were they not," he averred, looking at the detail of a crumbling archway before us.

"Certainly, Pons. The order still flourishes, I believe?"

"Most definitely."

Though Pons could not use his powerful magnifying lens, he certainly went over the ground in great detail, though the sightseers at this ancient monument would not have gathered it from his casual manner.

I sat down on a large flat stone and smoked for a while, content to let my companion wander; the sun was a little warmer in this enclosed space, though it was still bitterly cold and I did not linger long in that position. When Pons rejoined me his face had cleared.

"This is not the place, Parker. That seems self-evident."

"You have found something, Pons?"

He shook his head as we hurried down the far side of the knoll and back into the marshy ground.

"These walkers have saved us time, Parker. The old ruins are too public. They came by the main road. There is a new, paved path not marked on my map, which leads direct to the ruins, which are listed as an Ancient Monument."

He smoked on in silence for a moment or two, his face looking worried.

"Our final destination this morning must bear out my theory or I shall have to rethink our tactics."

He said nothing further and we went on and on into the bleak wilderness, the cold forgotten in the exercise I found in treading in exactly the same places as those just vacated by my friend. We had been proceeding in this manner for some while when Pons stopped casually and turned to me. He made an elaborate ritual of clearing out the bowl of his pipe before tamping it with fresh tobacco.

"Solitude is a wonderful thing, Parker," he said. "It becomes more precious as we advance farther and farther into the 20th century."

"I am not so sure, Pons . . ." I began when my companion rudely interrupted me.

"Come, Parker, solitude is at a premium. Even in the middle of a deserted swamp one cannot escape from the madding crowd. Good morning, Doctor!"

To my astonishment a thick clump of bushes at the right of the path just ahead of us wavered, though there was no breeze. A moment later the bull-like form of Dr. Strangeways stepped on to the path. The doctor looked considerably embarrassed.

"Well, Mr. Pons," he rumbled. "I trust you did not think I was spying upon you?"

"I did not know what to think, Doctor," said Pons blandly. "But if you wish to keep an eye on people without being observed it is as well to keep your binoculars in shadow. The sun was shining directly on to the lenses there."

The doctor bristled as though he were keeping his temper with difficulty.

"I was looking not at you, Mr. Pons, but at a pair of rare birds. I was concerned at their safety when I heard in the village that the walkers were on the marsh."

"I see," said Solar Pons, giving him a searching look. "However, I do not think you need be worried. They are not likely to go beyond the Abbey ruins. You seem to have completed your post mortem rather quickly."

The doctor's eyes were clouded and blank as he turned them upon Pons.

"It was a routine matter after all. There is no doubt in my mind old Jessel died of drowning."

Solar Pons frowned.

"Yet you seemed to have some doubts earlier this morning, Doctor. It was almost as though you yourself believed in the phantom of the marsh."

Strangeways drew himself up and his face looked troubled.

"I would not care to tell everyone this, Mr. Pons, but I felt guilty about Jessel. I had been deriding his stories, regarding them as mere drunkard's tales, but I myself saw something very strange after I left you last night."

"Indeed."

Strangeways nodded.

"I was called out after midnight to an emergency case. The farmer's cottage was up along the main road beyond Grimstone Manor. I was driving beside the rim of the marsh when I saw a weird blue light bobbing about, a considerable way off. It looked like a human figure but there was something unearthly about it."

Dr. Strangeways swallowed and there was doubt in his eyes as he looked at Pons sombrely.

"It gave me quite a turn, Mr. Pons, I don't mind telling you. And I felt quite ashamed at disbelieving old Jessel. And when I saw him dead this morning my shock can be imagined. He was found, you see, quite near where I saw the figure last night. Ought I to tell the police and the Coroner, do you think?"

There was an unexpected gentleness in Solar Pons' voice as he replied. He put his hand on the other's arm.

"Discretion for the time being, Doctor, I feel. The fewer people who know about this the better."

The doctor nodded; there was a strange expression in his eyes as he gazed at Pons.

"Tell me," my companion continued, "what was this phantom like?"

Impatience was already returning to Strangeways' voice.

"I have already told you, Mr. Pons. It was a fiery, bluish figure. It was too far away to see any detail."

"But how did it appear or disappear?"

The doctor stared at Pons in exasperation.

"How should I know, Mr. Pons? It was already visible when I first became aware of it. As soon as I saw it I was so startled I almost drove down into the dyke. When I saw it again it suddenly disappeared."

"Just so."

Solar Pons nodded, an expression of satisfaction on his face.

"As we have already heard. Like the pulling down of a blind, was it not?"

He turned to me.

"We shall be at the inn this evening, Doctor, if we are required. Come, Parker."

We left the burly figure of the medical man standing in perplexity on the path. I glanced back once and saw the sun glinting on the rim of his binoculars, an expression of bafflement on his face.

Some half an hour of cautious casting about in the marsh brought us at last to our final destination, a huddle of squalid brick buildings that looked like an abandoned tenant farm. Solar Pons' eyes were quick and alert.

"Aha, Parker, this is more like it."

He bent down at the edge of the reeds and I made out the heavy impression of a foot. Pons had his lens out and was making a minute examination. He cast about him for a few minutes and then traced the fading impressions up on to firmer ground, where they were lost on a rocky outcrop.

I followed Pons over toward the dilapidated brick sheds, for they were little more. Their corrugated iron roofs were red with rust and it was obvious they had been abandoned for years.

"D'Eath Farm," said Pons, consulting his map. "A most appropriate name."

"What did the tracks tell you, Pons?"

He gave me a quizzical look.

"Quite a lot, Parker. Many people have been here. Some of the footprints I cannot make out. Certainly Strangeways has been here within the past few days. And possibly Tebble. I could not, of course, make out the welts of his shooting boots themselves, as he was wearing them just now. But the imprints at the edge of the marsh there are similar to the ones he made in the soft earth when he was standing talking to us and the paw-marks of his retriever are unmistakable."

I looked at him wide-eyed.

"You could tell all that from this jumble of muddy marks on the ground, Pons?"

My companion chuckled.

"You forget I have made a study of such things, Parker. I could deduce a good deal more also. A lady has been here too. Though she wears heavy gum-boots, the lighter indentation is quite distinctive and entirely different from that made by a child."

"You should write a monograph on the subject, Pons," I said drily.

Pons' wry smiled widened.

"I have published four, Parker. But let us just look at these buildings yonder."

His aquiline nostrils were already sniffing the air as we approached the brick buildings and a moment later I caught what his keen sense of smell had already told him.

"Chemicals, Pons?"

Solar Pons nodded.

"Undoubtedly."

"Perhaps these sheds are used as an agricultural store, Pons?"

"Perhaps, Parker," was the cautious reply.

My companion stepped to the door of the largest building and frowned. He tried the handle carefully. It was obviously locked. He looked through the grimy window but when I joined him it was impossible to make anything out; the windows had apparently been painted white on the inside. We moved round. The next lean-to had its door secured by a heavy padlock.

"These do not appear to be disused after all, Parker," he said.

His eyes were twinkling as he ejected coils of blue smoke from his pipe. He thrust his hands deep into his pockets as he stared over my shoulder.

"For a swamp, this area of Kent is becoming remarkably crowded, Parker," he said mildly. "Good morning, Miss Grimstone!"

I turned to find our eccentric client's niece striding down a knoll toward us. She was sensibly and tweedily dressed and I saw at once that she wore stout gum-boots which were plastered with mud.

"Good morning, Mr. Pons! Good morning, Dr. Parker!"

There was a smile on Miss Grimstone's face but it was obvious she was disconcerted.

"I come here often to search for wild flowers and plants," she said somewhat defensively.

"Indeed," said Solar Pons. "I am glad to have seen you for I intended to call at the Manor on the way back. How is your uncle?"

"Well, Mr. Pons. But he is a badly frightened man. Could I persuade you to take lunch with us?"

Pons was obviously taken aback but he concealed the fact well; perhaps we had been mistaken and Miss Grimstone was not so miserly as we had been led to believe.

"I must talk to you, Mr. Pons, and there will be little opportunity otherwise. I was just going back and I have the pony and trap on the high road only half a mile from here."

Pons smiled as I looked thankfully from him to Miss Grimstone. Truth to tell I was not keen to retrace my steps over the miles of marshland we had already traversed.

"If you have quite finished here . . ."

"By all means."

Pons fell into step with Miss Grimstone and the two of them led the way diagonally down the slope and in a direction at right-angles to the way we had come. I was content to follow in their rear, keeping a sharp lookout still to make sure I was treading exactly in their footprints.

Miss Grimstone did not seem quite so forbidding as she had first appeared and I noticed her shooting shrewd glances at Pons from time to time. Eventually she seemed to come to some decision for she said, with an ironical inflexion in her voice, "You do not seem to think much of our mènage, Mr. Pons. Please do not judge me too harshly. I have had to fight for everything I have and such early struggles tend to distort one's character."

I saw that Pons' features bore a reassuring expression as he turned his head back over his shoulder to include me in the conversation.

"I can assure you, Miss Grimstone, that I do not lightly judge people. I am too used to human nature to be surprised by anything I find; neither do I adopt a censorious attitude."

"Nevertheless, you have certain reservations about Silas Grimstone," said the grey-haired woman shrewdly. "I have a number myself."

"You are frank at any rate. It is true that I do not approve of miserliness, neither do I regard it as one of the major virtues, particularly when the person in whom it appears has more than his fair share of the world's goods."

Miss Grimstone nodded, a deep sign escaping her lips.

"You are right, Mr. Pons, and I am afraid that my uncle's habits have become somewhat ingrained in me."

"It is often so in such enclosed households, Miss Grimstone. There was no need to mention it. And what of your uncle's earlier struggles . . .?"

"Business matters, Mr. Pons. He and his brother were engaged in many rancorous battles for control of the firm."

Solar Pons' brow knotted and he turned sharply toward our companion.

"I did not know Mr. Grimstone had a second brother."

The niece shook her head.

"He would not have mentioned it of his own accord, Mr. Pons. It was a sore point between them. In the end he bought out his brother's share of the firm. Mr. Jethro Grimstone emigrated to Australia, I understand."

"Indeed. When did all this take place, Miss Grimstone?"

"Many years ago, Mr. Pons. Over twenty, I believe. I was not living at the Manor in those days, of course. But I heard all about it from my father, who died shortly after. There were three brothers, you see, but my father abhorred Silas Grimstone. He was an openhearted and generous man."

She smiled shyly at Pons.

"I was only thirty or so then and much more personable. I was hoping to be married when my father died and there was such a change in my circumstances."

There was a brooding sadness in her eyes as I glanced at her as we slowly traversed the marshland path and I glimpsed in that moment all the long years of housekeeping for Silas Grimstone and all the hopes for a happier life with her own husband and family she must long since have given up. Pons stared at her for a moment, compassion shining in his eyes.

"I am truly sorry to hear that, Miss Grimstone. What you have just said interests me. You say your second uncle went to Australia."

"So I understand, Mr. Pons."

"From Silas Grimstone?"

"Yes. He mentioned it a number of times."

"And after he had gained control of the firm, things greatly improved."

"I believe so, yes."

"Hmm."

Solar Pons paused on the path and pulled reflectively at the lobe of his right ear.

"You have not said much about this apparition of the marsh, Miss Grimstone. What is your theory about it? And why should your uncle be so frightened?"

"Well, if you had seen it, Mr. Pons, you might have been frightened too."

Pons smiled ruefully.

"Perhaps you are right, Miss Grimstone. I understand it has been seen again last night."

He held up his hand to avoid any further questions and at that moment we came up the narrow path on to level ground where a patient pony harnessed to a shabby old trap cropped the winter grass as it stood tethered to the roadside fence. Solar Pons turned to me as he waited for Miss Grimstone to ascend to the driving seat of the vehicle.

"I think perhaps it might be best if we remained and kept watch at the Manor tonight, Parker. This will-o'-the-wisp may strike again and it is as well to be on our guard."

IX

"I hope this is not going on my bill, Mr. Pons!"

Silas Grimstone's voice was thick and clotted with greed as he glared at my companion. We were sitting in the parlour at Grimstone Manor, the blinds drawn, our chairs close to the smouldering fire on the hearth. We had already eaten and I was beginning to forget the dampness and chill of the marsh as we had seen it in the morning, though the room was far from over-warm as the temperature had dropped considerably with the coming of nightfall.

Pons had spent the afternoon in going over the grounds of the Manor and had made sure that all the doors and windows were secure before dusk. Now we waited for Miss Grimstone to bring the coffee and the brandy she had promised, against the querulous protests of her uncle.

"Our vigil here this evening?"

There was contempt in Pons' voice.

"Do not trouble yourself about that, Mr. Grimstone. There are some other matters I would like to discuss. You did not tell me about your brother. Your business partner; the one who went to Australia."

There was a long hush in the room and the old man's complexion seemed to have turned yellow. He struggled up in his fireside chair and put a shrivelled hand to the shawl at his throat.

"It was all a long time ago, Mr. Pons. That rascal went abroad and I have neither seen nor heard from him to this day, thank God!"

"Why do you say that, Mr. Grimstone?"

"Because he was a villain. The firm would have crashed if I had not taken control."

"That is your supposition, Mr. Grimstone?"

The old man put his head on one side and surveyed my companion grimly.

"It is indeed, Mr. Pons. And it is true. The affair is an old one and may be consulted in the Stock Exchange records."

The eyes expressed malevolent distrust as he stared at Pons.

"You seem to be forgetting your purpose here, Mr. Pons. My life is threatened by this ghastly thing from the marsh and you are talking ancient history."

Solar Pons smiled thinly and put up his hand to stop the flow of splenetic accusations that were beginning to tumble from our client's mouth.

"I have not been idle, Mr. Grimstone. I have a mind to put my theories to the test this evening. You have no objection to taking part in a little experiment?"

Silas Grimstone stared at Pons suspiciously as he went to the window and drew the curtain. He rubbed his thin fingers together. "Excellent! There is a mist coming up from the marsh. Ideal for our purposes. You have no objection to a little walk in an hour or so, suitably wrapped up? If we cannot find the Phantom of the Marsh— and it is pointless to go looking for him in such a wide area—then we must call him to us."

"Mr. Pons!"

The old man's voice was high and cracked in his agitation. He glared at my companion, pushing aside Miss Sylvia Grimstone as she went to offer him a cup of coffee.

The old man's niece had a faint smile on her face as she turned to me. She put the cup of coffee at my elbow and another in front of Pons who had now resumed his seat.

"You want me to go out there? You are using me as some sort of decoy, sir?"

Solar Pons nodded over the rim of his coffee cup.

"By all means, Mr. Grimstone," he agreed cheerfully. "You were out in your stable yard yesterday evening when we arrived, quite unprotected. I shall not require you to do much more tonight. Merely to show yourself and leave the rest to Parker and myself."

There was suppressed excitement in Miss Sylvia Grimstone's eyes.

"Ah, you intend to be on hand, Mr. Pons."

"Of course, Miss Grimstone. I would not risk your uncle's health or wellbeing for one second," said Solar Pons smoothly. "Parker here has his revolver and we will see whether this phantom is vulnerable to bullets or something more ethereal."

There was a strange, twisted expression on old Silas Grimstone's face and he nodded his head once or twice, as though he agreed with my companion's suggestion. He put his head on one side.

"What is your plan, Mr. Pons?"

"That is better, Mr. Grimstone," said Solar Pons, tenting his fingers on the table before him. "I have formed certain theories and considered a number of suppositions. Now I have to test them in the field as it were, I cannot do that unless we have some tangible reason for this creature venturing out tonight. He will not do so unless he knows that you are abroad."

Grimstone's expression became one of extreme alarm and he looked furtively around him as though he expected to find the subject of his fears at his elbow in the flickering firelight.

"You do not mean to say he is watching us?"

Solar Pons inclined his head.

"He must do so, Mr. Grimstone. That is the only possible conclusion one can draw. Otherwise, how can he appear only to you, except when others may be about by accident? No, Mr. Grimstone, there is a person of some cunning and persistence at the bottom of this business. And we must draw him out if we are to apprehend him."

"What do you wish me to do, Mr. Pons?"

Solar Pons put down his coffee cup with a faint chink in the silence.

"You must follow my instructions absolutely to the letter, Mr. Grimstone, if things are to be brought to a successful conclusion."

The old man looked at Pons soberly, fearful thoughts reflected in his cadaverous face.

"Very well, Mr. Pons. I will do as you say. What are your proposals?"

X

"There he goes, Parker! Quickly! It is vitally important that we keep him in sight at all times."

I followed Pons through the thick mist, marvelling once again at the unerring manner in which my companion found his way. The fog was thickening and even Pons, I think, was hard put to it to make out the indistinct figure of old Silas Grimstone. The night was dark and cold, the mist rising thickly from the surface of the swamp; altogether it was ideal for Pons' daring plan though it would be extremely dangerous if things went wrong.

I had my revolver in my pocket, the safety-catch on, but with my hand on the butt ready for action if need be. A number of disconnected thoughts were chasing themselves through my mind as we hurried along. Pons' plan was simple but like all such things, brilliant in its very elementariness. It combined daring, with some danger to ourselves, but with a minimum of risk to our client.

Miss Grimstone had driven us out in the trap along the main road toward the spot where it met the path which led through the swamp to the ruined buildings of D'Eath Farm. Silas Grimstone was to leave his niece at a predetermined time and walk along the path, keeping to the firm and high ground which led to the farm before it reached the swamp proper.

Pons and I had left the stopping place half an hour earlier; my companion had marked out another path on the map which led to the heart of the swamp. Once in position, we were to walk along our path of the morning in the direction of the farm. In this way, if the apparition appeared, we should be between it and the farm buildings and cut off any possible retreat into the swamp.

The most practical feature to my mind was Pons' inspiration in making Grimstone carry a small but powerful electric torch, ostensibly to light his way; instead, it would serve two purposes. To draw the apparition to its intended victim and at the same time denote Grimstone's exact position to us in order that we could protect him. Unfortunately, mist had closed in soon after we had gained the old path and Pons had been extremely anxious at the success of the plan.

Grimstone was due to leave his niece at exactly seven p.m. and at precisely that moment as indicated by the second hand of my watch, Pons had led the way back in the direction of the farm buildings. He had allowed fifteen minutes for old Grimstone to get to the farm and we should be in sight of him long before that.

But the mist grew thicker and I was becoming extremely anxious until Pons' reassuring cry; a moment later I saw the thin beam of light, low down on the ground, which was coming along the causeway, far off to our right. It was only a momentary glimpse and then the thick white vapour closed in again.

"We must hurry, Parker. I should never forgive myself if anything went wrong."

"We are within striking distance now, Pons. You could not have foreseen this thickening of the weather."

"Even so, Parker, we are dealing with an old man, who is deliberately exposing himself to danger at my request."

Pons hurried along the path so rapidly that I was hard put to keep up with him. The mist was thinning a little now and we again saw the beam of light dancing across the ground. Pons halted and took stock of the situation.

"We must be careful now, Parker. We have to make sure we do not alarm whoever may be concealed out here. Ah, that is better."

For, as we stepped forward from behind a screen of bushes we had a clear view of the high ridge of ground some two hundred yards off along which old Silas Grimstone was advancing with his torch. Far to the right, invisible behind the hump was the road on which Miss Grimstone was waiting with the trap. We were in the hollow of the swamp and to our left the almost invisible path wound until it reached the higher ground on which stood D'Eath Farm.

Pons led the way, stepping meticulously along a path that was quite invisible to me. All around us in the icy night was the presence of the swamp; I was uneasily aware of it as though it were some living, sinister presence in the darkness, just waiting for a false step aside to drag us down into the bottomless depths. Pons' iron nerves seemed to armour him against such treacherous thoughts and I fingered the chill surface of my revolver, taking comfort from the reassuring metal.

The beams of the torch were momentarily invisible to us, due to a rise in the ground and I realised that we were coming out on to the firmer terrain which led to the abandoned farm buildings. As we started uphill I was suddenly brought to a halt by an anguished cry which resounded through the silence of the night. It was repeated three times, each time more urgently and there was such fear in it that I felt the hairs on the nape of my neck rising and my flesh began to crawl.

Solar Pons gave an exclamation of anger and seized my arm.

"He is more clever than I thought, Parker! If I do not mistake the situation he is coming from the roadside and not from the farm. There is not a moment to lose!"

I tucked my arms into my sides and ran until my lungs were bursting but Pons was fleeter still, covering the uphill path at a tremendous rate. As we rose we were able to see the drama that was being played out on the rough upland track that led to the abandoned farm.

To my relief Silas Grimstone appeared to be unharmed, for we could see his torchlight bobbing about not more than a hundred yards in front of us. Behind him, seeming to hover over the ground and moving at an alarming speed was a horrific apparition whose spectacle stays with me yet. Bluish-yellow, seen first as a halo of crawling flame, then as a hard-edged figure, it appeared to float erratically.

The figure was tall but indeterminate and the hideous face with which it was surmounted, lapped in baleful fire, seemed to undulate and change shape as we watched. It was gaining on Grimstone with every second and with a last terrified look over his shoulder he at last apparently saw us coming to the rescue, for his torch altered course as our paths closed.

"For God's sake save me, Mr. Pons!" he croaked with the last of his breath before sinking down exhausted on to the path about fifty paces away.

"Your department, Parker," said Solar Pons coolly. "Two rounds and aim high, if you please."

The baleful blue figure of the phantom was still coming on, now making short hopping motions. The thing could not have seen us against the dark background of bushes as we ran up the path but as it was now alarmingly close to the fallen figure of the old man, I fired two shots into the air. The flash of flame and the detonation of the explosions seemed incredibly loud. I was momentarily blinded but when I opened my eyes again the marsh was empty; the blue, writhing figure might never have existed.

"Good heavens, Pons!" I ejaculated. "The thing has disappeared."

"Never mind that," said Solar Pons crisply. "Let us just make sure that no harm has come to old Grimstone."

We hurried over the short stretch of ground that separated us from our client and found him lying exhausted; winded but still choleric. I put down my revolver on the stump of a nearby tree and examined him by the light of his own torch.

"He is all right, Pons," I said, feeling his irregular pulse. "Just a fright."

"It might have meant my death!" the old man snarled with astonishing vindictiveness. I helped him up.

"We had better get him back to the Manor, Pons."

Solar Pons put up his hand. There was irritation on his face in the torchlight.

"There will be time enough for that later, Parker. Just douse the light. The game is far from over yet."

His rigid attitude and rapt attention to the matter in hand affected even Grimstone for he stopped his mumbling and went to stand quietly by the tree-trunk. Pons had sunk to his knees and now that I had switched off the torch, was almost invisible in the darkness. He moved forward, urging me to follow and I kept close behind him, leaving Grimstone behind. I had not gone ten yards before I realised I had forgotten the revolver, but subsequent events happened so quickly that it became immaterial.

Pons put his hand on my arm and I came to a halt beside him. He bent down beside the path and there was just enough light to see that he was searching about on the ground with his disengaged hand. He gave a grunt as he found what he wanted; a loose stone which was bonded to the earth with frost. He prised it loose and rose to his feet.

He threw it outwards into the swamp; we waited a few seconds with straining ears. The sudden, sharp crack of breaking ice and then the loud splash which followed sounded thunderous in the silence. At the same moment there was a loud rustling of branches and the same ghastly blue phantom figure reappeared not thirty feet in front of us.

"Come on, Parker!" Pons rapped out exultantly. "My theory was correct."

There were blundering noises ahead as I followed Pons, all fear forgotten in the sudden conviction that we had to deal with a mortal being and not some real phantom of the marsh. Ahead of us the bluish figure ducked and twisted with incredible agility, now appearing and then suddenly disappearing. The outline was curiously elongated and narrow and sometimes the blackness of night intervened for seconds at a time as the thing fled before us.

I stumbled on a root and Pons slackened a moment, turning back toward me. We were up among the farm buildings now and with the respite afforded the apparition had again disappeared.

"What was it, Pons?" I said breathlessly.

Solar Pons chuckled with satisfaction.

"It is mortal enough I fancy, Parker," he said. "There is no time to explain now. We shall find the answer to our problems at D'Eath Farm unless my reasoning is very wide of the mark."

We were close by the buildings and crept cautiously along in their shadow. Pons stopped once or twice and listened intently. He tried the door of one of the sheds. It opened quietly to his touch. He put his lips against my ear.

"As I thought, Parker. This has been used as the phantom's changing-room."

"He is not here now?"

"We shall see."

Abruptly and without any attempt at silence he flung open the door. At the same moment a strong beam of light from the pocket-torch he carried stabbed out across the room. The place appeared to be empty. It was simply a brick and wood shell, with an oil lamp hanging from the dusty beams. It was a sombre place, full of shadow and darkness. In the centre were two wooden boxes; on the top of one a tin was standing, together with a mirror and some brushes.

Solar Pons chuckled. Once again I caught the acrid chemical flavour. He tentatively tested the material in the tin with his fingertip, held it against his face, sniffing deeply.

"A solution of phosphorus, Parker! As I suspected from the beginning. There is your phantom."

"That is all very well, Pons," said I. "But how can he disappear in such a manner?"

"We shall find out in a moment or two, Parker," he said calmly, his sharp eyes stabbing about the room.

Then he did an astonishing thing. He stooped and quickly picked up the smaller of the two boxes, which had evidently served as a seat. He hurled it into the darkest corner of the shed. There was a sudden howl of pain. Then Pons had flung himself on to a vague shadow which stirred from the wall; there was a brief scuffle and the torch fell to the ground.

It was unbroken and I hastily ran to pick it up. By its light I could see that Pons was struggling with an astonishing creature that alternately glowed with unearthly blue light and then as rapidly disappeared as they rolled over. I ran to help him but my companion was already ripping the hideous mask from the creature. The dishevelled, almost pitiful face of a young man was revealed. He had been standing flat against the wall and in the black material he wore had been almost invisible.

"Allow me to present Mr. Norman Knight, our fellow guest from The Harrow Inn. Better known hereabouts as the crawling horror of Grimstone Marsh!"

XI

Pons chuckled grimly, looking down at the baffled figure on the ground.

"You seem to have recovered from your limp in an admirably short time, Mr. Knight."

I stared at the strange tableau in bewilderment.

"I do not understand any of this, Pons."

My companion held up his hand.

"All will be made clear in a very few moments, Parker."

He crossed to the fallen man and helped him up on to the wooden box where he sat, an abject and dejected figure, his head in his hands.

"As you can see, Parker, an ingenious though simple stratagem. The figure of the marsh phantom is painted with the phosphorescent solution on the front only. By simply turning away from the viewer, Mr. Knight could render himself to all intents and purposes invisible on a dark night."

I could not repress a gasp.

"So that was the answer, Pons!"

My companion nodded.

"On the occasions when the phantom suddenly disappeared, he was simply standing still in the centre of the marsh, keeping his back turned. As soon as he heard his victim move away he slipped off this hooded garment, returned to the farm here and secreted the evidence of his wicked charade."

"But what was the point of all this, Pons?"

"You may well ask, Dr. Parker," said young Knight, suddenly

standing up and turning a white but composed face to us. "My masquerade may not be as wicked as you think. Rather regard it in the light of an angel with a flaming sword come to right a great wrong."

"I am not denying your motives," said Solar Pons, with a strange smile, "but you were very mistaken in adopting this particular method to achieve your ends."

We were interrupted at this moment in a highly dramatic fashion.

We had been so absorbed in the drama before us that no one had noticed the faint shadow creeping closer from the door of the shed. Now a figure materialised in the faint beam of Pons' torch. Silas Grimstone's face was distorted with pain and anger and it was with a shock that I saw my pistol clutched in his trembling hands. Pons shot me a reproachful glance but his voice was firm and steady as he turned toward the old man.

"What does this mean, Mr. Grimstone?"

Grimstone stared at us with an ashen countenance; it was obvious his glazed eyes saw nothing but the form of young Knight. His voice, when it came was thick and clotted.

"So, you have come back from the marsh, have you? Well, I put you there once and I can do so again!"

He raised the revolver with a hoarse cry but Pons' reaction was as quick as that of a striking snake. He cannoned into young Knight and the crack of the explosion and the tinkle of glass that followed showed that the bullet had gone through the window.

"Run for your life!" Solar Pons commanded.

He extinguished the torch and I just caught a glimpse of Knight against the lighter square of the doorway before he had gone. There was another shot and then old Grimstone had rushed after him at a lurching run.

"I am sorry, Pons," I said, as the lean form of my friend got to its feet.

Pons switched on his torch again and as he did so we heard the faint crack of an explosion outside on the marsh. "No time for recriminations, Parker. Pray that we shall be able to avoid another tragedy."

Outside, we found the mist thickening a little but it was not difficult to see the direction our quarry had taken. Knight had wisely gone down into the swamp area, where he was obviously at home, instead of across the uplands where he would have made a good target for the revolver.

But the way soon grew twisting, among thick bushes and Pons twice stopped and examined broken reed-stems by the light of the torch. His lean, feral face bore the stamp of great anxiety.

"He has turned aside from the path, Parker. I fear the worst."

A few seconds later we came upon my revolver, where it had fallen barrel first among the reeds. I bent to pick it up and found Pons' hand on my arm.

"It would be unwise to venture farther, Parker."

As he spoke there came an unearthly scream from the misty depths of the marsh ahead. It had such fear and horror in it that I think I shall remember it to my dying day and even Pons' iron nerve was shaken. We stood there as it echoed and reechoed until it finally died away.

"It is all my fault, Pons," I said. "After all your efforts on behalf of your client."

Pons shook his head, a strange expression on his features in the light of the torch. He led the way back to the firmer footing of the path.

"Client or no, Parker, I think the world has seen the last of a damnable villain. If he has not been scared into permanent flight young Knight is the only person who can fill in the missing pieces for us."

I put the revolver back into my pocket and as we stepped up on to the higher ground there was a low rustling in the bushes.

The dishevelled figure of young Knight stepped out on to the path, an obviously shaken and frightened man.

"I swear I did not mean it to end like this, Mr. Pons," he said wildly.

Solar Pons looked at him for a long moment.

"Explanations will keep, Mr. Grimstone," he said slowly. "I suggest we return to the Manor immediately and break the news to your relation."

XII

"I am deeply shocked, but I cannot say I am entirely surprised at this ending, Mr. Pons."

Miss Sylvia Grimstone's face was grey and full of strain but she was quite in command of herself as she sat by the fire in the parlour at Grimstone Manor and poured the thick, hot coffee.

I took the cup from her gratefully, for I was frozen to the bone and the fire in the grate had sunk to a few glowing embers. Young Knight sat at a round table near the fire, midway between myself and Pons and our hostess.

"The police will be here within the hour, Miss Grimstone," said Solar Pons, his restless eyes probing round the room. "I think some explanations are in order before they arrive."

"I would be grateful for some light in this business, Pons, for I am completely in the dark."

My companion smiled wryly as he put down his cup and looked across at the young man who sat, grey-faced and trembling before us.

"As I have said on more than one occasion, Parker, patience is not always your strong suit. However, let me get briefly to the point. As soon as Silas Grimstone had told me his extraordinary story I realised that there would be some perfectly simple explanation. Phantoms do not walk in my book, neither do the dead return to plague the living. Therefore, I was looking for an elaborate masquerade. I wanted a man who knew the marshes; a stranger possibly, who had taken the trouble to map the secret paths; one who probably knew something about Grimstone's past and intended to frighten him by dressing up in the phosphorescent clothing we have already seen."

"But for what purpose, Pons?"

"We are coming to that, Parker. I first needed the method by which the phantom appeared and disappeared in such a startling manner; then a possible refuge in the marsh where he could hide and don his disguise; and finally, some corroboration from others that the apparition was not limited to Grimstone alone. I obtained all three in fairly short order."

Solar Pons stood up and went over to the fireplace; he kicked the fallen embers into life and Miss Grimstone hurried to put on some fresh billets of wood to feed the blaze thus engendered.

"It soon became evident that the costume which our friend here adopted and the method of the lightning disappearances could be explained by only one set of circumstances. My travels round the marsh made it self-evident that such appearances and disappearances would have to be extremely carefully stage-managed or the person involved in the masquerade would rapidly end a victim himself.

"It merely meant that the apparition—created by a luminous chemical solution—was painted on one side of the hooded cloak only. The person wearing it would then merely have to turn his back on his victim to become invisible. Jessel put me on to it when he said it disappeared as though someone had pulled down a blind. My deductions were proved right this evening in all respects when, as I suspected, I saw that the facial image strongly resembled Silas Grimstone himself."

"Pons, you cannot mean it!"

"I was never more serious, my dear fellow," said Solar Pons with a grim smile. "Our walk this morning and the conclusions I drew from the evidence presented to me, made it equally obvious that D'Eath Farm was the only conveniently situated building that would suit. Knight here could not only escape into the marsh but easily reach the main road. When I saw the padlocked door of the abandoned farm building and smelt the distinctive odour of phosphorus, my conclusions were hardened."

"What about your third point, Pons?" I asked.

"That was the most important of all, Parker. The entire deception was designed as an accusation; to appeal to old Silas Grimstone's guilty conscience. He had to be convinced that he—and he alone—had seen a ghost. Unfortunately for our friend here, others became aware of the deception. Among them Dr. Strangeways and the late Tobias Jessel."

Knight was already on his feet with a white face.

"I was not responsible for Jessel's death, Mr. Pons! I swear I only intended to frighten Grimstone into a confession."

"I am well aware of that," said Solar Pons gently. "Jessel undoubtedly fell into the dyke in a drunken stupor."

"What about the cuts on his hands, Pons?" I asked.

My friend shook his head.

"They were typical of death under those circumstances, Parker. The cuts were caused by Jessel's frenzied efforts to get out of the marsh before the cold overcame him. The wounds were made by the jagged edges of the broken ice."

Solar Pons turned away from Miss Grimstone and Knight, who slowly resumed his seat.

"To get back to my point, Parker. I strongly suspected that the so-called phantom had carefully prepared his scheme and that he wished no one but Grimstone to see the figure he had created. You may remember I was particularly careful to ask Grimstone about the circumstances of the occasion when both he and his niece saw the apparition."

"I remember, Pons."

"You will recall that Miss Grimstone suddenly appeared from behind a fringe of bushes, and I commended that fact to you. Knight did not even know she was there. In fact he was himself frightened by her sudden shriek and immediately made off. Is that not so?"

"Indeed, Mr. Pons."

Young Knight lowered his head and looked the very figure of contrition. I shot a puzzled glance at Pons and then at Miss Grimstone, who sat behind the coffee pot with tightly compressed lips. The clock ticked sonorously in the corner and it seemed impossible that the incredible drama of an hour ago had taken old Silas Grimstone so dramatically from us.

"You may remember also, Parker, that I was particularly intent on discovering the circumstances of the phantom's appearances to the old man. No true apparition, if such a thing existed, would make a noise when it appeared or disappeared; therefore, it was manufactured. We have already dealt with the matter of any traces it made being swallowed up by the mud and water, though there was enough evidence from the reeds and broken grasses to establish the passage of some heavy body. The zig-zagging motion the thing made was because it had to keep to the firm paths to avoid being sucked under.

"You may also recall, Parker, I took some trouble when we were out on the marsh, in examining the dyke near Grimstone Manor, the spot where both old Grimstone and Tobias Jessel had their frightening experiences with the fiery blue figure. Jessel was not meant to see the phantom. Knight was hanging about in his guise, down below the dyke, waiting to see if old Grimstone was coming out. He did not hear Jessel walking along the road above and thus blundered on him accidentally. I submit that this reading is correct as I could not hear your footsteps, Parker, when I was at the foot of the bank, a long way below the level of the road."

"You are perfectly correct, Mr. Pons," said Knight with a groan. "It happened exactly as you said. And I can swear that I was nowhere near poor Jessel on the night of his death."

"I believe you, Mr. Knight," said Solar Pons slowly. "And can so testify to the police if necessary."

I looked at my companion in amazement.

"This case began with a client being terrified by a phantom, Pons, and now it appears to be ending with the client as the villain and the attempted murderer as an innocent man!"

"Does it not, Parker," said Solar Pons with a dry chuckle.

There was silence for a brief moment. It was broken by young Knight who seemed to be recovering his spirits as Pons proceeded. "How did you come to suspect me, Mr. Pons?"

"I had a good many people who might have superficially fitted the bill," said Solar Pons. "They included Dr. Strangeways and a farmer on the marsh; our man might even have been concealed in a party of walkers who descended on the village. But I was looking for a young and active man; one who had a strong motive for treating old Grimstone so; one who had mastered all the paths and tracks of the marsh."

I looked at Pons in rising irritation.

"But how on earth could you have reasoned all this, Pons? We hardly knew Mr. Knight."

Solar Pons smiled, sending out a stream of aromatic blue smoke toward the ceiling.

"All this came to me very slowly, Parker. And there was not a great deal of data to go on. But when I inspected the hotel register and found that Mr. Knight had come to The Harrow in September, only a few weeks before Mr. Grimstone's ghostly manifestations began, my suspicions began to crystallize. Then, when Mr. Knight boldly introduced himself and I was able to study him close at hand, I immediately saw light. It was a masterstroke, Mr. Knight, to make such a dramatic entrance, though there was some risk that Dr. Strangeways might have examined your supposedly injured ankle."

To my astonishment young Knight gave a low chuckle.

"There is no getting around you, Mr. Pons. I reasoned, quite correctly, as it turned out, that Dr. Strangeways would not want to be bothered with anything so trivial, especially as he was enjoying a social evening at the hotel. Where did I go wrong?"

Solar Pons smiled thinly.

"When you came into the saloon bar you were limping with the right leg. The following morning, when we saw you just after breakfast, you limped on the left."

I looked at Pons thunderstruck and even Miss Grimstone had to smile.

"But why all this masquerade and why the limp, Pons?"

"To provide an alibi, Parker," said my companion patiently. "An injured man could not leap agilely about the marsh in that fashion. The solution came to me rather late. It was the facial resemblance, you see."

"Facial resemblance, Pons?"

Solar Pons nodded dreamily, his eyes half-closed.

"Unless I miss my guess, Mr. Knight is a close relative of Silas Grimstone. I would hazard his nephew."

Miss Grimstone closed her eyes and appeared much moved by the disclosure.

She breathed heavily.

"You are perfectly right, Mr. Pons."

"But why would Grimstone's nephew want to drive him out of his wits, Pons?" I cried somewhat wildly.

"One of the oldest motives known to mankind, Parker. Revenge. Miss Grimstone herself supplied the missing fragments of my pattern on the marsh this morning. She said that Jethro Grimstone, the partner in the firm, went to Australia many years ago. It can never be proved now but I submit that his body is lying out there in the depths of the marsh somewhere. Mr. Knight—or rather Mr.

Grimstone here—had come back from Australia and decided to take the law into his own hands to obtain a confession from his uncle. He would need an accomplice for that, Miss Grimstone, would he not?"

Our hostess drew herself up, tiny spots of red burning on her cheeks.

"I know how it must look, Mr. Pons, but there was great justification for what young John Grimstone did."

She looked across at him as though for silent corroboration. Grimstone stirred himself and stared at us with sombre eyes.

"It is an old story, Mr. Pons, and goes back many years but I want you to know the truth. My father was a good man; he built the family firm, though there was always bad blood between the brothers. Old Silas Grimstone was a dreadful and miserly man. My mother told me a great deal about the situation as I grew older. As I have said, I was only a child when the events I am referring to occurred. My family were well-off and we lived at Grimstone Manor here in some style. All that was soon to change. My father told my mother a good deal about his suspicions but she was never able to prove anything.

"To bring a long story to a speedy end, Mr. Pons, my father simply disappeared one day. He was out on the marsh and never returned. Neither was his body recovered. A man resembling Silas Grimstone was seen at the nearest railway station, but my uncle maintained that he was in London all that day. He told us that my father had to go to Australia on business suddenly. The idea was ridiculous, particularly as he and mother were very close. He would never have gone off like that without discussing it beforehand. In any case he had taken neither clothing nor luggage. It is my firm belief that Silas Grimstone waylaid my father on a lonely path in the marsh, attacked him from behind, perhaps with a heavy stone as a weapon, and then threw him into the quicksand."

The young man paused and stared at us with a haggard face.

"But a strange thing happened. A letter eventually came from Australia. It is my belief it was a forgery, committed at Grimstone's instructions. It was from a hotel in Adelaide and said father had to go out there on business for the firm; that we were not to worry; and that he would return eventually. My mother showed the letter to a number of friends but the forgery had been skillfully done and everyone said it was father's hand. Grimstone then put it about that the firm's affairs were in disorder and that father had fled to avoid being compromised in unscrupulous conduct.

"The final bombshell was a will, drawn up in Silas Grimstone's favour and apparently signed by my father. It left the house and the business to his brother. Of course, my mother fought the matter in the courts, but after some years the decision went against us. She was penniless and had to give up the house. Eventually she scraped some money together and we sailed to a new life in Australia. But mother was broken in mind and body and she herself hardly knew what to believe. She had some hope that we would be reunited with father in Adelaide but of course there was no such hotel as that in the letter and we never did find him. She had told me of her suspicions as I grew older, and I progressed to manhood with a burning desire for revenge. Mother died a few months ago and I felt free to return, the remainder of the family being settled, and myself a bachelor. I heard that Silas Grimstone still lived, made my way to Kent and perfected my plan. It seemed perfectly apposite to me. I modelled the phosphorescent hood on an old photograph of my father's features. I met Miss Grimstone on the marsh from time to time. She recognized the family likeness and I confided in her."

There was a long and deep silence, broken only by Pons knocking out his pipe in the fireplace.

"What have you to say to that, Miss Grimstone?"

"It is true, Mr. Pons. My uncle, by his manner, and furtive behaviour over the years regarding his brother had aroused my suspicions. He was pathologically frightened of anything to do with the marsh, though paradoxically, he felt compelled to go out at night on occasion."

"Perhaps he wished to make sure the body of this young man's father remained undisturbed in its burial place on the marsh," said Solar Pons sombrely.

Miss Grimstone shuddered and her face changed colour.

"Perhaps, Mr. Pons. But with this background, rightly or wrongly, my sympathies were with John Grimstone, once I had heard his story. I have suffered a good deal under my uncle's regime here all these years. I am afraid I am not at all sorry at how it has turned out. But I must make it clear I did not know anything of the apparition, or exactly what John Grimstone intended."

"I did not say I condemned either of you," said Solar Pons quickly. "And Silas Grimstone would certainly have killed young Mr. Grimstone had not the marsh claimed him at an opportune moment."

"I helped John Grimstone to his revenge," said Miss Grimstone slowly and deliberately. "I informed him of the old man's movements and when he might be going out. We hoped for a full confession."

"You need say no more," said Solar Pons. "I think we might leave it there."

Both Miss Grimstone and the young man turned surprised faces toward my companion.

John Grimstone cleared his throat.

"I am not quite sure I understand you, Mr. Pons."

"I am not a moral judge, Mr. Grimstone," said Solar Pons. "I think we will leave the dead to bury the dead. I am convinced of the truth of your story and that rough justice has been done."

Miss Grimstone let out her breath in a long sigh.

"You are a good man, Mr. Pons."

Solar Pons chuckled.

"Let us just say, Miss Grimstone, that little would be served by further scandal. We will inform the police when they arrive that Silas Grimstone has disappeared on the marsh. There will be a search but nothing will be found. It will be a nine-day wonder and nothing more."

There was silence for a moment and then Miss Grimstone gave Solar Pons her hand.

"I will myself settle your fee, Mr. Pons."

There was an awkward silence.

"It was providence, Mr. Pons. This young man has been robbed of his patrimony. We cannot recompense him for the death of his father or the injustices he has suffered. But I feel free, as Silas Grimstone's beneficiary, to offer him his rightful half-share in the company and a place here at the Manor with me. On my death the property and the business would revert to him, as I have no other kin."

"Justice, indeed, Parker," said Solar Pons softly. "Providence moves in mysterious ways."

And he said no more on the subject.

The Gumshoe
SEVEN STARS EPISODE THREE

THE TROUBLE WITH BARRYMORE
by KIM NEWMAN

This PI narrator works in the mean streets of Raymond Chandler's Los Angeles. He's not quite Philip Marlowe—less Humphrey Bogart or Dick Powell and more Ed Bishop (who played Marlowe on BBC Radio 4 in the 1970s).

The character first appeared in the 'The Big Fish' (originally written for Shadows Over Innsmouth *[1994] but first published in* Interzone *#76 [1993]), which also featured the versions of Edwin Winthrop and Geneviève Dieudonné who appear in 'Seven Stars'. The Gumshoe is also featured in 'Castle in the Desert' (*Anno Dracula: Johnny Alucard, *2013), while Special Agent Finlay turns up again in the forthcoming 'Red Jacks Wild'. Raymond Chandler's Marlowe first appeared in the novel* The Big Sleep *(1939).*

The anecdote about Errol Flynn and John Barrymore's corpse is told with several different supporting casts. The author first came across it in Otto Friedrich's book City of Nets *(1986). Special Agent Finlay previously appeared in the stories 'The Big Fish' and 'The McCarthy Witch Hunt' (*The Original Dr. Shade and Other Stories, *1994).*

Anyone interested enough in psychic detectives to read this book will recognise the little group gathered at Winthrop's house.

"YOU ARE A private detective?" asked the little pop-eyed man with the Peter Lorre voice. "Yes?"

"That's what the sign says," I quipped.

My caller stepped nervously around the office door, and giggled the way he did in the movies. He *was* Peter Lorre.

"Can you be trusted with a confidential matter?"

"If I couldn't, I might be tempted to fib about it."

His giggle became a laugh. The laugh you usually heard when he was torturing someone. It made a person nervous.

"I should have thought of that. You are an astute fellow."

"In my business, it sometimes helps to be honest. If I weren't, would my office look like this?"

Lorre looked at my filing cabinet, and took in the fizzing neon sign out in the street too close to my window. The sun was just down, and night people were rising from their murphy beds and coming out of their holes. My place of business did not look much like the elegant suite Bogart has in *The Maltese Falcon*. Then again, Sam Spade was a San Francisco dick.

"You were recommended to me by Janey Wilde."

That figured. They had been in a Mr. Moto movie together, two years ago when Hollywood could make films with Japanese good guys. I hadn't seen Janey since I handed back her missing child three months ago. She had called me in on a case I didn't like to think about, a case that didn't jibe with the way I had always assumed the world went.

If she had sent the talking screen's premier sadist to my office, I had a suspicion that the world was about to take another kink. I'd crossed that line once, from the place where mysteries can be wrapped up and the bodies stayed buried, into *Weird Tales* country.

"She impressed upon me your abilities at locating and returning missing persons."

Besides everything else, I had got her back her baby. That made me a hero, I guess. She'd given me a big bonus but, what with the war and everything, the town had forgotten to throw a parade and give me the key to the girls' locker-room.

"Who's walked away?" I asked, hoping to jog Lorre out of his circumlocutory flirtation.

" 'Walked' is not such an apt expression. You have heard, of course, of the Great Profile, John Barrymore." He pronounced it 'profeel', which—judging by what I had heard of Prince Jack—was not inappropriate.

"He died last week," I said.

I was sorry as hell about it. I'd never met the man, but he had great talent and had drank it away. It was hard not to feel something about that.

"I hope you don't want me to investigate a murder. That's the cops' business and they'd rather I left them to it. Besides, I understand Mr. Barrymore succumbed to what might best be called 'natural causes'. "

Lorre shrugged.

"John Barrymore is dead. There is no doubt about that. As dead as Sessue Hayakawa's career prospects. But he is also a missing person. I want you to find him, and bring him back to the Pierce Brothers Mortuary on Sunset Boulevard. For this, I will pay one hundred dollars."

"For this, you will pay twenty-five dollars a day. Plus expenses. My fees are not on a sliding scale."

Lorre spread his hands and hunched his shoulders, accepting my terms.

"Someone has snatched Barrymore's body?"

"Regrettably, that is so. I am ashamed to confess that I am that someone. Do not think me callous. I am a European as yet unused to the brutalities of this frontier culture. I was suborned into the act by a well-respected father figure, the director Raoul Walsh.

"As an amateur of psychology, I have been conducting extensive self-analysis for years. I recognise in myself a lamentable need to accept the authority of a patriarch. It is a common European failing, most tragically represented by the general adulation of Hitler. He offered me a high position in the Reich film industry, despite my 'mongrel' Hungarian background. I wired him that Germany had room for only one mass murderer of his talents and mine.

"I digress. I'm sorry. It is through embarrassment. Mr. Walsh, a forceful individual who is in a position to advance my career should he so choose, suggested I join him in a cruel practical joke at the expense of his friend, Mr. Errol Flynn."

Lorre wandered around my tiny office as he spoke, picking up and putting things down, as if given bits of business by the director. I wondered if, after years of self-analysis, he realised he was repeating his act from *The Maltese Falcon*.

"Mr. Flynn was greatly upset by the passing of Mr. Barrymore. He also has a tendency to idolise father figures, and saw in Barrymore perhaps the end result of his own dissolution. He organised a wake at the Cock and Bull, a bar catering to the more theatrical type of alcoholic. John Carradine recited speeches from *Hamlet*.

"David Niven recounted anecdotes of dubious provenance. A great deal of liquour was consumed. Flynn himself told stories of Barrymore's genius and tragedy. He became extremely intoxicated and was struck with a fit of melancholy. At that point, Mr. Walsh suggested a somewhat macabre practical joke, which we hurried to put into action."

Lorre paused. I was following the story. Working in Hollywood, you get used to the namedropping.

"At the end of the evening, Flynn was incapable of returning to his home unassisted. A taxicab was arranged. With drunken difficulty, he opened the front door of his house and switched on the lights, to be confronted with John Barrymore, unembalmed, sprawled in a chair in his hallway. The effect must have been considerable.

"You see, while Flynn was drinking, Walsh and myself surreptitiously left the Cock and Bull and made our way to the mortuary, where we bribed an attendant. We borrowed the body and transported it across town in Walsh's car, broke into Flynn's house, and propped up the corpse where he would find it. Imagine the ghastly sight it presented. Corpses have an unhealthy, pale glow in the moonlight. And Barrymore's face, empty of life, was a puffy mask of his former self. A truly grotesque thing."

This sort of thing happens more than you'd think. As Lorre said, Hollywood is a frontier town. Nobodies are elevated to positions of wealth and power in a few short months and then transformed back into nobodies again. Every prince has his court of hangers-on, jesters, assassins, freaks, witch doctors and courtesans.

"So Barrymore is at Flynn's house?" I deduced. "Why don't you just go over there and snatch him back? Flynn must be out cold by now."

Lorre smiled again. His teeth were not good.

"Naturally, that was our plan. But when we returned at dawn this morning, we found Flynn's front door hanging open, the chair knocked over, and no sign of either Flynn or the *corpus*. Various of our party have been searching the predictable sinkholes of vice and depravity all day, but we have reached the end of our resources. It has been decided that you are to be commissioned to bring this regrettable matter to a swift, happy and most of all unpublicised conclusion."

I sensed that under all the irony and his *mysterioso* screen image, Lorre was pretty much disgusted at what he had done. Then again, ninety-nine out of a hundred actors in this town would French-kiss a leper if a big-shot director like Walsh suggested it. Father figures and idolatry aside, it made sense to keep happy someone who could turn you from a drunken Tasmanian pretty boy into Errol Flynn.

"You think Flynn still has the corpse?"

Lorre shrugged again. "It is most likely. Unless both have been kidnapped by another party."

"You've left someone at Flynn's house? In case he comes back."

Lorre nodded. "Of course. Mr. Walsh took charge, and made sensible arrangements. He is a man of action."

Lorre gave me a hundred dollars as a retainer. It came in whiskey-circled five- and ten-spots, with a few crumpled singles, probably from a bar-room whip-round. I imagined Walsh not having small enough bills on him to contribute.

We shook hands on it. I had a client. I had a case. I had a headache.

"Hold, sirrah!"

A long-legged figure, cloaked in darkness (and a cloak), stood tall in Errol Flynn's hallway, an accusing foil pointed at my breast pocket. He had shoulder-length hair and a Buffalo Bill beard. His eyes were watery with a whiskey-ish tinge. I recognised John Carradine.

"I'm the detective," I said. "Peter Lorre sent me."

He stepped back, and saluted, slapping his long nose with the edge of his foil.

"Enter freely, friend. Thou most worthy servant of the higher law."

Flynn lived in a big house up on Mulholland Drive. I'd heard the stories and expected *boudoir* decor, complete with velvet curtains and pictures of fat little naked people on fat little naked cushions. In fact, the place was in disappointingly good taste.

He even had books. Not sawn-off spines glued together to make a novelty door for a hidden cocktail bar. Not privately published, gorgeously illustrated pornography. Proper books, by fellows such as Shakespeare, Scott, Stevenson and Conrad.

On its side in the hallway was a comfortable armchair. I imagined it stood up, with a dead actor sprawled in it. Not a lovely image.

Carradine bobbed around like a scarecrow on strings as I inspected the scene of the crime. Like Lorre, he knew how to cast himself. In his life, he was a courtier. Others might be Hamlet or Claudius, but he was down for Horatio or Osric. He knew when to put in a "fie on it" or a "message, sire!" and could swish his sword with the best of them. At this precise moment, he was getting in my way more than was advisable.

There were two possibilities. Flynn had taken the body and run off, either in a fit of insanity or as a joke to get back at Walsh. Or someone had intervened and snatched the both of them.

Actually, there was a third possibility. Three months ago, I'd have ruled it out altogether. But on a derelict gambling ship out in the Bay my opinion of the world had taken a tumble. Barrymore could have got up, and taken Flynn with him to the world of the dead.

To Flynn, Barrymore might be Jacob Marley. His fate was a hideously plausible prediction of the destination at the end of the road the younger man was taking. Was Flynn even now being shown the drunken ruination he could expect if he didn't reform?

No. That sort of thing didn't happen.

In books and movies, the supernatural has a point. The ghosts teach Scrooge a lesson. My experience was that nothing could be learned from the inexplicable. Like in the cartoons, pianos sometimes fell from the sky and squashed random people into pancakes.

There was no point in trying to make sense of this. If Barrymore were dragging a dead leg around the Hollywood hills like Tom

Tyler in *The Mummy's Hand*, was that any more insane than the idea of propping up a dead matinee idol in a movie star's hallway just for laughs?

I looked around, for clues. The door-lock was smashed in, showing raw wood where the mechanism had been wrenched away. That didn't square with what Lorre told me.

"When they planted the body, how did they get in?"

Carradine hung his head to one side in a posture classically intended to display thought to the gallery.

"French windows at the back," he said.

Lorre told me Flynn came home and, with drunken difficulty, unlocked his front door. But Lorre hadn't been there. He was imagining the plan as Walsh intended it. Had Flynn been so drunk that he decided not to bother with keys and smashed down his own front door?

It depended on what kind of drunk he was. If he were so soused he couldn't use a key, he would most likely be incapable of the physical task of kicking in a door—not an easy thing off the screen, even if you are Captain Blood and Robin Hood in one. In any case, it was more probable that Flynn would go round the back and get in easily through the French windows (as demonstrated by Walsh's body-snatching party) or take the easy option of sleeping it off in the garden.

I examined the lock. It had been professionally broken. A hefty shoulder had been applied. And a telltale black gouge suggested the involvement of a crowbar.

So someone else had broken in after Walsh. Someone better at smashing down doors but not as familiar with the property.

I reconstructed the crime, crossing the Flynn threshold and imagining myself as the wobbly movie star.

Dropped off in his driveway, he weaves his way up to his front door and finds it broken in. Lorre, in his reconstruction, imagined Flynn coming face to face with the dead Barrymore. That was possible. But he must be alerted by the broken lock to the fact that something is wrong. That percolates through even the most drunken brain. He steps warily into the hallway, imagining himself the hero of his movie, too drunk to be as cautious and cowardly as anyone who didn't think he was Errol Flynn would be.

Standing in his doorway, in a sort of vestibule between the door and the hall, I thought it through. There was a table by the door. In a bowl on the table were a bunch of keys, a money-clip well-filled with bills and a five-hundred dollar watch. Flynn goes through the ritual of divesting himself of these items after stepping into his house, all the while trying fuzzily to think about the broken door. Is there danger inside?

I stepped out of the vestibule and reached out. I touched the light-switch he must have flicked. I turned the lights off and then on again.

Flynn's eyes would be dazzled.

And he sees?

Barrymore, certainly. Maybe Walsh's joke goes as planned, and Flynn is terror-struck by the apparition. A puffy-faced, bloodless corpse.

But someone else—most likely, several someones—is there too, about their own business. Probably ill-doing of some sort. This place stank of it.

"Something is rotten in the state of Denmark," I opined.

"You can say that again, buddy," Carradine nodded sagely.

As I drove to the Pierce Brothers Mortuary, I thought about the case. The most likely and comforting solution, ridiculous as it sounds, was that Walsh chose to play his prank by coincidence on the night some entirely unconnected thieves decided to break into the Flynn mansion. The thieves get a surprise when they find Barrymore and are themselves surprised by a returning Flynn, and flee the scene, kidnapping the living and the dead.

It didn't play in Peoria. No matter how spooked they were by the body-snatching business, I couldn't imagine thieves who specialise in homes of the rich and famous but leave behind several thousand dollars of untraceable notes and an expensive watch. Not the sort of oversight you expect of the larcenous professional.

That meant the two break-ins at the Flynn place were connected. The second was a consequence of the first. The unknown persons were after Barrymore's body.

I wondered about the more fanatical fans. All the women who supposedly committed suicide when God took Valentino away. With a queasy stomach turnover, I remembered whispers about corrupt morgue attendants who took back-handers to let ghoulish busybodies peer and pry and poke at celebrity corpses. There were stories about Jean Harlow you don't want to hear.

This was California, central clearing house for cults. Mostly harmless kook groups, but there were others—I had shivery memories of the Esoteric Order of Dagon in Bay City—who were deeply dangerous.

Did some crazed John Barrymore worshipper out there have enough *tana* leaves to bring him back for one last private performance?

It was a fine spring night. With the windows of the Chrysler rolled down, I could smell orange blossom and gasoline on the Los Angeles breeze. There was a war on, of course. But there were always wars on.

The Mortuary was a single-story structure with a lot of stucco, and a couple of palm trees in the sidewalk outside. They had a marquee, presumably to announce their big funerals. Barrymore, lucky to get work in Bulldog Drummond "B" pictures these last few years, was back on top again, name in big black letters. This was the last place a star wanted to get billing. Though when Carradine went, he'd be lucky to rate a mention on the "Also Dead" roster posted outside.

There's a guy who always plays mortuary attendants in movies. A little, skinny, bald, pockmarked character with a voice that reminds you of Karloff and eyes that light up when he thinks of a nice, cold grave. His name is Milton Parsons.

I could swear he moonlights at Pierce Brothers. He was behind the desk, a bellhop in a mausoleum, reading a funeral directors' trade magazine. The cover story was about a shortage of coffin materials, what with the war effort claiming most of the nation's lumber and brass. Wasn't that just like the government, making the undertaker's job difficult at the same time it was supplying him with more corpses?

I showed him my badge. It's very impressive.

"I've come about Barrymore," I said.

I didn't have to ask if he were the attendant Walsh had bribed. He gulped, adam's apple bobbing over his wing-collar. He looked sallow and guilty.

"I was assured by Mr. Walsh . . ." he began.

"That's okay, fella. There's a war on. Rules don't necessarily apply."

He smiled, displaying a creepy slice of dentition that made his face even more skull-like. I wondered how much he'd have charged for a feel of Jean Harlow. I tried to keep my stomach down.

"Have there been any other unusual inquiries concerning Mr. Barrymore?"

His eyes glittered. "A great many have called to pay their respects. Several studio heads . . ."

None of whom would have given him work last week.

". . . and a remarkable number of ladies."

Barrymore had been famously profligate in that department since the turn of the century.

"If I might say so, it is becoming an embarrassment that the star is not, as it were, appearing on stage. An understudy will not suffice."

"I'm doing my best to get him back."

"I should hope so."

I imagined Barrymore laughing. Wherever he was.

"Since Walsh took him away, have there been any other *insistent* inquiries?"

"Oh, all of them."

"Unusually insistent. Groups of people, not single mourners. With perhaps a hefty member of the party, a chauffeur or bodyguard."

I was thinking of the type of muscle used to smash in doors.

"Maybe of an occult bent. You know, creepy types?"

He thought about it. He shuddered.

"Yes, sir. Indeed. Groups of that description have called. Two of them."

I closed my mouth. "Two?"

"Shortly after Mr. Walsh and Mr. Lorre departed, an Irish fellow demanded to be allowed to see the corpse. He offered quite a considerable emolument."

The attendant must have been sick to have gone with the first offer.

"He became quite abusive when we were unable to strike an agreement. He was accompanied by two unusual individuals. I didn't get much of a look at them, but they struck me as *wrong* somehow. I had the impression that they wore rather too much scent. To cover another smell, perhaps."

"This Irishman. I don't suppose you got his name?"

The attendant shook his head. He did not enjoy remembering this encounter. I had hit upon something that spooked him.

Imagine how that made me feel.

"Didn't he give you some way to get in touch with him, when the corpse was returned, so you could do business?"

The attendant froze, and clammed up. I filled it in for him.

"You told him about Walsh. You told him who had the body. He paid you."

He didn't contradict me.

"You said Barrymore was at Errol Flynn's house."

"No," he admitted. "Is that true?"

"Did Walsh have much of a start on the Mystery Man?"

"An hour or so."

It was impossible that the Irishman had tailed Walsh. Somehow, he had homed in on Barrymore. Did the dead actor come equipped with some sort of beacon?

My head was hurting more.

"And the second group?" I asked. "You said two suspicious groups made inquiries."

"I told them nothing."

"So they weren't paying. Who were they?"

"An Englishman, a French-accented woman and an American who claimed to be a federal agent. The Englishman did most of the talking. He left his card."

He left that up in the air. I didn't reach into my pocket. There was no need to put a bribe down to expenses yet.

"Do the Pierce Brothers still own the mortuary?" I asked. "And are they aware of your sideline?"

The attendant scowled and pulled the card out of thin air like a conjurer. He handed it over.

I knew the name before I saw it.

EDWIN WINTHROP. THE DIOGENES CLUB. LONDON.

He had been around the Janey Wilde business also, along with a French woman named Geneviève Dieudonné and a fed called Finlay.

I had the impression that Winthrop's special field of interest was *Weird Tales* country.

There was a telephone number on the back of the card.

"Because no money was involved, you didn't tell Winthrop about the Irishman, did you?"

The attendant looked down at his shoes. I shook my head, almost in admiration.

If Edwin Winthrop was surprised to hear from me, he didn't betray it in his even, chatty tones. I mentioned that I was looking for an actor, a recently deceased one, and that his name had come up in the investigation.

"In that case, you better pop out here for a chat. We're holed up in Coldwater Canyon. Just a couple of houses down from Boris Karloff."

He laughed that off. If Bela Lugosi was involved in this, then all the screen's bogeymen would be represented. That wasn't my kind of movie.

I took the address, which was on Bowmont Drive.

"Careful how you go," Winthrop advised me. "The turns get a bit sticky. And a lot of the signs have been taken down, to fool Japanese invaders."

I knew that.

I drove out to Coldwater Canyon. This was going to be an all-night case. It seemed to me that everyone involved slept only in the day, like Dracula. Except Barrymore, and he was supposed to be sleeping all the time.

I knew next to nothing about Winthrop. He had some official position, but wasn't keen on specifics. There were worse things waiting man than death, Hamlet had said—and John Carradine would agree with him—and that was something princes and governments had always known, and always done their best to conceal from the rabble. I knew that all governments must have people like Winthrop—or our own Special Agent Finlay—to take care of those things, discreetly and without public honour. I didn't like to think how busy they might be.

I couldn't spot Karloff's house, and it took me a while to find Winthrop's hideout. The whole street was ordinary. It was an ordinary house. A Flippino houseboy led me out onto the patio, where a group of people sat around the swimming pool. The moon was bright, and the only artificial light came from the glowworm ends of cigars and cigarettes.

Winthrop wore a white dinner jacket and was smoking a foot-long Cuban cigar. A black cat was nestled in his arms, blinking contentedly. Winthrop grinned to see me.

Geneviève Dieudonné, who wore something silvery and clinging that suggested a resistance to the quiet cool of the night air, arose elegantly from a recliner and gave me a dazzling smile. She said she was pleased to see me again.

A grunt from the other man I knew, Special Agent Finlay, suggested he disagreed with his French associate. He waved a paw at me, sucked his cigarette dead, then lit another.

There were other people around the pool. I would have thought them a party, but the only drink in sight was tea, served in mugs not the best china. This was a meeting and, from the slightly electric air, I guessed an urgent one.

Winthrop introduced me around.

A behemoth of a man whose weight was barely supported by a reinforced deckchair was Judge Keith Pursuivant, a jurist I had never heard of but who greeted me in oratorical Southern style. He wore a voluminous cloak and a wide hat, and might have been Carradine inflated to the size of a dirigible. Also present were a fellow called Thunstone, an academic named Leffing, a little Frenchman whose name I missed, a physician named Silence, and an American with too many Gs in his name to be credible.

"Have you heard of the Jewel of Seven Stars?" Winthrop asked.

"A racehorse?"

Winthrop laughed, and chucked the cat under the chin. "No.

A gemstone. One of the treasures of Ancient Egypt. An item of immense occult significance."

"*Nom d'un nom*," cursed the Frenchman. "A psychic *bombe*, of incalculable magnitude."

"Let me guess, someone else has it, and you want it?"

"You see through us entirely."

"It's for the war effort," Finlay said, dourly.

"We're throwing stones at Japan now?"

Strangely, nobody laughed at that. Which gave me a chill. This group might have its comical aspects, but they were deadly serious about their fabulous jewel.

"If it comes to that," Geneviève said, "the War might be well lost."

"Set against us in this business are a crew of very dangerous characters," Winthrop explained.

"An Irishman?" I ventured.

"You are up on this. Yes, Bennett Mountmain is the man to watch. A worse dastard than his uncle, if that's possible."

Bennett Mountmain. I had a name.

"He was kicked out of Ireland by the priests. He still claims to be the rightful king or some such rot. We know he's been knocking about in bad places. Haiti, Transylvania, Berlin. Like that swine Crowley in the last show, he's been working for the Huns. He's in close with Hitler's crackpot mages. And he's after the jewel.

"We think the Nazis have the spear of Longinus. Combine that with the Jewel of Seven Stars, and they might trump our Ark of the Covenant. We'd need Excalibur *and* the Holy Grail to beat that."

"And the Maltese Falcon?" I asked.

"Oh, that's real too. The Knights Templar still have it. By now, it might be charged with some minor power. We don't need to bother with that. Do we, Gees?"

The fellow with all the Gs nodded. These people had a complex private history I didn't want to go into.

You might not think it to look at me, but I do know what the spear of Longinus is. Also known as the *heilige lance*. And everybody's heard of Excalibur and the Holy Grail. From that, I could deduce the sort of item this Jewel of Seven Stars was supposed to be.

"Mountmain has the jewel," Judge Pursuivant boomed. His tones were impressive enough to disturb coyotes out in the canyon. "All is lost."

"He may have the jewel," Winthrop said. "But that's not the half of it. Getting it out of its vessel is notoriously a sticky business. We know that it is to be done at dawn, and in this mysterious White House of the prophecy. Mountmain's uncle couldn't manage it, which is why we're here all these years later. And the last twenty years will have shaped its aura in all manner of configurations. When you think of the life John Barrymore has lived. The heights, the depths, the triumphs, the humiliations, the genius, the despair. How much was Barrymore and how much the jewel? And how has all this *experience* affected the stone?"

Winthrop was excited, whereas the rest of his company was scared. Maybe he was a man of greater vision than they. Or maybe he was mad.

"We should be in Washington," Finlay said, gloomily. "We've missed the thing here. We should be there at dawn. The President himself might be in danger."

Winthrop wasn't convinced.

"We have Washington covered. And North Africa. And *Maison Blanche* in New Orleans."

Finlay killed another cigarette.

"This jewel," I asked. "You say it's in a vessel?"

Winthrop nodded, happily.

"What kind of vessel?"

"Why, John Barrymore's body, of course."

About midnight I was back in my office in the Cahuenga Building, telephoning hospitals and morgues, asking if a surplus stiff might have washed their way, one that seemed oddly familiar if looked at from the side. It was proper detective work, and as tedious and pointless as hell.

Someone—most likely this Bennett Mountmain bird—had John Barrymore, and inside the Great Profile was a rare and fabulously valuable jewel. Of course, if Mountmain hacked out the Seven Stars and dumped the body somewhere I could find it, then I'd still be living up to the letter of my mission. Lorre wanted the body back, not some priceless MacGuffin hidden inside it.

I was not yet suspicious enough to wonder whether Lorre had known about the Jewel of Seven Stars. He was only a sinister conspirator in the movies.

After the call-round was finished, I hit a few bars where newsmen hang out and invested some of Lorre's money in buying drinks and pumping for information. You can imagine the sort of newsman who has to stay behind in Los Angeles while all the decent writers head off to become war correspondents, and who also happens to be an after-midnight boozer.

I knew a lot of fellows like that.

Having struck Milton Parsons, I wondered if I'd come across a convenient squealer who was the spitting image of Elisha Cook, Jr. a shifty, sad-eyed little man who had the secret of the plot and was willing to swap it for a pathetic sliver of conversation. Of course, if I found an Elisha it was most likely he would wind up horribly dead by dawn, as an example.

Sometimes, it doesn't work out like that.

Nobody had even heard of Bennett Mountmain.

I got back to my office at about three, and found men waiting for me. I walked right into trouble. A fist sunk into my gut before I could get my hat off. Someone tried to take my coat off without unbuttoning it, yanking it from my shoulders to improvise a straitjacket. I heard my spiffy coat rip as I was trussed.

The man-handlers were a couple of blank-faced goons in shabby overcoats. They smelled like Tijuana whores, but I didn't get fairy vibrations off them. They wore the scent to cover another smell. That was a familiar note.

In my chair sat a man with a gun. It was a very nice gun, an automatic. He showed it to me without actually pointing it anywhere, twirling it by the trigger guard. I happened to notice that the safety catch wasn't on. My visitor was a locked-room murder mystery waiting to happen.

"Twenty years I've waited," my visitor said.

He had an Irish accent, soft but sinister. I knew who this was, but didn't say so.

"And before that, my uncle wasted a lifetime. To be so close to the achievement of such a purpose and have it snatched away. Do you have any idea, you foolish little detective, what that kind of frustration can make a person do?"

I was just deducing something when the gun went off. A bullet spanged off my filing cabinet, putting a dent in it and ringing the mostly empty thing like a coffin-shaped bell. The bullet ricocheted my way, and thunked into the meaty shoulder of one of the men holding me.

He didn't say a thing. He barely even moved. I saw a slow trickle of dark blood seep into his sleeve. The man's lack of complaint frightened me.

Mountmain was pointing the gun now. At me.

"Where is it?" he asked.

"This is where I say, 'I don't know what you're talking about,' and you sneer, 'but of course you do, foolish little detective' "—I liked the phrase—"and try to beat it out of me for an hour or two. The flaw in your plan is that I really don't know what you're talking about."

There was no harm trying it on.

"You are working for the Diogenes Club," he sneered. His favoured mode of expression was the sneer.

"I am working for Mr. Moto."

Deliberately, he shot the man he had wounded. This time, he put a bullet in the man's forehead. His hat blew off in a red cloud. No matter how John Barrymore looked, this fellow looked worse. The trickling hole between his eyebrows didn't help.

"That's someone I rely on and, in a strange sort of way, am fond of," Mountmain said. "Now imagine what I'll do to you, whom I've never met before and to whom I've taken an intense dislike."

"This would have something to do with a recently deceased Sweet Prince?"

"Give the man a goldfish."

"And a rock?"

Mountmain's sneer verged on a snarl.

"A rock? You could call it that. If you were a very stupid person indeed."

I did my best to shrug. Not easy.

Until five minutes ago, I'd assumed Mountmain had Barrymore. Certainly, that was what Winthrop thought. And he had read the program, which gave away all the story I had missed.

Not so.

"Your response time is excellent," I said. "I only started asking about you two hours ago."

Mountmain sneered away the compliment.

"Ten thousand dollars," he said. "If you lead me to the jewel. If not, you'll be tortured until you tell what you know. In unspeakable ways."

"I've never been tortured in a speakable way."

"Americans are such children. You always 'crack wise'. But you don't know what wise means in Europe."

He took my letter opener from my desk. He flicked his cigarette lighter, raising a flame. He held the flame under the blade, looking from it to me.

"I'd have taken the ten thousand dollars," he said.

"You've waited twenty years for something. If you wouldn't put up with torture after that, then you're not the man I think you are."

He almost smiled.

"Very cleverly put. Indeed, I'd endure anything. But that's because I know what's at stake."

The blade was red.

"You, *ma cushla*, know nothing."

I tried to wrestle free, but the two goons—if that was all they were—held me fast. Mountmain stood up. He put his lighter away and spat on the redhot blade. There was a hiss.

My office is on the sixth floor. Behind Mountmain was the window, and beyond that the irritating neon light. A face hung upside down at the top of my window, a fall of blonde hair wavering.

I was impressed. Geneviève had either climbed up from the street or down from the roof.

She clambered like a lizard, her arms and torso visible through the window, and lunged forwards, breaking through the glass.

Mountmain turned as her arms went around his waist. He stabbed with my letter opener, and she grabbed it with her bare hand. I smelled burning flesh and heard the sizzle. She bared sharp—unnaturally sharp—teeth and hissed, but did not scream. Mountmain bent backwards.

He shouted words in a language I didn't know.

I was let go and the goons rounded on Geneviève.

The office was too small for much of a fight. Geneviève took hold of the first goon, the one with the holes in him, and stuffed him out of the window. He fell like a stone. I felt the building shake as he smacked against the sidewalk.

The other goon hung back.

Mountmain scrambled to the doorway and tipped an invisible hat, sneering another command in old Irish or whatever. Then he left us with the goon.

This was a bigger specimen. It had an acre of chest, and eyes like white marbles. Geneviève made a face at it.

"It's been around too long," she said. "The binding is coming loose."

I had no idea what she was talking about.

Come to that, I was only just taking in the subtle changes in her. She still wore the evening gown, and had even scaled the building in heels, but her face was a different shape, sharper somehow. She had pointed teeth and diamond-shaped claw-nails.

We were in the world of the weird.

Geneviève held out her wounded hand. I saw the weal shrivel and disappear, leaving her white palm unmarred. The goon lurched towards her.

She knelt down, scooped up the letter-opener, and stuck it into his head. He halted, like a statue, but his eyes still rolled. He fell over, rattling the floorboards, and lay on his back.

"Do you keep foodstuffs here?" she asked.

"Is this the time to eat?"

"Table salt. I need salt."

She was on the mark. I've had too many meals in the office, while working odd hours. I have a hoard of basic groceries stashed in the bottom drawer of the filing cabinet, below the liquor. Without questioning her, I found a half-full bag of salt. It must have been there for years.

She smiled tightly as she took it, never looking away from the goon. With a pointed finger, she yanked his jaw open. Then she poured salt into his mouth, filling it entirely until trails spilled out.

"Needle and thread would be too much to ask. Do you have an office stapler? A first-aid kit?"

There was a small box of pills and salves. She took a roll of bandage and wound it around the lower half of the goon's head, mummifying the salt inside his mouth. Then, she stood up.

The goon shook, and came apart. He dissolved into what Mr. Edgar Allan Poe once described as a "loathsome mass of putrescence".

"Zombies," she spat. "Hateful things."

I drove, with Geneviève beside me, legs up on the seat like a child. She chattered and I interjected, and we tried to figure it out.

"Mountmain must have had Barrymore, but lost him," I said.

"He'll have him again soon. More importantly, he'll have the jewel. I'm surprised he bothered to call on you. It shows an impatience that is not good for him."

"How did he find Barrymore in the first place? The mortuary attendant couldn't have known where Lorre and Walsh took him."

"That's a nasty business. Scrying. It involves disembowelling a cat. Twice in one night would be pushing it, but my guess is that having failed to get what he wanted from you, he'll be here-kitty-kittying in some alleyway."

"He can find Barrymore by gutting a cat?"

"Magic. Hocus pocus. It works, you know."

"With so much at stake, couldn't you find a cat willing to give its life for the war effort?"

"It's not as easy as that. You have to be steeped in black magic for it to work. And that's not a good thing to be. It has long-term implications."

"But Mountmain doesn't care?"

"I should think not. That's why black magic is a temptation. You get ahead easily, delaying the payoff until it's too late."

"What are you, a white witch?"

She laughed, musically.

"Don't be silly. I'm a vampire."

"Bloodsucking fiend, creature of the night, accursed *nosferatu*, coffin-dwelling undead . . ."

"That sort of thing."

I let her go with it. Obviously, it wasn't worth arguing.

"Where are the rest of you? Winthrop and the others?"

"I'm afraid we have certain differences among ourselves. The War makes for odd alliances. I have a distaste for government work, which has been set aside for the moment. I've been keeping track of the Jewel of Seven Stars since its rediscovery. Edwin is a servant of the crown. The Diogenes Club, and its equivalents in the allied nations, wants to get hold of the Seven Stars to use as a weapon of war."

"How can a jewel win the War?"

"Think of it as a lens. It can focus intense destructive power. It seems to have a specific purpose. It is a device for destroying empires."

"Like Germany and Japan? Sounds good."

"You don't mean that. You haven't thought through what it means. It's not enough to win. You have to win without tainting yourself, or you're just piling up debts future generations will have to pay. Edwin can rationalise that; I can't. Of course, it's likely I'll be around to go through whatever future generations have to put up with."

"Mountmain wants the jewel to help Hitler?"

"And himself. His family believes in a destiny. He is the head of something called the Order of the Ram. It is foretold that the Ram will reign over the last days of the world. You know who Nostradamus is?"

"Fortune teller?"

"That's the bimbo. In his suppressed quatrains, Nostradamus is surprisingly specific about the MontMains. An expression disturbingly equivalent to 'thousand-year reich' crops up quite a lot."

"Errol Flynn has the body," I said.

She was quiet, and thoughtful.

"He's the only player left in the game. Mountmain wouldn't have taken him seriously, a drunken hero. He got hold of the body and escaped. Then, Mountmain must have revised his first impression and assumed Flynn was acting to a deliberate plan rather than careening at random. He'd start looking around for confederates, and that would lead to the person rattling his cage, to whit: me."

"I loved him in *The Adventures of Robin Hood*," she said. "'It's injustice I hate, not Normandy!'"

"But where is Flynn? It's a shame your prophet didn't say where we could find him."

"Michel de NostreDame wasn't always accurate. Sometimes, he didn't understand what he saw. Sometimes, he filled in with nonsense. He does describe a crisis, but his suggestion is absurd. He says that the jewel is to be found at the White House. Edwin has someone in Washington. And Finlay is on a plane, racing the sun. Just in case the jewel is spirited across country by dawn."

"*Dawn?*"

"Two hours' away. That's where the quatrain is highly specific. Even allowing for changes in the calendar since 1558."

I shook my head.

"There are white houses in California."

"To be frank, it could mean anything. The expression Nostradamus uses is '*Maison Blanche*'."

I stopped the car. We were outside the Warner Brothers lot. Lorre's home base. And Errol Flynn's. The pre-dawn light was already turning the water tower into a Martian War Machine.

I laughed out loud.

This was what it was like. When you saw it, and nobody else did. This was what made a detective.

"It's here," I said.

"How can you know that?"

"*Variety*. The trade paper. Most of my work is related to the studios. I keep up with the industry. Peter Lorre's shooting a film at Warners at the moment. With Humphrey Bogart and Ingrid Bergman."

Geneviève was prettily puzzled. Her face had settled down to her ingenue look again.

"I don't see . . ."

"It's called *Casablanca*, Geneviève. Casa Blanca. Maison Blanche. White House."

She looked across the lot, to the sound stages.

"Not the White House in Washington, not the city in North Africa. Here, *Casablanca*, Hollywood."

I drove onto the lot.

* * *

There were night-watchmen around, and a few early arriving or late staying technicians. I asked a uniformed guard if he'd seen Flynn. The man didn't want to say anything.

"I know he's on a bender," I said.

Finally, he nodded to a stage.

"He'll be sleeping it off now," the guard said. "He's a good lad, and we don't mind covering for him. The stories you hear don't mean anything."

I thanked him.

I could not resist a little triumph when I told Geneviève I had been right. We walked rapidly to the stage and found an unlocked door.

Inside was an Alice world. Half the stage was converted into a nightclub, with ceiling fans, a beat-up piano, twenty-five yards of bar, a backroom full of gambling equipment and row upon row of bottles of cold tea. Glasses and guns and hats were strewn around, each precisely in the spot they would need to be for shooting to resume. There were black cameras, like huge upright insects, halted where the club carpets gave way to bare concrete. Unlit lights hung from frames above.

In the centre of the set were two men, slumped over a bottle.

Flynn was so drunk and scared that he was drinking cold tea as if it were best bourbon. Barrymore was dead, but moving. The supposedly dark set was lit by a ruby glow from inside the dead man's chest.

Flynn raised a glass to his idol.

"What's it all for, Jack?" he asked. "All this mess, this nightmare, this fantasy, this horror? Is it just for play, just a game? To be packed up and put away by some snot-nosed kid who's lost interest?"

He slammed his glass down.

"I don't want it like that. I want Hamlet and Sherlock Holmes and Don Juan and Robin Hood and Custer. I want us to be heroes, to save something worth saving, to respect maidenly virtues and reflect manly ones. We shouldn't just be pathetic, whore-mongering drunks, Jack."

Barrymore was nodding.

There was no life in him. At least, none of his own. It was the Jewel of Seven Stars, animate. Geneviève took my arm, and gripped like a vice.

"To the glorious damnéd," Flynn toasted, tossing his glass away, wreaking hell with the continuity.

Barrymore's starched shirt was open and his chest was bulging. A cinder glowed inside his translucent flesh, outlining the black bars of his ribs.

"If Flynn takes the jewel, he'll be John Barrymore all over again," Geneviève said. "Personal triumph and degradation. But only personal. It will be shielded from the world. Rather, the world will be shielded from it."

"But it'll kill him," I suggested.

Geneviève nodded.

"Everybody dies," she said.

"Except you."

In a tiny, long-ago frightened little girl's voice, she repeated, "Except me."

Streaks of sunlight were filtering through the unshuttered glass roof of the stage. I wondered if Geneviève Dieudonné would shrivel at dawn, like the salt-stuffed zombie in my office.

A shot sounded.

Geneviève yelped. She looked down at a scarlet patch on her silver chest. Blood spread and her eyes were wide with surprise.

"Except me," she said, crumpling.

I turned, my gun out.

Bennett Mountmain strolled onto the stage.

He wore a stinking cat's skin on his forehead and upper face, like a caul, eyeholes ripped in the blood-matted fur.

"Silver bullet," he explained.

Geneviève moaned and held her wound. She seemed for the first time helpless. She was muttering in French.

Mountmain walked past me, with contempt.

Flynn stood up and barred his way, shielding Barrymore.

"You again," he snarled. "The treasure-hunter. You'll have to fight your way past my cold steel to snatch Cap'n Blood's doubloons for your coffers."

Wearily, Mountmain held up his gun.

"Go ahead, varlet, and shoot," said Flynn. His face was red and sunken, but he was twice the hero he seemed on the screen. He appeared to grow, to have some of the ruby glow, and he threw open his mouth and laughed at Mountmain.

The Black Magician fired, and his gun exploded in his hand.

Flynn's laughter grew, filling the stage, setting ceiling fans whirling. There was a demonic overtone to it. He stood with his legs apart, hands on hips, eyes shining.

Barrymore tipped forward, and a large stone fell out of his chest onto the prop table.

The light of Seven Stars lit up the *Casablanca* set.

Mountmain was on the floor, rolling in agony, weeping tears of bloody frustration. Geneviève was trying to sit up and say something. I knelt by her, to see what could be done.

There was blood on her back too. The bullet had shot right through her. The holes in her were mending over and coming apart again as I looked. Her blonde hair was white. Her face was a paper mask.

"Take the jewel," she said. "Save Flynn."

I crossed the room.

Flynn looked at me. He was unsure. He had recognised Mountmain for what he was. But not me.

"Pure and parfait knight," he said.

That was just embarrassing.

He stepped aside. I picked up the Jewel of Seven Stars. Tiny points shone inside it. I expected it to be warm and yielding, but it was cold and hard. I wanted to throw it into the sea.

"You've found it," a British voice said. "Good man."

Winthrop had left his scrying caul outside, but his forehead was still smeared. As he wiped the last of the blood away, I remembered the cat he had been cradling in Coldwater Canyon.

"Edwin," Geneviève said, weakly, shocked. "You haven't . . ."

"Can't make an omelette without breaking eggs," he said, unapologetically. "You don't approve, of course. Catriona wouldn't either. But you'll thank me for it in the long run. May I?"

He held out his hand. I looked at the jewel. I wanted to be rid of it. Flynn was still there. I sensed an attraction from the gem to the star. The sun was not yet up. I could plunge the stone into Flynn's chest and hide it for another generation. At the cost of a man's life.

Who's to say Errol Flynn wouldn't ruin himself without supernatural intervention? Plenty have.

Mountmain yelled hatred and defiance and frustration. He was bleeding to death.

Winthrop's hand was still extended. It was my decision.

People were pouring onto the stage. Winthrop's colleagues, cops, studio guards, Warners staff, uniformed soldiers, uniformed Nazis. I saw Peter Lorre, and other famous faces. Everybody was in this movie.

"Catch," I said, tossing the jewel up like a bridal bouquet.

Mountmain stood up, extending his ruined hand. Judge Pursuivant landed on him, crushing him to the floor.

Winthrop made a cricketer's catch.

"Owzat," he said.

Geneviève sighed through pain. I think she had stopped bleeding.

Someone asked in a loud Hungarian voice what the dead body of John Barrymore was doing on his set. Lorre breathed soothing sentiments, and a couple of grips removed the untenanted vessel from the site. Flynn, now merely drunk, further infuriated the director with cheery idiocies. That part of the story was swept aside. Hollywood hi-jinks. They happen all the time.

It came down to Winthrop, Geneviève and the jewel. And me.

"We must be wise, Edwin," Geneviève said.

The Britisher nodded.

"We have a great responsibility. I swear we shall not misuse it."

"We may not have the chance to decide. You can feel it, can't you? As if it were alive?"

"Yes, Gené."

Mountmain was dead, his spine snapped by Pursuivant. It had all come back on him, the black magic. Just as Geneviève had said it would.

Winthrop seemed sobered, shaken even. He couldn't get the last of the cat-blood off his face. He had done his duty, but now he was asking himself questions.

I hated that. I knew I'd be doing the same thing.

A soldier was beside Winthrop, with a lead box.

"Sir," he prompted.

Winthrop dropped the Jewel of Seven Stars into the box, and the soldier hesitated, eyes held by the red light, before clamping shut the lid. He marched off, other soldiers trotting at his heels, drawing Pursuivant and the others.

Winthrop helped Geneviève onto a stretcher. She was fading, bare arms wrinkling like a mummy's, face sinking grayly onto her skull.

"What wash that?" someone asked me. "The red shtone in the boxsh?"

I turned towards the star of *Casablanca*, a man satisfyingly shorter and older than me.

"That," I said, "was the stuff that dreams are made of."

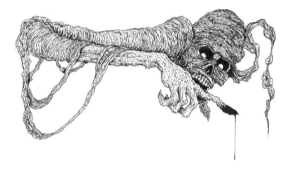

John Thunstone

ROUSE HIM NOT
by Manly Wade Wellman

Manhattan playboy and dilettante John Thunstone is almost too big to be reassuring, and most of his clothes have to be tailored especially for him. His hands and his eyes are sensitive, his big nose has been twice broken, and his black hair and moustache show a little streaking of grey.

A serious student of the occult and a two-fisted brawler ready to take on any enemy, he is armed with potent charms and a silver swordcane as he stalks supernatural perils through the exclusive night clubs of New York or in backwater towns lost in the countryside—seeking out deadly sorcery wherever he discovers it.

John Thunstone first appeared in 1943, after Farnsworth Wright retired as the editor of Weird Tales *and was succeeded by Dorothy McIlwraith. She and her associate, Lamont Buchanan, sat down with Manly Wade Wellman (1903–1986) for several careful discussions about how the character might look and act.*

The result of these meetings was the publication of 'The Third Cry of Legba' in the November 1943 edition of Weird Tales. *Over the next eight years, fourteen more stories appeared in the famous pulp magazine, concluding with 'The Last Grave of Lill Warren' in the May 1951 issue.*

Several of the Thunstone stories pitted the investigator against a wizard named Rowley Thorne, who the author admitted he had based on the real-life occultist Aleister Crowley, as well as a fearful race of beings called The Shonokins.

All these stories were collected in Lonely Vigils *(1981), and Wellman subsequently revived the character for two novels, transplanting Thunstone to the author's beloved England for* What Dreams May Come *(1983), and once again pitting the psychic adventurer against his sworn enemy Rowley Thorne in* The School of Darkness *(1985). All the John Thunstone short stories (plus those featuring his fellow phantom-fighter Lee Cobbett) were collected by editor John Pelan in* The Third Cry to Legba and Other Invocations *(2000), the first volume in the "Selected Stories of Manly Wade Wellman".*

The following tale was originally published in the special Occult Detectives issue of Kadath *(July, 1982), and it was later adapted by Michel Parry for a 1988 episode of the TV series* Monsters, *starring Alex Cord as John Thunstone.*

THE SIDE ROAD in from the paved highway was heavily graveled but not tightly packed except for two ruts. John Thunstone's black sedan crept between trees that wove their branches together overhead. Gloom lay in the woods to right and left. Once or twice he thought he heard a rustle of movement there. Maybe half a mile on, he came to the house.

It was narrow and two-storied, of vertical planks stained a soft brown. A tan pickup truck was parked at a front corner. Thunstone got out of the sedan. He was big and powerfully built, with gray streaks in his well-combed dark hair and trim mustache. He wore a blue summer suit. In one broad hand he carried a stick of spotted wood with a bent handle and a silver band, but he did not lean on it. Walking the flagged path to the front steps, he studied the house. Two rooms and a kitchen below, he guessed, another room and probably a bath above.

A slender girl in green slacks and a paint-daubed white blouse came to the open door. "Yes, sir?" she half-challenged.

He lifted a hand as though to tip the hat he did not wear. "Good afternoon. My name is John Thunstone. A researcher into old folk beliefs. I came because, yonder at the county seat, they told me an interesting story about this place."

"Interesting story?" She came out on the stoop. Thunstone thought she was eighteen or nineteen, small but healthy, with a cascade of chestnut hair. Her long face was pretty. In one hand she held a kitchen knife, in the other a half-peeled potato. "Interesting story?" she said again.

"About a circle in your yard," said Thunstone. "With no grass on its circumference. It's mentioned briefly in an old folklore treatise, and I heard about it at your courthouse today."

"Oh, that," she said. "Here comes Bill—my husband. Maybe he can tell you."

A young man carrying a big pair of iron pincers came around the corner of the house. He was middle-sized and sinewy, in dungarees and checked shirt, with a denim apron. He had heavy hair and close-clipped beard and a blotch of soot on his nose. No older than, say, twenty-two. This couple, reflected Thunstone, had married early.

"Yes, sir?" said the young man.

"This is Mr. Thunstone, Bill," said the girl. "Oh, I didn't say who we were. This is my husband Bill Bracy, and my name's Prue."

"How do you do?" said Thunstone, but Bill Bracy was staring.

"I've seen your picture in the papers," he said. "Read about your researches into the supernatural."

"I do such things," nodded Thunstone. "At your county seat, I looked up the old Colonial records of the trial of Crett Marrowby, for sorcery."

"Yes, sir," said Bill Bracy. "We've heard of that, too."

"Mr. Packer, the clerk of the court, mentioned this house of yours," went on Thunstone. "He called it the Trumbull house. And said that there's a circular patch in the yard, and some old people connect it with the Marrowby case."

He looked around him, as though in quest of the circular patch.

"That's around in the backyard," said Prue Bracy. "We've only lived here a few months. When we bought from the Trumbulls, they said we'd do well to leave the thing alone."

"Might I see it?" asked Thunstone.

"I'll show it to you," said Bill Bracy. "Prue, could you maybe fix us some drinks? Come this way, sir."

He and Thunstone rounded the corner of the house and went into the backyard. That was an open stretch of coarse grass, with woods beyond.

"There it is," and Bracy pointed with his tongs.

Almost at the center of the grassy stretch lay a moist roundness, greener than the grass. Thunstone walked toward it. The circle seemed nine or ten feet across. It was bordered with a hard, base ring of pale brown earth. Thunstone paced all around, moving lightly for so large a man. The inner expanse looked somewhat like a great pot of wet spinach. It seemed to stir slightly as he studied it. It seethed. He reached out with the tip of his spotted stick.

"Don't," warned Bracy, but Thunstone had driven the stick into the mass.

For a moment, something seemed to fasten upon the stick, to drag powerfully upon it. Thunstone strongly dragged it clear and lifted it. Where it had touched the dampness showed a momentary churning whirl. He heard, or imagined, a droning hum.

"I did that when we first came here," Bill Bracy said, a tremble in his voice. "I put a hoe in there, and the hoe popped out of my hand and was swallowed up before I looked."

"It didn't get my cane." He looked at Bracy. "Why did it take your hoe?"

"I've wondered myself. I haven't fooled with it again." Bracy's bearded face was grave. "I should explain, Prue and I came here from New York, because the house was so cheap. She paints—she's going to do a mural at the new post office in town—and I make metal things, copper and pewter, and sell them here and there. Mr. and Mrs. Trumbull wanted to get rid of the house, so we got it for almost nothing. They told us what I told you, leave that sinkhole thing alone. 'Do that,' Mr. Trumbull said, 'and it will leave you alone.'"

"But you lost a hoe in it," Thunstone reminded.

"Yes, sir," Bracy nodded heavily. "And when it came to evening that day, we heard noises. Sort of a growling noise, over and over. I wanted to go out and check, but Prue wouldn't let me. She was frightened, she prayed. And that's the last time we've meddled in it, and how about a drink now?"

"In a moment."

Thunstone studied the outer ring intently. It was of bald, hard earth, like baked pottery. Again he measured the distance across with his eye. Rings of that dimension had been common in old witchcraft cases, he reflected; they were about the size to hold a coven of thirteen sorcerers standing together, perhaps dancing together. Circles were always mysterious things, whether they were old or new. He turned back to Bracy.

"I'll be glad for that drink you mentioned," he said.

They returned to the house and entered a small, pleasant front room. There were chairs and a table and a sofa draped in a handsome Indian blanket. A small fireplace was set in a corner. Prue Bracy was making highballs at the table. They sat down and drank.

"I explained to Mr. Thunstone how we were advised to leave that thing alone," said Bracy.

"I'm not sure it should be left alone," said Thunstone, sipping. "Let me tell you some things I found out earlier today, when I was at the courthouse."

He referred to a sheaf of notes to read some of his conversation with the clerk Packer. He quoted what brief record the ancient county ledgers had of the execution, long ago, of Crett Marrowby. At that time in Colonial history, George II's act of 1735 obtained to repeal the death penalty for witchcraft; but for a mass of odd charges Marrowby had been put in jail for a year, with a public appearance in the pillory every three months. His execution had been simply for the murder of a minister of the local church, the Reverend Mr. Herbert Walford.

"And it was ordered that he be buried outside the churchyard," Thunstone finished.

"Confession or not, they thought he was evil," suggested Bill Bracy. "Is that all you have on the case?"

"So far, it is," replied Thunstone. "Yet I hope for more. Mr. Packer spoke of an old resident named Ritson—"

"That one!" broke in Bill Bracy, not very politely. "He's one of those crusty old characters that got weaned on a pickle. We met him when we first came here, tried to make friends, and he just turned the acid on us."

"I'll try to neutralize his acid," said Thunstone, and rose. "I'll go now, but I have a cheeky favor to ask. I want to come back here tonight and stay."

Prue blinked at him, very prettily. "Why," she said, "we don't have a spare room, but there's this sofa if you don't have a place to stay."

"I'm checked into the Sullivan Motel in town, but right here is where I want to be tonight," said Thunstone. "The sofa will do splendidly for me." He went to the door. "Thank you both. Will you let me fetch us something for supper? I'll shop around in town."

He went to the soft-lighted grill-room of the Sullivan Motel, for there, Packer had told him, old Mr. Ritson habitually sat and scowled into a drink.

Sure enough, there at the bar sat a gray man, old and hunched, harshly gaunt where Thunstone was blocky. It must be Ritson. He was dressed in shabby black, like an undertaker's assistant. His lead-pale hair bushed around his ears. His nose and chin were as sharp as daggers. Thunstone sat down on the stool next to him. From the bartender he ordered a double bourbon and water. Then he turned to the old man.

"I think you're Mr. Ritson," he said.

The other turned bitter, beady eyes upon him, clamped the thin mouth between sharp nose and sharp chin. "So you know who I am," came the grumpiest of voices. "I know who you are, too—this Thurston fellow who's come to poke into what ain't none of his business, huh? And you want to ask me something."

"Yes," said Thunstone evenly. "I thought I'd ask you what you'd like to drink."

"Eh?" The beady eyes quartered him, then gazed into an empty glass. "I'll have what you're having."

The bartender brought the drinks. Ritson gulped at his. Thunstone lifted his own glass but did not sip.

"I've been told that you know past history here, Mr. Ritson," he tried again. "About the case of a man named Marrowby, long ago hanged for murder and buried here."

Skimpy gray brows drew down above the unfriendly eyes. "Why in hell should I tell you a word of what I know?"

"If you don't," said Thunstone, "I'll have to go to Mr. Packer, the clerk."

"Packer?" Ritson squealed. "What does he know? Hell, mister, he wasn't even born here. He doesn't know old-time town history, he just sort of mumbles about it."

"But if you won't talk to me, I must look for information wherever I can get it."

"What information could Packer give you? Look here, my folks was here ever since the town was built, away back before the Revolution. Sure I know about the Marrowby thing. When I was a boy, my great-grandmother told me what she'd heard from her grandfather, who was young here at the time—better than two hundred and forty years back, I calculate."

Ritson swigged down the rest of his drink.

"Bring this gentleman another," Thunstone told the bartender, putting down some money. "Now, Mr. Ritson, what did you hear from your great-grandmother?"

"It happened long lifetimes ago. They'd had Marrowby up for his magic doings—he could witch people's dinners off their tables to his house, he'd made a girl leave her true love to come to him. All the law gave him for that was just a year in the jailhouse."

"But he was hanged at last," said Thunstone.

"That he was, higher than Haman," nodded Ritson above his second drink. "The way it was told to me, he killed a preacher—can't recollect the preacher's name—who'd read him out of the church."

"The preacher's name was Walford," supplied Thunstone.

"Whatever the name was, he died of a stab in the heart. And at Marrowby's house, they found a wax dummy of the preacher, with a needle stuck in it."

"Where was Marrowby's house?" asked Thunstone.

"Why, out yonder where the Trumbull house is, where them young folks took over. Maybe the charge wouldn't have stood, but Marrowby pleaded guilty in court. And they built a scaffold in the courthouse yard and strung him up." Ritson drank. "I heard the whole tale. He stood up there and confessed to black magic, confessed to murder. He said he had to repent, or else he'd go to hell. He warned the folks who watched."

"What was his confession?" Thunstone asked.

"Seemed like he warned all who were there not to follow black magic. Said he must confess and repent. And he said a thing I don't know the meaning of."

"Here," said Thunstone, "I haven't touched this drink." He shoved the glass to Ritson's hand. "What did he say?"

"It didn't make sense. He warned them not to be familiar."

"Familiar?" echoed Thunstone, interested.

"Said, 'Let familiar alone'. The like of that—strange words. Said, 'Rouse him not.' And swung off."

"And that's all?"

"Yes. They buried him outside the churchyard, and drove an ash stake into his heart to make sure be wouldn't rise up. That's the whole tale. But don't you go writing it."

"I won't write it," Thunstone promised him.

"Mind that you don't. Now, I've told you what I heard, and I hope it's enough."

"I hope the same," said Thunstone. "Will you excuse me? Good afternoon."

"What's good about it?" snorted Ritson, halfway through his third drink.

Thunstone went to his motel and changed into rougher clothes, chino slacks and a tan shirt and a light brown jacket. He thrust a flashlight into the jacket pocket. Around his neck hung a tarnished copper crucifix. He found a lunch stand and bought a plastic bucket of barbecued ribs, a container of slaw, and bottles of beer. Then he drove to the Bracy house.

The Bracys welcomed him in and enthused hungrily over the barbecue. "It just so happens that I'm baking cornbread," said Prue.

"That will go well with it."

As the sun sank toward the trees, they ate with good appetite. Prue asked about Thunstone's crucifix, and he told her he had inherited it from his mother. When they had finished eating, Prue carried the dishes to the kitchen and came back with blankets over her arm.

"Will these be all right for tonight?"

"They'll be splendid, many a night I've lain on harder beds than your sofa. But before I do that, there's business to be done outside, as soon as it gets dark."

"I'll come along," volunteered Bill, but Thunstone shook his massive head.

"No, two of us out there will be a complication," he said quietly. "This business will require careful handling, and some luck and playing by ear."

"Whatever you say," granted Bill, and Prue looked relieved.

"I won't promise to win ahead of things," went on Thunstone, "but I'll be specially equipped. Look here."

He grasped the shank of his cane in his left hand and turned the crook with his right. The cane parted at the silver ring, and he drew out a lean, pale-shining blade.

"That's a beautiful thing," breathed Prue. "It must be old."

"As I understand, it was forged by St. Dunstan, something like a thousand years ago. See what these words say at the edge?"

Both Bracys leaned to study. Bill moved his bearded lips soundlessly.

"It looks like Latin," he said. "I can't make it out."

"*Sic pereant inimici tui, Domine*," Thunstone read out the inscription. "So perish all thine enemies, O Lord," he translated. "It's a silver blade, and St. Dunstan was a silversmith, and faced and defeated Satan himself."

Bill was impressed. "That must be the only thing of its kind in the world," he ventured.

"No, there's another." Thunstone smiled under his mustache. "It belongs to a friend of mine, Judge Keith Hilary Pursuivant. Once I defeated a vampire with this blade, and twice I've faced werewolves with it. As well as other things."

"I don't feel right, letting you go out while I stay here," said Bill, almost pleadingly.

"Do me a favor and stay here with Prue," Thunstone bade him. "Stay inside, even if you hear trouble out there."

He got to his feet, the bared blade in his hand.

"It's dark now," he said. "Time for strange things to stir."

"Stir?" Bill echoed him, his band to his bearded chin. "Will that old sorcerer stir, the one they called Marrowby?"

"Not as I see it," said Thunstone. "Not if they drove an ashen stake through him to keep him quiet in his grave. No, something else I judge. I expect to see you later, when things are quieter."

He went to the front door and through it, and closed it behind him.

Night had crawled swiftly down around the house. Thunstone's left hand rummaged out his flashlight and turned it on, while his right hand carried the silver blade low at his side. The light showed him the grass of the yard, the corner of the house. He went around to the open space at the back. He heard something, a noise like a half-strangled growl. It led him toward the circle, while the bright beam of the flash quested before him. He came to where the ring of hard brownness bordered the soft, damp greenness. Again the noise stole, upward, the strangled snarl of it.

Thunstone stooped and directed the beam of the light, then thrust the mess with the keen point of his blade. Powerfully he stirred it around.

"All right," he said, hoping his words would be understood. "All right. Come out and let's settle things."

The snarl rose to a reedy shrillness, and he felt a clutch on his silver weapon. He drew it out, and thought the edge sliced something. Louder rose the voice, a true scream now, and something showed itself there in the swampiness.

A lump like a head rose into view, with two larger lumps like shoulders just below it. Thunstone made a long, smooth stride backward, keeping his light trained on what was there. Two slab-like paws caught the bald rim of the circle, and a great, shaggy shape humped itself up and out and stood erect before him.

It was taller even than Thunstone, broader even than he was. And it looked nothing natural. In the dancing light of the torch, it seemed to be thatched over with dark, wet fronds and tussocks. Its head was draped with such stuff, through which gleamed two closely set eyes, pale as white-hot iron.

A mouth opened in the tangle and out came a rumbling shout, like the roar of a great beast. It slouched heavily toward him, on two feet like shovels.

Thunstone slid warily to one side, keeping the beam of the light upon the creature, at the same time poising his blade.

"So here you've stayed," he said to it. "Marrowby repented, forswore you. He's dead, but you're alive. You're evil."

It roared again. Its great, long forelimbs rose like derricks. Thunstone saw talons, pale and deadly.

"Well, come on," said Thunstone, his voice quiet and steady. "Come on and see what you can do, and what I can do."

It approached in a squattering charge. Thunstone sidestepped at the last instant and sped a slashing cut at the bulk as it floundered past. This time it screamed, so shrilly that his ears rang. It swung around toward him, and he turned the ray of his flash back upon it.

"Hurt you, did I?" said Thunstone. "That's the beginning. Come again. Maybe I won't dodge this time."

It rushed at him with ungainly speed. He stood his ground. As it hurtled almost upon him, he lunged, a smooth fencer's lunge.

His point went home where its chest should be. The blade went smoothly, sleekly in, with a whisper of sound. It penetrated to the very hilt, and liquid gushed upon Thunstone's hand. He smelled an odor as of ancient decay.

A louder, more piercing scream than before. The weedy bulk almost forced him back. Then, abruptly, it fell away and down, and as it went he cleared his point with a strong, dragging pull. He stood over his adversary, shining his light to see it thrash and flounder on the ground.

"Did that do your business?" he asked it. "Perhaps not quite. Here, I'll do this."

He probed with the point where the neck would be, and lifted the blade and drove it down with all his strength, as he would swing an axe.

The head-lump went bounding away on the coarse grass, a full dozen feet. The body slumped flaccidly and lay still.

"*Sic pereant inimici tui, Domine*," intoned Thunstone, like a priest saying a prayer for the dead. He stood tense and watched. No motion. He walked to where the head lay. It, too, was as silent as a weed-tufted rock.

A moment, and then he turned back and went to the house,

finding his way with the flash beam. His feet felt tired and heavy as he mounted the steps. Pocketing his flashlight again, he opened the door.

Bill and Prue Bracy stood inside, arms around each other, eyes strained wide in terror.

"It's all over," Thunstone comforted them, and went to the sofa and sat down heavily. He fished out a handkerchief and wiped his silver blade. The liquid on it was thick and slimy, like blood, but it was green and not red.

"When old Mr. Ritson said that Marrowby had warned about something familiar, I felt pretty sure," he said.

"F-familiar?" stammered Prue.

"A sorcerer makes his pact with the powers of evil," said Thunstone, "and from the powers of evil he receives a familiar. Marrowby repented and died repenting, but his familiar stayed here, stayed hidden, without guidance, but wishing to do evil. I've put an end to that."

"What was it?" wondered Bill Bracy.

"It's hard to describe. When it's light tomorrow morning, maybe you and I will take spades and bury it. It's not pretty, I promise you that. But its evil is finished. I know words to say over its grave to ensure that."

He smiled up at the blank-faced Prue.

"My dear, could we have a fire there on the hearth? I want to burn this filthy handkerchief."

Still smiling, he slid the cleaned blade into the cane again.

Titus Crow

DE MARIGNY'S CLOCK
by Brian Lumley

Titus Crow is tall and broad-shouldered, and it is plain to see that in his younger days he had been a handsome man. Now his hair has greyed a little and his eyes, though they are still very bright and observant, bear the imprint of many years spent exploring rarely trodden paths of mysterious and obscure learning.

During World War II, as a young man, he was employed by the War Department; his work in London was concerned with cracking Nazi codes and advising on Hitler's predilection for the occult: those dark forces which Der Führer attempted to enlist in his campaign for world domination.

Following the end of the war, he fought Satan wherever he found him and with whichever tools of his trade were available to him at the time. Crow became a world-acknowledged master in such subjects as magic, specifically the so-called "Black Books" of various necromancers and wizards, and their doubtful arts; in archaeology, palaeontology, cryptography, antiques and antiquities in general; in obscure or avant-garde works of art—with particular reference to such as Aubrey Beardsley, Chandler Davies, Hieronymous Bosch, Richard Upton Pickman, etc.—in the dimly forgotten or neglected mythologies of Earth's prime, and in anthropology in general, to mention but a handful.

Brian Lumley's Titus Crow made his debut in 'Billy's Oak'

in the sixth issue of August Derleth's magazine/catalogue The Arkham Collector *(Winter, 1970). He made another appearance the following issue in 'An Item of Supporting Evidence' (Summer, 1970) and both stories were included in the author's first book, the Arkham House collection* The Caller of the Black *(1971), which also featured Crow in the title story plus 'The Mirror of Nitocris' and 'De Marigny's Clock'.*

Next, Crow and his assistant Henri-Laurent de Marigny became the main protagonists of a trio of Lovecraftian novels: The Burrowers Beneath *(1974),* The Transition of Titus Crow *(1975) and* The Clock of Dreams *(1978). Two more Crow stories, 'The Viking's Stone' and 'Darghud's Doll', were included in Lumley's second Arkham House collection,* The Horror at Oakdeene and Others *(1977), and the novellas 'Name and Number' and 'Lord of the Worms' appeared in the July 1982* Kadath *and* Weirdbook #17 *(1983), respectively.*

De Marigny himself was the hero of In the Moons of Borea *(1979), a sequel to* Spawn of the Winds *(1978), and a coda to the series, 'The Black Recalled', was published in the* World Fantasy Convention 1983 *souvenir book. All the Titus Crow stories are collected in* The Compleat Crow *(1987).*

ANY INTRUSIONS OTHER than those condoned or invited upon the privacy of Titus Crow at his bungalow retreat, Blowne House, on the outskirts of London, were almost always automatically classified by that gentleman as open acts of warfare. In the first place for anyone to make it merely to the doors of Crow's abode without an invitation—often even *with* one—was a sure sign of the appearance on the scene of a forceful and dogmatic character; qualities which were almost guaranteed to clash with Crow's own odd nature. For Blowne House seemed to exude an atmosphere all its own, an exhalation of impending *something* which usually kept the place and its grounds free even from birds and mice; and it was quite unusual for Crow himself to invite visitors. He kept strange hours and busied himself with stranger matters and, frankly, was almost antisocial even in his most "engaging" moments. Over

the years the reasons for this apparent inhospitality had grown, or so it seemed to Crow, increasingly clear-cut. For one thing, his library contained quite a large number of rare and highly costly books, many of them long out of print and some of them never officially *in* print, and London apparently abounded with unscrupulous "collectors" of such items. For another his studies, usually in occult matters and obscure archaeological, antiquarian or anthropological research, were such as required the most concentrated attention and personal involvement, completely precluding any disturbances from outside sources.

Not that the present infringement came while Crow was engaged with any of his many and varied activities—it did not; it came in the middle of the night, rousing him from deep and dreamless slumbers engendered by a long day of frustrated and unrewarding work on de Marigny's clock. And Titus Crow was not amused.

"What the hell's going on here? Who are you and what are you doing in my house?" He had sat bolt upright in bed almost as soon as the light went on. His forehead had come straight into contact with a wicked-looking automatic held in the fist of a most unbeautiful thug. The man was about five feet eight inches in height, thick set, steady on legs which were short in comparison with the rest of his frame. He had a small scar over his left eye and a mouth that slanted downward—cynically, Crow supposed—from left to right. Most unbeautiful.

"Just take it easy, guv, and there'll be no bother," the thug said, his voice soft but ugly.

Crow's eyes flicked across the room to where a second hoodlum stood, just within the bedroom door, a nervous grin twisting his pallid features.

"Find anything, Pasty?" the man with the pistol questioned, his eyes never leaving Crow's face for a second.

"Nothing, Joe," came the answer, "a few old books and bit of silver, nothing worth our while—yet. He'll tell us where it is, though, won't you, chum?"

"Pasty!" Crow exclaimed, "Powers of observation, indeed! I was just thinking, before hearing your name, what a thin, pasty creature you look—Pasty." Crow grinned, got out of bed and put on his flame-red dressing-gown. Joe looked him up and down appraisingly. Crow was tall and broad-shouldered and it was plain to see that in his younger days he had been a handsome man. Even now there was a certain tawniness about him, and his eyes were still very bright and more than intelligent. Overall his aspect conveyed an impression of hidden power, which Joe did not particularly care much for. He decided it would be best to show his authority at the earliest opportunity. And Crow obligingly supplied him with that opportunity in the next few seconds.

The jibe the occultist had aimed at Pasty had meanwhile found its way home. Pasty's retaliation was a threat: "Lovely colour, that dressing-gown," he said, "it'll match up nicely if you bleed when I rap you on your head." He laughed harshly, slapping a metal cosh into his open palm. "But before that, you will tell us where it is, won't you?"

"Surely," Crow answered immediately, "it's third on the left, down the passage . . . *ugh!*" Joe's pistol smacked into Crow's cheek, knocking him sprawling. He carefully got up, gingerly fingering the red welt on his face.

"Now that's just to show you that we don't want any more funnies, see?" Joe said.

"Yes, I see," Crow's voice trembled with suppressed rage. "Just what do you want?"

"Now is that so difficult to figure out?" Pasty asked, crossing the room. "Money . . . we want your money! A fine fellow like you, with a place like this—" the lean man glanced appraisingly about the room, noting the silk curtains, the boukhara rugs, the original erotic illustrations by Aubrey Beardsley in their rosewood frames "—ought to have a good bit of ready cash lying about . . . we want it!"

"Then I'm sorry to have to disappoint you," Crow told him happily, seating himself on his bed. "I keep my money in a bank—what little I've got."

"Up!" ordered Joe briefly. "Off the bed." He pulled Crow to one side, nodding to Pasty, indicating some sort of action involving the bed. Crow stepped forward as Pasty yanked back the covers from the mattress and took out a sharp knife.

"Now wait . . ." he began, thoroughly alarmed.

"Hold it, guv, or I might just let Pasty use his blade on you!" Joe waved his gun in Crow's face, ordering him back. "You see, you'd be far better off to tell us where the money is without all this trouble. This way you're just going to see your little nest wrecked around you." He waited, giving Crow the opportunity to speak up, then indicated to Pasty that he should go ahead.

Pasty went ahead!

He ripped open the mattress along both sides and one end, tearing back the soft outer covering to expose the stuffing and springs beneath, then pulling out the interior in great handfuls, flinging them down on the floor in total disregard of Crow's utter astonishment and concern.

"See, guv, you're a recluse—in our books, anyway—and retiring sorts like you hide their pennies in the funniest places. Like in mattresses . . . or behind wall-pictures!" Joe gave Pasty a nod, waving his pistol at the Beardsleys.

"Well for God's sake, just *look* behind them," Crow snarled, again starting forward, "there's no need to rip them off the walls."

"Here!" Pasty exclaimed, turning an enquiring eye on the outraged householder, "these pictures worth anything then?"

"Only to a collector—you'd never find a fence for stuff like that," Crow replied.

"Hah! Not so stupid, our recluse!" Joe grinned, "But being clever won't get you anywhere, guv, except hospital maybe. Okay, Pasty, leave the man's dirty pictures alone. You—" he turned to Crow "—your study; we've been in there, but only passing through. Let's go, guv, you can give us a hand to, er, shift things about." He pushed Crow in the direction of the door.

Pasty was last to enter the study. He did so shivering, an odd look crossing his face. Pasty did not know it but he was a singularly rare person, one of the world's few truly "psychic" men. Crow was another—one who had the *talent* to a high degree—and he sensed Pasty's sudden feeling of apprehension.

"Snug little room, isn't it?" he asked, grinning cheerfully at the uneasy thug.

"Never mind how pretty the place is—try the panelling, Pasty," Joe directed.

"Eh?" Pasty's mind obviously was not on the job. "The panelling?"

His eyes shifted nervously round the room.

"Yes, the panelling!" Joe studied his partner curiously. "What's wrong with you, then?" His look of puzzlement turned to one of anger. "Now come on, Pasty boy, get a grip! At this rate we'll be here all bleeding night!"

Now it happened that Titus Crow's study was the pride of his life, and the thought of the utter havoc his unwelcome visitors could wreak in there was a terrifying thing to him. He determined to help them in their abortive search as much as he could; they would not find anything—there was nothing to find!—but this way he could at least ensure as little damage as possible before they realized there was no money in the house and left. They were certainly unwilling to believe anything he said about the absence of substantive funds! But then again, to anyone not knowing him reasonably well—and few did—Crow's home and certain of its appointments might certainly point to a man of considerable means. Yet he was merely comfortable, not wealthy, and, as he had said, what money he did have was safe in a bank. The more he helped them get through with their search the quicker they would leave! He had just made up his mind to this effect when Pasty found the hidden recess by the fireside.

"Here!" The nervous look left Pasty's face as he turned to Joe. "Listen to this." He rapped on a square panel. The sound was dull, hollow. Pasty swung his cosh back purposefully

"No, wait—I'll open it for you." Crow held up his hands in protest.

"Go on then, get it open," Joe ordered. Crow moved over to the wall and expertly slid back the panel to reveal a dim shelf behind. On the shelf was a single book. Pasty pushed Crow aside, lifted out the book and read off its title:

"The . . . what? . . . *Cthaat Aquadingen!* Huh!" Then his expression quickly turned to one of pure disgust and loathing. "*Ughhh!*" He flung the book away from him across the room, hastily wiping his hands down his jacket. Titus Crow received a momentary but quite vivid mental message from the mind of the startled thug. It was a picture of things rotting in vaults of crawling darkness, and he could well understand why Pasty was suddenly trembling.

"That . . . that damn book's *wet!*" the shaken crook exclaimed nervously.

"No, just sweating!" Crow informed. "The binding is, er, human skin, you see. Somehow it still retains the ability to sweat—a sure sign that it's going to rain."

"Claptrap!" Joe snapped, "And you get a grip of yourself." He snarled at Pasty. "There's something about this place I don't like either, but I'm not letting it get me down." He turned to Crow, his mouth strained and twisting in anger: "And from now on you speak when you're spoken to." Then carefully, practicedly, he turned his head and slowly scanned the room, taking in the tall bookshelves with their many volumes, some ancient, others relatively modern, and he glanced at Pasty and grinned knowingly. "Pasty," Joe ordered, "get them books off the shelves—I want to see what's behind them. How about it, recluse, you got anything behind there?"

"Nothing, nothing at all," Crow quickly answered, "for goodness sake don't go pulling them down; some of them are coming to pieces as it is. *No!*"

His last cry was one of pure protestation; horror at the defilement of his collection. The two thugs ignored him. Pasty, seemingly over his nervousness, happily went to work, scattering the books left, right and centre. Down came the collected works of Edgar Allan Poe, the first rare editions of Machen's and Lovecraft's fiction; then the more ancient works, of Josephus, Magnus, Lévi, Borellus, Erdschluss and Wittingby; closely followed by a connected set on oceanic evil: Gaston Le Fe's *Dwellers in the Depths*, Oswald's *Legends of Liqualia*, Gantley's *Hydrophinnae*, the German *UnterZee Kulten* and Hartrack's *In Pressured Places* . . .

Crow could merely stand and watch it all, a black rage growing in his heart, and Joe, not entirely insensitive to the occultist's mood, gripped his pistol a little tighter and unsmilingly cautioned him: "Just take it easy, hermit. There's still time to speak up—just tell us where you hide your money and it's all over. No? Okay, what's next?" His eyes swept the now littered room again, coming to rest in a dimly lighted corner where stood a great clock.

In front of the clock—an instrument apparently of the "grandfather" class; at least, from a distance of that appearance— stood a small occasional table bearing an adjustable reading-lamp, one or two books and a few scattered sheets of notepaper. Seeing the direction in which Joe's actions were leading him, Crow smiled inwardly and wished his criminal visitor all the best. If Joe could make anything of that timepiece, then he was a cleverer man than Titus Crow; and if he could actually *open* it, as is possible and perfectly normal with more orthodox clocks, then Crow would be eternally grateful to him. For the sarcophagus-like thing in the dim corner was that same instrument with which Crow had busied himself all the previous day and on many, many other days since first he purchased it more than ten years earlier. And none of his studies had done him a bit of good! He was still as unenlightened with regard to the clock's purpose as he had been a decade ago.

Allegedly the thing had belonged to one Etienne-Laurent de Marigny, once a distinguished student of occult and oriental mysteries and antiquities, but where de Marigny had come by the coffin-shaped clock was yet another mystery. Crow had purchased it on the assurance of its auctioneer that it was, indeed, that same timepiece mentioned in certain of de Marigny's papers as being "a door on all space and time; one which only certain adepts—not all of this world—could use to its intended purpose!" There were, too, rumours that a certain Eastern mystic, the Swami Chandraputra, had vanished forever from the face of the Earth after squeezing himself into a cavity hidden beneath the panel of the lower part of the clock's coffin shape. Also, de Marigny had supposedly had the ability to open at will that door into which the Swami vanished—but that was a secret he had taken with him to the grave. Titus Crow had never been able to find even a keyhole; and while the clock weighed what it should for its size, yet when one rapped on the lower panel the sound such rappings produced were not hollow as might be expected. A curious fact—a curious history altogether—but the clock itself was even more curious to gaze upon or listen to.

Even now Joe was doing just those things: looking at and listening to the clock. He had switched on and adjusted the reading-lamp so that its light fell upon the face of the peculiar mechanism. At first sight of that clock-face Pasty had gone an even paler shade of grey, with all his nervousness of a few minutes earlier instantly returned. Crow sensed his perturbation; he had had similar feelings while working on the great clock, but he had also had the advantage of understanding where such fears originated. Pasty was experiencing the same sensations he himself had known when first he saw the clock in the auction rooms. Again he gazed at it as he had then; his eyes following the flow of the weird hieroglyphs carved about the dial and the odd movements of the four hands, movements coinciding with no chronological system of earthly origin; and for a moment there reigned an awful silence in the study of Titus Crow. Only the strange clock's enigmatic and oddly paced ticking disturbed a quiet which otherwise might have been that of the tomb.

"That's no clock like any I've ever seen before!" exclaimed an awed Joe. "What do you make of *that*, Pasty?"

Pasty gulped, his Adam's apple visibly bobbing. "I . . . I don't like it! It . . . it's shaped like a damned *coffin*! And why has it four hands, and how come they *move* like that?" He stopped to compose himself a little, and with the cessation of his voice came a soft whispering from beyond the curtained windows. Pasty's eyes widened and his face went white as death. "*What's that?*" His whisper was as soft as the sounds prompting it.

"For God's sake get a grip, will you?" Joe roared, shattering the quiet. He was completely oblivious to Pasty's psychic abilities. "It's *rain*, that's what it is—what did you bleeding think it was, spooks? I don't know what's come over you, Pasty, damned if I do. You act as if the place was haunted or something."

"Oh, but it is!" Crow spoke up. "At least, the garden is. A very unusual story, if you'd care to hear it."

"We don't care to hear it," Joe snarled. "And I warned you before — speak when you're spoken to. Now, this . . . *clock*! Get it open, quick."

Crow had to hold himself to stop the ironic laughter he felt welling inside. "I can't," he answered, barely concealing a chuckle. "I don't know how!"

"You what?" Joe shouted incredulously. "You don't know how? What the hell d'you mean?"

"I mean what I say," Crow answered, "so far as I know that clock's not been opened for well over thirty years!"

"Yes? S . . . so where does it p . . . plug in?" Pasty enquired, stuttering over the words.

"Should it plug in?" Crow answered with his own question. Joe, however, saw just what Pasty was getting at; as, of course, had the "innocent" Titus Crow.

"Should it plug in, he asks!" Joe mimed sarcastically. He turned to Pasty. "Good point, Pasty boy—now," he turned back to Crow, menacingly, "tell us something, recluse. If your little toy here isn't electric, and if you can't get it open—*then just how do you wind it up?*"

"I don't wind it up—I know nothing whatsoever of the mechanical principles governing it," Crow answered. "You see that book there on the occasional table? Well, that's Walmsley's *Notes on Deciphering Codes, Cryptograms and Ancient Inscriptions*; I've been trying for years merely to understand the hieroglyphs on the dial, let alone *open* the thing. And several notable gentlemen students of matters concerning things not usually apparent or open to the man in the street have opinionated to the effect that yonder *device* is not a clock at all! I refer to Etienne-Laurent de Marigny, the occultist Ward Phillips of Rhode Island in America, and Professor Gordon Walmsley of Goole in Yorkshire; all of them believe it to be a space-time machine—*believed* in the case of the first two mentioned, both those gentlemen now being dead—and I don't know enough about it yet to decide whether or not I agree with them! There's no money in it, if that's what you're thinking."

"Well, I warned you, guv," Joe snarled, "space-time machine!— My God!—H. G. bloody Wells, he thinks he is! Pasty, tie him up and gag him. I'm sick of his bleeding claptrap. He's got us nervous as a couple of cats, he has!'

"I'll say no more," Crow quickly promised, "you carry on. If you can get it open I'll be obliged to you; I'd like to know what's inside myself."

"Come off it, guv," Joe grated, then: "Okay, but one more word— you end up immobile, right?" Crow nodded his acquiescence and sat on the edge of his great desk to watch the performance. He really did not expect the thugs to do much more than make fools of themselves. He had not taken into account the possibility—the probability—of violence in the solution of the problem. Joe, as a child, had never had much time for the two-penny wire puzzles sold in the novelty shops. He tried them once or twice, to be sure, but if they would not go first time—well, you could usually *make* them go with a hammer! As it happened such violence was not necessary.

Pasty had backed up to the door. He was still slapping his cosh into his palm, but it was purely a reflex action now; a nervous reflex action. Crow got the impression that if Pasty dropped his cosh he would probably faint.

"The panels, Pasty," Joe ordered. "The panels in the clock."

"You do it," Pasty answered rebelliously, "that's no clock and I'm not touching it. There's something wrong here."

Joe turned to him in exasperation. "Are you crazy or something? It's a clock and nothing more! And this joker just doesn't want us to see inside. Now what does that suggest to you?"

"Okay, okay—but you do it this time. I'll stay out of the way and watch funnyman here. I've got a feeling about that thing, that's all." He moved over to stand near Crow who had not moved from his desk. Joe took his gun by the barrel and rapped gently on the panel below the dial of the clock at about waist height. The sound was sharp, solid. Joe turned and grinned at Titus Crow. There certainly seemed to be *something* in there. His grin rapidly faded when he saw Crow grinning back. He turned again to the object of his scrutiny and examined its sides, looking for hinges or other signs pointing to the thing being a hollow container of sorts. Crow could see from the crook's puzzled expression that he was immediately at a loss. He could have told Joe before he began that there was not even evidence of jointing; it was as if the body of the instrument was carved from a solid block of timber—timber as hard as iron.

But Crow had underestimated the determined thug. Whatever Joe's shortcomings as a human being, as a safecracker he knew no peer. Not that de Marigny's clock was in any way a safe, but apparently the same principles applied! For as Joe's hands moved expertly up the sides of the panelling there came a loud click and the mad ticking of the instrument's mechanism went totally out of kilter. The four hands on the carven dial stood still for an instant of time before commencing fresh movements in alien and completely inexplicable sequences. Joe stepped nimbly back as the large panel swung silently open. He stepped just a few inches too far back, jolting the occasional table. The reading-lamp went over with a crash, momentarily breaking the spell of the wildly oscillating hands and crazy ticking of de Marigny's clock. The corner was once more thrown in shadow and for a moment Joe stood there undecided, put off stroke by his early success. Then he gave a grunt of triumph, stepped forward and thrust his empty left hand into the darkness behind the open panel.

Pasty sensed the *outsideness* at the same time as Crow. He leapt across the room shouting: "Joe, Joe—for God's sake, leave it alone . . . leave it alone!" Crow, on the other hand, spurred by no such sense of comradeship, quickly stood up and backed away. It was not that he was in any way a coward, but he knew something of Earth's darker mysteries—and of the mysteries of other spheres—and besides, he sensed the danger of interfering with an action having origin far from the known side of nature.

Suddenly the corner was dimly illumined by an eerie, dappled light from the open panel; and Joe, his arm still groping beyond that door, gave a yell of utter terror and tried to pull back. The ticking was now insanely aberrant, and the wild sweeps of the four hands about the dial were completely confused and orderless. Joe had braced himself against the frame of the opening, fighting some unseen menace within the strangely lit compartment, trying desperately to withdraw his arm. Against all his effort his left shoulder abruptly jammed forward, into the swirling light, and at the same moment he stuck the barrel of his gun into the opening and fired six shots in rapid succession.

By this time Pasty had an arm round Joe's waist, one foot braced against the base of the clock, putting all his strength into an attempt to haul his companion away from whatever threatened in the swirling light of the now fearsome opening. He was fighting a losing battle. Joe was speechless with terror, all his energies concentrated on escape from the clock; great veins stuck out from his neck and his eyes seemed likely at any moment to pop from his head. He gave one bubbling scream as his head and neck jerked suddenly forward into the maw of the mechanical horror . . . and then his body went limp.

Pasty, still wildly struggling with Joe's lower body, gave a last titanic heave at that now motionless torso and actually managed to retrieve for a moment Joe's head from the weirdly lit door.

Simultaneously Pasty and Titus Crow saw something—

something that turned Pasty's muscles to water, causing him to relax his struggle so that Joe's entire body bar the legs vanished with a horrible *hisss* into the clock—something that caused Crow to throw up his hands before his eyes in the utmost horror!

In the brief second or so that Pasty's efforts had partly freed the sagging form of his companion in crime, the fruits of Joe's impulsiveness had made themselves hideously apparent. The cloth of his jacket near the left shoulder and that same area of the shirt immediately beneath had been *removed*, seemingly dissolved or burnt away by some unknown agent; and in place of the flesh which should by all rights have been laid bare by this mysterious vanishment, *there had been a great blistered, bubbling blotch of crimson and brown—and the neck and head had been in the same sickening state!*

Surprisingly, Pasty recovered first from the shock. He made one last desperate—fatal—grab at Joe's disappearing legs—and the fingers of his right hand crossed the threshold of the opening into the throbbing light beyond. Being in a crouching position and considerably thinner than his now completely vanished friend, Pasty did not stand a chance. Simultaneous with Crow's cry of horror and warning combined—he gave a sobbing shriek and seemed simply to dive headlong into the leering entrance.

Had there been an observer what happened next might have seemed something of an anticlimax. Titus Crow, as if in response to some agony beyond enduring, clapped his hands to his head and fell writhing to the floor. There he stayed, legs threshing wildly for some three seconds, before his body relaxed as the terror of his experience drove his mind to seek refuge in oblivion.

Shortly thereafter, of its own accord, the panel in the clock swung smoothly back into place and clicked shut; the four hands steadied to their previous, not quite so deranged motions, and the ticking of the hidden mechanism slowed and altered its rhythm from the monstrous to the merely abnormal . . .

Titus Crow's first reaction on waking was to believe himself the victim of a particularly horrible nightmare; but then he felt the carpet against his cheek and, opening his eyes, saw the scattered books littering the floor. Shakily he made himself a large jug of coffee and poured himself a huge brandy, then sat, alternately sipping at both until there was none of either left. And when both the jug and the glass were empty he started all over again.

It goes without saying that Crow went nowhere near de Marigny's clock! For the moment, at least, his thirst for knowledge in *that* direction was slaked.

As far as possible he also kept from thinking back on the horrors of the previous night; particularly he wished to forget the hellish, psychic impressions received as Pasty went into the clock. For it appeared that de Marigny, Phillips and Walmsley had been right! The clock was, in fact, a space-time machine of sorts. Crow did not know exactly what had caused the hideous shock to his highly developed psychic sense; but in fact, even as he had felt that shock and clapped his hands to his head, somewhere out in the worlds of Aldebaran, at a junction of forces neither spatial, temporal, nor of any intermediate dimension recognized by man except in the wildest theories, the Lake of Hali sent up a few streamers of froth and fell quickly back into silence.

And Titus Crow was left with only the memory of the feel of unknown acids burning, of the wash of strange tides outside nature, and of the rushing and tearing of great beasts designed in a fashion beyond man's wildest conjecturing . . .

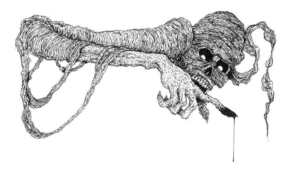

Richard Jeperson
SEVEN STARS EPISODE FOUR

THE BIAFRAN BANK MANAGER
by KIM NEWMAN

Richard Jeperson is an amnesiac who could be aged anywhere between thirty and fifty. A coal-black mass of ringlets spills onto his shoulders Charles II style, and he wears a pencil-line Fu Manchu moustache. His face is gaunt to the point of unhealthiness and dark enough to pass for a Sicilian or a Tuareg. Thin and tall and bony, he wears a fluorescent explosion of different multi-coloured outfits and has several rings on each finger. He looks as if he'd be just as happy on the foredeck of a pirate ship as in a coffee bar on Chelsea's King's Road.

Only slightly less striking is his associate Vanessa, who is in her early twenties and could be a model with her seamless mane of red hair down to her waist, Italian mouth painted silver, Viking cheekbones and unnaturally huge, green eyes. Along with ex-police constable Fred Regent, the trio travel around in Jeperson's silver-grey Rolls-Royce ShadowShark, investigating the strange and bizarre as representatives of the Diogenes Club.

Kim Newman created Richard Jeperson in the early 1970s in his very first efforts at fiction. The character originally appeared in a short play called Dracula Returns, *which is now lost, and the author wrote a series of stories and even a novel about him while still a schoolboy.*

When Newman decided to write a series of 1970s-style occult adventures, in the tradition of Jason King, The Avengers and Peter Saxon, he pulled the character—along with sidekicks Fred and Vanessa—out of mothballs. Jeperson made his official debut with the novella 'The End of the Pier Show' in the anthology Dark of the Night *(1997), and seven further tales were collected in* The Man from the Diogenes Club *(2006). The character also turns up in the stories 'The Man on the Clapham Omnibus' (*The Time Out Book of London Short Stories Volume 2, *2000), 'Cold Snap' (*The Secret Files of the Diogenes Club, *2007), 'Moon Moon Moon' (*Subterranean Online, *Summer 2009) and 'Who Dares Wins: Anno Dracula 1980' (*Anno Dracula: Johnny Alucard, *2013).*

ON THE ROAD to Somerset, Richard Jeperson drove into an anomaly. It was after midnight, a clear night in May. Behind the leather-covered wheel of his Rolls-Royce ShadowShark, he mulled over the urgent message that had brought him from Chelsea to the West Country.

Then the quality of the dark changed.

He faded the dashboard-mounted eight-track, cutting the cool jazz theme that had underscored his drive. He braked, bringing the wonderful machine to a dead halt within three yards.

He heard no night-birds.

"Weirdsville," he mused.

After slipping his flared orange frock coat over a purple silk shirt, he got out of the car.

He was parked on a straight road that cut across the levels. The stars and the sliver of moon were bright enough to highlight the flat fields of the wetlands, the maze of water-filled rhynes that made a patchwork of the working landscape.

Nothing wrong there, on the dull earth.

But in Heaven?

Tossing his tightly curled shoulder-length hair out of his eyes, he looked up.

An unaccustomed spasm of fear gripped him.

He saw at once what was anomalous.

He skimmed the constellations again, making sure he had his bearings. The North Star. Cassiopeia, the seated woman. Orion, the hunter.

Ursa Major, the Plough, was gone.

A black stretch of emptiness in the universe.

He had chanced on wrongnesses before, but nothing on such a cosmic scale. This could not be a localised phenomenon. If the seven stars were really gone, then the whole universe had been altered. He found himself shivering.

The moment passed. He looked up, and the constellations were aright again. The Plough twinkled on, seven diamond-chips in the Heavens. Richard was cold, with a heart-chill that was more than the night. The world was not aright just yet.

He got back into the ShadowShark and drove on.

Two hours earlier, he'd been in the basement of his home in Chelsea, meditating. He was halfway through a ritual of purification involving a week of fasting. He had gone beyond the hunger that had chewed his stomach for the first three days. He had shifted up a plane of perception. Strength was pouring into him, and his mind was forming pearls of understanding around grits of mystery.

Against all his express orders, Fred—one of his assistants—had interrupted his meditation, calling him to the telephone. He didn't waste time in protest. Fred had been selected for his reliability. He'd not have broken in unless it was something of supreme importance.

After exchanging a few words with Catriona Kaye, Richard had ordered Fred to get the Rolls out of the garage and despatched Vanessa, his other associate, to pick up three portions of cod and chips wrapped. Throughout the drive, he had been working the wheel and gear-shifts one-handed, while feeding himself with the other. He could not afford the physical weakness of fasting. His stomach knotted as he stuffed himself. He overcame the side-effects of such a sudden imposure on his body by mental force alone. By breaking off the ritual, he lost much. Wisdom leaked from his mind as fish and chips filled his belly.

It was a haunting. Normally, he'd have taken Fred or Vanessa with him. But this was not one of his usual exploits on behalf of the Diogenes Club, the venerable institution that referred many problems to him. This went to the heart of his whole life. Now, the Diogenes itself—or rather, its most respected elder statesman, Edwin Winthrop—was under siege from forces unknown.

He drove with both hands now. He had a sense of the enormity of the interests at stake.

Jeffrey Jeperson, the man who adopted him—a boy with no memories—from the rubble of war, had served on the Ruling Cabal of the Diogenes Club with Winthrop. Richard had been brought up with stories of Edwin Winthrop's secret services to his country. He had taken his first tentative steps into the arcane as Winthrop's most junior assistant. With old Mr. Jeperson dead and Brigadier-General Sir Giles Gallant retired, Winthrop was the last serving member of the Cabal that had seen the Diogenes through the tricky postwar years, when its many enemies had worked to see its ancient charter revoked and its resources dissipated.

Winthrop, nearly eighty, took little active part in the working of the club that was more than a club. He knew well enough to withdraw and let younger men have the reins, just as he had taken over from his own mentor.

Richard wondered if Winthrop entirely liked or trusted the people who now belonged to the club. The likes of Cornelius and King, who puffed *kif* in the smoking room, and toted transistor radios, where an inadvertent cough was once grounds for instant expulsion, to keep up with the cricket. The new generation, among whom Richard counted himself, seemed to dabble in the occult like dilettantes, rather than marching into the darkness like Victorian explorers or mapping plans for the conquest of the unknown like imperial generals.

But Winthrop had been a firebrand before he was a blimp. He still had his secrets.

Now those secrets were crawling into the open.

The anomaly convinced Richard the haunting was even worse than Catriona, Winthrop's lifelong companion, had indicated.

The ShadowShark cruised into the village of Alder. All the farmhouses were dark. The Manor House was a little way out of the village, on its own grounds. Richard drove past the small church and the Valiant Soldier pub, then took the almost-hidden road out to Winthrop's family home.

The car tripped an electric eye and the wrought-iron gates swayed open automatically. Lights burned on in the house, which seemed bigger after dark than Richard remembered it.

Catriona Kaye was waiting for him on the porch. A small, pretty woman, as old as the century, she seemed fragile, but Richard knew her to have a rugged constitution. Now, she seemed her age, nervous and worried.

"Richard, thank God you've come."

"Peace, Cat," he said, hugging her.

"It's worse than you think."

"I think it's pretty much as bad as it can get. Sometimes, stars are missing."

"You've noticed?"

They looked up, reassuring themselves. The Plough was there.

"How often?" he asked her.

"More and more."

"Let's go indoors."

The paneled hallway was empty. Richard noticed at once that the Turkish carpet had been taken up and was rolled into a giant sausage against one wall, like a record-breaking draught excluder. The floor was polished wood tiles, in a herringbone pattern, discreet charms of protection carved in corners.

Catriona gasped in horror.

"It was here," she said. "Moments ago."

She scanned the floor, dropping down on her knees, and feeling the wood with gloved hands.

"Just here," she said, almost at the foot of the main staircase. It was still carpeted, a claret weave held down by brass rails.

Catriona began tugging at the stair carpet, wrenching tacks loose. Richard went to her and helped her stand. Her knees popped as he got her upright. She was alarmingly light, as if she might drift away.

"Lift the carpet," she said.

He took out his swiss army knife and used the screwdriver to extract the bottom five rails. Like a conjurer whipping a table-cloth out from under a complete dinner service, he pulled the carpet loose, popping tacks, and tossed it back in a great flap onto the upper stairs.

Catriona gasped again. Richard knew how she felt.

Burned into the bare wood of the stairs was the black shape of a man, like a shadow torn free and thrown away. It seemed to be crawling up to the landing, one hand reaching up, fingers outstretched, the other poised to overreach its fellow, pulling the bulk of the shadow upwards.

"It was on the ground floor just now," Catriona said. "Before that, outside, a burnt patch on the lawns, the driveway—on gravel!—the front steps. It lay under the mats on the doorstep."

"You've seen it moving?"

"Watched kettles, Richard. I've sat and stared for hours, keeping it still, keeping it at bay. But look away for a moment, and it shifts."

He sat on the stairs, just below the man-shape. The outline was distinct. The light wood around the outline was unaffected, a little dusty, but the shape was matt black. It seemed like a stain rather than a brand. He touched it with his fingertips, then laid his flat palm where the small of the man's back would have been.

"It's warm," he said. "Body temperature."

It was as if someone with a high fever had lain there. He looked at his fingers. No black had come off on them. He flipped the longest blade out of his knife and scored across the ankle. The black went into the wood.

"There are others, out on the moor, gathering."

He turned to look at Catriona. The woman was strung taut, and he knew better than to try and soothe her. She'd been around the weird long enough to know how serious this was.

"It's an attack," he said, standing up, brushing dust from the knees of his salmon-coloured flared trousers. "But from what quarter?"

"Edwin won't talk. But it's to do with the War, I'm sure."

When people said "the War", depending on their age, they meant the First or Second World War. But Catriona meant a greater conflict that included both World Wars. It had started a great deal earlier, in the mid-19th century—nobody could agree quite when—

but finished in 1945, with the defeat not only of Germany and Japan but of an older, not entirely human, faction that had used the axis powers as catspaws.

Outside of the Diogenes Club, almost no one understood that War. Richard, who had no memory of his childhood, had lived through the aftermath. He'd heard Edwin's account of the War, had examined many of the documents kept in the secret library of the club, and saw all the time the lingering effects, written into the ways of the world in manners untraceable to most of humankind but as glaring as neon to the initiate.

"He says it's not over. That we made a great mistake."

Richard looked into Catriona's pale blue eyes, struck breathless by their lasting loveliness, and sensed her controlled terror. He embraced her and heard her squeal of shock.

"We looked away," she said.

He turned back, still holding Catriona by her shoulders.

An orange score-mark, where he had scratched the wood, shone in the stairs. The shape's feet were on the next step up, its head and arms were under the still-attached carpet. "If it gets completely under the carpet, it'll be able to move like lightning. Once it's out of sight, it's free."

He left Catriona and started working on the stair-rails. In minutes, he'd exposed the shadow's head and skinned the carpet up to the first-floor landing.

"I'll stay here and watch," she said. "You should go and see Edwin. He's in the *camera obscura*."

Two staircases led up from the first-floor landing. One was the ingress to an attic apartment mysteriously occupied by an ancient female dependent Edwin in happier times referred to as "Mrs. Rochester". The other led to the *camera obscura*, a large space in which an image of the house and its surroundings was projected by an apparatus of reflectors installed around the turn of the century by Edwin's father.

Richard paused on the landing. It was carpeted by a linked series of Indian rugs, which could be easily pulled up. The far staircase, to Mrs. Rochester's rooms, was in shadow. He thought he could hear her breathing, as he had often done twenty years ago. Most boys would have had nightmares about the asthmatic invalid, but Richard had no dreams at all, no memories to prod his night-thoughts to fancy.

He climbed up to the *camera obscura* and stepped into the dark room.

Edwin stood, leaning under a giant circular mirror, looking down at the mostly shadowed table. The distinct shapes of the house, the grounds, the village and the moor were outlined. By moving the mirror, Edwin could spy further afield.

Nothing was moving.

"Shadows," Edwin said, his voice still strong. "Reflections and shadows."

He dipped his hand into the image, waving through the church, scaling his skin with old stone.

"Richard, I'm glad you're here."

"It's not a happy place, Edwin."

Edwin's dark face twisted in a smile.

"How would you put it, 'a bad vibes zone'?"

"Something like that."

"It's a Hiroshima shadow."

"Yes."

At the sites of the atom bomb detonations, vaporised people left such shapes on the walls and streets, permanent shadows.

"I'm to pay for what I did."

"You weren't the only one, Edwin. You're not even the only one left."

"But I'm special. You see, I played it both ways. I had two chances. The first time, I was wise or cowardly and let it go. The second time, I was foolish or brave and took hold of it."

"There was a War on."

"There was always a war on."

"Not now."

"You think so?"

"Come on, Edwin. This is the Age of Aquarius. You more than anyone should know that. You helped throw the foe back into the outer darkness."

"You've grown up being told that, boy."

"I've grown up knowing that."

The darkness that lay like a veil in his mind, blacking out the first years of his memory, throbbed. Things were shifting there, trying to break the surface.

"Do you want to see something pretty?"

Edwin Winthrop did not ramble. Even at his age, he was sharp. This was not a casual question, addressed to a child who had long grown up.

"I love beauty," Richard said.

Edwin nodded and touched a lever. The table parted, with a slight creak.

Red light filled the room.

"It's the Jewel of Seven Stars," Richard said.

"That's right."

The gem lay on black velvet, its trapped lightpoints shining.

"The Seven Stars. They weren't there earlier. In the sky. That's not supposed to happen."

"It's a sign, boy."

"What isn't?"

"Very good. Everything is a sign. We won the War, you know. With this, essentially. People cleverer than I looked into it and saw a little of how the universe worked."

Richard looked behind him. In the darkened room, shadows could glide like serpents.

"And I gave this to them. Not the Diogenes Club, me. Just as twenty years earlier, I let the jewel go. The club has always been people like you and I, Richard. We like to pretend we're servants of the Queen or the country. But when it comes to this bauble, we're on our own. As far as it belongs to anyone, it's mine now. Can you imagine Truman letting Oppenheimer *keep* his bomb? Yet the club let me take this souvenir when it was all over."

"Men can be trusted, Edwin. Institutions change. Even the Diogenes Club."

"Do you want this?"

Edwin indicated the jewel.

It seemed to pull on Richard's gaze, sucking him into red depths. A moment's contact made him squirm inside. He broke the spell, and looked away.

"Very sensible. It can bring great gifts, but there are prices to be paid. A talented man was once elevated to genius by it, but his life dribbled away in waste and pathetic tragedy. We won a War, but we changed so much in the winning that I'm not sure we even came through it. I don't just mean Britain lost an Empire. It's more than that. Mrs. Rochester told me I took too many shortcuts. So I must pay. You've always seen the dark in me, Richard. Because, through no fault of your own, there's a dark in you."

Richard shook his head, vigorously. He could not let this pass.

"I'd have died in a concentration camp if it were not for the Diogenes Club, if not for men like my father and for *you*, Edwin. I was a boy with no memory. You've given me more than life. There's been a purpose."

"I've a terrible feeling we've just left a mess for you to clean up. All these, what do you call them, 'anomalies', all these wrongnesses in the world. Think of them as fall-out. And the other horrors, the ones everyone notices—the famines, the brushfire wars, the deaths of notable men. When I laid my hand on this"—he grasped the jewel, his hand a black spider over the red glow, flesh-clad bones outlined by the gem's inner light—"I took the worst shortcut, and I made it acceptable. There used to be, in Beauregard's time, an absolute standard. I destroyed that."

Richard did not want to believe his old friend. If there was chaos where once there had been order, he was a child of that chaos. Where Edwin had gone by intellect, he ventured with instinct.

"Now, I must pay. I've always known."

"We'll see about that," Richard said, determined.

A flash of light filled the room. Not from the jewel. It was lightning, drawn into the *camera obscura* from outside. Violent rain drummed the roof. A storm had appeared out of cloudless night sky.

Down below, in the hallway, there was a hammering.

As they emerged onto the landing, light fell onto Edwin's head. Richard did not have time to be shocked by the new lines etched into his friend's face.

They made their way to the main staircase. Catriona lay in a huddle on the stairs. The shadowman was gone. The front doors stood open, and someone stood on the mat, looking down.

The polished floor of the hallway was crowded. A dozen shadowmen, overlapping, reaching out, were frozen, swimming towards the foot of the stairs.

The house was invaded.

"Ho there above," shouted the newcomer at the door, a woman.

Lights flickered as thunder crashed. Rain blew into the hall, whipping the woman's long coat around her long legs.

Richard was by Catriona, checking her strong pulse. She was just asleep. He looked at the woman in the doorway. The door slammed shut behind her, nudging her into the hall. She stepped gingerly onto the tangle of shadows.

She had a cloud of white hair, medusa-snaked by the storm, with a seam of natural scarlet running through it. Despite the white, her face was unlined. The flicker of the lights made her freckles stand out.

The woman was of Amazon height and figure, well over six feet, extra inches added by her hair and stacked heels. Under a deep-green, ankle-length velvet trench coat, she wore a violet blouse, no bra, frayed denim hot pants, fishnet tights and calf-length soft leather pirate boots. She had a considerable weight of jade around her neck and wrists and pendant gold disc earrings the size of beer-mats.

Richard, though immediately impressed, had no idea who this woman was.

"All in this house are in grave danger," she intoned.

"Tell us something we don't know, love," he replied.

She strode across the chaos of shadowmen, slipping off and shaking out her wet coat. Her arms were bare. High up on her right upper arm was an intricate tattoo of a growling bear, with the stars of the constellation picked out in inset sequins.

"I'm Maureen Mountmain," she announced, "High Priestess of the Order of the Ram."

"Richard Jeperson, at your service," he snapped. "I assume you know this is Miss Catriona Kaye and the gent whose house you are invading is Mr. Edwin Winthrop."

"There's someone else here," she said, looking up at the ceiling. "I sense great age, and a strong light."

"That'd be Mrs. Rochester. She's sick."

Maureen laughed open-mouthed. She was close enough for Richard to catch her scent, which was entirely natural, earthy and appealing. Maureen Mountmain was extremely attractive, not just physically. She had a fraction of the magnetism he'd felt from the Jewel of Seven Stars.

"I don't know her real name," he admitted.

"It's God-Given," Maureen said. "Jennifer God-Given."

"If you say so, love."

"I told you my name was Maureen, Richard. Not 'love', 'darling', 'honey' or 'pussycat'."

"I stand corrected, Maureen."

"Do people call you Dick?"

"Never."

"There's always a first time, Dick."

There was a tigerish quality about Maureen Mountmain. The claws were never quite sheathed.

"Mountmain," said Edwin, shakily. "I know that name."

"Do not confuse me with any of my family, Mr. Winthrop. My Uncle Bennett and my Great-Uncle Declan, for instance. I believe you were present at their happy deaths. Mountmain men have always been overreaching fools. The women-folk are wiser. If you heed me, you might live out the night."

Richard wasn't sure whether he wanted to trust Maureen. He knew about the relatives she'd mentioned, from Edwin and from a comprehensive study of dangerous crackpots. If she was as well up on the War as he thought she was, she might fancy herself the Witch Queen of the Western Isles.

Come to that, she might earn the title.

"Don't just stand there gaping, idjits," she said, indicating the shadowmen at her feet. "You have other visitors. This is serious."

Catriona stirred. Richard helped her sit up.

"Very well, Miss Mountmain," Edwin said, a little of his old iron back. "Welcome to the Manor House. I am pleased to meet you."

Edwin slowly made his way down the stairs, past Richard and Catriona. He stood at the foot of the stairs and held out his hand to Maureen.

"There's been bad blood between the Diogenes Club and your

family," he said. "Let it be at an end."

Maureen looked at Edwin's hand. It occurred to Richard that the woman could snap Edwin's neck with a single blow. Instead, Maureen Mountmain embraced Edwin fiercely, lifting him a little off his feet.

"Blessed be," she announced.

Richard felt Catriona's fur rising. A feud might be over, but enmities lingered.

"I remember Declan Mountmain," Catriona said. "An utter bastard."

"Quite right," Maureen said, releasing Edwin. "And Bennett was worse. If either of them had been able to make use of the weirdstone, there'd be precious little of the world left by now."

Catriona stood, daintily, and nodded a curt acceptance of Maureen Mountmain.

"What Declan and Bennett wished for may still come about," Maureen said, urgently. "They were bested, and the greater forces who used them checked, by the rituals your Diogenes Club used in the War. But you woke up the Seven Stars, bought a short-term victory at the cost of long-term trouble."

Edwin nodded. "I admit as much," he said.

"Do not bother justifying your actions. All men and most women would have done the same."

Most *women?* thought Richard.

"And you could have done it earlier, when victory would have seemed even cheaper and been far more costly. For that, the world owes you, Miss Kaye, a debt that'll never be understood. Your influence, a sensible woman's, tempered this man's instincts. Like my uncles, Edwin and, I intuit with certainty, Dick here, are fascinated by the weirdstone. To them it is like a well-made gun that should be fired or a showoff's automobile that must be driven. Men never think that guns have to be fired *at* something or cars driven *to* somewhere."

Richard bristled. This bedraggled demigoddess had the nerve to barge into someone else's home and deliver a lecture in occult feminism.

"Women have faults too," she said, in his direction. "Men like guns and cars, women like men who like guns and cars. Who is to say which is the more foolish?"

"What's happening here?" Richard asked.

Edwin looked down. Maureen stepped in.

"A crisis, of course."

"It's coming for the Seven Stars," Edwin said, "swirling about the house, converging on the gem."

"What is coming?"

"The Biafran Bank Manager," Edwin chuckled, blackly.

"*What?*"

It was a strange thing to say. But Edwin was no longer the firm-minded man Richard remembered.

"A joke in poor taste," Maureen explained. "He means the Skeleton in the Closet."

Richard had heard it before, a reference to a television advert. It was one of a wave of desperate jokes made in response to the heart-breaking photographs of starved men, women and children that came out of Biafra during the famine. Any disaster that couldn't be contained by the human mind spilled over in sick humour, graveyard comedy.

"Why now?" Richard asked.

"It's been coming a long way, my boy," Edwin said, "for a long time."

"He's been building you up for this," Maureen said. "Your life has been a series of initiations."

Edwin looked at her sharply, with new respect.

"I've had to teach myself, old man. But I've been coming along too."

"It's true," Edwin said. "Richard, I knew I wouldn't be capable of facing what is coming. I thought, almost hoped, I'd be dead by the time the changes really got underway, and you were the one we chose to take over. You're stronger now than I ever was. You have talents. We had to work for things which are easy for you. I know that's no comfort."

Richard felt a deep resentment. Not at the way his life had been shaped, but that the great purpose he had always sensed was imperfectly revealed to him while an outsider, the daughter of old enemies, had understood.

Thunder crashed again, and the lights went out. They came

back again and the shadowmen on the floor were crowded around the foot of the stairs, black fingers reaching upwards. The quality of the light was different, wavering. Filaments fizzed at the end of their tether.

It was the anomaly again, and they were inside it.

The lights strobed, leaving photo-flash impressions on his eyes. The periods of darkness between the periods of light lengthened. The shadowmen were in motion, revealed by a pixellation of still images. They crowded together as they swarmed up the stairs, passing under Richard and Catriona. A fresh wave spread out from under the closed front doors, scrambling around Maureen's boots. Richard held Catriona and tried to gather his spiritual strength, controlling his breathing, feeling the focus gather in the centre of his chest, preparing for an assault.

The shadowmen flowed up onto the landing, gathering around Edwin, arms seeming to lift from the floor, as insubstantial yet sinewy as steel cobwebs.

From inside his jacket, Edwin took the Jewel of Seven Stars.

The lightbulbs all exploded at once. Glass tinkled onto polished wood.

The shadowmen were frozen.

Red light filled the hall, spilling down from the landing. Edwin held the jewel up. The Seven Stars shone, like the ones no longer in the Heavens. The constant light held the shadowmen back.

"So that's it," Maureen said, awed. "I never dreamed."

"You feel it, like everyone," Edwin said. "The *temptation*."

"I can't blame you," she admitted.

Edwin set the jewel on the floor. Once out of his hand, the jewel changed. Its light, fuelled by the wielder, dimmed. The shadows around Edwin grew. A thin arm, like a black stocking on a wind-whipped washing line, wrapped around Edwin's leg. He sank to one knee, pulled down. Another shadow latched onto his arm.

Catriona broke free, suddenly strong, and ran up the stairs, Richard and Maureen at her heels. They hesitated at the landing.

Edwin lay on the floor, twisted. Shadowmen twined around him, pinning him down, growing tight. The light-points of the jewel, lying nearby, glowed like drops of radioactive blood.

Catriona released a single sob, and clung to the bannister. Richard felt Maureen's strong hand on his arm, sensed the warmth of her body close to him. This was entirely the wrong time to be aroused, but he had no control over his surging blood.

The shadowmen wrapped Edwin like a mummy's windings. He disappeared under black, elongated forms. The shadowmen coalesced into one man and flattened, leaving a final Hiroshima shadow.

"It took him," Maureen said.

The anomaly wasn't passed. It wasn't over.

Maureen stepped past him and reached down for the jewel. Richard took her arm, holding her back, feeling the warmth of her bare skin, fighting the fog of desire in his mind, torn by a deep need to throw her aside and take the jewel for himself. With Edwin gone, it was up for grabs.

"No," he said, finding his strength.

Maureen's outstretched fingers curled into a fist.

"No," she agreed.

They separated and stood either side of the jewel. It was changed, somehow. Edwin had passed into it or beyond it.

"It'd make a novel doorstop," he suggested.

She laughed, with an appealing edge of hysteria.

Catriona still stood, clinging to the bannister, eyes sparkling with unshed tears, the life she had shared with Edwin torn away and crumpled up.

"This is like a blasted relay race," Richard said. "Do we pick up the baton?"

"We have to do something with it."

"Take it upstairs," Catriona said. "She'll know what must be done."

"She?" Richard and Maureen both asked.

"Mrs. Rochester. Geneviève, her name is. She'll be waiting. I'll be up myself, when I've composed myself. I'd like to be alone now, anyway. Alone with . . ."

She indicated the last shadowman. This one would stay put.

"Together," Maureen said.

They lifted the jewel between their right hands. Richard felt

Maureen's cheek against his, and the side of her body as they slipped arms about each other. She had a few inches on him. Between their palms, the Seven Stars glowed.

They made their way to the far staircase.

Mrs. Rochester—Jennifer God-Given—Geneviève Dieudonné lay on a narrow, coffin-shaped pallet. A tie-dyed blanket was gathered over her legs. She looked a thousand years old, and was plugged into a standing drip-feed. A bandage was fixed to her side, stained with greenish seepage.

Her million wrinkles arranged themselves into a smile.

"I apologise for my appearance. Your uncle shot me, dear. With silver. If he'd had better aim, I'd not be here."

"You know who I am?" Maureen asked.

"Madame Sosostris knows all," Geneviève intoned.

Another name? No, a joke.

They set the jewel down at the old woman's feet. It nestled in the folds of her blanket, like a hot-water bottle.

"Edwin's gone," Richard said.

"I know. He stepped into the shadows. Against my advice, but it's too late to bother with all that. He was, at heart, a good man. Despite everything."

Maureen was clinging closer to Richard. For the first time, he had a sense that she too was afraid. Her obvious courage was in need of the occasional injection of bravado.

"Will you die?" Maureen asked the ancient woman.

"No, no, no," Geneviève chuckled. "At least, not just yet. You might not think it to look at me, but I'm getting better. The tide of years caught up with me, but it's drawing away from the shore now."

"Do you need our blood?"

Richard noticed only now the sharp little teeth in the old woman's shrunken mouth.

"Not yet," Geneviève said. "You mustn't think of me until you've bound the jewel. We've a chance to damp down the ill effects of its use, just briefly. There's a ritual which will truly end yesterday's War, which will pack back into the stone all the nastiness that has trickled out since we opened it up back in '44."

"Will everything be . . . better?" Richard asked.

"Not really," Geneviève admitted. "Nuclear reactions will still be part of physics, and you all have to live with the consequences. All the rest of it, you must take responsibility for. The Jewel of Seven Stars didn't make men stupid or venal or mad. It just fed on those things and spewed them out a thousandfold. But with the stone wrapped, the old world will have a chance."

"Why didn't Edwin perform this ritual?" Maureen asked.

"He'd spoiled himself for it. Something sad about a cat. And Catriona couldn't stand in for you. The participants have to be from both factions. You're a Mountmain, dear. And Richard is the creature of the Diogenes Club. Adversaries whose allegiances run counter to the official history. Churchill and Hitler were equally opposed to Diogenes and aligned with your uncles. There were great villains on Edwin's side and saints tied up with the Mountmains. It's too late to blame anyone. You just have to end the cycle, to make way for that Aquarian nonsense."

As Geneviève spoke, Maureen took his hand in a tigerish grip.

"This ritual," he began, "what exactly . . .?"

"What do you think?" Geneviève laughed.

Richard looked up into Maureen's eyes, and saw understanding in them.

Magical sex always struck Richard as somehow contrived, requiring the consideration of mathematics in a process that worked best when run on sheer instinct. You had to keep your head full of angles of the compass and meaningless rituals, locked up within your own skull when your body wanted to flow mindlessly into another. And magick rituals tended to be performed on cold stone floors hardly suited to comfort or arousal.

This was not like that at all.

They were together on cushions spread over the *camera obscura* table, the jewel between them. In their own anomaly, they ebbed and flowed like the tides, bloodstreams and bodies pushed and pulled by primal forces. Daybreak brought fields and woods and buildings into the room, patterning their bodies. At the centre of a harmonious universe, energies poured in through their open minds, bound up and redirected by their coupling. Mirrors shone warm sunlight down on them.

Tantric sex, the most common form of sex magic, was all about building up spiritual energy by making love at length but never reaching the dissipation of climax.

This was not like that at all.

They peaked three times apiece.

"The seventh," she whispered.

They passed the jewel between them, running it over their bodies. Richard looked through the stone, past the stars, seeing Maureen's face rubied with joy. They kissed the Jewel of Seven Stars, and Maureen took it, pressing it to her yoni.

He entered her again, pushing the weirdstone into her womb.

Joined by the jewel, they came again, finally, together, completing the pattern of seven stars.

Then, they slept.

Richard awoke, all sense of time lost. His coat had been arranged around him.

Maureen was gone.

He still felt her, tasted her, scented her.

The Jewel of Seven Stars was gone too.

Dressed, clothes abrading the tender spots of his body, he explored the house.

The Hiroshima Shadow marked Edwin's passing.

Catriona was in Mrs. Rochester's room. Geneviève was sitting up, hidden behind a veil of mosquito netting.

"She took the stone," he said, weakly.

"Her family have been after it for years," said a voice from behind the netting.

"She visited," Catriona said, "after she left you, she came here. She was glowing, Richard."

"Like a ripe orange," the voice—so unlike Mrs. Rochester's frail whisper—said, "so full of *life* that she had some to share. Edwin made up for what he did with the stone, and she made up for what her uncle did to me."

The veil fell.

The woman on the bed was not Mrs. Rochester. She was lithe, red-lipped and unhurt. But it was Geneviève, young again.

"Now," she said, "the old War is over."

The anomaly was gone. The War was finished. A great purpose of his life, undefined in his mind until last night, was concluded. But he still had his darkness, the shadowed part of his mind and memory. Because a part of his life was gone, he clung tenaciously to what he could remember, fixing memories like butterflies pinned to a card. Edwin Winthrop was a memory now, and Mrs. Rochester. And Maureen.

Their coming together ended something, cleared the stage for many beginnings. But that was it. Her taste would fade. But the memory would stay.

Geneviève got out of bed for the first time in thirty years. Her old woman's nightgown hung strangely on a body barely grown. Underneath her years, she was impossibly young. She hugged Catriona, and Richard. She danced on the points of her toes. The jewel-light shone in eyes reddened by Maureen's blood.

Catriona was bereft, Geneviève reborn.

A fresh cycle would begin.

Francis St. Clare and Frederica Masters

SOMEONE IS DEAD
by R. Chetwynd-Hayes

Francis St. Clare is a wealthy young man and an authority on the occult who describes himself as "the world's only practising psychic detective". When he first met Frederica Masters, an extremely attractive and gifted materialistic medium, he at once realised the enormous psychic power she possessed and convinced her that by becoming his assistant she could fulfil her potential. Despite their friendly bickering with each other, Fred and Francis are consulted by clients who need their unique knowledge and gifts to investigate cases involving the supernatural.

'Someone is Dead' (The Elemental, 1974) was their first adventure from author Ronald Chetwynd-Hayes (1919–2001), and it set the tone for all the subsequent stories in the series with the authors' trademark blend of horror and humour. This is best exemplified by such titles as 'The Wailing Waif of Battersea' (1975), 'The Headless Footman of Hadleigh' (1977), 'The Gibbering Ghoul of Gomershal' (1980), 'The Astral Invasion' (1984), 'The Phantom Axeman of Carleton Grange' (1986) and 'The Cringing Couple of Clavering' (1988).

Published in 1993, the novel The Psychic Detective *revealed how Fred and Francis first met and, for a while, was destined to be a Hammer Film Production. A final short story featuring the duo, 'The Fundamental Elemental', appeared in* The Vampire Stories of R. Chetwynd-Hayes (*aka* Looking for Something to Suck and Other Vampire Stories, *1997*).

HE WAS A tall, lean young man with a pale face and the smile of one who is hiding his natural shyness under a mask of easy self-confidence. The girl by his side was extremely pretty: ash blonde hair, white skin, and wearing an expression of cynical amusement as though her blue eyes had seen more than her years warranted. In contrast to her companion's neat black suit, she wore a colourful costume that bordered on the bizarre. The mauve blouse had a dangerous split down the centre that revealed the valley between her breasts; there was a corresponding parting at the rear which offered the masculine eye a tantalizing glimpse of a white, smooth back. The black miniskirt was the stunted offspring of a broad belt and her splendid, nylon-clad legs riveted every man's attention and raised a storm of feminine envy.

"I," announced the young man, "am Francis St. Clare, the world's only practising psychic detective."

He paused, as though to allow time for applause, then nodded in the girl's direction. "This is my assistant, Frederica Masters. She answers to Fred."

The silence suggested embarrassment. Six people looked, first questioningly at each other, then back at the ill-matched couple standing just within the open doorway. At last a plump young man with receding hair came forward and held out a soft, moist hand.

"I'm Reggie Smith."

Francis St. Clare briefly touched the offered hand and said: "Pleased to meet you," while the girl nodded.

"We are delighted you could come." Reggie Smith poured out the statement. "Delighted and relieved. When we read your advertisement in *The Ghost Hunter's Weekly*, I said to my wife . . ."

"That's me," an equally plump young woman stated. "I'm Betty."

Francis murmured that he was charmed and the girl nodded again.

"I said to Betty," Reggie went on, "this is the man for us. Didn't I, Betty?"

"You sure did," his wife nodded violently. "Your very words."

"Can we sit down?" Fred spoke for the first time and there was a fusillade of "Sorry," "Of course," until soon they were seated in a circle, eight voices searching for something to say.

"I expect you'll want to hear all about the—er—phenomenon," Reggie suggested at length.

"No." Francis produced a gold cigarette case, fitted a cigarette into a grotesquely long holder and lit it with a lighter that was shaped like a miniature coffin. "No. Eyewitness accounts are never accurate. They embellish, over-dramatise. If there is a psychic phenomenon here, I prefer to see and hear it with an unbiased mind. Tell me about the setup."

"Setup?" Reggie raised his eyebrows and looked questioningly round the circle with an amused smile. "We all live here."

"I didn't imagine you were visiting." Francis watched a smoke ring drift up to the ceiling. "But are you all related, or what? This is a large house and, frankly, none of you are my idea of county."

A large man near the fireplace grunted and a petite little brunette next to him said "Indeed" in tone of voice which suggested a knife being drawn across ice.

"We are three separate couples that share," Reggie Smith explained. "The housing problem is pretty acute nearer town, so we all got together and bought this place. It is divided into three reasonably large apartments and altogether it works very well."

"Do you swap?" Fred asked.

"I beg your pardon!" The big man all but exploded and Francis smiled.

"You mustn't mind Fred. She's naturally depraved. Now, I think it might help if I knew all your names."

"Surely." Reggie motioned to the large man. "This is Roland Taylor and next to him is his wife, Nina. Roland is chief clerk at Hackett's Designs."

"How's the designing business?" Francis enquired.

"Fair," Roland grunted and Nina smiled sweetly.

"And this," Reggie said, indicating a red-haired young man who sat beside a cool, serene young creature with the face of a Madonna, "is Jennifer and Leslie Halliday."

"Your occupation?" Francis asked.

"Chartered accountant," Leslie Halliday replied, "and I don't believe in the supernatural."

"Indeed." Francis flicked ash onto the carpet and Betty Smith hastened to put an ashtray on the arm of his chair. "Suppose you were to meet a headless man in the back garden, what would be your reaction?"

"I'd look for an explanation," Leslie said shortly.

"Very sensible. Now, you er—Reggie, how do you earn the necessary crust?"

"I'm a car salesman."

"I see." Francis sat back and stared thoughtfully at the fireplace. "We have a chief clerk, a chartered accountant and a car salesman all living in a haunted house. One might say the mundane married to the outrageous. What time does the phenomenon occur?"

"Anywhere from nine o'clock to midnight," Reggie replied in a low voice.

"Good." Francis consulted a gold wristwatch. "That gives us time to bath, shave and eat dinner. Tell me, do you eat separately, or *en masse*?"

"All together in the original dining-room," Reggie stated. "It's more economical and labour saving."

"Right, if you will kindly show us to our room, we'll prepare for the worst."

"I've prepared two rooms," Betty Smith said coyly.

"Fine," Francis nodded. "We don't sleep together."

"Only on alternate Sundays," Fred added.

The dining-room was oak-panelled and rather gloomy. The long table wore two white starched table-clothes; a collection of neatly placed plates and stainless-steel cutlery reminded Francis of a well-dressed hardware shop, and two tall wax candles assisted the overhead chandelier in keeping the shadows at bay. Everyone had "dressed". That is to say, the men wore mass-produced dinner jackets and the women long evening gowns. Francis was attired in faultless evening dress, while Fred appeared in a glittering silver creation that approached the frontiers of near nudity by having a strip of material at the front, leaving the back and ribs bare. The other three women greeted this apparition with unmistakable signs of disapproval, which was wasted on the recipient who seated herself at the table and examined the empty plates with greedy expectancy.

"What's all this, then? Fast day at the monastery?"

"Really, Fred," Francis sighed. "One can't take you anywhere." He apologised to the assembly. "Sorry about this, but she is a genius, and is only trying to let you know. Shall we get on? I'd like to be well fortified before whatever happens—happens."

There was a slight easing of the tension and Betty Smith rang a small brass cowbell, which was a signal for the door to open and a large raw-boned girl to enter, pushing a loaded food trolley.

"This is someone I haven't met," Francis said.

"Gertrude," Reggie announced. "She does for us."

"How-dew," Gertrude announced, placing a plate of soup in front of Fred. "I does for them."

"Has Gertrude experienced the phenomenon?" Francis enquired, wagging an admonishing finger at Fred who had already laid eager hand to spoon.

"She leaves before nine," Reggie stated.

"Nutting," Gertrude said, apparently anxious to stress her non-observation, "nutting would make me stay in this 'orrible 'ouse after dark."

"Why?" Francis asked.

"It's bleeding 'aunted." Gertrude presented Reggie with the final plate of soup and departed.

"Not very bright," Betty informed Francis. "She's never seen anything, but imagines a lot."

"But she's rather sweet." Nina Taylor smiled at Francis and thereby earned herself a glare from Fred.

"What do you know about your house?" The world's only practising psychic detective addressed the entire table. "For example, how old is it?"

"Pretty old." Roland sipped his soup with an expression of distaste. "Too much salt again. Elizabethan, I'd say."

"Balls," said Fred, scraping her plate with fast-moving spoon.

The shocked silence was broken by Francis saying softly: "Fred does the research. Never go on a job until we've looked into the background."

"Pseudo-Elizabethan," Fred went on, examining with a critical eye the plate of roast beef which Gertrude deposited before her. "Built in 1880."

"Oh." Reggie Smith looked depressed, then he brightened. "I could have sworn the estate agent chap said it was genuine Elizabethan, but he must have meant the original house."

"Prison," said Fred, attacking the roast beef.

"Pardon!"

"This house was built on the site of a 17th-century prison. It was knocked down in 1830. Your place was shoved up fifty years later."

"That's what made me decide to take the case," Francis explained. "You get a lot of interesting phenomena on the sites of old prisons. Do you remember the case of the headless strangler of Marshalsea, Fred?"

"Do I not?" Fred grimaced. "The bastard kept taking swipes at me with a dirty great rope."

"How awful for you," Jennifer Halliday gasped. "What on earth did you do?"

"Bashed him in the unmentionables with me handbag. Turned out to be some joker dressed up."

"We come across any number of fakes," Francis observed airily. "Surprising the people who get their kicks out of imagining they have a ghost on the premises. Still, I suppose it's better than taking to drink."

"I can assure you . . ." Reggie began.

"I think our friends will be convinced in a few hours' time," Nina observed softly. "It was possibly a good idea not to tell them the details. Surprise is a great educator."

"I'm convinced already," Fred said, cleaning her plate with a piece of bread. "Francis, my love, something has just come into the room."

"Indeed?" Francis filled his glass with some inferior red wine. "Malignant?"

"No, I don't think so." Fred was peeling a peach. "Rather sad— frightened. Nothing visual, but I can feel. It's near the fireplace."

All eyes were drawn in the general direction of the marble

fireplace and Francis murmured softly: "Keep your shirts on—don't stare."

"But it's too early," Betty Smith wailed. "Nothing happens before nightfall."

"Nothing you can see," Francis commented dryly. "Power comes with darkness. Fred, where is it now?"

"Behind me," said that young lady cheerfully. "I think it would like to tell me something, but it doesn't know how."

"Masculine or feminine?"

Fred closed her eyes.

"Don't know. Very weak . . . said . . . frightened . . . very . . . very frightened. Hold on a sec . . . it's gone."

"Sure?" Francis watched the girl's face with some anxiety. "Put out mental feelers."

Fred remained motionless for a full minute, her eyes closed and her face devoid of expression. The silence was heavy with subdued fear and Betty Smith whimpered.

"Shut up," Francis snapped. "This is not the time for an attack of the vapours. Well, Fred?"

"Gone." She opened her eyes, but the cynical, irresponsible expression was missing; her body was rigid, the face paler than usual. "It's a strange one, Francis. Rather like the wailing waif of Battersea, but weaker."

His eyes were like chips of blue granite as his glance flickered from face to face.

"You say nothing happens before nine o'clock or thereabouts, but has anyone experienced a strange coldness? As though a door had been left open?"

"I have," Nina confessed, "and once or twice it seemed that someone was staring at me. You know, a feeling of eyes boring into the back of your neck."

Francis nodded. "Right. Anyone else? And don't start imagining. I want facts."

Five heads were shaken and St. Clare smiled grimly.

"One latent psychic and the rest gross materialists, which means five of you shouldn't see or hear anything at all. Let's have that girl in again."

"You mean Gertrude?" Reggie asked.

"I didn't mean the Queen of Sheba. Ring that bell so I can find out what she knows, sees or imagines."

Betty shook the cowbell violently and presently Gertrude entered, wearing her outdoor coat and seemingly not happy at being summoned.

"Jew want me? Got to be off, me mum don't like me out after dark."

"Gertrude," Francis smiled genially, "you said a while back nothing would make you stay in this house after sunset. If I recall correctly, you stated it was haunted. What makes you think that?"

Gertrude hung her head and swung her left foot back and forth like a tongue-tied schoolgirl.

"Everyone knows its 'aunted."

"You mean you have been told it is haunted. You've never seen anything unusual yourself?"

Gertrude did not answer, but continued to swing her foot; her face was a sulky mask.

"Well," Francis insisted gently, "have you seen anything?"

Almost reluctantly, Gertrude shook her head.

"So," Francis said relaxing slightly, "how can you be certain the house is haunted?"

"Want to go 'ome. Me mum said I must be 'ome before dark."

"When you have answered my question. How can you be sure the house is haunted?"

"Me—me gran." The words poured out in an unbroken torrent. "She was passing 'ere one night, the moon was bright it was and a bloody great man was walking the garden a bloody great man in black and his eyes glared so me gran fair split 'er drawers and he were walking on nutting . . ."

"You mean," Francis interrupted, "he was walking on air?"

Gertrude nodded violently.

"Yus, walking on air. 'E was three or four feet up but me gran could 'ear his feet treading on summat 'ard and she ran like billy-o."

"I bet she did." Francis smiled gently. "Right, that will be all, Gertrude. You can go now."

Gertrude escaped. She went through the doorway with great speed as though anxious to demonstrate her grandmother's long-ago retreat, and presently they heard her footsteps running down the garden path.

"So far, so good." Francis rubbed his hands with boyish glee. "The pattern is familiar up to a point, but from then on . . . I don't know. By the way, where does the phenomenon take place?"

"Mostly in the hall," Reggie volunteered, "but you can only see it from our sitting-room. The sound effects can be heard all over the house."

"I gather the experience is rather disturbing."

They all nodded and Reggie added, "You can say that again."

"Well, that being the case—forgive the question—why do you stay here?"

"Because we've nowhere else to go." Reggie raised his voice. "Damn it, man, we've all sunk our last pennies in this place and we like it. Frankly, you're our last hope."

"Hope is a white horse galloping towards a limitless horizon," Francis murmured softly. "Very well, you lot scamper upstairs when the time comes, and Fred and I will sweat it out in the sitting-room."

"You sure?" growled Roland Taylor. "There's a natural explanation of course, but the whole damn business is pretty bloodcurdling."

"Quite sure." Francis rose. "You'd only be in the way. Your united fears would build up and feed whatever materialises."

"I think we really ought to tell you what to expect," Betty Smith said. "I know you've had lots of experience with this sort of thing, but . . ."

"No." Francis shook his head. "Under no circumstances. It is important I have no preconceived opinions. I do not wish to be told the plot before I read the book. So upstairs with all of you and leave Fred and me to make some necessary preparations. When it is all over, I will call you."

There were a few half-hearted attempts to discourage him, but finally they trooped upstairs while Francis and Fred retired to the Smith sitting-room. The girl grimaced.

"This is going to be a tough one, Frankie. I can feel the atmosphere building up."

"Not to worry." He opened a small suitcase and took out a bottle of water, a roll of tape and five little wooden crosses mounted on silver bases. "I don't know if it will be of any use, but we might as well set up a pentacle, just in case a nasty gets rough. Let's clear a space."

They cleared the floor of furniture, rolled back the carpet, then proceeded to pin the white tape into the outline of a five-pointed star. On the apex of each point, Francis stood a cross, then, having opened the bottle, poured some of its contents into five little silver bowls which he placed on the tips of the inner points. He straightened up and rubbed his hands.

"Well, that's done. Let's hope it works. Do you remember the demon of Colchester Road?"

"Do I not?" Fred shuddered. "He chucked the crosses at us and threw me around the room."

"We've had a lot more experience since those days. Put a couple of chairs inside, we might as well be comfy."

They lifted two chairs over the taped lines, then Francis drew the curtains and switched on all the lights.

"Storm coming up," he announced, "beginning to rain and the wind is rising. Listen to it."

A gust of wind buffeted the house and the rain could be heard lashing the garden. Fred shivered.

"I hope it is not going to thunder. I don't mind spooks on the rampage, but I can't stand thunder."

"Shouldn't think so," Francis comforted. "Just a downpour—do the gardens good. Right, as the actress said to the bishop, all we have to do is wait for something to happen."

They sat on two spindle-legged chairs in the middle of the star, like two children playing some bizarre game. Francis whistled and stared thoughtfully at the ceiling; Fred examined her fingernails and once she yawned.

Francis spoke at last. "I wonder what shape it will take? I can't help thinking the disturbance here has nothing to do with the present house. Probably goes back to the old prison. Listen to that wind. A few chimney pots will go if it keeps up. What do you think of that lot upstairs?"

Fred shrugged her white shoulders.

"Pretty commonplace crowd. That Nina creature is probably psychic, although she doesn't know it."

Suddenly, as though a switch had been pulled, or a vast curtain had been dropped about the house, the sound of wind and rain ceased. An abrupt, absolute silence rushed in from all sides and Francis gasped.

"This is it, my sweet. Hang on to your seat."

For the space of two minutes nothing happened, then, from afar-off, they heard a door slam, followed by the sound of bolts being driven home. Then footsteps; loud, heavy treads that seemed to be crashing down on a paved floor. They grew steadily louder and nearer before the sitting-room door crashed open and Francis saw that, instead of the carpeted hall, a long, door-lined passage lay beyond. Coming towards them was a tall man dressed completely in black.

"Quick, Fred!" Francis snapped his fingers, "What do you feel? What is it?"

"I don't know." Fred shook her head. "I can't feel anything. No coldness, no sense of a presence—nothing."

"What?"

Francis stared at the approaching figure in astonishment. "But you must, girl. Look, there's a complete reconstruction out there. I'd say yer actual 17th-century prison, and that charlie must be governor or something, and a nasty-looking brute he is too."

The tall man approached as far as the open doorway. There he stopped and appeared to be staring at the wide-eyed couple seated in the pentacle. He was at least six and a half feet tall and had a dark, intelligent, but evil face, framed with long black hair. He was dressed completely in black: black cut-away coat, black shirt and cravat, black buckskin trousers and black, silver-buckled shoes. He carried a long riding crop which he slashed spasmodically against his leg.

"Here goes," Francis murmured, then raised his voice. "Who are you?"

The black, sinister figure continued to stare straight at him; there was a gloating expression in the dark eyes.

"What is it you want?" Francis spoke slowly. "You don't belong here."

The figure switched the riding crop several times, then, raising his left hand, began to prod with a rigid forefinger the empty space that lay between the door-posts. It was as though he were feeling an invisible wall.

"What the hell . . . ?" Francis stood up, an expression of dawning comprehension lighting his eyes. "No, mate, it's not ready for you to come through yet. I'd push off if I were you and come back another day."

The black figure dropped its hand and looked at Francis with deepening interest; the thin lips slowly parted and a set of magnificent white teeth were bared in a mirthless grin. After a few moments, he turned slowly and began to walk back down the passage, trailing his riding crop along the right-hand wall, so that it made a rattling sound, slithered from brick to wooden door, then back to brick again. Without warning, the sitting-room door slammed, and instantly the sound of pelting rain and howling wind flashed back into being. Francis jumped to his feet and raced for the door. He flung it open, tore out into the hall and shouted:

"Downstairs all of you! Hurry!"

Way up on the first landing a solitary door opened, proving they had all been huddled in a single room for comfort, then they came down the stairs, every face alive with fearful expectancy.

"In here." Francis led the way back into the sitting-room and the Smiths pretended not to see the rolled-back carpet or the displaced furniture.

"Now," Francis said closing the door and taking up a position in front of the fireplace, "we have just witnessed a scene which is without parallel in my experience. The present—the now—was blocked out and we saw a stretch of corridor that rightfully belonged to the past. A tall, dark man walked up to that doorway and seemed to prod an invisible wall. Is this the phenomenon you have all seen at various times?"

They all nodded and Roland Taylor muttered: "Time picture."

"What?"

"I said, a time picture." The big man raised his voice. "An image that builds up under certain conditions. Rather like television waves, and we are the receiving sets."

"I know all about time images," Francis snapped, "only they rarely come equipped with sound and the viewer is usually a high-sensitive person and she felt nothing. Why?"

"I don't understand," Reggie Smith sounded and looked very

distressed. "What's it matter if she felt hot or cold? The place is still haunted."

"No," Francis shook his head, "apart from the unknown presence Fred detected in the dining-room, I have found no trace of psychic phenomena here."

"But . . ." Betty Smith was near tears. "The man, that awful passage?"

"Is the result of what I can only describe as a time slip. For a short while, part of this house reverts, for reasons I have yet to determine, to the original prison which stood on this site some two hundred years ago."

"Rubbish," Roland Tyler growled. "Don't listen to him. All we have seen is a picture of how the passage used to look."

"Ever thought of going through that door and meeting that bloke in the black gear, halfway?" Francis enquired.

Roland Taylor shook his head.

"Frankly, no. I was too scared. But if I had done so, the entire picture would have disintegrated."

"Fancy trying your luck tomorrow night?"

Taylor flushed and growled, "Certainly not. We're paying you to do the investigating."

"Exactly." Francis smiled grimly. "I'm the expert. The policeman you are paying to catch the criminal, the soldier you have engaged to fight your war. Now, let's go one step further. Think carefully. How long would you say the passage was when you first saw it?"

"Four—six feet," Betty Smith ventured.

"Oh, no." Nina shook her head. "Ten feet I'd say. The man came out of a—kind of mist."

"Eight to ten feet," Halliday stated. "Certainly not longer."

"This evening," Francis said softly, "I'd be willing to bet my braces on it being all of thirty feet long."

No one spoke for a full minute, then Roland Taylor asked quietly: "What are we supposed to deduce from that?"

Francis St. Clare stared thoughtfully at the speaker, then shook his head. "I'm honestly not certain. Perhaps when I said the house had slipped back into the past, I should have said 'was slipping.' Sliding down a time precipice. But why? Some people—special people—have entered the past for brief periods, but purely as spectators. We seem to be on the verge of becoming actors."

"That's absolute nonsense," Roland protested. "There's no way back into the past. Shadows, images of bygone years can manifest if the conditions are right, but the idea of living people being transported back is ludicrous."

"Suppose," St. Clare said quietly, "you come to a river. It cannot be forded and only one of you can swim. How can you cross?"

"Build a bridge?" Jennifer Halliday suggested.

"Bright girl. But how? You have plenty of rope, there are trees on both sides, but the tallest cannot span the river. A rope can be thrown across, but there is no way to anchor it. What is the solution?"

"A strong swimmer . . ." Leslie Haliday began.

"Ah!" Francis nodded, then chuckled with boyish glee. "Go on."

"Could swim across taking the ends of two ropes with him. These tied to a convenient tree would make a rope bridge."

"Exactly." Francis began to walk from one person to another, staring into each frightened or bewildered face, pouring out a torrent of words, clearly in the grip of some intense excitement. "Two ropes and agile men could cross; the river—the limbo—would be bridged. But the important first step, the essential action, is to get a man over to the other side. Without him, the would-be travellers can only stand and . . ."

He paused, looked back into the empty hall, then swung round to face the seven bewildered people. ". . . stare into the future."

"What the hell?" Roland exploded.

"One of them came across," Francis was shouting. "It's no use shaking your heads. No use mouthing platitudes—impossible, farfetched, it couldn't happen . . . It *has* happened and one of you bloody well know it's happened."

The babble of voices rose. Roland Taylor sneered and seemed on the point of striking the tall, elegant young man who appeared to be enjoying their discomfort.

"You're stark, raving mad. I was against you being called in from the start, but I never dreamed you'd come up with such a harebrained, cracked stunt as this."

"Shut up!" Francis roared. "I said, shut up and listen. There's no other explanation. I know it must sound fantastic to people who have only travelled along the narrow road that runs between house and office, but reason it out for yourselves. Someone—some intelligence, has bridged the great gulf that divides the past from the present. It cannot—I repeat—it cannot be a one-way operation. An anchor man was sent over and he's here with us—now."

They stared at him openmouthed, half convinced, on the verge of full belief.

"You mean . . ." Jennifer Halliday was the first to speak. "There's a ghost—here?"

Francis raised a slim eyebrow.

"Yes, indeed, there is a ghost. Fred sensed it in the dining-room. The ghost of someone recently murdered."

"Murdered!" Roland Taylor looked helplessly round the room. "No one has been murdered here."

"But you're wrong." Francis nodded several times. "Someone has certainly been murdered. One of you has had the life force—the essential essence—the soul if you will, driven from his or her body, and you are now possessed by an entity from the past. Or, to put it another way, one of you is dead. The question is—which one?"

They went back to their rooms, where doubtlessly they conjectured, denied, toyed with their fears, and Fred and Francis were left alone.

"Can you contact the late departed?" Francis asked. "A simple communication, a materialization, and our problem would be solved."

"I doubt it," Fred shook her head. "You know what the newly departed are like. Frightened, not sure what has happened. They shy away from psychic contact like a tee-totaller from whisky. But I can try."

"Do that." Francis guided her to a chair. "Put out feelers and see if he or she is around. Then we'll take it from there."

Fred seated herself and closed her eyes. Francis stood behind her and gently stroked the smooth forehead.

"Relax," he instructed in a low voice, "but be careful. You never know what might be prowling around. Now, search this room. Is there anything at all?"

"No," Fred said softly, "nothing at all."

"Right. Now the hall. Put out feelers into the hall, but slowly—take it easy—is there anything in the hall?"

Fred did not answer for some time; there was an expression denoting great mental effort on her pale face. Then she whispered: "I can feel something. Wait a minute . . . Yes . . . fear . . . bewilderment . . . almost total darkness . . ."

"Can you make contact?" Francis asked. "Try to bring it nearer. Bring it in."

"Hold your horses, this is bloody hard work. Every time I make contact it shies away like a virgin from a . . ." She sat up and faced the closed doorway with tight-shut eyes. "All right now . . . don't panic . . . we want to help. Get it? Help . . . friends . . . we're friends . . . don't get your knickers in a twist . . . come nearer . . . that's the ticket . . . nearer . . . keep your cool . . ."

"Keep it up," Francis rubbed his hands in anticipation. "Keep going, you're doing fine."

"Through the door, ducky." Fred was leaning forward, her eyes still closed. "Come on . . . wood don't mean a thing to you now. Follow the blue light, all trains go to Waterloo . . . What the hell . . .?"

"What's wrong, Fred?" The eager smile died and he watched the girl with growing anxiety. "Snap out of it. What's the trouble?"

"Interference. Fear . . . terror . . . the bastard is on to us. Oh, my God!"

She began to jerk violently, writhing from side to side, and her voice rose to a scream. "The pain . . . get if off . . .!"

"Break contact!" Francis shouted. "Let go, clear your mind, it's only auto suggestion. Break contact, you silly cow."

Suddenly the girl went limp and flopped back in her chair; two tears crept from under her closed eyelids and trickled down her pale cheeks. Francis rubbed her hands, then gently shook her.

"Okay. It's all over. Wake up, there's a good girl."

Fred opened her eyes and for a while she stared up into the lean, anxious face. Francis kissed her, then straightened up.

"All right now?"

"Yes. I made a bit of a fool of myself, didn't I?" She shuddered. "I was caught off guard. The sudden flash of cold terror—and the pain. It was as though I was being flogged."

"Possible." Francis nodded. "Our tall friend would be accustomed to dealing out such treatment. Go on."

"Well, that's all. When I broke contact, I passed out. I fear we will never find the newly departed again. My own discomfort was only a reflection of what he or she must have gone through."

"Well, one thing is certain," Francis said, taking out his cigarette case and putting a cigarette between the girl's lips. "We have to make it the hard way. Watch every one of them, and wait for the anchor man to slip up."

"Nina has a psychic potential." Fred puffed at her cigarette. "She could have been the magnet that attracted them in the first place. There again, Roland Taylor is always protesting, and he seems to have been against you being called in. I think he's a prime suspect."

"There's no more we can do tonight." Francis yawned. "So to bed. Tomorrow we must wrap the case up or call it a day, for I doubt if we can hold them here for longer than twenty-four hours. When the big fellow comes into this room, they'll forget their investment and be off."

Three men and three women sat in a rough half-circle; each face wore a suitably grave expression and returned Francis's searching glance with disarming innocence. The psychic detective took up his favourite position on the hearthrug, with Fred standing to his left.

The girl was wearing the bizarre costume in which she had arrived, the white letters E.V. standing out over her right breast.

"I've gathered you together," Francis began, "to report progress and in military jargon, to put you fully in the picture. Today, I did some research in the local library and was fortunate enough to find this." He took a fat volume from the mantelpiece. *Pilbeam's History of Clarence and Surrounding Districts*. There's an entire chapter devoted to Clarence Grange. It seems there was a prison on this site. It was built in 1629 and demolished in 1830. Now I don't have to tell you that a 17th-century prison was not the best place in the world to land up in, and if the wrong man was in charge, almost anything could happen. This brings me to the year 1742, for it was then, according to contemporary records, that a Mr. Royston Wentworth was appointed governor. There's little doubt he bought the post. Let me quote."

He opened the book and began to read, but occasionally raised his eyes, as thought to observe the expressions on the faces of his audience.

" 'Royston Wentworth was a man of goodly proportions and was well versed in the arts that pertain to a scholar and a gentleman. But he did not follow the path of the godly, but did pursue the hound of dark knowledge so that righteous men shunned his presence.

" 'When in the year of Our Lord 1742 he did take up the appointment of Governor of His Majesty's Prison at Clarence, he did make one Christopher Wyatt his chief officer and certain other men of ill-repute were installed as turnkeys . . . By 1743, all the former staff had been turned away and only Governor Wentworth's men were to be found in authority, and there was much talk of evil deeds performed behind those grim walls . . .

" '. . . At his trial, one prisoner: a forger and by name of Jeremiah Watts, did testify that Governor Wentworth and the aforesaid Christopher Wyatt did cause a wall to disappear and beyond did he see things that made his bowels move with fear . . .

" 'He did see a room where lights burned without flame and a glass-fronted box in which tiny images moved . . .

" '. . . Many of the inmates had become lunatics and one was so bewitched, he swore upon Holy Writ he was not of this time, but had been born in a century yet to come.' "

Francis closed the book and carefully replaced it on the mantelpiece. When he spoke his voice was low, like an accomplished preacher preparing to enjoy himself.

"He swore upon Holy Writ that he was not of this time, but had been born in a century yet to come." Francis paused, then raised his voice. "Which one of you was—or will be—he or she? Do not dismiss the idea of time transportation lightly. Many people have claimed to have been switched from one age to another, and when they have tried to explain their predicament to the authorities, have been treated as madmen. Remember, ten to fifteen thousand people disappear every year in Great Britain alone, and are never seen again. Who is to say they are not wandering about the streets of medieval London, or rotting in some 17th-century madhouse?"

Jennifer Halliday raised her hand, rather like a schoolgirl who wishes to ask Teacher a question.

"Please, if what you say is true and these—people—succeed in making their bridge, what will happen? Will they kidnap us?"

"There is one present who can answer that question better than I," Francis answered dryly. "But I'd say the transfer will be one of souls, not bodies. Royston Wentworth was looking—or is looking—for an escape. He must have known his activities would sooner or later lead him to the gallows. By swapping personalities with someone in a far-off age, he would be safe. It would seem he intends to bring his staff with him."

"It's unbelievable." Roland Taylor shook his head. "Too far fetched."

"Really!" St. Clare raised an eyebrow. "I would have thought you of all people would have found the situation most plausible."

"What is that supposed to mean?"

"It is supposed to mean this." Francis suddenly pointed a forefinger at the large, red-faced man. "I believe you are the anchorman. The one they sent over to take possession of the real Roland Taylor's body. The bridge isn't complete yet, so the ghost of the poor wretch is still trying to make itself felt. Only you scared it off. That's why you did not want me called in. That's why you have poured cold water on the very idea from the start, that's why . . ."

"You're bloody mad." Taylor got up, his face congested with rage. "You poor fool, your theory is full of holes. I can sink it with a few words. Firstly, if I, or, for that matter, anyone here, is a refugee from the 18th century, how is it we all talk 20th-century English? Eh? If you wish, I'll take that television set to pieces and put it together again. Want to know who my mother and father were? When they were born and when they died? Shall I give you a rundown on the history of the last thirty years? Care to watch me drive a car? Go and lock yourself up in the nearest loony bin."

"How about that?" Reggie Smith smiled. "I can drive a car, name the Prime Minister of England from 1920 upwards. That puts me in the clear."

"I can type," Betty Smith said demurely. "Sixty words a minute."

"I can ride a bicycle," Nina Taylor announced, "type, do shorthand, use a telephone and an adding machine—and I saw *Gone with the Wind* three times."

"I," Jennifer Halliday said, ticking off the list of her accomplishments on the fingers of her left hand, "can type, do shorthand so long as it's not too fast, tell you the entire plot of *Love Story* . . ."

"All right." Francis raised his hand. "So, you are all clever boys and girls. Doesn't mean a thing. Messrs. Wentworth and Co. were brilliant men. Far ahead of their time. They might not be able to type or take a television to pieces, but they knew the human mind. They had to for this little caper to work. When our unknown anchorman took over a contemporary body, he also inherited a 20th-century brain. A fully-active computer, with a first-class memory bank. No doubt he was scared stiff when his new body entered a car, but so long as he did not interfere, the memory bank would instruct the brain on what must be done. Sorry, Mr. Taylor, but you can recite the *Encyclopaedia Britannica* backwards, and I'll still not be convinced you're not an 18th-century black magician on the rampage."

"Come to think if it," Jennifer Halliday said shyly, "Mr. Taylor was never particularly frightened when the—er—phenomenon took place. I often wondered why. I know *I* was."

"Because I didn't run round like a headless chicken, it doesn't mean I wasn't scared." Taylor glared at the girl, then turned to Francis. "You've got a lot to answer for, St. Clare. Before you came we were scared of ghosts, now we're terrified of each other."

"True." Francis nodded. "And with just cause. One of you is an alien, a forerunner of a diabolical invasion. And don't think Mr. Taylor is my only suspect. For example, Mrs. Taylor could well be our—forgive me—our man. She has a certain latent psychic power which could well have drawn the alien to her."

Nina Taylor started as though she had been struck.

"I find that remark to be insulting, Mr. St. Clare. If you think I would allow the spirit of some strange man to take possession of my body, you must be madder even than my husband believes. Really!"

Just then Gertrude put in an appearance and announced: "Denner is sarved," and they all trooped into the dining-room, where they sat round the table in complete silence. Once, when Reggie Smith coughed, everyone jumped and stared at the offender as though he had suddenly sprouted horns. The rattle of cutlery on plates, the murmured request that someone pass the salt, the flopping of Gertrude's slippered feet as she moved round the room—all contributed to an atmosphere so sinister, it could almost be tasted. Francis noted that Roland Taylor put down his knife and fork after a few mouthfuls and stared glumly at the opposite wall.

"Francis," Fred said suddenly, "you might be interested to know our wandering recently departed is back."

"Really?" Francis registered faint surprise. "Surely you don't mean that the ghost of the newly dead is in this room?"

Gertrude screamed, dropped a tray of sherry trifle, and ran from the room.

"I didn't mean your grandmother had dropped in for high tea," Fred retorted indignantly. "The poor coot is hovering behind our Roland's chair."

"Damnation!" Roland Taylor pushed back his chair and crashed a clenched fist down upon the table. "What game are you playing, St. Clare? You've scared that wretched girl out of the few wits she has, and frightened the rest of us into the bargain."

"I'd better go and see if she's all right." Betty Smith rose. "I don't want to lose her, help is hard to find."

"You scared, Taylor?" Francis enquired. "In a tizzy, are you?"

"Of course I'm scared," Taylor roared, "I've never pretended to be anything else."

"Then why don't you go away? I don't mean for ever, just until this matter is cleared up."

"Why should I?"

"Why shouldn't you?" Francis turned his attention to the others. "Why not all of you? Get into your cars and drive to a hotel for the night. Tomorrow, I might have some good news for you. Well, how about it?"

Before anyone could answer, Betty Smith returned and resumed her seat at the foot of the table.

"I think Gertrude will come in tomorrow, but she's in a hell of a blue funk at the moment. We really must be careful what we say when she is present."

"St. Clare wants us to move out," Taylor said, "pack our bags and spend the night at a hotel."

"Is that necessary?" Betty asked. "I mean, up to now we've been perfectly safe upstairs."

"Up to now, I agree," Francis nodded, "but if Charlie-boy succeeds in completing the bridge, I'll not be responsible for your safety."

Nina shivered. "I say, let's go. I keep imagining that great brute lumbering up the stairs."

"I don't see why we have to leave our house because some blighter from the past sees fit to strut along a nonexistent passage," Roland Taylor grumbled. "Besides, think of the expense."

"Your bank account won't be of much use when you've changed places with Royston Wentworth and friends," Francis retorted grimly. "But the main point is, with you out of the way, Fred and I will only have ourselves to worry about."

"I suppose we could ring up the Green Boy," Betty suggested. "I mean, they could be full up."

"They aren't." Francis grinned. "I took the liberty of making three reservations."

"Bloody cheek," Roland growled.

"Of course," Francis shrugged. "I expected one of you to object. I would imagine that Master Wentworth will be livid when he finds his anchorman is not at his post."

Half an hour later three cars went roaring down the drive and a heavy silence descended on the house.

"Are you sure it's going to work?" Fred asked for the third time.

"Nothing is certain in this world." Francis drew the curtains, then opened the sitting-room door. "But I'd say one of them will find his or her way back. A lot depends on the anchorman being present between nine and midnight. He might be able to operate from a distance, but I doubt it. It's the atmosphere in this place which is their greatest asset. No, the intruder, the possessed, must come back or the bridge will begin to crumble. What time is it?"

"Eight fifty-five." Fred consulted her wristwatch.

"Any minute now. Might as well make ourselves comfy. No need to take precautions—they wouldn't help us anyway."

Fred sank down into an armchair while Francis helped himself to a stiff drink from the sideboard.

"What about me?"

"No." He shook his head. "A sniff from the cork and you're away. I want your precious sixth sense fully alert."

"You're a pig."

"Yes, I know. People have remarked on my swinish aspect before."

"By the way, have you considered what our palsy-walsy from the other side will do when he finds his anchorman is missing?"

Fred shrugged. "I don't know. Belt for the nearest church and demand sanctuary?"

"Not on your nelly. A high master of the black art wouldn't find much sanctuary in a church. No, he'll send another man over, who'll make a beeline for the nearest psychic medium to hand."

"You don't say?" Fred considered this possibility for a few moments, then an expression of alarm widened her eyes. "Eh, wait a minute. That's me."

Francis nodded. "You have keen perception."

"But . . . if he succeeds . . . then it's the same as if I was killed."

"I have always observed," Francis commented dryly, "that you have a remarkable gift of summing up a situation in a few words."

"Oh, thank you very much. I'm to be a Judas goat."

"Really, I wouldn't call you a goat. Let us say, irresistible bait."

"You unfeeling bastard. I thought you loved me."

"I do." Francis nodded violently. "If the worst should happen, it will be a great sacrifice."

"Suppose—I'm killed?" Fred demanded. "What will you do?"

He sighed deeply.

"I'll have to learn to love someone else."

Somewhere, a little way off, a door slammed.

"Is that our wandering boy returned?" enquired Francis thoughtfully. "Or can it be Master Wentworth taking his evening stroll?"

They waited, ears strained to catch the merest sound, eyes alert for the unexpected. Then there came the sound of approaching footsteps, pacing a hard surface: a slow vibrating tread that made a table-lamp quiver, a resounding picking-up and putting-down of heavy feet. But the hall remained perfectly normal: the thick carpet, the umbrella stand, the shaded lights—all belonged indisputably to the 20th century. The footsteps came up to the open doorway, then stopped. They heard the sound of heavy breathing.

"Sound but no picture," Francis said softly. "Come on, Charlie, whoever you are. Master is going to be very cross."

Suddenly there was a loud crash, as though someone had kicked a wooden partition. After the lapse of a few moments, the sound was repeated, and Francis grinned.

"Temper, temper."

"Frankie, love." Fred spoke in a small voice. "I'm just the teeniest bit frightened."

"Well don't be," he growled. "You're a professional and you know that fear is a key that will open any door. You also know what might come through an open door. I remember . . ."

He was cut short by a tremendous shout—a mighty roar of rage that seemed to echo down a long corridor. And then came the sound of more footsteps, only now they were lighter—running.

"Stand by." Francis got up. "Reinforcements."

"Can they see us?" Fred asked in a voice that was not quite steady.

"I don't know." He shrugged. "Maybe. They certainly know we're here."

"I don't know if I fancy being watched by some weird characters from the 18th century." Fred shuddered, then clutched her head with both hands. "Someone is trying to get in."

"What!" Francis spun round, his eyes cold, his face an impassive mask. "Explain. Quick, girl."

"Cold fingers probing my brain . . . pain . . . trying to get in . . ."

He reached her in two giant strides and gripped her arm. "Blank your mind, use your will."

"I can't . . . they're strong. . ."

"Look into my eyes." He released her arms and clamped her face between his two hands, then tilted her head until their eyes were only a few inches apart. "Fight. Think pain—for them. He's burning up, his stomach's on fire . . . there's a bloody great fire in his belly . . . red hot knives are slicing through his head . . . he's drowning in a sea of white hot cinders . . . He's going . . . he can't hold on . . ."

From behind them, from beyond the open doorway, came the

scream of a man in mortal agony, followed by the sound of retreating footsteps. There was another bellow of rage, then silence. Francis slumped down into a chair and wiped his forehead.

"That was a near thing," Fred gasped.

"Well, they won't try that again." Francis got up and poured himself another drink. "Ye gods, I needed that. For a while I thought I'd have to go out girl hunting."

"What now?" Fred enquired.

"They'll wait for their anchorman to show. Which reminds me— where the hell is he?"

"It's not going to work." Fred shook her head. "Whoever it is, he or she could never get away from the others without raising suspicion."

"But he's got to." Francis banged his clenched fist down upon the chair arm. "Don't you understand? The bridge is being built slowly, night after night; if there is a break, all their work will be wasted."

"Then why don't we pack it in and leave 'em to it?"

"Because they would start again. If not on this lot, then on someone else. We've been hired for a job of work, and I'll be damned if . . . What's that?"

Again there came the sound of approaching footsteps, only now they came from outside. The crunch of feet on gravel: slow, fugitive treads that were barely perceptible, but conjured up a picture of someone approaching the house with extreme caution.

"Can it be?" Francis took a deep breath and his eyes glittered with intense excitement. "Yes, I do believe this could be our wandering boy. Fred, my love, may your seed be as the sand on the seashore, in a few minutes from now, the undead will come ambling in through that there door. Any bets?"

"Taylor." Fred nodded. "I'll put me best pair of drawers on Roland Taylor."

"And very fetching he'll look in 'em too. Maybe. But I rather fancy that little Nina number. Quiet, not much to say for herself. Well, here goes."

The faint, hesitant footsteps were coming up the front steps; a key was inserted in the Yale lock, then after a while the door creaked open, then was closed with elaborate care. A shadow fell across the hall carpet; it elongated, then crept slowly up the right-hand wall as its owner advanced towards the sitting-room. A figure gradually emerged into the open doorway.

"Oh, there you are," said Reggie Smith.

Francis St. Clare bowed.

"Good evening, Mr. Christopher Wyatt."

"I tell you I came back because I was worried," Reggie Smith repeated. "I was worried out of my mind."

"I bet you were," Francis grinned maliciously. "The master was very angry. Can't say I blame him."

"But damn it all, I called you in. If I was the—the guilty one, would I send for the one person who could muck up the entire exercise?"

"Yes." Francis closed his eyes, then opened them again. "Only I wasn't suppose to do anything. I was just the poor bloody crank who plays at ghost hunting. No, Fred was the ace-in-the-hole. A strong psychic who could produce that little extra something. A mere girl with a highly developed psychic gift. A push-over for a take-over. One more lad across the river. Perhaps the great man himself."

"Really, of all the bloody rot," Reggie Smith protested.

"Only I wasn't the silly crank I was supposed to be," Francis went on remorselessly. "I gave her the will to fight back and your man retreated with a bloody nose."

"Look," Reggie appeared to be on the verge of tears. "I felt awful about leaving you two alone to face—whatever is going to happen, so I sneaked back."

"Why did you creep up the drive? Where's your car?"

"I came by taxi. The hotel garage was locked up for the night. I walked softly because I was scared."

"You know something, F.S.?" Fred enquired. "I think he's telling the truth."

"Maybe." Francis sighed. "It's crazy enough to be true—or an elaborate cover story. I'm reserving judgment, Mr. Smith, but should circumstances prove my worst suspicions, look out. Don't forget that."

Reggie Smith made a gurgling sound and looked fearfully at the open doorway.

"Perhaps I'd better get back," he suggested.

"Perhaps you'd better not," Francis countered. "Since you're here, I'd be obliged if you would answer a few questions. Has anyone in your crowd been behaving at all strangely?"

"No." Reggie shook his head. "I can honestly say I've noticed nothing out of the ordinary. Everyone has been on edge lately, of course, but that's only to be expected."

"It would be strange if they were not. Tell me, what do you usually do between nine and midnight?"

"Eh?"

"When our friend Royston takes his evening stroll, what's the usual practice? Do you always go upstairs?"

"Not at first," Reggie said thoughtfully. "No, we all went out into the garden. But after a while someone found the disturbance never troubled the upper storeys, so we got into the habit of trooping upstairs."

"What was the matter with the garden?" Francis asked, his eyes closed.

Reggie shrugged.

"Nothing, only it was damned cold."

Francis's eyes opened and he stared intently at the empty hall.

"Cold, you say?"

"Yes." Reggie frowned. "Well, the wind springs up over the downs at sunset."

"So it does. Tell me, did you lock all the doors before you all trotted out this evening?"

"Of course we did."

"Sure?"

"Of course I'm sure." Reggie frowned again and his voice carried the faintest suggestion of a peevish tone. "We decided you had enough to contend with, without having burglars breaking in. We've been robbed twice, you know. Betty said . . ."

"You even locked the back door?" Francis insisted, "—and you doubtless ensured that all the windows were securely fastened?"

Reggie was staring at him in astonishment.

"Yes, it was my turn to be security man. One has to have organization in a setup like this . . ."

"Fred," Francis drawled, a smile lighting his face, "I'm a stupid block-headed fool."

"Confession is good for the soul," that young lady quoted. "I wondered how long it would be before the penny dropped."

"A bloody, benighted, blind, deaf, half-witted cretin," Francis added. "There was the answer being served to me on a plate and I hadn't the gumption to see it."

"You can't help it," Fred comforted, "it's the way your mother put your hat on."

"You, of course, spotted the missing link," Francis suggested.

There was a short pause.

"No," said Fred.

"But you've cottoned on now?" he asked, glaring at her over one shoulder.

She shook her head.

"I haven't your brains. I'm only the hired help."

"But damnation, girl, it's as plain as the nose on your face."

"Speak for your own nose. I haven't a clue of what you are talking about."

"I'm talking about the anchorman. You must realise who it is. We've been so concerned with the impossible, we've overlooked the obvious. Think, girl."

"I am thinking and it hurts."

"Jumping beanstalks, Reggie, be a good fellow and do something for me."

"Sure." Reggie brightened like a Boy Scout about to do a good deed. "Anything."

"Good. Open up the old lugholes and listen. Go and unlock the back door. Then walk round the house whistling 'Rule Britannia'. When you reach the front door, come in, shut the door and turn out all the hall lights. Got that?"

Reggie concentrated.

"Unlock the back door, walk round the house whistling 'Rule Britannia', come in front, shut door, turn out lights. Got it." He frowned. "Why?"

"Never ask 'why'," Francis shook his head gravely. "That word has ruined more kingdoms than you wot of. Just trot away and do your little act."

"All right, if you say so. But for the life of me . . ."

"When you come back I'll give you a big kiss," Fred promised.

"Oh!" Reggie flushed a bright red and almost ran to carry out his appointed task. Francis glared at his assistant.

"You want him to break a blood vessel? Behave yourself, the balloon will go up in about five minutes."

From far off came the sound of a door opening, then, after a considerable period a shrill rendering of "Rule Britannia" that was accompanied by the crunch of approaching footsteps.

"Never make the top ten," Francis observed.

"But he's lovely," Fred stated.

The front door opened with an abruptness that suggested Reggie was grateful to leave the night behind, then the hall lights went out and he stood in the doorway, beaming like a schoolboy who has successfully broken bounds.

"Did it!" he exclaimed.

"You're dead clever," Francis pronounced gravely. "Now switch off all the lights and go and sit beside Fred. You can have a little slap and tickle before the fireworks begin."

Reggie tore round the room, switching out lights, and in no time at all they were sitting in total darkness, like three ghosts waiting for midnight. Once, Fred exclaimed, "Hey, watch it!" and Francis swore.

"Cut it out. Someone is supposed to think the entire bottom floor is empty. If you can't control him, suffer in silence."

"Really," Reggie's voice protested plaintively, "I never . . ."

"Shut up," Francis growled.

Fifteen minutes passed, then the hall clock struck eleven, and scarcely had the last vibrating chime died away, when they heard the first sound. A tiny bang. Possibly a slight miscalculation when someone carefully closed the back door. Then, for a while, nothing, save a growing tension as they became aware of an approaching presence. Reggie whimpered.

"One more sound out of you," Francis whispered, "and I'll knock you for six."

A chair stirred in the next room and bumped against the dining-table; a voice muttered a curse; then they heard the soft pad of feet muffled by the thick carpet. A dark figure, a shape of deeper darkness, slid obliquely across the room and became silhouetted against the rectangular blur of the open doorway. The voice was harsh: a shouted whisper.

"Master—master, they locked me out."

Light crashed through the darkness, and the sudden transition caused eyes to blink, so for a few more seconds the identity of the figure in the doorway remained a mystery. Then Francis St. Clare spoke.

"So, we meet at last, Master Christopher Wyatt."

Gertrude sprang round, her face contorted with fear and rage.

The two men bound the long, raw-boned figure to a straight-backed chair while she made raucous cries like a she-bear caught in a trap. Once or twice the cries merged into words—words spoken in an accent which was a mixture of raw Cockney and West Country, the vowels slurred so as to make the speech well nigh unintelligible.

"Master . . . don't leave me alone in this awful place . . . I'm shut off . . ."

"Right," said Fred, once the binding operation was completed, "I know you're just itching to show off. When did you realise it was Gertrude?"

"When Reggie said it was only cold in the garden. You may remember Gertrude told us her gran had seen a man walking about the ground, thereby implying the phenomenon manifested itself in the garden. It doesn't. A closed place, steeped in atmosphere, is essential for the bridge building. I should have suspected before, of course. Gertrude was a natural for a takeover. Simple, a limited vocabulary that made the intruder's task easy, she was, if I can use the expression, made for the job."

"But she was always out of the house well before nine o'clock," Reggie protested. "Unless, of course . . ."

"She came back," Francis finished the sentence. "I've no doubt the back door was left unlocked until you retired to bed. But tonight you locked up before departing, hence we were treated to a show without vision. The camera was missing. The question is—what now?"

"You mean . . .?" Reggie stared with evident apprehension at the open doorway.

"All this supplication should get results sooner or later," Francis observed, watching the erstwhile Gertrude with some satisfaction. "Our future depends on how well we handle the situation when it occurs."

Gertrude/Wyatt twisted her head to one side and glared at Francis with dilated eyes.

"Master Wentworth . . . 'ee know . . . 'ee make you twist . . ."

"He's a bit slow off the mark," Francis remarked cheerfully. "I should give him another shout, if I were you."

"Master . . ." The mouth was open, revealing an assortment of bad teeth. "Master . . ."

"That's the stuff." Francis nodded his approval. "Bellow away."

"Look here," Fred protested. "I'm not all that keen to see old nasty-chops. Can't we get Gertrude—or whoever she is—certified, and leave the house to itself for a bit? You said the bridge would disintegrate once the anchorman was removed."

"And what about the real Gertrude? If we can't get her back into her rightful habitation, at least her death should be avenged. Besides, we've been hired to do a job of work and I don't like leaving it half-completed. So here we sit until Charlie-boy puts in another appearance."

He tapped the writhing figure on the shoulder.

"Come on now, a couple of more good bellows. Let rip with some of the old psychic influence."

"Anyone fancy a cup of tea?" Reggie asked. "I can soon put the kettle on."

"Not a bad idea," Francis agreed. "Make sure you warm the pot and none of those bloody teabags."

"No sugar," Fred called out after Reggie's retreating figure, "and not too strong."

"Master Wentworth . . . oi am 'ere!" Gertrude/Wyatt's voice sounded a little hoarse. "Gongi . . . Deliverenti . . . woti . . ."

"That sounds a bit technical," Francis said, grinning. "The devil alone knows what it means."

"Mattermass . . . Satanus." Gertrude/Wyatt was shouting with all his/her might. "Smackmuckus . . . bumoninus . . . Pondocronous . . . cunmontus . . ."

"Did you hear the like?" Francis enquired.

"Sounds a bit indecent to me," Fred retorted. "I bet they were a filthy old lot back in seventeen-something. I say, what must it be like for a man to be in a woman's body?"

"It's been done before." Francis shrugged. "Now shut up, I think someone is receiving loud and clear."

There was the sound of many doors opening, followed by the clattering of running footsteps. The hall seemed to dissolve; the walls fell inwards and in the blink of an eyelid, the long, door-lined passage flashed into being. The tall, dark man was hurrying towards the open doorway, his face a mask of terrible rage. The wretched figure in the chair seemed to shrink; speech babbled off the tongue in a cascade of words.

"Locked out, Master, 'ee locked me out . . . found out, powerful 'ee be. Oi tried to contact . . . oi tried, but too far, Master . . . oi were too far off . . ."

Royston Wentworth clenched his fists and hammered them against the invisible wall. The dull thud gradually gave way to a terrible cracking sound, as though a brick or rock wall were splintering, then there was a mighty crash as the tall, black-clad figure stepped into the room. Several other men were creeping along the passage; they stopped at the doorway, seemingly unwilling, or perhaps lacking the courage, to cross the barrier.

Royston Wentworth stood looking down at the bound figure that cringed in the chair.

"An ass has more wisdom in its head than thou," he stated.

"Yes, he wasn't very bright," Francis agreed. "A spare key would have saved you a lot of trouble."

The arrogant eyes turned slowly in his direction; the thin lips were parted in a mirthless grin.

"I will pluck your soul from your body and toss it down upon the dark plains, where it will be hunted by the hounds of death."

"There again," Francis continued, "you aren't all that smart."

"Try to talk English," Fred instructed. "He hasn't a clue what you're on about."

"I said," Francis shouted, "your head has lost its wisdom. Oh, damn, I can't talk this jargon. The idea was for your souls to come across, not your flipping bodies. You're on alien ground, son.

You're in my territory. Get it? Savvy?"

"'Course he doesn't," Fred protested. "He probably thinks you're taking the mickey."

It was not clear if Royston Wentworth understood what was being said or not, but his intention was unmistakable. He was moving towards Francis, his arms outstretched, the fingers slightly curved, and he was growling, deep down in his throat. Francis sidestepped, then began to retreat; he slid a small table across the floor so that it bumped against the ledge of the approaching giant, causing him to stumble. Wentworth recovered at once, kicked the table to one side, then continued his relentless advance. Fred picked the table up and threw it at the broad back. It struck Wentworth between the shoulder blades and instantly he turned with incredible speed and made for the petrified girl.

"Move!" Francis shouted. "Run!"

His warning was unheeded. A hand that looked as if it might have been hewn out of granite swung round and slashed across Fred's left cheek. She went hurling backwards, bounced off a chair, then collapsed on to the floor. Francis forgot his cautious tactics and went in like a boxer going all out for a knock down. He slammed a combination of punches into the hard belly, then executed a perfect upper cut to the jutting chin. He repeated the process three times. Finally, he rubbed his raw knuckles and looked up.

Wentworth's face wore a derisive grin.

"Bloody hell!" Francis swore as he tried to back away, but the great hand found his throat and he was being forced down to his knees, while the ridiculous thought flashed across his mind: "Is this the story where the baddie wins?"

Consciousness was dissolving into a bottomless pit; his soul was preparing to depart for an unknown destination, when a brown object flew across the room and smashed against Wentworth's face. The steel fingers were jerked from Francis' throat and he sank to the floor, gasping for breath.

Wentworth was screaming; his hands were clasped over the cut, inflamed face. Reggie Smith looked down at Francis and shrugged.

"What else could I do? I threw the teapot at him."

Francis came gradually back to life and gazed upon the writhing giant with speechless astonishment. Not until he had clambered to his feet was he able to give utterance.

"The cup that cheers," he said slowly. "The lifesaving brew. Reggie, you're a bloody marvel. Hand me that small table."

Reggie obeyed and Francis crashed the table down on Wentworth's head, just as the giant was about to take a more active interest in the proceedings.

"Sleep," he advised, "and wake up in a more depressing yesterday."

Wentworth acceded to this request by crashing to the floor, where he lay like a felled oak waiting for the jack-saw. Francis began to straighten the prostrate figure as Fred climbed slowly to her feet and rubbed the ugly red weal that marred her left cheek.

"Rope," he said, snapping his fingers, "curtain cords, nylons, your knickers—anything."

After a hurried scramble, which Reggie watched with an appreciative eye, Fred handed Francis a pair of sheer nylons which he used to secure the giant's ankles and wrists. He then straightened up and surveyed his handiwork with a certain justified pride.

"Number one ungodly laid low. Now to put him back where he belongs. Reggie, do you feel strong?"

"No."

"Good. Catch hold of his legs, while I take a firm grip of his manly shoulders."

Reggie displayed a certain reluctance to lay hands on the enemy, particularly as four sinister-looking individuals were watching the operation from the open doorway. They had not moved since Wentworth had invaded the sitting-room, but were now showing signs of disquiet as it became evident their leader was being returned unto them. Reggie looked fearfully back over one shoulder.

"What about—those men?" he whispered.

"Don't worry your little head," Francis advised, then shouted to Fred: "Switch the television on."

"Which channel?" Fred enquired.

"Independent. A few commercials should put the fear of the devil in them. They do me."

Slowly, with great effort, they dragged Wentworth towards the open doorway. The silent audience retreated a few steps and one shook his head.

"That's interesting," Francis observed, "they don't seem keen on having laughing-boy back. That's too bad. Back he goes, whether they like it or not."

It proved impossible to throw the body through the doorway for the simple reason, it was too long. Wentworth's weight negated any idea of tossing him in head first, and Francis was coming to a reluctant conclusion when signs of extreme agitation among the silent audience made him look round.

The television screen was depicting a monkey dressed in 18th-century costume. It was drinking from a teacup.

"There's nothing I like better than a cup of Rosy Lee," said the monkey.

The four men turned on their heels and raced down the passage. Their flight was followed by the sound of many doors opening and closing. Then silence.

"You know," Francis said, taking a firmer grip on Wentworth's shoulders, "I never realised before the true virtue of tea. Right, let's get him in there."

After much straining, heaving and grunting, they deposited their burden upon the stone floor, then looked around. Reggie was shaking like a jelly in an earthquake.

"We're . . ." he stopped. The situation robbed him of words.

"In the 18th century," Francis nodded. "In the Clarence old prison, and heaven help us if the bridge disintegrates before we get back. Still, it would be a shame if we didn't have a look round."

Beyond the doorway the sitting-room and the colour television was indisputably 20th-century, but on either side and behind, the distant past was as real as Monday morning. Francis opened one of the doors and entered a cell which was bare save for a plank-bed and an iron bucket. He went back into the passage and was greeted by a terrified Reggie, who was gazing longingly at the cosy sitting-room.

"I think we ought to get back. There are those—men, they keep looking round the corner."

Even then a fearful face was peering at them from round the

nearest corner, but when Francis shouted: "Boo!" quite loudly, it instantly disappeared.

"Perhaps you're right," he admitted reluctantly, "but it would have been nice to explore a little longer, particularly if I fetched a camera. Think what the Sunday papers would pay for a photograph of yer actual 18th century."

"Francis," Fred called, "come quickly. Gertrude is playing up and I can't do anything with her."

They tore back into the sitting-room and there was the possessed Gertrude staring at the television screen with obvious terror.

"Hasn't she ever seen a TV before?" Francis asked Reggie. "The real Gertrude, I mean."

"She certainly never saw ours, and I don't suppose her old mother owns one."

"Then there's no memory to draw upon," Francis remarked thoughtfully. "Turn over to the other side."

Fred pushed a button and there was an instant picture of a big man hitting a little man with all his strength. Gertrude/Wyatt screamed.

"We will put you in yon box," Francis promised, "and you will be hit by a big man for all eternity."

The camera moved in to a close-up of the little man's face. It looked like a lump of raw meat.

"Back to the other channel," Francis ordered.

A man was running towards the camera; suddenly, a shot rang out and a nasty red stain appeared on the man's shirtfront. He made an interesting gurgling sound and crashed to the pavement.

"We will make you small, shrink you smaller than small, then put you in yon box," Francis informed the speechless Gertrude/Wyatt, "for that is the gateway to Hell . . . Turn over to BBC2, Fred."

The screech of brakes, the roar of guns, the thud of fists on bare flesh, followed by an ear-splitting scream. Something grey, a wisp of mist, streaked towards the open doorway and instantly the passage vanished, to be replaced by the familiar hall. Francis wiped his brow.

"Never thought it would work. Lucky they chose a simple mind. Any sign of the real Gertrude, Fred?"

"No need to worry." Fred was untying the confining cords. "As soon as she wakes up, the rightful spirit will return. Just as ours does when we wake each morning."

"Has—has the bridge gone for good?" Reggie asked, looking anxiously at the empty hall.

"Sure thing. The anchorman has belted back across the river. It might be as well if you did some alterations to the hall. Replaced the floorboards, did a spot of redecoration, so that the vibrations are changed. But I think your house will behave itself from now on. Ah, I see our wanderer has returned. Best turn the television off."

Gertrude opened her eyes. She looked slowly round, then up at Reggie Smith.

"Mr. Smith, sir, I's 'ad a funny dream. I was walking round the 'ouse and nobody took notice of me."

"Now you must go home, Gertrude, for night has fallen."

She rose from the chair, looking fearfully at the overhead lamp, then at the drawn curtains. "My mum says I'm not to be out after dark. And me asleep in your best armchair, sir."

"Why mustn't you be out after dark?" Francis asked slyly. "Afraid of ghosts."

"No, I doesn't believe in that nonsense. It be the men with evil in their 'earts, that do prowl around in the darkness."

Francis smiled.

"May wisdom always be with you, Gertrude."

They crowded round the car expressing gratitude, the women cooing, the men doing their best to be hearty, their minds already forgetting. It was Betty Smith who asked the final, so far unanswered question.

"Miss Masters . . . Fred, I hope you don't mind my asking, but surely your initials are F.M.?"

"That's right." Fred climbed into the seat next to Francis.

"Then . . . why the letters E.V. that are so beautifully embroidered on your dress? What do they stand for?"

The car began to glide slowly away; Fred's voice came back to them, clear, untroubled: the voice of Helen calling over the walls of Troy.

"Ex-Virgin."

Reuben Calloway and Roderick Shea

VULTURES GATHER
by BRIAN MOONEY

Reuben Calloway was born in 1928. Abandoned at birth, he lived in a series of foster homes until adopted at three years of age by widowed archaeologist Simeon Calloway. He subsequently travelled the world with his father, who encouraged an early interest in the occult developed in Egypt and India. After working for the British Intelligence Corps, serving in West Berlin in the early 1950s, he accepted a position with Southdown University in Hampshire, where he prefers research and investigation into the outré to teaching.

Father Roderick Shea was born in 1940. He first met Reuben Calloway in 1967 and his life has never been the same again. He has some psychic gifts (as did several of his Irish ancestors) but has never been happy about this.

Brian Mooney describes Calloway as being "Something of a scruffy Orson Welles, with all the arrogance but without the charm." He made his first appearance as a minor character in an unpublished Lovecraftian story that the author never bothered to rewrite, and his name is mentioned in 'The Guardians of the Gates' (Cthulhu: Tales of the Cthulhu Mythos #2, 1977). *The first story to properly feature Calloway and Shea, 'The Affair at Durmamny Hall', appeared in the special Occult Detectives issue of* Kadath *(July, 1982). Calloway is by himself, on the trail of a European* *werewolf, in 'The Waldteufel Affair' (*The Anthology of Fantasy & the Supernatural, *1994), and the pair returned in 'The Tomb of Priscus' (*Shadows Over Innsmouth, *1994), in which they discover a Roman archaeological site is being used as a gateway to bring back the Ancient Ones.*

REUBEN CALLOWAY, REPLETE with rich food and vintage wine, was only slightly surprised when his host interrupted sleepy contentment by announcing: "I have good reason to believe that I'm going to be murdered and I'd like to ask your help." He had half-expected something like this. After, there was no such thing as a free lunch—or as in this case, a free country weekend with all meals thrown in.

Calloway had always enjoyed the good things of life when he could get them and the dinner he had just eaten—from the *paté* with melba toast to the overgenerous portion of syllabub followed by a selection of cheeses—had been a glutton's delight. But he did not know Sir Isaac Pryce well—he had only briefly met the baronet during a somewhat pompous university ceremony—and he had wondered why he should be invited to the millionaire's home.

Still, Calloway wasn't proud and his stipend as a university reader didn't stretch to much in the way of good living. He had accepted the summons, had cancelled several tutorials with students both brilliant and hopeless, and had journeyed to the remote Yorkshire mansion as quickly as his creaking old pre-war car would allow.

Following pudding, the two men had gone from the dining room into Pryce's library where they sat by a huge log fire. A spacious octagonal room, the library was furnished with floor-to-ceiling cases crammed with all manner of books, ranging from sturdy volumes bound in beautiful leather to a collection of well-thumbed paperbacks.

While they waited for Elmore, Pryce's butler, to serve coffee, Calloway explored the bookshelves. A devoted book-man, he revelled in eclectic collections such as the one he found here, a collection which encompassed almost every subject that a right-minded person (that is, someone like himself) would find interesting and entertaining.

There were books on philosophy, ancient and modern, ranging from Democritus through the Athenian and Platonic schools to Hegel, Kierkegaard and Russell. There were classics in no particular order: tightly packed collections of Dickens and Scott squeezed an unfortunate Jane Austen between them while a slightly more relaxed George Eliot leaned for support against Wells and Kipling. The Brontës were more aloof, sharing a top shelf only with Collins. The French and Russians were well represented, Dumas, Zola and Balzac intermingling with Tolstoy and Turgenev.

There were works on medicine and astronomy, botany and entomology. Most of Eleanor Omerod's books were there together with a particularly fine edition of the Reverend Wood's *Illustrated Natural History* which Calloway recognised as being worth several months of his salary. Another case contained several different versions of *The Thousand and One Nights*. Not only were there the more common Burton and Madrus and Mathers translations but also, Calloway noted, an English version of the early Galland edition together with Torrens's 1838 book and Paynes's collection from 1882. In the same cabinet, a tired-looking Boccaccio swapped quips with that jolly vulgarian Rabelais.

There was humour: Wodehouse, Thurber, Belloc, Thorne Smith. And crime fiction. The near-fascist Bulldog Drummond vied for honours with a debonair Saint, prissy Poirot, supercilious Holmes and a regiment of their like. There was Golden Age SF, and one book-case was devoted entirely to supernatural fiction. It amused Calloway to see among the latter almost every one of the cheaply printed anthologies issued by various Fleet Street newspapers during the Thirties. Excellent collections all, but many wealthy persons might have shunned them as being beneath their pockets' dignity. Then there were editions of Stoker, M. R. James, the Americans Poe and Bierce and Lovecraft, many others.

What pleased Calloway most was the fact that all of these books appeared to be well used and not just installed on the shelves as furnishings. "You really are a man after my own heart, I think," Calloway said as he returned to his chair by the fire.

"Here, have a look at these," the baronet said, almost shyly as if wary of being thought trivial. "They are my very favourites, for they were the first books that I chose for myself as a school prize." He passed over two books which he had picked up from a coffee-table.

Calloway turned the books over. Respectively, they were titled *The Boy's Book of General Knowledge* and *The Boy's Book of Puzzles and Brain-teasers*. Inside they were inscribed: *To Isaac Pryce, for exceptional effort—June 1904.*

"You couldn't better those books for content and entertainment," Pryce said. His smile was charming and proud, as if he were ten or eleven again.

"I agree," Calloway replied gently. "Thank you for showing them to me."

Sir Isaac Pryce was a strange man in some ways, Calloway had decided earlier. The millionaire had been born wealthy through various inheritances and had made a substantial second fortune in Africa; he was obviously well educated and well read; yet much of the time he acted the Victorian dinosaur or vulgar *nouveau riche* character, as if he inhabited a short story by Somerset Maughm. For instance, he had told Calloway—in fact, practically bragged—that he spoke no word of any foreign language. "There's always someone around who speaks English," he asserted, "And if not they'll always understand English if it's shouted loudly enough."

Then on the subject of business he had been almost a bore. "Always keep it simple," Pryce had instructed Calloway. "That was my maxim in business life. Always keep it simple. If your systems are simple, solutions to problems are generally simple. Occam's Razor, you know."

Yet otherwise he could be a delightful companion. The two had discussed radio programmes, sharing a common joy in *The Goon Show* and Hancock and *Journey into Space*. (It was then that Calloway had started to appreciate Pryce, deciding that on balance he approved of his host.)

They discussed politics, deploring the Suez action as a pathetic, desperate act by a pathetic, desperate Prime Minister. Both men admitted to liking the new rock and roll music—"I've always had a taste for the blues and similar music and this is just a natural extension," said Pryce—dismissing as narrow fuddy-duddies those older people who condemned it. They discussed films, deriving much pleasure from horror films and Capra's comedies and De Mille's epics.

Elmore, gaunt and probably much less old than he actually looked, served them Blue Mountain coffee while Pryce poured generous measures of spirit into balloon glasses. "Armagnac," he said, passing a glass to Calloway. "Marquis de Montesquiou. The company was established by a descendant of Charles de Batz Castelmore, believed to be the man upon whom D'Artagnan was based. I'd never drink anything else."

"Not even one of the fine cognacs, Hine or Otard, say?"

"Not even those. If I can't have the Marquis, then I'd just as soon have a cup of tea."

As soon as the butler retired, Sir Isaac offered Calloway a cigar from a beautifully carved wooden humidor.

"Thank you." The big man sniffed with appreciation at the fine tobacco and read the name on the band. "Hoyo de Monterey. I once met an elderly French nobleman who smoked nothing else."

"I know of him," observed Sir Isaac. "An occultist like yourself, I believe."

"I don't know where you heard that," was Calloway's disgruntled reply. "It's certainly not true. Nor do I think that *Monsieur le Duc* would relish such a description."

"Well, I have heard some strange stories about him." Sir Isaac trimmed the end of his own cigar with care. "As indeed I have of yourself. You are comparatively young, Calloway, but they say you have substantial knowledge of the outré. An amateur detective, too, I believe."

"I've read a few books in the British Museum's proscribed section," muttered Calloway. "I've also read Conan Doyle."

"Do you know Africa?" Sir Isaac changed the subject abruptly.

"Not really," Calloway told the baronet. "I have spent a little time in Egypt, mainly involved with University work of one kind or another. And a stopover in Capetown while on a flight to India. Those apart, no, I don't know Africa."

"Interesting place. When you're out on the savannah, you can always tell when there has been a kill. Vultures gather. You can see them wheeling about the skies from miles away." Sir Isaac drew for a moment on his cigar and continued. "Human scavengers aren't that much different. When anyone fairly wealthy dies, watch the vultures gather, all of them hoping for pickings regardless of how slim. It's going to be like that when my time comes."

Calloway grunted. The coffee was good, the brandy and cigars excellent. (If he could afford them, he thought, the cigars might even wean him away from his beloved Turkish cigarettes.) Calloway settled himself a little more comfortably into his wing-chair; he was patient and he guessed that Sir Isaac would get to the point in his own good time.

Sir Isaac studied his guest for some moments then he said: "Feathered vultures don't make their own kills. On the other hand, human vultures might. I'm going to die, Calloway: I have good reason to believe that I'm going to be murdered and I'd like to ask your help. I don't think it will happen for a very long time yet but happen it will."

If Calloway had been commonplace in attitude he might have thought he was dealing with a crank or a neurotic. But Calloway was not commonplace in attitude. He looked carefully at the other's lean, sun-weathered face and decided that Sir Isaac was serious.

"Have you proof of this?" Calloway asked. "Do you have any suspicions as to who your possible killer might be? And have you spoken to the police about it?"

"No, no and no. In that order." Sir Isaac grinned suddenly. "Thank you for not treating me as if I'm a crazy man, Calloway. I have no proof for reasons which I will tell you shortly. I suspect that my assassin will be someone close to me, someone as yet very young, perhaps not even born. Can you imagine trying to explain that to the police? Anyway, if I did tell the police why I believe I will be murdered at an indeterminate date in the future, they would never again take seriously anything I told them."

Sir Isaac rose from his chair and stretched his long body. At seventy-five inches he was as tall as his guest but lean and stringy, quite unlike Calloway's great bulk. "I'd like you to come and see something, Calloway," he said. "Bring your drink with you."

Calloway pulled himself up, spilling cigar ash down the front of his old dress-shirt. (He had earlier discarded his scruffy dinner-jacket, the place being like a hothouse. "Can't stand the cold," Pryce had explained. "Not since Africa.") An ineffectual effort to brush away the ash served only to add another stain to the garment. Pausing just long enough to refill his glass from a nearby decanter, Calloway trudged after his host who led him from the library.

Crossing a heavily carpeted corridor, the two men came to a beautifully carved oak door. Pryce reached into a trouser pocket and pulled out a length of chain to which was attached a solitary key. "No one comes in here unless with me," he explained. He unlocked the door and the two men passed through. Sir Isaac pressed a switch and a rectangular room of impressive dimensions was instantly illuminated by softly glowing lamps mounted around the panelled walls.

At one end of the room was a great, open fireplace in which yet another fire blazed despite the fact that no one was there to appreciate it. Several large wing-chairs were grouped in front of the hearth and to one side was a small drinks trolley with decanters and glasses.

Starting midway down the room, and occupying a considerable area, was a great glass-topped table standing on eight sturdy legs while in a far shadowy corner Calloway could see what looked like a life-sized statue. The table was deep-based, perhaps slightly larger overall than a billiards table, and Pryce led his guest straight to it. He touched a switch hidden beneath one edge and the table's whole interior was suffused with a golden light of surprising clarity. So cleverly placed was the concealed lighting system that no hint of a source could be seen.

Calloway gasped, overcome with sudden wonder. He was looking down at the most exquisitely realistic diorama that he had ever seen. Spread out below him rolled mile upon mile of African savannah, seen as if from a height of several thousand feet. There were grasslands and water-holes and distant hills interspersed with sparsely dotted clumps of acacia trees in miniature, and there were figures—almost pinpoint tiny, it was true, and yet instantly recognisable for what they were.

Great herds grazed, antelope, wildebeest and zebra, closely shadowed by packs of wild dogs and jackals and hyenas. Elephants and giraffes browsed, dust-clouds seeming to stir beneath their feet. A somnolent pride of lions rested in what little shade they could find, dozing off the effects of a heavy meal. A distant group of tribal hunters, concealed behind a group of termite hills, pointed towards the game, anticipating full cooking pots and bellies.

Then Calloway rubbed his eyes and peered again. He could not be certain, and yet . . . weren't those vultures wheeling in the skies, not set into the glass but apparently hovering free?

He turned to Pryce. "My congratulations," he said. "I have never seen anything like this before. I doubt that I ever will again. Did you create this?"

Isaac Pryce shook his head. "I manufactured the setting: the table, the lighting . . . The rest—illusion, reality, who knows?"

He refused to elaborate. Instead he took Calloway's arm and led him to the statue in the corner. Another switch and two spot-lamps cast a gentle glow. It was not exactly a statue but something else, mounted regalia, some form of armour . . . Calloway was unsure.

What appeared to be an all-in-one garment of tanned reptile skin, long and lean and embellished with metal ornaments and feathers was surmounted by a grim, basilisk-like mask in time-blackened wood, with staring eyes of some precious stone, possibly agate. The mask was crowned with a high, pharisaic head-dress and about the neck was a massive collar of interwoven gold and silver. Clasped in each hand was a long wooden wand or sceptre, the delicately carved rods borne as if they were symbols of authority. For some reason, Calloway found it difficult to meet the implacable gaze of the grotesquely masked head.

"Disturbing, isn't it?" commented Pryce. "This is, or rather, was, Alchuan. *No, don't touch him you fool!—*" as Calloway reached out a massive fist.

"My apologies, Calloway," he said seconds later. "But you see, when I said that this is Alchuan, I meant that literally. Within the costume is the mummified corpse of a man called Alchuan." He switched off the lights. "Let's go back to the library and I'll explain."

"I met Alchuan almost forty years ago when I was quite a young man and newly arrived in Kenya," said Pryce when they were once more settled with fresh drinks and cigars. "I suppose for want of a better expression you might call him a witch-doctor, although that's not wholly accurate. Alchuan had attached himself to a local village but he wasn't one of them. For a start, he wasn't even negro, let alone Kikuyu.

"I don't really know what he was but more than anything he reminded me of the paintings and carvings one sees of Ancient Egyptians, with their long, narrow heads and fine features. Alchuan spoke a great number of African languages and excellent English too. He never quite explained his origins to me but he often made allusions that I never fully understood. For instance, he frequently referred to the lizard-men of Valusia, one of the legendary races of prehistoric Earth, I believe."

Calloway nodded agreement.

"It was Alchuan who created that wonderful display I showed you," Sir Isaac continued. "He instructed me to have the table made and then, somehow, he created the display. It happened overnight and to this day I don't know how or even why. But that was much later . . .

"Anyway, it's too long a story to go into but early on in our relationship I was responsible for saving his life. After that we became almost like adopted father and son. He told me that among his people, the sons would keep the father's dead and preserved body in a place of honour, for was it not the place of a father to oversee and protect his offspring. He made me promise to afford him that traditional courtesy."

Pryce suddenly laughed. "I had a bugger of a job getting the table and the body shipped home. Had to convince all sorts of carriers and authorities that they were genuine museum pieces."

The man's demeanour changed abruptly. "It was Alchuan who— shortly before he himself died—foretold that in late life I would be murdered by someone close. Normally I might have ignored this as so much mumbo-jumbo. But by then I had known Alchuan for many years and had witnessed some of the strange powers that he possessed, so I accepted what he said without question. He also said that through his intervention, I would be avenged swiftly. The channel for retribution, he asserted, would be through huge man of learning and prodigious appetites, even though his description was very much more flowery. I think that possibly you're that man, Calloway."

"I'm nobody's angel of vengeance," said Calloway. "You'd probably be better off going to Sicily or the States to hire a Mafia gunman. Some of them are men of quite gross appetites and they've learned plenty about death and revenge."

"I'm not saying that you will be the avenger *per se*," the baronet answered. "I believe that you, if it is you, will simply act as a faucet to let flow whatever power Alchuan has set about me." He thought for a moment, then argued: "Surely vengeance can take many forms. For instance, when a police officer investigates a crime which leads to the conviction of an offender, it could be claimed that he is the channel of society's revenge."

Without seeking permission, Calloway poured himself another half-glass of armagnac. "You could be right," he grunted.

"All I'm asking, Calloway, is that if I ever call upon you, you'll come, that if anything should happen to me, you'll endeavour to find the truth. Just promise me that."

"Didn't Alchuan say if there is any way of lifting or avoiding this . . . destiny?"

"I thought about that," Sir Isaac admitted. "Alchuan replied that it was written and what was written could not be undone."

"Very well," the big man grumbled. "If and when this happens, I agree to seek the truth. I can't imagine the police being very happy about it but I'll do what I can." Then he brightened a little. "Perhaps your local bobby will turn out to be a fat philosopher and I'll be able to stay at home . . ."

That had been twenty or so years ago and now Calloway and I were within a few miles of Sir Isaac Pryce's home. Calloway had long ago attained full Professorship at Southdown University and his disreputable old Ford had been relinquished in favour of a disreputable old Rolls. These were the only material rewards that life had brought him. He continued necessarily to smoke Turkish cigarettes rather than Havana cigars, and he still could not afford Marquis de Montesquiou armagnac.

During the journey he had described to me that first night at Sir Isaac's home. "And after that, not a word about the matter," said Calloway. "It could have been just a normal weekend at a friend's home. We did some walking, a little shooting, a lot of drinking, we talked, laughed, set the world to rights. We did not once mention Alchuan and his strange prophesy. And after that, not another word from Sir Isaac Pryce, not until I received his telegram yesterday evening."

Calloway had shown me the telegram. It could have been in the running for the year's terseness prize. "*Now. Pryce.*"

"You're sure he wasn't a hoaxer, or just plain eccentric?"

"It would have been an expensive hoax. He even paid my petrol costs as well as giving me one of the most luxurious weekends I've had in my life." Calloway fumbled one-handed for cigarettes and the Rolls started to veer across the thankfully empty road. I snatched the packet and lit one for him. It was vile. I've often thought that if chocolate tasted as disgusting as tobacco, nobody would ever want a second piece in their life. So why do people persevere with cigarettes?

Calloway muttered his thanks. "As for eccentric . . . well, aspects of his life might strike some people as eccentric but conversely they'd strike others as remarkably sane. He didn't have a television but TVs were not as commonplace back in the Fifties as they are now. And even today some wilder parts of the country still have reception problems. And he wouldn't have a telephone in the house. Said that he'd had more than enough of them during his working life. Can't say I blame him. I hate the bloody things myself, useful as they are."

Useful for calling me out on unwanted adventures, I could have added. I didn't trouble myself, though, for I knew it wouldn't bother Calloway one whit. Instead I peered out at the thickening snow storm and said, "I hope to God we get there before this gets too bad."

Had we been making this journey in summertime it could have been pleasant and enjoyable. Starting early and travelling first through the rolling downs of Hampshire and Wiltshire, we progressed via Gloucester and Warwickshire, by-passing the massive conurbation of Birmingham to reach the southern reaches of Yorkshire via Derby. Skirting the major cities of Sheffield, Bradford and Leeds we eventually found ourselves among the wild Yorkshire moors and dales, heading up toward the borders with Cumbria and Durham.

When we had set out early that morning, though, the skies had been heavy with dark grey clouds and for much of the distance there had been intermittent rain and sleet, which combined with the heavy spray thrown up by vehicles on the motorways had reduced visibility enormously. Calloway's driving style didn't help much either and he had given me several scares. "I don't know why you're worried," he had laughed. "I feel safe enough. Having a live priest in the car has got to be more reassuring than any number of St. Christophers."

Some way beyond the Midlands the rain and sleet had eased but the clouds had darkened, becoming purple-black and oppressive, and the very air seemed to fall silent, as if waiting for the bulky mass to crush our car beneath it. As we had turned onto the little used country road that covered the final few miles to our destination, the rain and sleet had turned to snow which gradually worsened until the car's headlights picked out nothing but a fine white covering on the road ahead and the wipers battled hard to keep the windscreen clear.

"Don't worry," said Calloway. "I think we're almost there." We continued ascending a gradually rising road and several minutes later we reached the crest. Below us, about a mile or so down in a valley, I could see the lights of a great house with a shadowy hint of crenellated turrets. Despite the dark, there was an overall impression of age and solidity. I muttered heartfelt thanks. Calloway just smirked, as if to say, "Trust me, Roderick."

Minutes later we were standing in a porch roughly the size of a small chapel, Calloway pounding away at the iron knocker of a metal bossed wooden door, not unlike that of my church. Each massive thud returned a series of fainter echoes and Calloway only stopped when we heard the rattle of bolts being withdrawn. Unoiled hinges rasped painfully as the door was hauled open and a skinny man in a loose-fitting suit peered out at us.

"Elmore!" Calloway boomed. "Not looking a day older, I swear it." We stepped through into a hallway which, had it been slightly less roomy, would have made a good set for *The Prisoner of Zenda* (probably an *avant-garde* nude production, for the heat in the place was like a thick blanket).

"Professor Calloway . . . by, it's been a long time. It's grand to sithee sir." A mouthful of overlarge dentures grinned at us. "Sir Isaac told us tha' was comin."

Calloway gestured in my direction. "I took the liberty of bringing my friend Father Shea," he explained. "I'm sure you can fit him in somewhere. Must be a couple of hundred rooms in this place. Sir Isaac about?"

The butler shook a bald head. "Nay, the maister were feelin' tired like. Went to bed some time ago. Tha'sll see him in the morning. Young Mr. Richard's here, though, along with Mr. Peter Lambourne. Last I heard, they were goin' down to t'games room to play billiards."

"And who are they?"

"Why, sir, Mr. Richard's Sir Isaac's nephew, Mr. Richard Theobald, that is. And Mr. Lambourne's Sir Isaac's solicitor, here on business I shouldn't wonder although both he and Sir Isaac have been close mouthed about that. Anyhow, come thee along, gentlemen, and I'll sithee to thy rooms. When tha'rt freshened up, there'll be a hot supper and drinks waiting."

We met our fellow guests while we were eating the very welcome meal that Elmore had set before us. The dining-room door was thrust open and a vigorous voice preceded its owner. "Come on, Lambourne, just one more drink as a night-cap—Hello, who are you?"

The speaker was a stocky young man, probably in his mid-twenties, casually dressed in flared corduroy trousers and flowered shirt. Dark hair tumbled to his shoulders and he wore a heavy Zapata moustache. A slightly older man with shiny black hair plastered to his skull followed him in. He wore a heavy, expensive-looking pin-striped suit. I didn't understand how he could stand the near-tropical heat in the house. Perhaps he was just impervious to it.

We introduced ourselves. The young man turned to Elmore, who had started to clear the supper table. "You didn't tell me other guests were due." While not exactly angry, there was displeasure in his tone.

"Well, Mr. Richard, happen I reckoned it was Sir Isaac's place to tell thee who he asks to his own house . . . sir." No love lost there.

Calloway had been staring at Richard Theobald. "Have we ever met?" he asked. "I'm sure I know you. Southdown University possibly?"

"I don't think so," the younger man said, adding, "After all, I went to Cambridge." There was arrogance in his smile and distaste for the lesser universities in his tone.

I didn't sleep too well that night, probably a combination of strange bed and oppressive heat. But towards morning I drifted off and as a result overslept a little by my standards. It was after nine that I went down for breakfast. I had awakened to the unnatural stillness and clarity which indicates heavy snowfall and this was confirmed when I drew back the light curtains at the bedroom window. Thick drifts piled their way up the hills and beyond, muffling all sound. Although not snowing at the moment, a louring sky threatened to send much more, and soon. I couldn't see us going anywhere for a while. "Just a quick trip," Calloway had promised when he had called at the presbytery. "Should be only a day or so." A time will come when I stop listening to him.

I mentioned the weather to Elmore while he was serving me with bacon and eggs. "Aye, sir, it can get bad up in these parts. Tha could find thisen stuck here for days now. Good job that we allus keep a well-stocked larder here. The nearest village is Felldike and that's nigh impossible to reach when t'snow cooms down."

Theobald and Lambourne came in at that point and started eating with no more than a perfunctory greeting. I couldn't help feeling that as far as these two were concerned, Calloway and I could depart and get lost in the snow-covered wilds. Then my friend drifted in, boomingly cheerful, a large bowl of steaming porridge in one hand and what looked suspiciously like a glass of brandy in the other. Throughout the oatmeal, bacon and eggs and endless toast and honey, he carried on a one-sided conversation, oblivious to the other men's almost curmudgeonly manners.

Spreading marmalade thickly onto a bread-roll, Theobald turned casually to the old servant and said, "Have you seen my uncle this morning, Elmore?"

"That I haven't, sir. But maister looked fair whacked last night as tha knows." The butler pulled out an ancient pocket watch and consulted it with grave concentration. "Not often he's this late, though. Maister may be in his eighties but he allus puts away a hearty breakfast. Mebbe I'd better call him."

Minutes later Elmore was back, puffing heavily as if he had put in an unusual effort. "I can't get any reply from maister, gents, and his room seems to be locked from the inside."

"Perhaps we'd better take a look, Richard," said the lawyer, Lambourne. They left the room and Calloway jerked his head to indicate that we should follow. As we reached the hallway we could hear the footsteps of our fellow-guests overhead. Elmore had waited for us.

"Coom on, Professor, I'll show thee to the maister's bedroom."

He conducted us up the stairs and then along a corridor in a separate wing from the one where Calloway and I were quartered. We reached our destination to find Theobald trying to open the door, rattling the handle and pushing his weight against it, while Lambourne knocked hard against the panels with his fist. Both men were calling out to the occupant to open up.

Without ceremony, Calloway used his great weight to thrust them aside with ease. Calloway often takes strangers by surprise that way. Most mistake his fat for flab. It isn't. It's more the solid weight of an old bruiser gone to seed.

Grunting an insincere "Sorry!" Calloway squatted by the door and peered through the keyhole. "Black as night in there," he commented, rising to his feet. "The curtains must still be closed. As far as I can make out, though, there's no key on the inside of the door."

"There must be something wrong with my uncle," said Theobald, "Lord knows we've been making enough noise."

"Perhaps we'd better break the door down," Lambourne suggested.

"More likely break your shoulder," Calloway told him. "These doors are solid. Is there a spare key, Elmore?"

"Nay, maister keeps only key. Best if someone goes in through window, sir. We've got ladders in the old stables. We'll have to dig our way across, likely. We keep spades in the house for this time of year and a fair old selection of gumboots and overshoes, so I should be able to fit you all up."

As it turned out, it was Theobald and myself who dug out a back-breaking path through a couple of feet of snow to the stables and then, with ladders, struggled our way back to the spot below Sir Isaac's bedroom windows. Calloway, probably far and away the strongest of us, shamelessly ignored all hints that he should help, while Lambourne smoothed down his already slick hair and muttered something about sedentary work having ill-prepared him for this.

We raised the ladders then looked at each other. I hate ladders but I made a half-hearted gesture to mount it. Theobald stopped me. "I'm the youngest here. I'd better go," he said. "If you could just make sure that the ladder stays firm." At last Calloway consented to do something useful, sauntering through the narrow channel cleared in the snow and applying his weight to the ladder's base.

Theobald shinned up the ladder far more quickly than I could have done, or would have tried, and there was the sound of breaking glass as he smashed a pane to reach in and release the lock holding the sash window fast closed. He pushed the window up and we saw his legs disappear through the gap.

There was the sound of curtains on ancient brass rings being ripped back and then a pause of several minutes before Theobald's head appeared once more. "You'd better all come up," he called. "I think that my uncle's dead."

Theobald admitted us to the bedroom which was stiflingly hot, although it would probably cool down fairly rapidly now that the window was open. "The key was on the bedside cabinet," said the young man. "My uncle's on the bed. It looks like he locked himself in for the night after we got him to bed and then just died."

"Indeed," Lambourne added. "Now I wish that we'd taken more notice when Sir Isaac said he felt unwell. I'm afraid I just put it down to the weariness of old age."

I went to the bed and sought a pulse at the wrist and throat of Sir Isaac Pryce. I noticed a slight crust of dried vomit around his mouth and similar stains down the front of the dressing-gown he wore. Even as I touched him I knew it was too late. The body was cold, but I tried. Nothing. I turned to my companions and shook my head. I don't know what religion, if any, that Sir Isaac had belonged to but I whispered the words of absolution and sketched a blessing in the air.

Theobald and Lambourne had adopted suitable expressions of sadness but I didn't get an impression that they were heartbroken. Calloway simply looked resigned. The only genuine grief came from poor old Elmore. He sat down on the edge of the bed and reached out one gentle hand to touch the still form. "He were a good maister," said the old man, a tear running down his cheek.

"You know, it's possible we have a tragic accident here," said Richard Theobald. "I think my uncle may have inadvertently taken an overdose—either that or it was deliberate. Look, there's a bottle of brandy on his bedside table and his bottle of his sleeping pills is empty. I'm sure that he had quite a few left yesterday." He made as if to pick up the objects.

"No, don't touch them please." Calloway's voice was quiet but there was unmistakable authority there. "The police could well need them later for forensic examination."

"The police?" Lambourne sounded scornful. "Just look out of the window, Calloway. With all that snow, we'll be lucky if the police can make it here within the next four or five days. More, probably, seeing that Sir Isaac would not have a telephone in the house. You know, if we're going to be isolated, it could get unpleasant in here." Suddenly he looked queasy.

Calloway had been gazing hard at Theobald. Without a by-your-leave he leaned over and plucked something from the younger man's sweater sleeve. "Loose thread," he explained, holding up a scrap of white cotton. "I can't bear untidiness." The others stared at him. When it comes to elegant dressing, Calloway is of the school of men who always appear to have forgotten to undress for bed on the previous night.

Then Calloway took charge. "I think that we can move the body to the stables or an outhouse later on. It will be cold enough out there for a few days at least. We'll handle matters as respectfully as we can.

"In the meantime, perhaps you two will take Elmore downstairs and see that he's all right. Roderick and I will stay here and do what needs to be done."

"Why you two? Why not us?" Lambourne's voice was querulous, that of a man who knows that inside he is only small and ineffectual but who is trying to establish his authority.

"Who better?" said Calloway soothingly. "You're both so close to him; we're more detached. And after all, Roderick's a priest and I'm a professor."

Okay, so he told the truth, but it was an amazingly flexible truth. Calloway is a professor neither of medicine nor pathology. Not that it matters. The others accepted our credentials without further question and, I'm sure, with some relief, and they led Elmore away.

Calloway closed the door firmly behind them. "Right, Roderick, let's see what we've got here."

I looked around me. The chamber was a large one, dark-panelled, with a high ceiling and a deeply luxurious carpet underfoot. Over to the left as you entered was an immense, old-fashioned hearth. There were similar fireplaces in the guest-rooms and even larger ones downstairs. The remains of a fire—ashes and glowing embers of wood—still smouldered in this one. Near to the hearth was an antique captain's chair of some dark wood with a worn, red leather seat. Directly opposite the fire was a sash window with broken glass beneath it from where Theobald had forced an entry. Crimson velvet curtains, far more thick and heavy than those in my room, had been pulled back roughly. A second set of curtains was still drawn, covering another window.

Sir Isaac's bed was a huge four-poster hung with crimson drapes to match the window curtains. The mattress was obviously substantial and the baronet's body lay on top of a thick eiderdown of a type rarely seen any more. To the right of the bed was a cabinet with an electric lamp and the bottles Theobald had referred to.

The old man himself, lying on his back, was clad—as already noted—in a long dressing-gown of royal blue, beneath which he was still wearing shirt and trousers. His feet were covered with a pair of dark blue slippers and I noted with mild amusement that he was wearing yellow socks. He looked peaceful enough. I guessed that when brought to his room, he had simply settled down to rest, perhaps vomited in his sleep and had died.

"Looks as if we've had a wasted journey," I said to my friend.

"Not at all." He was studying the bedside table, scratching one cheek and humming to himself. It sounded like an old Buddy Holly number. Abruptly he switched to a Beatles tune, picked up both bottles, examined them briefly and set them down again with care. "Come over here, Roderick. Tell me what you see."

I did as bid. "A bottle of Remy Martin, about one-third full, and an empty prescription bottle." I peered more closely at the latter. "Phenobarbitone, I think. There was a lot of fuss about that when I was a boy in the Forties."

"Yes, Remy Martin and phenobarbitones. Anything else?"

I could only guess that he meant the fine film of dust, disturbed only by the moving of the bottles, and said so.

"Right." The off-key humming started again as Reuben Calloway wandered around the room. Now it was Presley's turn to be treated discordantly. Calloway halted by the captain's chair, then stooped to fiddle with something. When he straightened he was half-smiling.

"Another thread," he told me. "Caught in a splinter in the arm of the chair."

"I know, you hate untidiness." Not to be outdone I glanced about and spotted a tiny piece of white stuck to the cuff of the dead man's dressing gown. "There's another!"

"Ah, thank you Roderick and well done. That's where I intended to look next." Smug glee lit his face and he said, "But you've missed some more." He pointed to the door of the bedside cabinet from which another thread protruded. He tugged at it and the door came open, spilling an untidy pile of white bandages on the floor. He picked them up. There were several raggedly cut lengths of material. "There you are," Calloway announced as if making a great revelation.

Straightening up, he said, "Now, I want you to help me with something which may seem ghoulish. We're going to get some of the clothes off Sir Isaac."

I made some sort of protest but only because I thought Calloway would expect it. I know my friend and accepted that he wouldn't do such a thing without good reason.

I eased off Sir Isaac's slippers and—at Calloway's insistence—his socks. While I was doing that, Calloway ran gentle hands over the body. "No rigor mortis yet," he muttered. "But then the room was stinking hot, what with the fire and the central heating. I don't know too much about it, Roderick, but I believe that rigor can be retarded or hastened depending on the ambient temperature. Right, let's get on."

We started on the difficult bit. Disrobing a corpse is tiring but we managed as far as was necessary for Calloway's purposes. We managed to lift the old man's dressing-gown and shirt to his shoulders and trousers and shorts down to his ankles. His buttocks, the backs of his thighs and his lower legs and feet were a dull, liverish colour.

Calloway pointed to the discoloration. "Hypostasis," he announced.

"Post-mortem lividity," I agreed. Two could play at one upmanship.

Calloway took the game a bit further. "So tell me what's wrong," he said.

"Good grief, Calloway, I'm a priest, not a mortician!" Calloway just frowned and so I looked at the body more carefully. Then I realised what he was getting at. "There's no lividity on his back," I said.

"Good, Roderick. Now doesn't that seem strange for someone who died sleeping in that position? And look, there are some very faint marks around his forearms and chest." Calloway pointed and I peered. There may have been something there. I wasn't sure but my friend's eyes are sharper than mine.

Calloway plucked at his lower lip. "I think Sir Isaac was right all those years ago," he mused. "He was to be murdered and the prophecy has been fulfilled."

Deep down I felt that Calloway might be right but I had to play the Devil's advocate. "This just isn't so much wishful thinking on your part?" I asked. "You're not trying to read too much into what's happened?" Then I had another thought. "The door was locked from the inside. Surely that casts doubt on any chance of foul play?"

"Ah, yes, the locked room. Thank you for pointing that out to me, Roderick. I'll be sure to keep that in mind."

Why did I have the odd feeling that I was being patronised?

We re-dressed Sir Isaac and laid him out as best we could. Then we left, locking the door behind us.

Lambourne and Theobald were waiting in the library. "Such a sad business," Calloway told them, "I think you were probably right, Theobald. Just another tragic misadventure. You read about it so often in the press, all too frequently with the elderly. They take one or two sleeping tablets, then wake up in the middle of the night, forget that they've had their dose and repeat it. Just so that we can be clear about matters, what happened last night before myself and Father Shea arrived?"

Between them, the two men related the sequence of events. During dinner, Sir Isaac had complained of feeling tired and unwell. At last he had asked to be taken to his room. His nephew and the solicitor had helped him and once there, he had just wanted to be helped onto his bed and allowed to rest. That was the last they had seen of him.

"Thank you, gentlemen," said Calloway, "And our condolences, Mr. Theobald. We'll just pop along now and see how Elmore is getting on."

We found the elderly butler in an echoing, stone-flagged

Victorian kitchen, drinking a cup of strong tea and being fussed over by a middle-aged woman whom I assumed to be the cook.

We sat down at the scrubbed refectory table and accepted an offer of tea for ourselves. The cook served us with steaming mugs and having thanked her profusely, Calloway turned on the charm and complimented her on the breakfast. "Best porridge I've ever had!" he boasted. Some simpering from the woman, a little more banter from Calloway and suddenly she found herself agreeing that, yes, she could find something to do elsewhere while the gentlemen had a word with Mr. Elmore. At times Calloway amazed me.

"A sad business, Elmore," said Calloway when we were left alone with the butler.

"Aye, sir," the man replied. "Sir Isaac were a good man and he'll be sorely missed. I know he were old, like, but he'd always kept healthy. Used to get tired sometimes, but that's understandable at his age."

"He didn't suffer from rheumatism or arthritis, anything like that? Use bandages for support at all?"

"Nay, sir, whatever gave thee that idea?" Elmore chuckled. "Sir Isaac were in fine fettle, better than me, happen."

"What occurred at dinner last night, before we arrived?"

"I'm not rightly sure at that, sir. The maister were as sprightly as allus when he came down to eat. Then a while after I'd served the coffee, when I came in to clear away the crocks, he were practically out on his feet—could hardly stand oop by himself. In the end yon other pair helped him oop the stairs and that were it until I tried to call him this morning."

"Do you know if he habitually took sleeping tablets?"

"He took 'em sometimes." Elmore scratched his thinning pate. "As he got older he didn't sleep so good. But when he did have a pill, it was usually just a half-a-one. Said he didn't want to rely on 'em."

"Did he have much to drink?" Calloway asked.

The old servant flared up. "Maister were no drunkard!" Calloway hastened to soothe his feelings and at last he continued. "He had mebbe a glass or two of wine wi' dinner and then coffee. He were so knackered he didn't even have his usual armagnac."

"Still liked his Marquis de Montesquiou, did he?"

"Oh aye, sir. Wouldn't touch owt else. Kept some good cognac and whisky for guests, though."

"And did he always keep a bottle by his bedside?"

"Nay, he never did that. But there was a bottle there, wasn't there?" Elmore's mouth slackened and his eyes widened with shock. "Here, mebbe the maister meant to kill hisself."

"Don't distress yourself, Elmore. I don't think he intended that at all." Calloway pulled out a packet of cigarettes, offering Elmore one. I poured us all some more tea then Calloway said: "I'm not criticising, just curious, but I noticed that your master's bedroom was a bit dusty. Surely that's unusual?"

There was pride in the reply. "Aye, well, that's Sir Isaac for you. A good maister. Place like this, sixty years and more ago, had dozens of servants. Now there's just me, Mrs. Hopkirk and a lass as cycles oop from t'village to clean like. She's been down wi' bad flu for a couple of weeks and maister wouldn't let me or Mrs. H. do any of the cleaning work.

"Now, sir, we've had us tea and we've had a smoke together, so let's go along to my room. Maister gave me a letter for you some weeks back, said if owt happened to him, see that you got it as quickly as could be. I've waited till now 'cos I didn't want them other two buggers to see it."

Elmore led us down a short corridor leading from the kitchen to his quarters. He had a small sitting room simply furnished with a couple of armchairs, a small bookcase and a highly polished old bureau. Several reproduction prints hung on the walls and there was a radio which must have dated from the early Fifties (I can recall my parents having one very similar). Through a partly opened doorway I could see a single bed and the edge of a wardrobe.

Elmore delved into the bureau and produced a heavy brown manilla packet with the single word CALLOWAY on the front. I could see that the flap was thickly sealed with red wax. "Here it is, Professor. Tha'll want to look at it in private, so I'll leave thee and the good Father here alone. Stay just as long as tha needs."

As the door clicked shut, Calloway broke the sealing and ripped the package open. Three other envelopes—one bulky, the others slim—fell out, together with a piece of folded notepaper and a key.

There was a card label tied to the key with a cryptic message. "*You can guess where this is for.*" "Yes indeed," Calloway muttered. He opened and read quickly through the note before passing it to me. It was hand-written, dated about two months previously.

Dear Calloway,
If you are reading this, Alchuan's prophecy has been realised and I am dead. I do hope you remember well our first dinner and conversation and your promise from all those years ago. Just in case this envelope falls into the wrong hands, I am leaving you a pair of simple puzzles to solve. When you have deciphered them, you should know what to do next. The locks are my favourite books, the key is seven.

Perhaps when you leave you would care to take with you a cabinet or two of Hoyo de Monterey and a case of the Marquis. Enjoy them to the full.

Your grateful acquaintance (or friend),

Isaac Pryce

(5,2,2,5)

8312149261422524254425798

While I was reading this, Calloway had ripped open the larger of the two inner envelopes and removed the contents. "Sir Isaac's will," he said. "And another note attached to it. Listen. '*This is my latest and only genuine will and testament. All previous wills have been destroyed and any other document found will be a forgery. Isaac Pryce.*'"

Calloway flicked through the document quickly. "Properly signed and witnessed," he commented. He turned his attention to one of the thin envelopes and produced a newspaper cutting. It was a photograph of Richard Theobald, Lambourne slightly behind him, the pair descending the front steps of an impressive-looking building. A caption read: RICHARD THEOBALD AND HIS SOLICITOR LEAVING MELDRUM'S, THE MERCHANT BANK, YESTERDAY AFTERNOON.

"Now I know why Theobald looked familiar when we met," exclaimed Calloway. "You may recall the business, Roderick. It was a year or two ago—there were City rumours of dodgy business at

Meldrum's, accusations of insider dealing, forgery, misappropriation and so on. Either nothing could be proved or there was a whitewash. Whatever happened, Richard Theobald had to resign and left under a cloud."

Two pieces of paper—or rather parchment, for it was far more heavy and of better quality than ordinary paper—fell from the third envelope. Calloway laughed. "A puzzle indeed," he commented.

The first read:

θκηβγβ ὠλ γνκ ωσηου φκεώδα νοβ λσκβυ

and the second:

θοαφβ ὠλ γνκ ηοα βιηγγκα νοβ θώυκβ

"What do you think, Roderick?" Calloway asked me.

"It's Greek, but from the little Greek I know it doesn't seem to make any sense," I replied.

"It probably wouldn't," said Calloway. "I'll wager anything that these notes are in English. I told you on the way here that Sir Isaac was surprisingly proud of his lack of languages."

There was a soft tap at the door and Elmore's head appeared. "I'm serving lunch now, gentlemen," he said. "Maister would want things to carry on as normal."

Calloway pushed everything back into the packet and stuffed it all under his shirt. I didn't think anyone would notice, Calloway's appearance generally being so untidy.

We ascended to the dining room and ate lunch, during which our fellow guests once more did their utmost to ignore us, maintaining normal courtesy but no more than that. At the end of the meal, Lambourne pushed back his chair and stood up, saying to Elmore, "Mr. Theobald and I have some private business to discuss concerning the late Sir Isaac's affairs. It will take much of the afternoon. If needed we'll be in the library although I trust that there will be no reason to disturb us."

Through the open door we saw them cross the great hall and enter the wing in which the library was situated. Calloway followed quickly and silently. I know of old how stealthily he can move when necessary but it still surprises me. Seconds later he was back.

"They've taken precautions against disturbance. I heard the key turn in the lock."

"That's a heavy hint," I observed.

"Did you notice anything odd about their actions, Roderick? No? When did you ever hear of a lawyer wanting to discuss business without having a case filled with documents? Never mind, it gives us a chance to do what's necessary."

"And what is necessary, Reuben?"

"Oh, didn't I say? We're going to search their rooms." I started to protest but Calloway just flapped a big paw at me. "We're not police, are we? The rules of search and evidence don't apply to us, do they? So come on."

I wasn't too certain about the legal accuracy of his arguments but I followed on, knowing that he'd just go ahead without me anyway. Calloway caught Elmore in the hall and muttered instructions about warning us if the others seemed likely to vacate the library.

We went into Theobald's room first. There was nothing very interesting there except for a small scrapbook filled with newspaper cuttings. All were concerned with the troubles at Meldrum's bank; it seemed apparent that Richard Theobald took pride in the part that he had played in the scandal.

A large brief-case lay on Lambourne's bed, fastened and locked, but Calloway was undeterred. He took out a pocket-knife and used the smallest blade to fiddle with the locks until they sprang open. The case was filled with papers and documents. After a quick glance at each, Calloway threw many aside as being of no interest but retained three. Not even bothering to repack and close the brief-case, he grabbed my arm and dragged me back downstairs where he hailed Elmore who was still keeping watch.

"A couple more questions," Calloway said to the old man. "What can you tell me of a Doctor Wragby of Felldike?"

"He's Sir Isaac's GP, sir," Elmore replied.

"And what sort of person is he?"

"He's a good doctor, right enough, but . . ." The butler paused, as if slightly embarrassed to be discussing the physician. Calloway gave him a cigarette and waited patiently. The cigarette was half-smoked when Elmore made up his mind. "It's this way, Professor. He's got a reputation, like, for being careless wi' money and so on . . . They reckon he's o'er fond of gambling and expensive women . . ."

"And what about our friends in the library?"

"Them?" Elmore snorted with contempt. "Yon Mr. Richard's a right wastrel. Expelled from school though he did well enough at college. And tha may have heard of yon bank shennigans. His mother's Sir Isaac's favourite niece, so he's been tolerated all these years. Only ever cooms here when he wants summat.

"As for Mr. Peter Lambourne, he's not Sir Isaac's real solicitor. That was Mr. Lionel Lambourne, Mr. Peter's father. Mr. Lionel is a lawyer of the old school. Tha could trust him wi' your life. Mr. Peter's another one like Richard, only cleverer, or more cunning mebbe, not having been caught out like. Mr. Lionel had a stroke awhile back, which is why the young 'un's here."

Calloway thanked the elderly servant. "I don't think you'll have to bother about those two much longer, Elmore. But we'll see, we'll see."

We were off again. Calloway ushered me into the library wing but instead of going there we approached the opposite door. Calloway took out the labelled key which had been with Sir Isaac's letter and tried it in the lock. "I thought so," he said, pleased. He opened the door to admit us. It was an attractive-looking room although a light layer of dust signified unoccupancy for some time. It was very warm because of the central heating and materials for a fire were laid in the grate. Calloway struck a match and within moments small flames were flickering around the logs which started to snap and crackle.

While he was tending the fire, he said: "The diorama I mentioned, it's over there. Go and have a look. I think you'll find the switch just under that left-hand corner of the table."

I did as bid and was overwhelmed by the beauty of the model, which was as close as I could imagine to seeing the real savannah from an aircraft. I stood there in such wonder that I became breathless, with a sense of vertigo, and could almost feel myself being drawn into the scene. I drew back, slightly shaken.

Having got a good blaze going to his satisfaction, Calloway had taken a Havana cigar from a cedar box and was now puffing cheerfully. The smoke was fragrant, a great improvement on his dreadful cigarettes. He came to stand by my shoulder.

"This is . . . well, it's just beyond description," I said.

"Yes, isn't it?" As he looked at the diorama, an expression of doubt crossed his face. I asked him what was wrong.

"I'm not sure." He walked around the table, cigar gripped between his teeth, stopping from time to time to gaze closely, nose almost touching the glass top. "I know it has been many years since I've seen this, and my memory may be playing tricks, but I'm almost certain that it's not the way it was then. Different groupings of animals, changes to the landscape, old trees down and new trees growing, things like that. Perhaps I'm getting old." He shrugged. "Anyway, come and meet Alchuan."

The image of Alchuan was even more astounding than the African diorama. It was as Calloway had described to me and yet there was more. He had not mentioned how tall and skeletally thin the thing was, nor just how sinister it truly appeared. And perhaps it was because I am occasionally sensitive, an unwanted and unappreciated inheritance from some Celtic ancestor, but for me the thing radiated power. And more than that. I felt a tacit approval of Calloway and myself but beneath that approval lurked menace, malevolence even.

I told Calloway this. "Do you really think that it contains Alchuan's remains?" I asked.

"Would you care to look under the mask?"

"No, I don't think that I would."

"Good, then let's get to work." Calloway stalked back to the fireplace and sat in one of the armchairs, gesturing me into another. He poured two armagnacs and pulled out the various documents and papers from under his shirt.

"This is the will that Sir Isaac noted as being the only genuine one. There are substantial bequests—all net of taxes—to Elmore and Mrs. Hopkirk, with a lesser amount to someone called Rosemary Garth, presumably the cleaning girl. Generous amounts to various charities and the bulk of the estate of Joanna Theobald—presumably Richard's mother. No mention at all of Richard. Lionel Lambourne and his partner Daniel Jason are named as joint executors." Calloway put the will carefully to one side.

"This is a will I took from Peter Lambourne's case. It appears good, but if Sir Isaac is to be believed, then it is false. There are some small bequests to the servants and the whole of the remainder goes to '. . . my beloved great-nephew Richard Theobald . . .' The sole executor is Peter Lambourne.

"Now turning to the other papers I filched, one is a promissory note from a Doctor Wragby of Felldike. He seems to owe Peter Lambourne ten thousand pounds. The second is a letter to Peter Lambourne from the Law Society, instructing him to attend a disciplinary hearing in the new year. There have been allegations made which, if proved, could result in him being struck off."

"Poor Sir Isaac seems to have surrounded himself with rogues," I observed.

"More likely the rogues chose to surround him. Pryce was sharp and I'm sure that he was on to them. Which brings us to our puzzles." Calloway produced the two pieces of parchment with the Greek lettering. "I said before lunch that these will be in English. And they shouldn't be too difficult to crack. As well as his pride in speaking no foreign languages, Sir Isaac impressed upon me his belief in simplicity.

"I'm just realising that what I thought to be somewhat boring dinner chat all those years ago was probably a preparing of the way. Sir Isaac was dropping hints."

Calloway pointed to the drinks table. "Pick up those books, Roderick." I did so and looked at the titles. They were *The Boy's Book of General Knowledge* and *The Boy's Book of Puzzles and Brain Teasers*. "Pryce mentioned in his letter to me that his favourite books were 'the lock'. Have a look through them. I'm sure that between them you'll find the Greek alphabet and a section on simple codes."

I riffled quickly through the thick pages. "Yes, here's the Greek alphabet, and here in the other book is a section on codes." Light dawned. "It says here that the simplest of all codes is the transposition of one letter or number for another. You think that Sir Isaac transposed Greek letters for Roman."

"That's the most likely thing, wouldn't you agree?."

"That could lead to other complications," I said. "There are only twenty-four letters in the Greek alphabet as compared with our twenty-six. And there's no exact correspondence. For instance, the third letter of the Greek alphabet is 'gamma' which is equivalent to our 'G', not 'C'."

Calloway poured himself another armagnac and rekindled

his cigar which had gone out. "I don't think so. Pryce wouldn't have wanted complications. I think he made a straightforward transposition. We'll write it down and to even things, we'll just try leaving out the final two letters of our alphabet."

Calloway scribbled on the back of the largest envelope and passed it over to me. "Does this look right?"

a b c d e f g h i j k l m n o p r s t u v w
α β χ δ ε φ γ η ι φ κ λ μ ν ο π ρ σ τ υ ώ ω

"Seems okay. Pass me the parchments and let's see what that gives us." This time it was my turn to scribble and I came up with two lines of mixed and senseless letters.

θκηβγβ ώλ γνκ ωσηου φκεώδα νοβ λσκβυ
hkgbcb vl cnk wsgou jkevda nob lskbn
θοαφβ ώλ γνκ ηοα βιηγγκα νοβ
hoajb vl cnk goa bigccka nob hvukb

"That's gibberish," I said. "Either the messages are nonsense or else there's another code buried underneath the first."

"You're right, Roderick," was the answer. "*The Boy's Book of Puzzles* probably didn't anticipate a reader substituting a foreign alphabet for the Roman. We're on the right lines though. What would be the simplest transposition?"

I thought for a moment. "I suppose using B for A or something like that. I'll give it a try." Several more minutes of work and the result still lacked logic.

ilhcdc wm dol xthpv opc mtlco
ipbkc wm dol hpb cjhddlb opc iwvlc

"Say that Pryce's transposition went deeper into the alphabet," suggested Calloway. "He liked things simple but there is such a thing as too simple. Let's have another look at his letter." He read briefly and then grinned. "We both need our backsides kicking, Roderick. Not only did he say that his books were the lock but also that the key was seven. What's the seventh letter of the alphabet? G? Try again, taking 'G' as the first letter of the alphabet."

Calloway doesn't need me, he needs a secretary. "There!" I said when I finished.

a b c d e f g h i j k l m n o p r s t u v w
g h i j k l m n o p r s t u v w a b c d e f

"I'll do the next bit, Roderick," he grinned. "Before you have to confess to the venial sin of losing patience."

Taking a fresh envelope, he started to work. Feeling that I now deserved another drink, I poured a liberal double into my glass. I was almost tempted to try a Hoyo de Monterey but why should I give up the good habits of a lifetime?

"That's it, Roderick. I've cracked it." He looked at my face and added hastily, "I mean, we've cracked it. Here, what do they look like to you?"

θκηβγβ ὠλ γνκ ωσηου φκεώδα νοβ λσκβυ

hkgbcb vl cnk wsgou jkevda nob lskbn

beasts of the plain devour his flesh

θοαφβ ὠλ γνκ ηοα βιηγγκα νοβ

hoajb vl cnk goa bigccka nob hvukb

birds of the air scatter his bones

I read and felt a slight chill. "They look like curses to me," I admitted. Calloway nodded. Then I had another thought. "We've forgotten something, Reuben. At the end of Pryce's letter there were some figures. What's the betting they're another code?"

"Yes, I overlooked that. Very likely that you're right. Let's see them again—"

(5,2,2,5)

831214926142252425798

I picked up the pencil. "Assuming that each number indicates a letter, I'll try the simplest conversion first. 'A' for one and so on until we have twenty-six for 'Z'.

(e,b,b,e)

hcabadibfadbbebdbegih

"Not much help," said Calloway. "But I didn't think it would be. The key is seven, so we'll start again with 'G' as one, which will give us . . . let's see . . . yes, 'F' as twenty-six, thus—"

g h i j k l m n o p q r s t u v w x y z a b c d e f

1 2 3 4 5 6 7 8 9 10 11 12 13 14 15 16 17 18 19 20 21 22 23 24 25 26

I had been wondering again about the first set of figures: (5,2,2,5). "You know what they remind me of, Reuben? The indicator in a cryptic crossword clue. You know what they're like. You have a written clue and then in parenthesis a series of figures with commas to show the number of words in the answer and how many letters there will be in each. So let's just go for a transposition of the second set of numbers."

"Good thinking," approved Calloway. "The first number is eight, which on our new scale is 'N', followed by three equivalent to 'I' . . . Therefore 8312 spells 'NIGH' and then we have 'G' and 'J', which are obviously wrong. How many English words start with 'N-I-G-H', Roderick?"

"I'd say about half a dozen or so . . . Supposing that after 8312 the one and four are actually fourteen . . ."

"Right! Fourteen is equivalent to 'T', giving us the five-letter word 'NIGHT'. So the next figure, nine, is 'O', followed by two and six, either 'H' and 'L' or twenty-six 'F'. Definitely twenty-six because the two-letter word 'OF' makes more sense that 'OH'." Calloway muttered on, more to himself than to me, then started to chuckle. "Very droll, Sir Isaac," he said. He showed me four words. NIGHT OF THE DEMON.

"What on earth does that mean?" I asked.

"I think it means a very nasty surprise for someone," was the reply. "First of all I'll get rid of this—" Leaning forward, Calloway threw the second, supposedly false, will into the fire and prodded at it with a fire iron until it was ashes.

Lighting another cigar, Calloway waddled over to a window and looked out. I joined him there. During the day there seemed to have been fresh snowfalls and now, mid-afternoon, it was almost dark outside. "I know that expression, Reuben. I think you're having one of your crises of conscience. Have you reached a decision about whatever the moral dilemma is?"

My friend reached up to pull the curtains closed, then answered me. "Yes, we'll have an end to this affair now. Wait here a moment, Roderick."

He stalked from the room and pounded on the library door which was snatched open. Lambourne's voice came to my ears, rasping, annoyed. "What do you want, Calloway? I said that we wanted to remain undisturbed!"

"I know," said Calloway. "You wanted to discuss matters concerning Sir Isaac's death. Well, so do I. If you would care to join myself and Father Shea I think we can give you some pertinent facts about the matter."

"Very well," grumbled the other. They followed Calloway in, Lambourne with bad grace, Richard Theobald with an air of arrogant detachment. Calloway's manner was jovial and expansive as he ushered them to the chairs that I had pulled forward to the hearth.

Calloway sat facing them, his manner relaxed, his expression benevolent. "Drinks, gentlemen? Cigars? No? Very well, to business. In my opinion, Sir Isaac Pryce's death was neither a natural one nor accidental."

"You mean you think that he killed himself?" asked Lambourne. "I suggest that you be sure of your facts before making such rash accusations."

"Oh, I'm so sure of my facts I've ruled out suicide. Sir Isaac was murdered."

Again, it was Lambourne who reacted. "Balderdash! Murdered? By whom?"

Calloway's expression became even more benevolent. "By whom? Why, by you two, of course."

Richard Theobald just smiled a lazy smile but Lambourne's face reddened to an extent that I momentarily expected him to keel over. "This is bloody nonsense!" he snarled. "I'm leaving . . ."

"*Sit!*" Calloway's command would have impressed a regimental sergeant-major. Lambourne collapsed back into his chair.

Richard Theobald continued to smile. "A ridiculous accusation," he drawled. "What evidence and motive can you come up with?"

"I came here expecting the worst," Calloway said. "You're probably unaware but I once stayed here with Isaac Pryce, many years ago. He told me of a prophecy that he would be murdered by someone close to him and he asked me to look into the matter when it eventually happened."

"And that's it?" Lambourne's voice rang with disbelief. "Years ago an eccentric old man told you he would be murdered and so when he dies you look around for someone to accuse?"

"Of course that's not it. Not alone, anyway." Calloway reached over for the decanter. "I was always a little sceptical about the prophecy until I saw the dead man and examined him and his chamber." Calloway held up his glass, letting the soft light play on the cut crystal and the pale amber fluid. "Armagnac, gentlemen. A very fine, very expensive armagnac called Marquis de Montesquiou. Sir Isaac told me that he never drank any other spirit. I'll bet that neither of you knew that. Odd, then, that the bottle by his bedside should be Remy Martin. A very good cognac, gentlemen, but a cognac nevertheless. Sir Isaac wouldn't have touched it."

"People can change," commented Richard Theobald. "And if he intended to kill himself, as may have been the case, would it matter what he used to wash the pills down with?"

Calloway shook his head. "Possibly not. I did ask Elmore today, though, and he confirmed that his master still only drank the Marquis, although he did keep other good liquor for any guests who wanted it.

"Then there were the bandages . . ."

"Bandages—just what the hell are you talking about now, Calloway?" Lawyer Lambourne was becoming very agitated.

"The cut bandages I found in Sir Isaac's bedside cabinet. You'll recall that when we were in your uncle's room this morning, Mr. Theobald, I plucked a piece of lint from your sleeve. We found matching pieces of lint on the cuff of Sir Isaac's dressing-gown, more caught on the arm of the wooden chair in the room, and also on the door of the cabinet. Inside the cabinet was a small bundle of bandages."

"There are any number of reasons why my uncle could have bandages in his room." Richard Theobald sighed. "This is becoming boring, Professor."

Calloway looked contrite. "I'm sorry for that," he said. "Bear with me if you will. I also asked Elmore if Sir Isaac had any need for bandages and he said not."

"Elmore's only a servant!" snapped Lambourne. "What could he possibly know?"

"Probably far more than you," was Calloway's dry observation. "Let's move on, though. We're all agreed that the brandy and bandages are good grounds for suspicion—well, perhaps not all of us but Father Shea and I certainly thought so. Therefore we delved a little further. We looked for hypostasis. I'm sure that Father Shea can tell you about that."

I was touched. It wasn't often that Reuben Calloway threw any glory my way. "Hypostasis—also known as post-mortem lividity," I explained. "When someone dies, after a time blood accumulates at the lowest point in the cadaver."

Calloway had given me my moment. "Thank you, Roderick," he butted in. "We found Sir Isaac lying on his back. Lividity should have been evenly distributed from the shoulders down. It wasn't. It showed on his buttocks, backs of his thighs and the lower part of his legs. Indications are that he died in a sitting position and remained so for quite a few hours after death. Now I'll tell you what I think happened . . ."

Throughout Calloway's exposition, Richard Theobald had remained calm and watchful, had even served himself with an armagnac which he sipped with apparent approval. Lambourne had ceased his bluster. His lips were now tight and I thought that I caught a whiff of fear.

Calloway steepled his fingers beneath his chin and regarded the two men, face still benevolent. "Earlier today you told me that Sir Isaac was complaining of feeling unwell during dinner last night. And yet Elmore has testified that when his master appeared for dinner he was quite well. 'Sprightly', I think, was the word he used. I surmise that somehow during the meal you contrived to feed him one or two of his sleeping tablets, possibly in strong coffee which would disguise the taste.

"Eventually you had to help him to his bedroom, apparently unwell, almost falling asleep. Once there, you sat him in his chair, carefully secured him in place with the bandages around his arms and body then poured a mixture of cognac and crushed sleeping pills down his throat. After which, you callously left him to die.

"When you broke into the bedroom this morning—" Calloway pointed an accusing finger at the seemingly unflustered Richard Theobald "—you hastily cut the bandages free and laid the old man out on his bed before calling us. It wouldn't have been too difficult. The room was stiflingly hot and rigor mortis had not yet set in. You had to hide the bandages somewhere in a hurry and so you stuffed them into the bedside cabinet."

"Very clever, Professor Calloway." Richard Theobald looked amused. "An interesting theory but haven't you overlooked the fact that my uncle's room was locked from the inside? This being the fact, how could we have done what you accuse us of?"

Calloway grinned. "Ah, the famous locked-room mystery. Locked room, bah! You may not be aware that during the Thirties and Forties several British detective story writers had very successful careers by specialising in locked-room mysteries. And you know what? At the dénouement, the solutions were simple to the point that the reader wanted to kick himself for not working it out."

"And am I going to kick myself?" Theobald sneered.

"I think so. There is no locked-room mystery. When you left Sir Isaac last night, you just locked the door from the outside. The key was in your pocket when you climbed that ladder this morning. You see, you told us that the key was on the bedside cabinet but it couldn't have been.

"The place has remained undusted for a couple of weeks because the cleaning girl has been off work sick. The dust on the bedside cabinet was disturbed where the brandy and sleeping pill bottles had been but there was no sign that said the key had been placed there."

For the first time since Calloway had accused them, Richard Theobald seemed unsure of himself. "That would have been careless of me if your theory's correct," he muttered. "You've given us what you obviously consider evidence. How about motive?"

"Greed, what else?" Calloway nodded at each man in turn. "I don't know if you were summoned here by Sir Isaac so that he could warn you off, or whether you invited yourselves. You are both men whose integrity is questionable and both of you probably needed a lot of money and fairly quickly. Whatever the circumstances, I think you came here quite prepared to kill the old man.

"You, Mr. Theobald, were compelled to resign from one of the City's top merchant banks under a cloud. No criminal charges were brought against you, but the old boy network—well known for closing ranks against outsiders—does not expel one of its own unless they are very suspect indeed.

"As for Mr. Lambourne, he is due to appear before the Law Society to answer some embarrassing questions about misappropriation of clients' funds. Again, the Law Society is a conservative organisation which does not turn easily on its own."

"You've been nosing in my property," gasped Lambourne, astounded.

"Of course I have," was the unabashed reply. "I'll even tell you how you thought you'd get away with murder. You got your hooks into another weak man, one Doctor Wragby of Felldike. Doctor Wragby is in your debt, Lambourne, for quite a few thousand pounds. I take it that when Sir Isaac's body was discovered, Doctor Wragby would be summoned and would sign a death certificate without question. His debt would be expunged and he could go his way. If Elmore had queried this, he would have been told that you were doing it this way for the sake of his master's memory, so that it would not appear that Sir Isaac had either killed himself or accidentally drunk himself to death.

"What you couldn't reasonably have expected was for us to turn up here nor could you have expected the heavy snowfall which would make it impossible to summon the profligate Doctor Wragby."

Calloway drained his glass and leaned back in his chair, grinning like an unpleasant schoolboy who has just perpetrated a nasty practical joke. "Of course," he said, "All this is speculation on my part. It might be very hard to prove anything in a court of law. Why, I've even destroyed one piece of vital documentary evidence. The will that you so beautifully forged between you went into that fire some time ago. Father Shea saw me destroy it."

Lambourne pulled out a handkerchief and wiped his brow. I could see that his hand was trembling. Richard Theobald's face contorted with hideous fury and for a moment I thought that he was going to spring at Calloway. Something in Calloway's calm stopped him and he relaxed. After a few seconds, Theobald even managed a shaky laugh. "Not that I'm admitting anything but it looks as if we're off the hook," he said as he stood up. "So if you don't need me any more . . ."

"A moment, please. These were in a letter to me from Sir Isaac. I think he meant them for you." Calloway passed each man a piece of the parchment bearing Greek lettering. They looked at them in puzzlement.

"Just what's this supposed to mean?" cried Lambourne.

"That's from the Greek alphabet," Calloway told him. "Perhaps Mr. Theobald can read it, being a Cambridge man."

"No. I did Latin," said the younger man.

"No matter. The lettering is Greek but the messages are in English. And that's not much help to you, either. They're in code. Sir Isaac loved simple puzzles. To save you effort, Father Shea and I solved them this afternoon. I'll tell you what they say, shall I? Mr. Theobald, your piece of parchment reads: 'Beasts of the plain devour his flesh'; while yours, Mr. Lambourne, transcribes as: 'Birds of the air scatter his bones.'"

"What sort of nonsense is that?" yelled Lambourne, bravado starting to return.

Calloway shrugged. "Precisely, it's just nonsense. The ramblings of an eccentric old man. Best place for that sort of rubbish is the fire. That's what I'd do if I were you. I'd throw it on the fire."

Lambourne's face screwed up like a child in tantrum. "Damn right!" he screamed, as if burning a piece of paper would solve his problems. He crumpled the parchment and cast it into the flames and then snatched Richard Theobald's slip and repeated his action.

"Is that it? Can we go now?" The lawyer's voice was petulant.

"One last thing," said Calloway. "Sir Isaac left us another little code to solve, a numerical one this time. I won't bother showing it to you. The answer was in four words: NIGHT OF THE DEMON."

"So what?" Lambourne asked.

"Obviously you are not a cinema fan," said Calloway, "Whereas I enjoy a good film, as did Sir Isaac. About eighteen or nineteen years ago there was a film titled *Night of the Demon*. Dana Andrews played the lead."

Richard Theobald shook his head. I think he was becoming convinced that Calloway was a bit mad. "Is there a point to this cinematic reminiscence?"

"Oh yes, a very good point." Calloway's tone remained light. "*Night of the Demon* was based on 'Casting the Runes', a short story by M. R. James. In the tale, an occultist lays a curse on his enemies. The curse is passed on a ribbon of parchment which, once the victim has accepted it, is whisked away by a supernatural wind into the nearest fire. Consequently, the victim has no chance of allaying the curse."

The bantering look faded from Calloway's face and he became deadly serious. "You have just destroyed by fire a curse placed upon you." He turned to me. "I think we'd better leave this room now, Roderick. *Quickly!*"

He hustled me towards the door. As he did so, I thought I saw something out of the corner of my eye. I could swear that the figure of Alchuan was starting to move. Calloway pushed me into the corridor, slammed the door behind us and turned the key in the lock. Enraged voices bellowed behind us. "*What the hell are you playing at, Calloway?*" The door was kicked violently from the inside.

"Reuben, I thought I saw—"

"Don't remember seeing anything, Roderick," Calloway admonished. "It will be better that way." The shouts from inside the room took on a more frantic note, the kicks and blows to the door became more urgent, and then, abruptly, there was silence.

Elmore came gasping from the hall. "I heard yelling, sir. What's going on?"

"I don't know." Calloway's lie was glib. "Father Shea and I just came to investigate." He turned the key and entered the room. "That's strange, there's nothing here."

I followed him in. The room was empty, save for a collapsed heap of something on the floor near to the display table. A closer look and I recognised it as being Alchuan's regalia. The costume was flaccid and empty and I no longer had a sense of it containing any kind of presence. I pulled back the curtains to find the windows closed and secure, the snow on the ground outside undisturbed.

"Someone's been playing silly buggers in here!" muttered a disapproving Elmore.

I turned to Calloway who was standing musing by the diorama, drawing gently on his rekindled cigar. "Reuben, what happened to them? Where could they have gone?" I whispered.

He took the cigar from his mouth and after a moment's thought, said: "I'm not sure, but I think I have an idea . . . *Good grief!*"

He pointed at the display table with the glowing tip of the cigar.

Before our astonished gaze that wonderful diorama was fading,

fading until it had vanished as if it had never existed. The table was nothing more than an empty, glass-topped display cabinet.

The breeze blowing into their faces was hot, bearing with it alien odours, strange dry stenches of animals and vegetation, of dirt and death; while a furnace glare of sun beat down from a sky bleached almost white. Tall, waving grasses, sweeping to a far horizon, were pale brown and ochre, and the darker colours of thorn trees jutted starkly upwards, gnarled fists clutching at emptiness. Smoky clouds of dust flurried about the plain as the vast herds of herbivores wandered about in the eternal search for food. From somewhere close by came the coughing growl of an unknown animal quickly followed by answering noises.

Richard Theobald and Peter Lambourne gazed around in fear. "Where in the hell are we?" croaked Theobald. "And how the devil did we get here?"

Lambourne didn't answer him. Instead he just pointed a terrified finger towards an acacia tree. At first, Richard Theobald couldn't make out what it was his companion was indicating and then his eyes became accustomed to the glare. In the little island of shade cast by the acacia stood two figures, staring at them with unblinking intensity.

The one was tall and hideously emaciated, with pharaoh-like, elongated skull and skin dusty brown-grey in colour. Theobald was certain that there were no eyes in that sere and withered face although he could feel its relentless regard. The other watcher was more familiar. Tall, too, but less so. Skinny, also, but more naturally so. And clad in an old, blue dressing-gown. Sir Isaac Pryce, smiling at his killers with grim pleasure.

Theobald slumped to the ground and pressed his face against his knees. He was shaking now, and the more he tried to control it the more feverish it became. Lambourne still stood, unmoving, pointing, deep in shock. He was making low gibbering noises and tears flowed down his cheeks.

The first lioness came padding silently towards the two men, tawny eyes narrowed, then another, and then two or three more, until the whole pride was circling them. The beasts were just curious at first, then rumbling snarls slowly became more savage, more menacing.

One lion, bolder than the rest, patted tentatively at Lambourne with a great forepaw. When there was no reaction the paw struck again, harder, faster. At the smell of blood, the others joined in.

Richard Theobald raised a suddenly aged face and looked up. The lions were worrying at the now screaming Lambourne and several were looking towards himself. Yards away, jackals and hyenas were loping in, eager for scraps. High in the molten sky, Richard Theobald could see vultures gathering.

Harry D'Amour

LOST SOULS
by CLIVE BARKER

Harry D'Amour is a private investigator in his late thirties, with three days' growth of beard and the eyes of an insomniac. He has a long nose, strong jaw, wide brow, with grey hairs and frown-lines well in evidence.

He is repeatedly drawn to the dark side against his will. Unable to change it, he is forced to walk the line between Heaven and Hell. It is his destiny and he must accept it.

A devout Catholic, he fights his war alone and in secrecy and his chosen battleground is the streets of New York. Among his few friends is Norma Paine, a black blind medium who owns thirty televisions and never leaves her apartment. She communes with the spirits who come seeking her guidance to find the Hereafter.

D'Amour's cramped and chaotic office is near 45th Street and 8th Avenue. He depends upon a free Chinese dinner every week to vary his diet, drinks hard, hates crowds and carries a .38 pistol. His other weapons include nearly a dozen tattoos—talismans and sigils to ward off evil.

He is haunted by something that happened one Easter Sunday in Brooklyn. It was there, in a house on Wyckoff Street, that D'Amour first encountered the supernatural—a routine surveillance on an adulterous wife went literally to hell when her secret lover was revealed as a demon. The resulting confrontation left many people dead—including Father Hess, who had fought at the investigator's side—and D'Amour with a fear of stairs and a relentless passion to seek out the demons and destroy them.

Clive Barker's Harry D'Amour made his debut in the short story 'The Last Illusion', originally published in the sixth volume of Books of Blood *(1985). The Christmas story published here first appeared in the December 1986 issue of* Time Out *and D'Amour then turned up as a minor player, older and certainly wiser, in the novel* The Great and Secret Show *(1989). He returned to centre stage five years later in the sequel,* Everville, *and D'Amour is pitted against the author's demonic Pinhead and his fellow Cenobites in* The Scarlet Gospels *(2015).*

In 1995 the character was portrayed by Scott Bakula in the movie Lord of Illusions, *written and directed by Barker and inspired by his first story about D'Amour.*

EVERYTHING THE BLIND woman had told Harry she'd seen was undeniably real. Whatever inner eye Norma Paine possessed—that extraordinary skill that allowed her to scan the island of Manhattan from the Broadway Bridge to Battery Park and yet not move an inch from her tiny room on 75th—that eye was as sharp as any knife juggler's. Here was the derelict house on Ridge Street, with the smoke stains besmirching the brick. Here was the dead dog that she'd described, lying on the sidewalk as though asleep, but that it lacked half its head. Here too, if Norma was to be believed, was the demon that Harry had come in search of: the shy and sublimely malignant Cha'Chat.

The house was not, Harry thought, a likely place for a desperado of Cha'Chat's elevation to be in residence. Though the infernal brethren could be a loutish lot, to be certain, it was Christian propaganda which sold them as dwellers in excrement and ice. The escaped demon was more likely to be downing fly eggs and vodka at the Waldorf-Astoria than concealing itself amongst such wretchedness.

But Harry had gone to the blind clairvoyant in desperation, having failed to locate Cha'Chat by any means conventionally available to a private eye such as himself. He was, he had admitted to her, responsible for the fact that the demon was loose at all. It seemed he'd never learned, in his all too frequent encounters with the Gulf and its progeny, that Hell possessed a genius for deceit. Why else had he believed in the child that had tottered into view just as he'd leveled his gun at Cha'Chat?—a child, of course, which had evaporated into a cloud of tainted air as soon as the diversion was redundant and the demon had made its escape.

Now, after almost three weeks of vain pursuit, it was almost Christmas in New York; season of goodwill and suicide. Streets thronged; the air like salt in wounds; Mammon in glory. A more perfect playground for Cha'Chat's despite could scarcely be imagined. Harry had to find the demon quickly, before it did serious damage; find it and return it to the pit from which it had come. In extremis he would even use the binding syllables which the late Father Hesse had vouchsafed to him once, accompanying them with such dire warnings that Harry had never even written them down. Whatever it took. Just as long as Cha'Chat didn't see Christmas Day this side of the Schism.

It seemed to be colder inside the house on Ridge Street than out. Harry could feel the chill creep through both pairs of socks and start to numb his feet. He was making his way along the second landing when he heard the sigh. He turned, fully expecting to see Cha'Chat standing there, its eye cluster looking a dozen ways at once, its cropped fur rippling. But no. Instead a young woman stood at the end of the corridor. Her undernourished features suggested Puerto Rican extraction, but that—and the fact that she was heavily pregnant—was all Harry had time to grasp before she hurried away down the stairs.

Listening to the girl descend, Harry knew that Norma had been wrong. If Cha'Chat had been here, such a perfect victim would not have been allowed to escape with her eyes in her head. The demon wasn't here.

Which left the rest of Manhattan to search.

The night before, something very peculiar had happened to Eddie Axel. It had begun with his staggering out of his favorite bar, which was six blocks from the grocery store he owned on 3rd Avenue.

He was drunk, and happy; and with reason. Today he had reached the age of fifty-five. He had married three times in those years; he had sired four legitimate children and a handful of bastards; and—perhaps most significantly—he'd made Axel's Superette a highly lucrative business. All was well with the world.

But Jesus, it was chilly! No chance, on a night threatening a second Ice Age, of finding a cab. He would have to walk home.

He'd got maybe half a block, however, when—miracle of miracles—a cab did indeed cruise by. He'd flagged it down, eased himself in, and the weird times had begun.

For one, the driver knew his name.

"Home, Mr. Axel?" he'd said. Eddie hadn't questioned the godsend. Merely mumbled, "Yes," and assumed this was a birthday treat, courtesy of someone back at the bar.

Perhaps his eyes had flickered closed; perhaps he'd even slept. Whatever, the next thing he knew the cab was driving at some speed through streets he didn't recognize. He stirred himself from his doze. This was the Village, surely; an area Eddie kept clear of. His neighborhood was the high Nineties, close to the store. Not for him the decadence of the Village, where a shop sign offered EAR PIERCING. WITH OR WITHOUT PAIN and young men with suspicious hips lingered in doorways.

"This isn't the right direction," he said, rapping on the Perspex between him and the driver. There was no word of apology or explanation forthcoming, however, until the cab made a turn toward the river, drawing up in a street of warehouses, and the ride was over.

"This is your stop," said the chauffeur. Eddie didn't need a more explicit invitation to disembark.

As he hauled himself out the cabbie pointed to the murk of an empty lot between two benighted warehouses. "She's been waiting for you," he said, and drove away. Eddie was left alone on the sidewalk.

Common sense counseled a swift retreat, but what now caught his eye glued him to the spot. There she stood—the woman of whom the cabbie had spoken—and she was the most obese creature Eddie had ever set his sight upon. She had more chins than fingers, and her fat, which threatened at every place to spill from the light summer dress she wore, gleamed with either oil or sweat.

"*Eddie*," she said. Everybody seemed to know his name tonight. As she moved toward him, tides moved in the fat of her torso and along her limbs.

"Who are you?" Eddie was about to inquire, but the words died when he realized the obesity's feet weren't touching the ground. *She was floating.*

Had Eddie been sober he might well have taken his cue then and fled, but the drink in his system mellowed his trepidation. He stayed put.

"Eddie," she said. "Dear Eddie. I have some good news and some bad news. Which would you like first?"

Eddie pondered this one for a moment. "The good," he concluded.

"You're going to die tomorrow," came the reply, accompanied by the tiniest of smiles.

"*That's good?*" he said.

"Paradise awaits your immortal soul . . ." she murmured. "Isn't that a joy?"

"So what's the bad news?"

She plunged her stubby-fingered hand into the crevasse between her gleaming tits. There came a little squeal of complaint, and she drew something out of hiding. It was a cross between a runty gecko and a sick rat, possessing the least fetching qualities of both. Its pitiful limbs pedaled at the air as she held it up for Eddie's perusal. "This," she said, "is your immortal soul."

She was right, thought Eddie: the news was not good.

"Yes," she said. "It's a pathetic sight, isn't it?" The soul drooled and squirmed as she went on. "It's undernourished. It's weak to the point of expiring altogether. And *why*?" She didn't give Eddie a chance to reply. "A paucity of good works . . ."

Eddie's teeth had begun to chatter. "What am I supposed to do about it?" he asked.

"You've got a little breath left. You must compensate for a lifetime of rampant profiteering—"

"I don't follow."

"Tomorrow, turn Axel's Superette into a Temple of Charity, and you may yet put some meat on your soul's bones."

She had begun to ascend, Eddie noticed. In the darkness above her, there was sad, sad music, which now wrapped her up in minor chords until she was entirely eclipsed.

The girl had gone by the time Harry reached the street. So had the dead dog. At a loss for options, he trudged back to Norma Paine's apartment, more for the company than the satisfaction of telling her she had been wrong.

"I'm never wrong," she told him over the din of the five televisions and as many radios that she played perpetually. The cacophony was, she claimed, the only sure way to keep those of the spirit world from incessantly intruding upon her privacy; the babble distressed them. "I saw power in that house on Ridge Street," she told Harry, "sure as shit."

Harry was about to argue when an image on one of the screens caught his eye. An outside news broadcast pictured a reporter standing on a sidewalk across the street from a store (AXEL'S SUPERETTE, the sign read) from which bodies were being removed.

"What is it?" Norma demanded.

"Looks like a bomb went off," Harry replied, trying to trace the reporter's voice through the din of the various stations.

"Turn up the sound," said Norma. "I like a disaster."

It was not a bomb that had wrought such destruction, it emerged, but a riot. In the middle of the morning a fight had begun in the packed grocery store; nobody quite knew why. It had rapidly escalated into a bloodbath. A conservative estimate put the death toll at thirty, with twice as many injured. The report, with its talk of a spontaneous eruption of violence, gave fuel to a terrible suspicion in Harry.

"Cha'Chat . . ." he murmured.

Despite the noise in the little room, Norma heard him speak. "What makes you so sure?" she said.

Harry didn't reply. He was listening to the reporter's recapitulation of the events, hoping to catch the location of Axel's Superette. And there it was. 3rd Avenue, between 94th and 95th.

"Keep smiling," he said to Norma, and left her to her brandy and the dead gossiping in the bathroom.

* * *

Linda had gone back to the house on Ridge Street as a last resort, hoping against hope that she'd find Bolo there. He was, she vaguely calculated, the likeliest candidate for father of the child she carried, but there'd been some strange men in her life at that time; men with eyes that seemed golden in certain lights; men with sudden, joyless smiles. Anyway, Bolo hadn't been at the house, and here she was—as she'd known she'd be all along—alone. All she could hope to do was lie down and die.

But there was death and death. There was that extinction she prayed for nightly, to fall asleep and have the cold claim her by degrees; and there was that other death, the one she saw whenever fatigue drew her lids down. A death that had neither dignity in the going nor hope of a Hereafter; a death brought by a man in a gray suit whose face sometimes resembled a half-familiar saint, and sometimes a wall of rotting plaster.

Begging as she went, she made her way uptown toward Times Square. Here, amongst the traffic of consumers, she felt safe for a while. Finding a little deli, she ordered eggs and coffee, calculating the meal so that it just fell within the begged sum. The food stirred the baby. She felt it turn in its slumber, close now to waking. Maybe she should fight on a while longer, she thought. If not for her sake, for that of the child.

She lingered at the table, turning the problem over, until the mutterings of the proprietor shamed her out onto the street again.

It was late afternoon, and the weather was worsening. A woman was singing nearby, in Italian; some tragic aria. Tears close, Linda turned from the pain the song carried, and set off again in no particular direction.

As the crowd consumed her, a man in a gray suit slipped away from the audience that had gathered around the street-corner diva, sending the youth he was with ahead through the throng to be certain they didn't lose their quarry.

Marchetti regretted having to forsake the show. The singing much amused him. Her voice, long ago drowned in alcohol, was repeatedly that vital semitone shy of its intended target—a perfect testament to imperfectibility—rendering Verdi's high art laughable even as it came within sight of transcendence. He would have to come back here when the beast had been dispatched. Listening to that spoiled ecstasy brought him closer to tears than he'd been for months; and he liked to weep.

Harry stood across 3rd Avenue from Axel's Superette and watched the watchers. They had gathered in their hundreds in the chill of the deepening night, to see what could be seen; nor were they disappointed. The bodies kept coming out: in bags, in bundles; there was even something in a bucket.

"Does anybody know exactly what happened?" Harry asked his fellow spectators.

A man turned, his face ruddy with cold.

"The guy who ran the place decided to *give* the stuff away," he said, grinning at this absurdity. "And the store was fuckin' swamped. Someone got killed in the crush—"

"I heard the trouble started over a can of meat," another offered. "Somebody got beaten to death with a can of meat."

This rumor was contested by a number of others; all had versions of events.

Harry was about to try and sort fact from fiction when an exchange to his right diverted him.

A boy of nine or ten had buttonholed a companion. "Did you smell her?" he wanted to know. The other nodded vigorously. "Gross, huh?" the first ventured. "Smelled better shit," came the reply, and the two dissolved into conspiratorial laughter.

Harry looked across at the object of their mirth. A hugely over-weight woman, underdressed for the season, stood on the periphery of the crowd and watched the disaster scene with tiny, glittering eyes.

Harry had forgotten the questions he was going to ask the watchers. What he remembered, clear as yesterday, was the way his dreams conjured the infernal brethren. It wasn't their curses he recalled, nor even the deformities they paraded: it was the smell off them. Of burning hair and halitosis; of veal left to rot in the sun. Ignoring the debate around him, he started in the direction of the woman.

She saw him coming, the rolls of fat at her neck furrowing as she glanced across at him.

It was Cha'Chat, of that Harry had no doubt. And to prove the point, the demon took off at a run, the limbs and prodigious buttocks stirred to a fandango with every step. By the time Harry had cleared his way through the crowd the demon was already turning the corner into 95th Street, but its stolen body was not designed for speed, and Harry rapidly made up the distance between them. The lamps were out in several places along the street, and when he finally snatched at the demon, and heard the sound of tearing, the gloom disguised the vile truth for fully five seconds until he realized that Cha'Chat had somehow sloughed off its usurped flesh, leaving Harry holding a great coat of ectoplasm, which was already melting like overripe cheese. The demon, its burden shed, was away; slim as hope and twice as slippery. Harry dropped the coat of filth and gave chase, shouting Hesse's syllables as he did so.

Surprisingly, Cha'Chat stopped in its tracks, and turned to Harry. The eyes looked all ways but Heavenward; the mouth was wide and attempting laughter. It sounded like someone vomiting down an elevator shaft.

"*Words*, D'Amour?" it said, mocking Hesse's syllables. "You think I can be stopped with words?"

"No," said Harry, and blew a hole in Cha'Chat's abdomen before the demon's many eyes had even found the gun.

"*Bastard!*" it wailed, "*Cocksucker!*" and fell to the ground, blood the colour of piss throbbing from the hole. Harry sauntered down the street to where it lay. It was almost impossible to slay a demon of Cha'Chat's elevation with bullets; but a scar was shame enough amongst their clan. Two, almost unbearable.

"Don't," it begged when he pointed the gun at its head. "Not the face."

"Give me one good reason why not."

"You'll need the bullets," came the reply.

Harry had expected bargains and threats. This answer silenced him.

"There's something going to get loose tonight, D'Amour," Cha'Chat said. The blood that was pooling around it had begun to thicken and grow milky, like melted wax. "Something wilder than me."

"Name it," said Harry.

The demon grinned. "Who knows?" it said. "It's a strange season, isn't it? Long nights. Clear skies. Things get born on nights like this, don't you find?"

"*Where?*" said Harry, pressing the gun to Cha'Chat's nose.

"You're a bully, D'Amour," it said reprovingly. "You know that?"

"*Tell me . . .*"

The thing's eyes grew darker; its face seemed to blur.

"South of here, I'd say . . ." it replied. "A hotel . . ." The tone of its voice was changing subtly; the features losing their solidity. Harry's trigger finger itched to give the damned thing a wound that would keep it from a mirror for life, but it was still talking, and he couldn't afford to interrupt its flow. " . . . on 44th," it said. "Between 6th . . . 6th and Broadway." The voice was indisputably feminine now. "Blue blinds," it murmured. "I can see blue blinds . . ."

As it spoke the last vestiges of its true features fled, and suddenly it was Norma who was bleeding on the sidewalk at Harry's feet.

"You wouldn't shoot an old lady, would you?" she piped up.

The trick lasted seconds only, but Harry's hesitation was all that Cha'Chat needed to fold itself between one plane and the next, and flit. He'd lost the creature, for the second time in a month.

And to add discomfort to distress, it had begun to snow.

The small hotel that Cha'Chat had described had seen better years; even the light that burned in the lobby seemed to tremble on the brink of expiring. There was nobody at the desk. Harry was about to start up the stairs when a young man whose pate was shaved as bald as an egg, but for a single kiss curl that was oiled to his scalp, stepped out of the gloom and took hold of his arm.

"There's nobody here," he informed Harry.

In better days Harry might have cracked the egg open with his bare fists, and enjoyed doing so. Tonight he guessed he would come off the worse. So he simply said, "Well, I'll find another hotel then, eh?"

Kiss Curl seemed placated; the grip relaxed. In the next instant Harry's hand found his gun, and the gun found Kiss Curl's chin. An expression of bewilderment crossed the boy's face as he fell back against the wall, spitting blood.

As Harry started up the stairs, he heard the youth yell, "Darrieux!" from below.

Neither the shout nor the sound of the struggle had roused any response from the rooms. The place was empty. It had been elected, Harry began to comprehend, for some purpose other than hostelry.

As he started along the landing a woman's cry, begun but never finished, came to meet him. He stopped dead. Kiss Curl was coming up the stairs behind him two or three at a time; ahead, someone was dying. This couldn't end well, Harry suspected.

Then the door at the end of the corridor opened, and suspicion became plain fact. A man in a gray suit was standing on the threshold, skinning off a pair of bloodied surgical gloves. Harry knew him vaguely; indeed had begun to sense a terrible pattern in all of this from the moment he'd heard Kiss Curl call his employer's name. This was Darrieux Marchetti; also called the Cankerist; one of that whispered order of theological assassins whose directives came from Rome, or Hell, or both.

"D'Amour," he said.

Harry had to fight the urge to be flattered that he had been remembered.

"What happened here?" he demanded to know, taking a step toward the open door.

"Private business," the Cankerist insisted. "Please, no closer."

Candles burned in the little room, and by their generous light, Harry could see the bodies laid out on the bare bed. The woman from the house on Ridge Street, and her child. Both had been dispatched with Roman efficiency.

"She protested," said Marchetti, not overly concerned that Harry was viewing the results of his handiwork. "All I needed was the child."

"What was it?" Harry demanded. "A demon?"

Marchetti shrugged. "We'll never know," he said. "But at this time of year there's usually something that tries to get in under the wire. We like to be safe rather than sorry. Besides, there are those—I number myself amongst them—that believe there is such a thing as a surfeit of Messiahs—"

"Messiahs?" said Harry. He looked again at the tiny body.

"There was power there, I suspect," said Marchetti. "But it could have gone either way. Be thankful, D'Amour. Your world isn't ready for revelation." He looked past Harry to the youth, who was at the top of the stairs. "Patrice. Be an angel, will you, bring the car over? I'm late for Mass."

He threw the gloves back onto the bed.

"You're not above the law," said Harry.

"Oh *please*," the Cankerist protested, "let's have no nonsense. It's too late at night."

Harry felt a sharp pain at the base of his skull, and a trace of heat where blood was running.

"Patrice thinks you should go home, D'Amour. And so do I."

The knife point was pressed a little deeper.

"Yes?" said Marchetti.

"Yes," said Harry.

"He was here," said Norma, when Harry called back at the house.

"Who?"

"Eddie Axel; of Axel's Superette. He came through, clear as daylight."

"Dead?"

"Of course dead. He killed himself in his cell. Asked me if I'd seen his soul."

"And what did you say?"

"I'm a telephonist, Harry; I just make the connections. I don't pretend to understand the metaphysics." She picked up the bottle of brandy Harry had set on the table beside her chair. "How sweet of you," she said. "Sit down. Drink."

"Another time, Norma. When I'm not so tired." He went to the door. "By the way," he said. "You were right. There *was* something on Ridge Street . . ."

"Where is it now?"

"Gone . . . home."

"And Cha'Chat?"

"Still out there somewhere. In a foul temper . . ."

"Manhattan's seen worse, Harry."

It was little consolation, but Harry muttered his agreement as he closed the door.

The snow was coming on more heavily all the time.

He stood on the step and watched the way the flakes spiraled in the lamplight. No two, he had read somewhere, were ever alike. When such variety was available to the humble snowflake, could he be surprised that events had such unpredictable faces?

Each moment was its own master, he mused, as he put his head between the blizzard's teeth, and he would *not* have to take whatever comfort he could find in the knowledge that between this chilly hour and dawn there were innumerable such moments—blind maybe, and wild and hungry—but all at least eager to be born.

Sally Rhodes
SEVEN STARS EPISODE FIVE

MIMSY
by KIM NEWMAN

Like Anthony Boucher's Fergus O'Breen, Clive Barker's Harry D'Amour and F. Paul Wilson's Repairman Jack, Sally Rhodes is a private eye in the Black Mask *tradition. But her world has even darker darks than Philip Marlowe's or Sam Spade's, and because of these frequent incursions of the unbelievable, her stories also have a more pronounced streak of black humour.*

Sally's great inspiration in the PI business is not Marlowe, but Jim Rockford. She often solves her cases by wandering through a mystery until someone takes pity on her and explains the whole thing.

Born of filth in 1961, Derek Leech emerged fully formed from the River Thames, destined to found a multimedia empire from his dark domain, the steel and glass Leech Pyramid, in the heart of London's Docklands.

*Sally Rhodes first appeared in Kim Newman's short story 'Twitch Technicolor' (*Interzone *#28, 1989), followed by 'Gargantuabots vs the Nice Mice' (*Interzone *#33, 1990), 'The Man Who Collected Barker' (*Fantasy Tales *4, 1990) and 'Mother Hen' (*Fantasy Tales *6, 1991). The author gave her a slight career change and a baby in 'Organ Donors' (*Darklands *2, 1992), in which she first encounters evil media mogul Derek Leech, and the two crossed paths again in the novel* The Quorum *(1994), where she meets Neil.*

Leech himself originated in 'The Original Dr Shade' (Interzone #36, 1990) and he has reappeared in 'SQPR' (Interzone #52, 1992), Life's Lottery (1998), the 'Where the Bodies Are Buried' quartet published in the anthologies Dark Voices *and* Dark Terrors *(1993–96), 'Another Fish Story' (*Weird Shadows Over Innsmouth, *2005), 'Cold Snap' (*The Secret Files of the Diogenes Club, *2007) and 'Sorcerer Conjuror Wizard Witch' (*Mysteries of the Diogenes Club, *2010).*

ONE DAY IN Spring, the Devil called her.

"Sally Rhodes Investigations," she said brightly into the phone, trying to sound like a receptionist.

"Miss Rhodes," he said, voice distorted a little, perhaps addressed to a speaker phone, "this is Derek Leech."

She hung up.

The voice had scraped her bones.

She looked from the office half of her front room to the living-room half. Jerome, her son, was building a Lego robot, notionally supervised by Neil, her boyfriend, who was curled on the ancient sofa, making notes on a scribble-pad. Neil was still assembling an argument for the book he'd been thinking of starting for three years. Lego structures spread about the floor, weaving around the cat-basket and several of Neil's abandoned coffee mugs.

Normality, she thought.

Kid. Man. Pet. Toys. A mess, but a mess she could cope with, a mess she loved.

The phone rang again. She let it.

The office half of the room was ordered, different. A computer, a fax, files, a desk. This was where she thought. Over there, on the sofa, amid the lovable mess, was where she felt.

She was breaking her own rules.

The ringing phone jarred on her emotions.

At her desk, she was in business. She had to be harder, stronger.

She picked up the phone, but didn't announce herself.

"Miss Rhodes, for every second you don't hang up, I shall donate one hundred pounds to your favoured charity, which is, I believe, Shelter."

It did not surprise her that Leech knew she supported Help for the Homeless. The multimedia magnate knew everything about everyone. Atop his Pyramid in London Docklands, he had all the knowledge of the world at his disposal.

"Go ahead," she said.

"Regardless of our past differences, I admire your independence of spirit."

"Thank you. Now what is this about?"

"A friend of mine needs your services."

"You have friends?"

She imagined Leech had only acolytes, employees and possessions.

"The finest friends money can buy, my dear. That was a joke. You may laugh."

"Ha ha ha."

"My friend's name is Maureen Mountmain. She has a daughter, Mimsy, who has gone missing. Maureen would like to retain you to find her."

"You must have people who could do that. If this Maureen Mountmain was really your friend, why don't you turn the dogs loose?"

"You have resources no one I employ could have."

That was the most frightening thing anyone had ever said to her. Leech let it hang in the air.

"Sally, you've inconvenienced me. Twice. Your life would be much easier if you had chose not to stand in my way. You have something of the purity of a saint. No one in my organisation can say as much. Only someone of your virtues could handle this job. I appeal to you, as a secular saint, to help my friend."

She let seconds tick by.

"Do you accept?"

She counted slowly up to ten in her mind, making a thousand pounds for the homeless.

"I'll take the job," she said, "on the condition that I'm retained by this Mrs. Mountmain . . ."

"Miss."

". . . Miss Mountmain, and not by you personally or any sneaky subsidiary company."

"You'll not take the King's shilling."

"Cursed gold?"

Leech laughed, like ice cubes cracking in a bowl of warm blood.

"Once this call is completed, your business is with the Mountmains. I act, in this instance, only as intermediary."

She knew there was a hidden clause somewhere. With Leech, nothing was straightforward. His way was to rely on the fallibility of those he dealt with. Despite his stated opinion, she knew she was as likely to be gulled into a moral trap as anyone else.

Jerome pestered Neil for his expert opinion on the robot spider scuttling around the floor.

"My associate, Ms. Wilding, will give details of the appointment she has arranged for you with Miss Mountmain. I have enjoyed this conversation. Good-bye."

The phone clicked, and a woman came on. Sally took down an address and a time.

When she hung up, she realised her heart was racing. It had been a while.

She'd been working on everyday stuff these last few years. As it happened, she'd done a lot of work with runaway children. Though sometimes she walked away well-paid and satisfied from a tearful reunion, she more often traced some kid caught between a horrific home life and an ordeal on the streets, then wound up sucked into an emotional, legal and ethical Gordian knot.

But the weird stuff was in her past.

Even with Jerome and Neil, physical leftovers from that period of her life, in the flat, she'd almost convinced herself she didn't live in that world any more. She had kept up with the inescapable growth of Derek Leech's Earthly dominion, but tried to forget the strange devices at its heart.

Perhaps she was wrong. Perhaps he wasn't the Devil, but just an ambitious businessman. He had used magic in the past, but that was only trickery. Conjuring, not sorcery.

She tried and failed to convince herself.

"Mummy, look, I've made a monster."

"Lovely," she said to her son. "Neil, you're on kid-watch and the phone. I'm out on business."

Neil looked up at her and waved a cheery paw.

"I accept the mission," he said.

She kissed them both and left the flat.

The address she had been given turned out to be a Georgian mansion in Wimpole Street. It stood out among perfectly preserved neighbours, showing signs of dilapidation and abuse. By contrast, with polished brass door-trimmings and blue plaques announcing the former residence of the great and good, the Mountmain house looked like a squat. Over the lintel was spray-painted DECLAN MOUNTMAIN, TERRORIST AND DEVIL-WORSHIPPER, LIVED HERE 1888–1897.

Maureen Mountmain, who answered the door herself, was tall and thin, with a strange red streak through snow-white hair. She wore long black velvet skirts and a tatted shawl over a leather waistcoat. Her neck and wrists were ringed with jades and pearls. Her face was stretched tight, but Sally didn't see tell-tale face lift scars. As her shawl slipped, she showed a sparkling tattoo on her upper arm. There was a great strength in her but she lacked substance, as if every surplus atom had been sucked away over the years.

She wanted to ask Maureen how well she knew Derek Leech, and what their connection was, but that wasn't the point.

She was hurried into the hallway, which stank of patchouli. The original wooden panels had been painted over with dull purple. Childish patterns, like the crescent moons and stars on a cartoon wizard's conical cap, were scattered across the walls and ceiling. On a second look, Sally saw the painting-over extended to framed pictures which still hung, chameleoned, up the staircase.

"When she was little, Mimsy only liked purple," Maureen said, proudly. "She can be very insistent."

"Do you have any pictures of her?"

"At an early age, she heard about the aboriginal belief that photographs could capture souls. She would smash any cameras she saw. With a hammer."

Sally thought about that for a moment. She wondered if Mimsy took her hammer with her.

"Any drawings or portraits?" she asked.

Maureen shuddered.

"Even worse. Mimsy believes art not only captures the soul but distorts and malforms it."

"She's very concerned with her soul."

"Mimsy is extremely religious."

"Did she attend any particular church? That might be a good place to start looking for her."

Maureen shrugged. As Sally's eyes got used to the gloom of the hall, she noticed just how distracted Maureen Mountmain was. Her pupils were shrunk to black pinholes.

"Mimsy rejects organised religion. She has declared herself the Avatar of the Ram. She hopes to revive the Society of the Ram, an occult congregation my family has often been involved with."

"Devil-Worshipper and Terrorist?"

"Mimsy put that up there. She was proud of her heritage."

"Are you?"

Maureen was unwilling to say.

Sally knew something had broken this woman. Deep down inside her, there was extraordinary resilience, but it had been besieged and eroded. Maureen Mountmain was a walking remnant. It was too early to be sure, but Sally had an idea how Miss Mountmain had been broken and who had done the deed.

"Might Mimsy be with her father? You live apart?"

Again, Maureen was unwilling, but this time she put an answer together.

"Mimsy doesn't know her father. He is . . . unavailable to her."

"If it's not a rude question, do *you* know Mimsy's father?"

For the first time, Maureen smiled. In her wistfulness, she could be beautiful. Sally knew from the flicker of wattage that this woman had once shined like a lantern.

"I know who Mimsy's father is."

She didn't volunteer any more.

"May I see Mimsy's room?"

Maureen led her upstairs. The whole first floor of the house was a ruin. Several fires had started but failed to take. A medieval tapestry, of knights hunting something in green woods, was half-scorched away, leaving the men in armour surrounding a suggestive brown shape. There were broken items of furniture, statuary and ceramic piled in a corner.

Maureen indicated a door smashed on its hinges.

"You say Mimsy left?" Sally asked. "You don't think she was abducted?"

"She walked out of this house on her own. But she might not have been herself."

"I don't understand."

"She took with her a precious item. A keepsake, if you will. Something that was important once. It was her belief that this item communicated with her, issued orders. A large red stone."

"A ruby?"

"Not exactly. The weirdstone is known as the Seven Stars, because of a formation of light-catching flaws which look like the constellation."

Maureen dropped her shawl to show her tattoo. Seven blue eyes glinted in a green creature, also configured like the Great Bear.

"Is this jewel valuable?"

"Many might pay dearly for it. I certainly did, though not in money. But it's not a thing which can be owned. It is a thing which owns."

"Mimsy thought this jewel talked to her?"

Maureen nodded.

Sally looked around the room. After the build-up, it was a surprisingly ordinary teenager's bedroom. A single bed with a frilly duvet, matched by all the lampshades. Posters of David Duchovny, Brad Pitt and some pretty boy pop singer she was too out-of-date to recognise. A shelf of books: thick occult-themed paperback nonsense—*Flying Saucers from Ancient Atlantis*—mixed with black-spined, obviously old hardbacks. Outgrown toys were placed like trophies on a mantelpiece: Turtles, Muppets, a withered rag doll.

She tried to imagine Mimsy. Long ago, before all the weirdness, Sally had taken a degree in child psychology. It was just about her only real qualification.

"Imaginary friends are projections," she suggested. "Mimsy might have displaced onto the jewel, using its 'voice' to escape responsibility. It's more sophisticated than 'I didn't break the vase, the pixies did', it's 'I broke the vase, but I was obeying orders'."

"Mimsy is twenty-seven," Maureen said. "In her life, she has never made an excuse or obeyed orders. It is her belief that the jewel talks. I don't doubt this is true."

"A subjective truth, maybe."

"You don't believe that, Miss Rhodes. You know Derek Leech. You know better. There's such a thing as Magic. And such a thing as Evil."

Sally was off her balance. She had thought this was about a teenage runaway.

"Does she have a job? A boyfriend?"

"She can always get money from people. And she has lovers. None of them mean anything. Mimsy has only one emotional tie."

"To you?"

"No. To the weirdstone."

"Neil, pick up," she told her own answerphone.

She was calling from her mobile, out in the open in Soho Square. Merciless sun shone down, but the dry air was cold.

Neil came on, grumbling.

"I thought you were answering the phone," she said.

"Jermo and I were watching *Thunderbirds*."

She let that pass.

"I need you to do some research, historical stuff."

One of Neil's uses was trawling the Internet for ostensibly useless information. He had even been known on occasion to go physically to a library and open a book.

"Write these keywords down. The Jewel of Seven Stars, the Society of the Ram."

"Dennis Wheatley novels?"

"One's an object, the other's a cult. And see what you can find out about the Mountmain family. Specifically, a fellow named Declan Mountmain from the late 19th century, and a couple of contemporary women, Maureen—must be in her late forties though she doesn't look it—and Mimsy, twenty-seven."

"As in Borogroves?"

"Mimsy. No, it's not short for anything."

"No wonder she ran away from home. Calling a kid Mimsy is semiotic child abuse."

"There are worse kinds."

She folded up the phone and thought. Mimsy's father—whoever he might be—was out of the picture, supposedly. She'd accept that for now.

Unconsciously, she had come to the Square to make her call. It was where she had met Jerome's father. Connor had been lolling on the benches with the other bike messengers, waiting for jobs to come in. He had been killed in a street accident, also near here.

She was reminded not to trust Derek Leech.

Mimsy, obviously, was a horror. But how much of one? Spoiled brat or Anti-Christ? She found herself aching for Mimsy's Mumsy. Despite purple panels and hippie scent, and the timid dithering at the memory of her daughter, Maureen was a survivor. She wondered if she was looking at her own future in Maureen Mountmain.

Sally had a tattoo. A porpoise on her ankle. That didn't make her strange. She had worked a case once with Harry D'Amour, an American private detective who was covered in tattoos which he claimed worked as a psychic armour. You needed armour for what was most vulnerable, and you couldn't tattoo your heart.

"What's up, Sal?"

Her ex-boyfriend sat down next to her. He wore Lycra cycling shorts and a joke T-shirt with a thick tyre track across the chest.

"Hello, Connor," she said, unfazed.

"I've never thanked you for avenging my death," he said.

He looked impossibly young in the bright sunshine. He had been nearly two-thirds her age. Now he was just over half her age.

"You look good," he said.

"I dye my hair."

"But just a little."

"Just. You have a son. He's a good kid. Jerome."

"I didn't know."

"I thought you might not."

"She's a strange one, Sal. That's why I'm here. Why I've been allowed to talk to you."

"This is about Mimsy Mountmain?"

Connor looked sheepish. They hadn't been together long and, baby or not, it wouldn't have lasted. He had always been looking for an angle, less interested in a leg over than a leg up. But she was sorry he had been killed.

Jerome loved Neil—that was one reason Neil had lasted—but had grown up, like Mimsy, without a dad.

"It's not so much Mimsy, it's this rock thing. The jewel. You're to mind out for it. It can cause a lot of trouble. Not just for you there, but for me here. For us here."

"Where is here?"

"Somewhere else. You'd be able to explain it. I can't. Sorry, Sal. Gotta rush."

He stood up and looked around. She wondered if he'd come on his bike.

"Did I ever tell you I loved you?"

"No."

"Funny that."

He left. Sally wondered why she was crying.

When she got back to Muswell Hill, she heard the retch of the printer as she climbed the steps to her flat. After her ghostly encounter, she had spent an afternoon getting in touch with old contacts who knew something about what is euphemistically known as "alternative religion". Though a few of them had heard of Declan Mountmain as a historical fruitcake, no one could tell her anything about his present-day descendants.

She let herself in, and found Neil and Jerome busy downloading and printing out. In the last few months, Jerome had gone from helping Neil with the computer to being impatient with the grown-up's inability to get on as well with the machine as he did.

"There's a lot of dirt, Sal-love," Neil announced, proudly.

Sally hugged Jerome, surprising him.

"Gerroff," he said, wriggling.

She laughed. She had needed contact with Connor's flesh-and-bone offspring. It grounded her, dispersed some of the weirdness build-up.

"It wasn't Dennis Wheatley," Neil said. "It was Bram Stoker. He wrote a novel called *The Jewel of Seven Stars*. It was made into a Hammer Film with Valerie Leon."

Like a great many men his age, Neil had encyclopedic recall of the bosomy starlets who appeared in the Bond films, Hammer Horrors, Carry Ons and *Two Ronnies* TV sketches of the early 1970s.

"You know Stoker based Dracula on Vlad the Impaler. He also based this *Seven Stars* effort on scraps of truth. It's about an Ancient Egyptian witch who possesses a modern lass. There was, apparently, a real Jewel of Seven Stars, found in a proper mummy's tomb. It disappeared after a break-in at the British Museum in 1897. Guess who was the number-one suspect?"

"Is this like Jack the Ripper? Pick an eminent Victorian?"

"No. It's highly guessable. I'm talking Declan Mountmain, who was sort of a cross between Aleister Crowley and Patrick Bergin in *Patriot Games*. Half-mad warlock, half-psycho Irish separatist. He tried to blow up Lords, during a Gentlemen versus Players match. He had a nephew, Bennett, who was by all accounts even worse. He was in with the Nazis in World War II and was killed in Los Angeles while spying for Hitler."

"No wonder Maureen's off her head."

"I've got a great jpg from a Hippie History website, of Maureen at Glastonbury in 1968. She's got up as a fertility priestess, body-painted green all over and extremely topless. I had to send Jermo into the other room while I downloaded it."

"I saw the rude lady," Jerome piped up.

"Well, I tried to send him. Anyway, Maureen was not only the Wiccan babe of the Summer of Love but an early *Comet* knockout, one of Derek Leech's first Page Three girls. Those shots will be on the Net somewhere, but you have to pay a fee to get them. Do you think Leech is this Mimsy's father?"

She thought about it. It fitted together, perhaps a bit too neatly.

"There are other players in this. And the jewel comes into it somehow."

"I've got a big cast for you, going back a hundred years, snatched from a lot of occult and paranoid conspiracy sites, the type you have to play sword and sorcery games to get onto. Some famous names. But there are interesting gaps. Names rubbed out of the record, like those Pharaohs who were so disgraceful that they were removed from history. I keep coming across these references to 'the War' in contexts that make me wonder which one is being fought."

She looked at the sheaf of printed-out articles for a while, trying to piece it all together.

"It's this bloody stone," she said, at last. "That's what's wrong. In 1897, it supposedly disappears. Then it turns up in a treasure chest in Wimpole Street and waltzes off with Mimsy. But there's this one tiny mention of it in the reports of Bennett Mountmain's death in Los Angeles."

"So he took it on holiday? Maybe it was a talisman of his devotion to the Führer."

"But how does it come to Maureen, and Mimsy? In 1942, this Captain 'W' of the deleted name seems to have snatched it back for England. Or Egypt. Or Science. I think the jewel has been stolen back and forth between two crews down the years. The Mountmains and some other shower, the mystery 'W''s bunch. The others mentioned only by initials. Mr. 'B' from 1897, even this 'R.J.' from the '70s. We need more about the initials. Could you spend tomorrow on it? You might have to stir yourself to the British Museum and the Newspaper Library."

"I'll take Jermo to see the mummies."

Jerome stuck his arms out and limped across the room.

"How does he know what the Mummy walks like, Neil?" she asked. "Have you been showing him your Hammer videos?"

"He gets it from *Scooby-Doo*."

She playfully strangled him.

"So perish all unbelievers who defile the innocent minds of young children," she intoned, solemnly.

They kissed and cuddled, and Jerome told them not to be soppy.

If a grown-up woman of twenty-seven wants to go missing and not be found, the legal position is that it's very much her business. Here, the abandoned mother might be able to lay a charge of theft against the absconded daughter, but Sally now knew enough about the Seven Stars to realise accusing anyone of stealing it would result in a potentially endless series of criss-cross counter charges.

Mimsy had walked out of her mother's house a week ago.

Finally, Maureen had coughed up an address book, with Mimsy's friends marked by pink felt-tip pen asterisks. Sally spent two days making telephone calls. None of Mimsy's "friends"—current worshippers, cast-off ex-lovers, bedazzled sidekicks or bitter rivals—admitted any knowledge of her.

But the drudgery was useful.

Everyone she talked with revealed, by their attitude, a bit more about the quarry. The impression Sally had already formed from Maureen was strengthening by the minute.

Mimsy Mountmain was quite a package. In her early teens, she'd made a million pounds as a songwriter. Sally remembered the titles of a few pop hits whose tunes and lyrics had vanished from her mind. Mimsy hadn't needed to work since, but had published a series of slim volumes of poetry in an invented language.

At sixteen, she put a young man into a coma by battering him with a half-brick. The court returned a verdict of self-defence and she was written up, in the *Comet* among other papers, as a have-a-go heroine. Then, under less clear-cut circumstances, she did it again. This time, the cracked skull belonged to a married bank manager rather than an unemployed football fan. She did three years in Holloway, and came out as the undisputed princess of the prison.

Her ex-lovers were all standouts. Politicians, celebs, serious wealth, famous criminals, beauties and monsters. Some of them hadn't come through the Mimsy Mountmain Experience without sustaining severe damage.

It might be that Mimsy was more than just missing.

She tried to read one of Mimsy's poems. Without being in the least comprehensible, it gave her the shudders. She had the impression Mimsy was up to something.

"It's not a family," Neil said, without taking off his coat, "it's a club."

Sally looked up. Neil brought Jerome into the flat.

"We saw mummies!" her son said.

Neil flopped open a notebook.

"Ever heard of a journo named Katharine Reed? Irish, turn of the century, bit of a firebrand?"

Sally hadn't.

"She left a memoir, and in that memoir she alludes in an off hand way to a Charles Beauregard who is almost certainly your Mr. 'B'. The *DNB* has pages on him. Reading between lines, he was something between a spy and a spy-catcher."

"I know the feeling."

"He became something high up in the Secret Service, and his protegé was a Captain Edwin Winthrop."

"Him I've heard of. He co-wrote a book about authentic hauntings in the West Country. Sometime in the '20s."

"That's the one. And he is your Captain 'W', to be found in Hollywood in 1942."

Sally considered hugging Neil. But the mention of the Secret Service was unsettling.

"Have you a name for the last one, 'R.J.'?"

"Sadly, 1972 wasn't long enough ago for any of the secret stuff to have been disclosed yet. And a lot of the files on the others, even Beauregard, are sealed until well into Jerome's adult life. He'll have to finish the puzzle."

"I'm going to be a spy when I grow up," Jerome announced.

"That'll be useful," she said. "What did you mean about a club?" Neil grinned.

"You'll love this. Remember Mycroft Holmes?"

"Who?"

"Brother of the more famous . . .?"

"Sherlock?"

"Give the girl a kiss," he said, and did. "Yep, Mycroft, whom Conan Doyle informs us 'sometimes was the British Government', was, as it turns out, a real person. His private fiefdom was a gentleman's club in Pall Mall, the Diogenes. It was a cover for a special section of British Intelligence. When Mycroft retired or died, this Beauregard took over and played the hush-hush game even more seriously. For the best part of this century, the Diogenes Club was Britain's own Department of Weird Shit. You know what I mean."

"Only too well."

"Aside from the wonderful Kate Reed, none of the people mixed up in this thought to write memoirs—though I've found references to a suppressed issue of *Black Mask* which supposedly ran a story that gave away too much—which means it's all locked up in Whitehall somewhere. When you sort this out . . ."

"When!"

"When. I have confidence in you. Anyway, when you sort this out, there might be a book in the Diogenes Club. Britain's X-Files. There's a hook. And at this late date, the secrecy issue is long dead."

"I'm not so sure about that."

"Come on, Sal-love. It's great stuff. Look, mummy's curses, Sherlock Holmes, Hooray for Hollywood, spies and ghosts, a fabulous lost treasure, Nazi Irishmen, hippie chicks with extremely large breasts, politics and black magic, terrorism, old dark houses, the plague."

"Think it through, Neil. You say it's all still secret."

"Just bureaucracy. We can get in there."

"When the War is over, the secrets come out. We know about that Scottish island Churchill dosed with anthrax. The Eastern Bloc refugees we handed over to Stalin for genocide. All that came out. Why not this stuff about the jewel?"

"Too trivial to be taken seriously. I mean, it's absurd, right? Spooks."

"When the War is over, the secrets come out. These secrets aren't out. Because the War isn't over."

"You're being a wet blanket, love."

She backed off from an argument. Neil didn't like being a dependant, but none of his outside projects ever quite came together. And he resisted being brought into the firm as a partner.

"I'm sorry," she said.

While she was on the bus, her mobile bleeped. It was Maureen. Sally ran down the list of the people she'd talked with, and floated out some of the material Neil had gathered on the Diogenes Club. Surprisingly, a door opened. Then closed again.

"They're out of business," Maureen said. "Have been for a long time. Winthrop, I knew. At the end. That was the last War. This is something new."

"Is it about Mimsy or the Seven Stars?"

Maureen hesitated.

The bus was stuck in Camden High Street.

"Sally, when you find Mimsy . . . you won't hurt her, will you?"

She thought of the two coma men. Only one had got better.

"If she doesn't want to come home, that's fine by me. I just want to know if she's all right."

She had heard that on every missing child case. If Jerome wandered off, she wouldn't be convinced he was all right until he was back home. But Jerome wasn't twenty-seven.

"I think Mimsy can take care of herself," she said, trying to reassure Maureen.

"The Jewel of Seven Stars isn't important to me."

After Maureen had rung off and the traffic started moving again, Sally thought to ask herself the question. So, who is the jewel important to? A morphing billboard outside the bus shifted from an ad for the new *Dr. Shade* movie to one for the Daily Comet to one for Cloud 9 satellite TV. All Derek Leech products.

The traffic thickened again, and Sally felt trapped.

Despite what she had told Neil and Maureen had told her, she had to go to Pall Mall. It wasn't that she thought this Diogenes Club was germane to the investigation, but she wanted to look at it, to cut off that avenue before it took up too much time. Besides, she was curious.

It took several wanders up and down the Mall before she found the tiny brass plate on the big oak doors. All it said was MEMBERS ONLY. The building was shuttered and out of use. She hammered on the doors, to see if she could raise some member from a decades long sleep. No one came.

She stood away from the building.

The Mall was busy, with Easter Holiday tourists enjoying the country's new climate in short-sleeved shirts and pastel dresses. There might be a drought on, but she could get used to this Californian London. Doom-merchants, however, said it was a sign of the end of the world.

A slim blonde girl in white wafted across very green grass, towards her. She wore a wide-brimmed straw hat and dark glasses with lenses the size and colour of apples.

For a moment, she thought this was another ghost. It was something about the way the light hit the girl's hair. She reminded Sally of Connor.

"Nobody home," the girl said.

She was too young to be Mimsy, not yet out of her teens. She had the trace of an accent.

Sally shrugged.

"You're looking for the jewel," the girl said.

Through the green lenses, tiny red points shone. This pretty waif had enormously hungry eyes.

"I'm looking for the woman who has the jewel," Sally said.

"Mimsy," the girl said, head cocked. "Poor dear."

"I'm Sally Rhodes. Who are you?"

"Geneviève Dieudonné. Call me Gené."

"Are you Mimsy's friend?"

Gené smiled, dazzling. Sally realised this girl had an archness and composure that didn't quite fit with her initial estimate of her age.

"I've never met her. But I *feel* her. I share blood with her mother. That was a great sacrifice for Maureen. She was just pregnant. There's a sliver of me in Maureen, left behind like a sting in a wound. And a tinier sliver in Mimsy. Along with all the other stuff. She was conceived around the Jewel of Seven Stars. That's why it speaks to her."

Gené wasn't insane. But she was talking about things beyond Sally's experience.

"The bauble that causes the trouble, Sally," Gené said. "I've danced with the stone, like the gentlemen who used to doze beyond those doors, like the Mountmain Line. Down the years we all revolve around the Seven Stars. Sometimes, years and years slip by and I don't think of the thing, but always it's there, the knowledge that I share the planet with the Jewel of Seven Stars, that it'll be back."

"That's an odd way of putting it."

"I'm an odd sort of person."

"Are you one of Leech's?"

"Good Heavens, no. I've been called a leech, though."

When Gené smiled, she showed sharp little teeth, like hooks carved of white ice.

"What do you want from me?"

"A partnership. I help you find the girl, and you let me have the jewel."

"What do you want with it?"

"What do people want with jewels? I wish I knew. Since you ask, I'll tell you. If possible, I'll get rid of it. It was buried for thousands of years without causing too much trouble. If I could securely bury it again, or stow it away on a deep-space probe, I'd do it. It fell out of the sky once. For years, I wondered about those seven flaws, the seven stars. Then, when we launched *Voyager*, I understood. On our rocket we engraved a star map, to show where it came from. The jewel is dangerous, and I want to damp the fire. Satisfied?"

"Not really."

"I wouldn't be either. You remind me of myself at your age. Seriously, Mimsy—whether she knows it or not, and I think she does and welcomes it—is in danger so long as she has that stone with her. Your job, I understand, is to find Mimsy and make sure she's safe . . ."

How had this woman known that?

". . . and I can help you."

"If you can find Mimsy, why don't you? Why do you need me?"

"I'm not a solo sort of person. Difficult in my position, but there you are. I work best with a stout-hearted comrade. Someone to keep me down to earth."

"I like you, Gené. Why is that?"

"Good taste."

Gené kissed Sally on the cheek, with an electric touch.

"Come on, Sal. Let's get a cab. I think I know where to start."

Sally was usually sparing with taxi travel. It was still most practical to get around London on the bus and tube, and she had to account for her expenses. But Gené had a handbag full of money, in several different currencies. She got them into a black cab and ordered the driver to take them to Docklands.

"You rattled a lot of webs when you went through Maureen Mountmain's address book," Gené explained. "Bells rang, and I hopped on a plane from Palermo. I've read up on you. You're good.

They'd have liked you at the Diogenes Club, though they were funny about women."

It was evening, now. Not dark yet, but the light was thin and cold. They were venturing into Docklands just as most people were leaving. The '80s *moderne* office buildings were unnaturally clean in their emptiness, life-sized toys fresh from their boxes.

The black glass pyramid caught the last of the sun.

"It's coming back to Leech," Sally said.

"Not really. But I think you'd have come here yourself soon."

"If I can help it, I stay away."

"Understood. But you've covered Mimsy's human connections with no luck. You're drawing back and looking at the whole picture. That's what made you go to the Mall. What you have to do is think of yourself as part of the pattern, to see how you fit in, where you can be triangulated."

Sally saw what Gené meant.

"I'm in the pattern because of Leech. He doesn't do anything for no reason. This isn't a favour to a friend. This is part of a plan."

Gené clapped.

"I'm the last person Leech loves. He said—and he's always annoyingly truthful—that only I could do this job. He wants me to find Mimsy."

"And the Seven Stars."

"There's a link between Leech and Mimsy. It's broken, or at least played out to its full length. Is he after the jewel?"

"Leech's dominion is of this world," Gené said. "He only wants what I want, to keep the Seven Stars out of circulation. I'm not happy to share a common cause with him, but there you are. This business scrambles all your allegiances."

"I thought Leech might be Mimsy's father."

"Good guess, but no. That was Richard Jeperson, one of the Diogenes fellows. Mimsy is unpredictable precisely because she is the fruit of an opposition, the Mountmain Line and the Diogenes Club. And whatever I threw in didn't help. Whatever havoc she wreaks, we can all take the blame."

Gené had the cab stop a few streets away from the Pyramid.

When it had driven off, the road was empty. The last of the light was going. It was a cloudless night, but the blanket of sodium orange street-lighting kept the stars at bay.

"One of the reasons I like you, Sal, is that you believe me. Over the years, almost no one has. Not at first. But you've stepped into the dark enough times to know the truth when you hear it."

They looked up at the Pyramid.

"The Jewel of Seven Stars is a tool for ending empires," Gené said. "It ended the rule of a Pharaoh. Declan Mountmain wanted to use it on Britain. Bennett Mountmain thought he could win the War for Hitler. Edwin Winthrop turned it on Germany and Japan. It could be used on that Pyramid."

Sally imagined Leech's empire in ruins.

"But there's a cost. The world is still living with the consequences of the way Edwin and the Diogenes Club wound up the last War. I think Leech is one of those consequences. If the times weren't out of joint, he wouldn't have taken hold and grown like a cancer."

"Leech thinks Mimsy is a *threat*?"

She couldn't believe it. But it made sense.

"A mad woman from a long line of mad people? Armed with a chunk of dubious crystal? Do you have any idea of just who Derek Leech is? Of how far beyond human reckoning he is?"

"Why you, Sal? Why did he pick you?"

"He said I was a saint."

Gené spread her arms and opened her hands.

"I'm not a saint. I'm a single mum. I'm kissing forty. My life and business lurches from crisis to crisis."

"*Twice*, you've stopped him, Sal. You've saved people from him."

"In the end, that meant nothing. He had other plans."

"No one else has ever stopped him. Not once."

Sally saw what Gené meant.

"So I'm the only person he can think of who could stand between him and Mimsy."

"Not just Mimsy."

The night was all around. Gené took off her dark glasses. Her eyes were alive and ancient, points of red burning in their depths.

* * *

They had spent the night by the Pyramid. Nothing had happened. Her instinctive faith in Gené's inside knowledge was fraying. It would have been much more convenient if Mimsy had turned up in Derek Leech's lobby, brandishing the Jewel of Seven Stars like a *Star Trek* phaser.

Red light came up in the East, and Sally phoned for a minicab. She didn't think the night wasted.

She and Gené—Geneviève—had talked.

Without saying what she was, Gené had revealed a lot. She filled in, apparently from personal knowledge, a lot of the gaps. If Neil ever wrote his book, she'd be a prime source. But she wasn't scary, like Leech. She was proof that you could live with the weirdness and not be swallowed up by it. She had a real personality.

Gené had made mistakes. She said what she thought, without filtering it through a brain that framed everything as a series of crossword clues with hidden killer clauses.

In the cab, Gené was jittery.

"I'm sorry," she said. "I led you down the wrong path. Something happened last night. And we missed it. My fault. I thought the Seven Stars would revolve around Leech. Maybe they will, but not yet. Maybe there's too much Mimsy in the brew . . ."

Her mobile jarred her out of the half-sleep she had fallen into. The minicab was caught in the morning influx of commuters into Docklands.

It was Neil.

"The police have been round," he said. "It's to do with your client. She's been killed, Sal-love."

She was shocked awake.

"Maureen?"

"Yes. You'll have to check in and give a statement. The pigs know you were working for her."

Cold inside, she asked the question.

"Was it Mimsy?"

"She wasn't killed with a hammer. From what they let slip, I don't think it could have been murder. She had an allergic reaction to insect bites."

Sally hung up and redirected the cab driver to Wimpole Street. She told Gené what had happened.

"Bitten to death?" Gené mused.

There was a policeman at the door, but Sally got through by admitting she had been asked to give a statement. Gené looked at the man over her sunglasses and was waved in without comment.

"Neat trick."

"You wouldn't want to learn it."

The hallway was changed. All the purple paint was gone and there was a thick, crunchy carpet. Sally realised she was standing on a layer of bloated, dead flies. The purple paint had been stripped by a million tiny mouths, which had etched into the surfaces of everything. A cloud must have filled the house. The curtains were eaten away completely, dried white smears scabbed the window-glass.

"She's trying to use it," Gené said.

"I have to see," Sally said.

"I know."

They went upstairs. Policemen stood around the landing, and a couple of forensic people were expressing appalled puzzlement. Photographs were being taken.

A detective inspector issued orders that none of this was to be released to the press. He looked a hundred years old, and was too tired to shout at anyone for letting Sally and Gené into the house.

Sally explained who she was and that the dead woman had hired her to find her missing daughter. She admitted she hadn't managed to do so.

"If she's missing the way her mum is, you might as well give the money back."

"To whom?" she asked.

Actually, she hadn't been paid in advance. Leech would certainly cover it, but Sally didn't want to take his tainted money.

"It's not an allergic reaction," Gené said. "Flies don't sting."

"No," the inspector agreed. "They chew."

Sally looked into Mimsy's room. Maureen Mountmain lay on the bed. She was only recognisable by her distinctive hair, white with a red streak. Her naked bones lay in a nest of dead flies.

"It's started," Gené said.

She had tried to call Neil but not been able to get through. Gené was silent in the cab, seeming far older after the long night and the horrors of Wimpole Street. There was a long-shot suggestion that it was all down to the new climate, hatching flies early and driving them mad.

Sally tried not to be anxious. There was no home to bring Mimsy back to. She was off the case. In Muswell Hill, Gené dropped her off.

"Don't worry, Sal. It'll take years. I'm sorry to lose you, but you can get on with your life. It comes down to those of us who live outside human time, Leech and me and the Seven Stars. Give my love to your son. I'd like to meet him one day."

Sally watched the cab go. She wondered where Gené was headed. She had said something about needing to get in out of the sun. And getting something to drink.

If she was going to fail anyone, she was glad it was Leech—she thought now that he had wanted her to check Mimsy, somehow though—she was ripped open and bled empty about Maureen.

She went upstairs.

She had not been able to get a call through because Neil was using the modem, digging up material on the Fourth Plague of Egypt. He thought it was germane to the investigation.

"There is no investigation, dear," she said. "No client."

Jerome wandered in, dressed in his too-small pyjamas.

"Who was the pretty lady?" he asked.

"Were you peeking out your window?"

Her son didn't answer her.

"Okay," she said. "I give up. What was the Fourth Plague of Egypt?"

"You should know that," Neil said. "It's in *The Abominable Dr. Phibes*. Flies."

"You won't be out of pocket," Leech said. "I've authorised a payment. You may forward it to Shelter, if you wish."

"I don't deserve to get paid. I did nothing. I found out nothing.

Mimsy is still missing. And the Jewel of Seven Stars."

The phone was cool in her hand.

"You *have* found something out, then."

Leech sounded different. Tired? Maybe it was the connection?

"A little. Nothing relevant."

"I had hoped you might influence Mimsy, by your example. I see now that was overly ambitious of me."

Had he set Sally Rhodes, with her sword of righteousness, against Mimsy Mountmain, with her weirdstone, hoping they would cancel each other out?

"Can she hurt you, Derek?" she asked.

"This call is over. Goodbye, Sally."

She listened to the dead line. It was now a question of living with the fear, of getting through the plague years. Derek Leech had an empire, and she had a computer-crazed kid and a boyfriend who'd never grow up. She knew, at last, that she was more suitable to survive.

Marty Burns

THE MAN WHO SHOT THE MAN WHO SHOT *THE MAN WHO SHOT LIBERTY VALENCE*

by JAY RUSSELL

Martin Burns was born in 1955. As a child actor, he played precocious brat Sandy Salt in Salt & Pepper, *one of the many hugely forgettable Manny Stiles-produced TV sitcoms of the mid-1960s. Achieving a brief notoriety for his incessant use of the annoying catchphrase "Hot enough for you?", Burns flared as a minor hearthrob teen-idol, then fizzled in a series of woeful adult performances, leading to an inconsequential career in low-budget films.*

He reputedly quit The Business and spent nearly two decades working as a low-rent private investigator in Los Angeles. He made a surprise return to acting in the television series Burning Bright, *following his involvement in exposing the bizarre Jack Rippen/ Celestial Dogs scandal. His acting has not improved with time.*

Marty Burns first appeared in Jay Russell's debut novel Celestial Dogs *(1996), which mixed Hollywood moguls with ancient Japanese demons in a battle for the soul of humanity. Emerging as the surprise hero, Marty subsequently travelled to Britain, where he became involved with a neo-Nazi cult with mystical powers in the sequel,* Burning Bright *(1997), and he investigated a murder mystery which revolved around an old Hollywood noir movie in* Greed & Stuff *(2001).*

Apocalypse Now, Voyager *was a novella published in 2005, and further Marty Burns stories have appeared in the anthologies* Dark Terrors 4 *('Sullivan's Travails', 1998),* White of the Moon *('What Ever Happened to Baby June?', 1999) and* Psycho-Mania! *('Hush . . . Hush, Sweet Shushie', 2013).*

IT STARTED WITH a friendly game of strip Ouija; it ended in massive head trauma, a moderately broken heart, and the pink taffeta dress that John Wayne was buried in.

But I'm getting ahead of myself.

There's a ton of time to kill when you're on a shoot. It's kind of a cliché about how boring filmmaking is, but if you're an actor it's a simple truth: you spend most of the day sitting around *waiting* to act. (Of course, there are a few who say that even when the cameras are rolling I look like I'm waiting to act.) So you have to find ways to fill the day. The catering unit helps, but son-of-a-gun if the network doesn't insist on a weight clause in every actor's contract. I suppose that's what happens when you show up for negotiations carrying a sixer.

We were working on the third episode of the second season of *Burning Bright*: something or other to do with a missing kid, a deadly virus, a pretty girl—there's *always* a pretty girl. I used to question the logic of the show's plots, but I got too many stomach aches. Now, on the producer's advice, I read my lines and bank my cheques. Most of the day's shooting was occupied with a tricky action sequence requiring my stunt double. I had to hang around the set *just in case*, but with the Dodgers having an off-day and my iPad on the fritz, I couldn't think what to do until Karlbert, our story editor, pointed out the new wardrobe assistant.

"She can undress me any old time," Karlbert practically drooled.

Karlbert's a pig (though he may not be entirely responsible: what were his parents thinking when they named him Karlbert?), but this time he did have a point. Though my leching days are largely behind me, I sure enough could endure a blast from the past for this woman. She was one hundred and twenty immaculately proportioned pounds of delight, with generous handfuls of femininity in all the right places. Not to mention a killer Gene Tierney overbite.

That's a good thing, if you didn't know.

Bobbi was her name and as luck would have it, she was as free-thinking as she was attractive. You'd have to be to agree to play strip Ouija with Karlbert, who's on the thin side of bald and the fat side of rotund, and me. Now admittedly the rules of strip Ouija are a little *ad hoc*, but the essence of the game is to pose questions to the Other Side that generate a positive response. Provoke any bad karma and you lose an item of clothing. Given my extensive networking with things that go bump in the night (along with Karlbert's and my unashamed willingness to cheat), I figured Bobbi's good ship lollipop would be cresting the horizon quicker than you could say Madame Blavatsky.

Less than an hour later, I still had my pants and socks and Karlbert a very grey pair of very briefs. Bobbi'd lost an earring, but gained a smug expression. So much for networking. I tried to avoid glancing Karlbert's way; bad enough he had that name, he was hairier than a baboon to boot. It was his turn to ask a question, and he looked stumped before his face lit up.

"Was John Wayne a homo?" he asked the Great Beyond.

I took my finger off the planchette.

"What kind of fool question is that?" I demanded.

"It's a damn good question. And one to which the answer will be a resounding yes, if you'll be kind enough to oblige."

"John Wayne was not a . . . he wasn't gay," I said.

"Because he never hit on you?"

"No! I mean, I never met him. But we're talking the Duke here." I'm not much on Hollywood legends—if anybody knows just how strange a town this is, I do—but John Wayne for goodness sake!

"James Dean was queer," Bobbi said.

"James Dean partied with Sal Mineo, for chrissake. John Wayne hung with John Ford. And John Ford was a *man's* man." They both looked me at oddly. "Wait, that didn't come out right."

"John Wayne," Karlbert said, "was buried wearing a dress."

"You read that on TMZ or something?"

"It's true."

"It's not."

"Want to bet?" Karlbert pointed at the Ouija board. "Let's ask."

"No, no, no. Not good enough by half." Karlbert had big, fat fingers; teaming up to get Bobbi naked was one thing, but I wasn't about to thumb-wrestle him over the planchette with money on the line.

Karlbert thought for a moment. "Okay," he said, nodding to himself. "I know another way. If you've got the cash and the nerve."

Bobbi studied me with a will-he-or-won't-he look in her eyes, and a pout as sexy as all get-out on those delectable lips.

What was a boy to do?

The guy lived Hollywood adjacent—sorry, we talk like that in L.A.—right around the corner from three, count 'em, three nudie bars. It was awfully late to be so close to Little El Salvador for my lily white ass, but a bet was a bet. And Bobbi, who'd insisted on coming with us when shooting wrapped for the day, was nervous enough that she let me hold her soft-as-satin hand.

Karlbert rapped on the apartment door. I surveyed the field of broken syringes scattered in the grass out front. One fewer than the number of spent condoms. An L.A. zen garden.

"So what does this guy do exactly?" I asked.

"He's a psychic," Karlbert said.

"Huh-boy."

"Oh yeah, and a cartoonist."

"He's a psychic cartoonist?"

"Uh-huh, but the two careers are entirely separate so far as I know. Thing is, he's also a collector."

Before I could ask, Karlbert knocked again, then kicked so hard at the base of the door that the wood nearly splintered. Footsteps sounded from the other side.

"Whatever you do," Karlbert hurriedly whispered, "don't say anything about his weight."

"His weight?" I said.

The door opened. The frame was filled by an enormous black man wearing leather trousers and nipple rings. I knew because he was naked from the waist up. He had a broad belly like a bean bag chair, and coin slot eyes. He also wore a shoulder holster containing a very big gun.

"K.B.," he croaked. "What haps?"

"Yo, Montserrat. I've brought a couple of unbelievers for a history lesson. We seek a taste of your own brand of truth."

Montserrat—he was big enough to be an island—took me in with a bored glance, but his narrow eyes widened at the sight of Bobbi in a tight T-shirt. He actually licked his lips. Who wouldn't?

"All right," he said, tongue still dangling. "C'mon in."

The tiny apartment was filthy beyond belief. Fortunately, the disgusted eye was distracted from the ignorant armies of roaches and silverfish clashing over the mouldy remains of pizza crusts by the array of photographs gracing one long wall from floor to ceiling. Presumably this was Montserrat's collection. The pictures were pornographic in the extreme—stuff I didn't even know people outside Cirque du Soleil could do—but more amazingly, every damn shot featured a celebrity. Movie and TV stars past and present, politicians, baseball players, the first lady of the American theatre, Flipper . . .

Bobbi gasped. I gasped even louder.

"Virgins?" Montserrat mumbled.

Karlbert nodded. I probably should have been offended, but I was too stunned.

Montserrat seemed reluctant to take his eyes off Bobbi, but Karlbert took the big man by the arm and led him to the far side of the room. They spoke in hushed tones.

Bobbi pointed to a spot high on the wall. "Is that . . . Richard Nixon?" she squeaked.

I gawked and nodded. "A tricky dick, indeed."

"Poor Mrs. Nixon," Bobbi said.

"Poor Checkers!" I clucked.

"Yo," Karlbert called.

I walked across the room. Bobbi was glued to the spot, taking it all in. I let her be. Montserrat had disappeared.

"Give me the money," Karlbert said, holding out his hand.

We'd wagered five hundred bucks. Karlbert had actually made me stop at a cash machine to get the moolah on the drive over.

"You haven't won yet."

"Just give it to me," Karlbert insisted.

I sensed this was no place to argue. I slipped the folded bills into

Karlbert's palm just as Montserrat returned. He held a big photo album in his massive hands. With surprising gentleness, he opened the book and flipped through the laminated pages. When he found what he wanted, he turned the book around and held it up for the two of us to see.

It was an 8 x 10 glossy of John Wayne. He looked like he was about sixty-five in the picture, that revered face as battered as an old pair of shoes.

John Wayne: standing in the doorway of a western saloon—a film set, no doubt.

John Wayne: American hero and icon.

John Wayne: wearing . . . a pink taffeta dress.

The sonuvabitch really didn't have the legs for it.

"It's a fake, digitally fiddled," I said. "You did this with Photoshop or something."

Montserrat shook his head.

"Where'd you get it, then?"

Montserrat just stared at me.

"This is all bullshit," I said, pointing at the wall. "These kind of scams have been going down for years, they're old as Tijuana bibles. You manufacture these things. It's nice quality, I admit, but it's still a con." I turned to Karlbert. "Give me my money back."

Karlbert had gone wide-eyed, shaking his head.

"What?" I said. "Come on. The game's up. Hand it over."

"It's for real," Montserrat whispered. He didn't look mad so much as insulted.

"And how do you know that exactly?"

"Come from the horse's mouth. Man who took this picture the man who shot the movies."

"What?" I asked. "What movies? What are you talking about."

"Camera dude give it to me. Dude what lensed *The Man Who Shot Liberty Valence*. Ever hear of it?"

"Hey, I played poker with Woody Strode, okay? How do you know this guy took it, that it's for real? How do you even know him?"

"Cause I shot him."

There was a moment of deep silence. You could have heard a battleship drop.

"Sorry?"

"Camera dude got himself into trouble few years back. Liked to play the ponies, didn't like to pay. Had to shoot him some. Was my job back then. He give me this so I don't shoot him no more. It was a stressful situation."

Ex-button man psychic cartoonist. Great googly-moogly, I have got to get out of L.A.

I glanced over my shoulder at Bobbi. She'd gone to take a closer look at a photo—Fred MacMurry and William Demerest! Is nothing sacred?—but now stared at the three of us open-mouthed. I looked at Karlbert who rather eloquently communicated that it was a quarter-past time for me to shut the fuck up. I turned to Montserrat, who was again eyeing Bobbi's tits and licking his massive chops.

"Three bills, right Montserrat?" Karlbert asked.

Montserrat nodded. Karlbert passed over the money and the big man carefully removed the photo from the album and handed it to Karlbert.

"I've been wanting this puppy for a good while now," Karlbert told me. "I'm building a little collection of my own. Thank you very much."

I just nodded.

Karlbert started toward the front door, but I had to turn back.

"You, uh, got any of me in there?" I asked, pointing to the album.

Montserrat shrugged his whalish mass, sniffed once. "No demand," he said.

I didn't know whether to be flattered or insulted.

We were walking back up the path to the sidewalk, when Bobbi reached into her pocket and pulled out the small snapshot.

"What's that?" I asked, offering a dopey smile.

"I took it off the wall," she whispered. "While you guys were talking."

Karlbert spun around. "What? You did what?"

"I . . . I had to have it. I mean, he's a Beatle."

Before I could even make out which moptop, I heard the roar from behind. Montserrat, still shirtless, nipple rings flapping, charged up the path toward us, gun in hand. Karlbert started to curse, but the gunshots drowned out the words.

The first shot caught Karlbert along his left ear. I actually saw a piece of his dangly lobe fly off in a spurt of blood. The impact spun him around, so that the second shot caught him square in the back of the head. It was Zapruder time all over again.

I froze as Montserrat thundered up to me. He raised the gun in both hands and jammed the barrel between my lips. He didn't so much as blink before pulling the trigger.

No more bullets. Straight to shul for this boy come Saturday morning.

It seemed to take the big man a minute to realize what had gone wrong. I hadn't moved a non-intestinal muscle, even as he flipped the gun around to pistol whip me, but Bobbi, bless her curvaceous soul, was a she-devil on wheels. She'd found a hunk of two-by-four amid the garden debris and brought it down with all her might across the back of Montserrat's head.

That caught his attention.

Whether the blow to the noggin would have been sufficient to put an end to the evening's festivities, we'd never know, because quicker than a Michael Ironside film goes to video, Bobbi swung the lumber around and brought it up with testicle-crunching force between Montserrat's legs.

They must have heard the scream in Yokohama.

Montserrat was still squealing when the cops and ambulances arrived. I'd barely moved for thinking I should be dead, but Bobbi tore her shirt off and wrapped it tight around Karlbert's head to stanch the bleeding.

Turned out to be as close to seeing her naked as I'd ever get. I do dream, though.

It cost the network a few dollars with the L.A.P.D. Widows and Orphans Fund to keep my name out things, but then Hollywood adjacent violence doesn't really rate these days. Karlbert recovered, though he needed two months in the head trauma unit at Cedars. He had to give up his position as story editor on *Burning Bright*, but frankly the plots have gotten much better now that he's gone. Even after they released him, poor Karlbert lost the ability to tell the difference between sweet and sour. The doctors are puzzled.

I know the weed of crime bears bitter fruit and all, but not being able to enjoy a good Chinese meal seems a hell of a price to pay for your sins.

Bobbi left the show as well, albeit for a six-figure development deal with DreamWorks. I hear she's come out of the closet, too, but then lesbian chic is in monster fashion at the moment. Word is she's stalking Ellen DeGeneres.

It only occurred to me quite a bit later that even if it was real, the photo that started the whole mess—courtesy of the man who shot *The Man Who Shot Liberty Valence*—and which cost me five hundred bucks, wasn't proof at all that John Wayne was *buried* wearing a dress, much less that he was gay.

I still don't like to believe it, but for my own pathetic peace of mind (and admitted prurient interest) I had another go at the Ouija board. I went about it a little more seriously this time, thinking I had a shot at getting through to the Duke if I really put my mind to it. Hard as I tried, though, I couldn't make contact. The best I could manage was Ward Bond, so just for the hell of it I asked him. Any John Ford fan might have guessed the reply:

When the legend becomes fact, print the legend.

Jerome Rhodes
SEVEN STARS EPISODE SIX

THE DOG STORY
by KIM NEWMAN

Unlike his mother Sally, Jerome Rhodes relies on state-of-the-art technology in his investigations.

Conceived in the story 'Organ Donors' (Darklands 2, 1992), a toddler in The Quorum *(1994) and grown-up in 'Where the Bodies Are Buried 2020' (Dark Terrors 2, 1996), Jerome is named after the author's nephew and the adult character inhabits a world loosely connected with that of Kim Newman's early science fiction stories, 'Dreamers' (Interzone #8, 1984) and 'Patricia's Profession' (Interzone #14, 1986), and his debut novel,* The Night Mayor *(1990).*

Dr. Shade was originally a fictional scientific vigilante of the 1930–50s, created by "Rex Cash" (Donald Moncrieff) for Wendover's Magazine. *With his identity hidden behind a cloak and goggle-like dark glasses, he employed a group of semi-criminal bully boys in his never-ending war against foreign elements importing evil into the heart of the British Empire. The character became even more popular as an official agent of the British government in a daily comic strip in the* Evening Argus *(1935–52), illustrated by Frank FitzGerald and written by Harry Lipman under the Cash pseudonym from 1939 onwards.*

Introduced in Newman's British Science Fiction Award-winning novella, 'The Original Dr Shade' (Interzone #36, 1990), the

character took on a life of his own, later reappearing in the novel
The Quorum *(1994) as an alter-ego of Derek Leech.*

THE CLIENT HAD fixed the meetsite, Pall Mall. Neutral ground, equidistant from his Islington monad and her Brixton piedater. He was used to getting-about. Types who needed an Information Analyst didn't want the need known. It usually meant they were in a reverse, and even a rumour could key terminal panic. Vastcorps were conservative, prone to dump at the first smokesign, trailing a plankton-field of small investors who'd unload at decreasingly sensible prices. A whisper could drag down an empire toot sweet.

Though he spoke with what he knew from old teevee to be an English accent, Jerome thought of Pall Mall, like all else, as *Paul Maul.*

The London Board of Directors had gotten so weary of Former Americans visiting the Mall and asking where the stores were that the strip had been rezoned for commercial development. Preservation-ordered buildings, no longer needed after the out shifting of admin to Bletchley, were subdivided into franchise premises: Leechmart, Banana Democracy, Guns 'n' Ammo, Killergrams. Some stores here were so chic they had actual goods in stock, for real-life inspection.

The client had called the place *Pal Mal*, like an elderly person would. Her face ident, however, scanned as girlish. For an inst, he'd optioned asking her if her parents knew she was accessing their comm-hook.

She had a name, not a corporate ident. Geneviève Dieudonné. He'd worked for private citizens before, though he was usually indentured to corps or gunmints. He did not come low-budget. She'd have to meet his price, either in currency or access.

She had specified an old address, between fast outlets, clothes shops and the dream parlours. A prime site neglected in the redevelopment. He was to wait outside for her.

It was a cool day at street level. The cloud-kites were over the East End, which let unfiltered sunlight pour down here, bleaching everything pastel. A few other get-abouts strolled in the chill light, toting parasols. The odd unperson nipped out, though they were supposed to stay behind the scenes, darting across the open to shade, covering their eyes against the burning glare.

He sat on a pink play-bench and turned down his earpiece, lulling the info-flow. If the client had a problem, he needed to clear his mind.

He was distracted anyway, by a barking dog. A couple of gay get-abouts were shamed by their unruly Alsatian. The hom tried to calm the dog, adjusting the collar with the handset; the fem apologised to passersby, explaining there must be some glitch in the mood-collar.

A micro-event, but it rang a bell.

On the people-mover, there'd been another dog, a miniature of some breed yapping in an old woman's grip. Get-abouts had got about, shifting to another carriage.

Two geek dogs. Not info on which to build a case.

"Jerome Rhodes?"

She wore a thick wraparound eyeshade, a heavy sun-cloak and a wide-brimmed black straw hat with a scarlet silk band. She must have skin cancer in her genetic background, or be extra-cautious, or need the disguise. She was a pretty lady: he intuited he might have seen her before, once, long ago.

He stood and offered his hand, making a fist so the bar-code on the back was smooth. She did not produce a reader to confirm his ident. She also did not offer her hand.

"You conch that without ident exchange, no contract is legally enforceable?"

It was surprising how many of his clients were ignorant of the regs of Information Analysis.

She shrugged, cloak lifted a little by the airflow.

"I should terminate this meet," he said.

She took off her eyeshade and looked at him.

"But you won't," she whispered.

It was as if she saw through his eyeshade, accessing his brain.

"I want you to locate a ghost," she said.

That wasn't an unusual request. Ghosts were rogue idents, projected into the Info-World, often leashed to their physical persons by a monofilament of ectoplasm. Some spook-makers cultivated a swarm of ghosts. You had to mind it was a baseline form of Multiple Personality Disorder, that ghosts sprang from meat-minds.

Something about the way she had put it didn't quite scan. He was acute to precise meanings, even when words offered multiple readings.

She'd meant ghost the way he took it. But she had a B story minded, another meaning. "A ghost, as in . . .?"

She smiled at his prompt.

"As in Jacob Marley? As in Henrik Ibsen? Perhaps. But, primarily, the breed of ghost you know about."

He had a reputation as a ghost-buster. Two years ago, Walt McDisney hired him to bust a cadre of disgruntled ex-employees who assumed the idents of wholly-owned cartoon characters and harassed accessors of Virtual McDisneyland. That was a big case for Rhodes Information, involving Info-World banditry, pop culture terrorism, copyright violation and several different layers of obscenity law. The culprits were under Household Arrest for the rest of their lives, shut out of the Info-World forever.

The barking Alsatian had set off another animal, a snapping terrier. They were noisemaking in disharmony, not competition. Jerome heard a third canine whine, joining in from backstage. A lot of unpersons kept dogs on traditional strings.

The client was distracted, too. She slipped her eyeshade back on, but he'd caught the narrowing of her eyes. It was if she had suffered a sudden brainpain.

"What's the ghost's tag?"

"Seven Stars."

Jerome pulled out his earpiece, shutting off info-flow, suddenly concentrating on only the A story.

"Seven Stars?"

He needed a confirm. She gave it.

"Seven Stars isn't a ghost," he said. "Seven Stars is a terrorist-corp. Gunmints have gone after them. And vastcorps. What info do you have that puts us in a better start position than the heavy hitters?"

"Seven Stars is one person, physically. Of course, she might be considered a Legion."

He tagged the reference.

"Mark. Chapter Five. Verses Eight and Nine. 'For he said unto him, "Come out of the man, thou unclean spirit". And he asked him,

"What is thy name?" And he answered, saying, "My name is Legion: for we are many".

"King James Version, Jerome. Very impressive. I thought Post Christians used the Jeffrey Archer translation."

"I'm not a P-C," Jerome said. "The Bible is of cultural importance beyond religious significance."

"How are you on the Old Testament?"

He didn't want to get into a Trivial Pursuit session, so he shrugged modestly.

"Look up Exodus, Chapters Seven through Twelve."

"The Plagues of Egypt?"

"Very good. To answer your original question, I have the ident of Seven Stars. The meat-name."

He winced. He had not expected vulgarity from her.

"It's Mimsy Mountmain."

She spelled it for him.

He still didn't quite believe Seven Stars was one person. Most theorists put them down as an Info-Army, covertly funded by a consortium to disrupt the Info-World. The vastcorps all had their private security people out looking for them, not to mention various Global Information Police forces.

Over the last year, Seven Stars had been busy.

At first, the Scramble Bombs seemed random, disruptions of the info-flows. Vastcorps and gunmints set aside their info wars to post rewards for the expulsion of Seven Stars. Derek Leech himself, the visionary of the Information World, the ultimate stay-at-home, stepped out of his Pyramid for the first time in a dozen years to appear on a realwelt platform with the Managing Director of London, the CEO of McDisney-Europa and the Moderator of the Eunion.

Then came serious pranks, calculated to undermine client confidence. Jerome had been amused, with the cynicism about stay-at-homes endemic among get-abouts like him, when a hundred million people were convinced by a phreak edition of *OnLine Vogue* that the latest fashion was for rouged and exposed anuses. When a hundredth of the subscribers lipsticked their recta, it counted as a genuine fashion trend and the real *Vogue*, a Leech publication, was obliged by law to report it. The fact that the fashion followers' registration fees went to an untraceable account in Virtual Switzerland was an extra giggle.

The pranks became murderous, and Seven Stars seemed scarier. A few high-profile ident assassinations were costly embarrassments for heads of states and CEOs, deleted from the Info-World or metamorphosed so their access signatures made all users read them as unpersons. After an ident assassination, you could always get another life, even if it meant going back twenty years and starting all over. When a random percentage of Leech-Drug prescriptions were tainted, a substantial death-toll of meat-lives—realfolk—mounted. Stay-at-homes struck dead in their monads, were reclassified by their Households from home-user to waste material.

If the long-foretold Collapse were to come, Seven Stars might look good for the role of Anti-Christ. Empires were shaking, and a lot of independents were going psycho "in the tradition of" Seven Stars.

One person. One ident. Mimsy Mountmain.

Jerome had asked the client for back-up confirmations. She just knew. That was scary in itself.

He was as good at reading people as at conning info-mass. People had readouts and flagged items too. He believed the client. Though there was something about her that didn't scan.

Back at the monad, he jacked his earpiece into the Household and pulled in a few info-blips. He often started with a random trawl, seeing if connections could be made.

The dog story was an epidemic. The first theory was that a sound pitched only to sensitive canine ears was causing all dogs—including the few wolves left in realwelt zoos—low-level irritation. However, no such ultra-sound could be detected by instruments other than dog-brains.

Even through his monad-block's soundproofing, Jerome heard distinct animal noises. He was grateful that he didn't have a companion or minion dog. There were reports of minion dogs—gene-designed for guard and attack duties—savaging stay-at-home masters. It couldn't be an Info-Prank. Dogs weren't generally jacked into anything other than the Actual.

He set searchers on Mimsy Mountmain, cloaking himself for caution. For added coverage, he put a search out on Geneviève Dieudonné. It was always a smart keystroke to learn as much about the client as the quarry. Often, something the client didn't know about themselves was the breakthrough clue.

He subscribed to the usual police sites, from which he downloaded the surface material on Seven Stars. He didn't want to chance a full-on search yet. The last thing he wanted was to flag his own name. Seven Stars could have him wiped. Or killed.

Should he make a comm-link with Sister Chantal and initiate discussion on the Plagues of Egypt? Since the Fall of the Vatican, she was freelancing out of Prague but would still be up on Biblical scholarship. He skinned his thought package. He had a perfectly good reason to call Chan, but was reluctant to do so. He had an emotional case-file on her, and knew she'd interpret a call as personal rather than professional. Then they'd have to go forward or back. And he wanted to stay where they were.

He left it as it was.

The dog story was a mushrooming news-bomb, eclipsing other developing stories. Most channels offered feeble alternatives—something about an astronomical anomaly, a human interest orphan massacre, a new development in endocrinology—but the dog story was global, a stone mystery, affording a full response spectrum from farce to horror. He couldn't afford to get caught up in the mediamass of speculative coverage.

On Cloud 9, the premier Leech newsline, extreme theorists were getting the coverage: a canine groupmind, begging for a cosmic bone; a conceptual breakthrough, representing the sudden attainment of sentience in a competitor species; a literal curse of God, a rebuke for the collapse of most organised churches in the Religious Wars of '20.

Jerome forced himself to tune out on the dog story.

His search results were downloading. The first thing he learned was that Mimsy Mountmain was a real person, born 1973—which made her fifty-three now. Her mother was listed as Maureen Mountmain (d. 1998), her father was not known. There were sealed police records from the 1990s, which he'd take the trouble to gut later. Nothing much after the turn of the century. Hot links fed off to biographies of several family members, stretching back to the 1800s. They would be a distraction just now, but he made a mental flag to find out why they were supposed to be so interesting.

The real woman of mystery was Geneviève Dieudonné.

A person of that name had been born in France in 1416. She apparently died—there was some doubt about exact circumstances and date—in 1432. At sixteen.

A person of that name had been born in Canada in 1893 and died under her married name of Thompson in 1962. A life's worth of data on her scrolled past swiftly.

A person of that name was mentioned in the acknowledgements of *Some Thoughts on the Bondage of Womanhood*, by Katharine Reed. Published 1902.

And a person of that name was on the payroll of the Free French for several months in 1942. She worked in Los Angeles, presumably for the War Effort, though the nature of her service was not listed.

There was no record of the woman he had met this afternoon.

Geneviève 1893–1962 left a portfolio of photographs, from childhood through to old age. Geneviève 1902 and Geneviève 1942—definitely different from the 1893–1962 woman and probably from each other—left no pics.

It seemed likely his client had used an off-the-peg ident to contract with him she had not offered him her hand for reading, he minded—but must also have gone to some trouble to find a name that would not yield miles of scroll on many different people down through the centuries. Over a thousand people on record were called Jerome Rhodes.

An afterthought downloaded. A search gave you public record info first, then revisited any sealed files you'd previously accessed. This blip came from his own master contacts file. A Geneviève Dieudonné was listed as a contact of the Sally Rhodes Agency in 1998. Unless on some major rejuvenative surgery kick, this could not be the same woman.

His mother had, as usual, not kept a proper record. From the notation, it was ambiguous as to whether this Geneviève was a client or an informant. She did not seem to have paid anything, which was just like Mum. Too many deadbeats rooked her out of a fee for services rendered.

He would have been five or six. He minded the times. Neil, Mum's boyfriend, was teaching him how to find things out. They had even gone to paper-and-dust libraries to look things up. It was the start of his induction into the Info-World.

Had he seen Miss Dieudonné then? At first sight, the client had seemed to ring a distant alarm. But this couldn't be the same woman.

Was his client trying to tell him something by using a name that would be in his mother's records?

Logically, he could comm-link with his Mum, retired and living in Cornwall. But he didn't like to bother her yet. He could access info on his own, and didn't need to crawl to her when problems got thorny. She had taught him to be self-reliant. Maybe neurotically so. If that was the case, he'd get it seen to eventually.

As things were, he was employed, but not contracted, to find a ghost whose name he knew on behalf of a meat-woman who was anonymous. Nice irony. He appreciated it.

He had several favoured ports into the Info-World. He usually sidestepped the dreamwelt sites that impressed the neos and plugged straight into streams of pure data, not even bothering with a customised simile. Most of the ghosts he had busted revealed too much about their meat-selves in their self-designed wish-fulfilment avatars. They all had an unhealthy preoccupation with self.

It always amazed him that the geek gunslingers were so locked into games-playing they never took in the view. It was like ignoring the stars. To him, the thrill was in the info landscape, the waves and currents and trends and collapses. He could endlessly access, anchored on a loose chain, becoming one with the world, letting it flow around and through him.

But this time, he wanted to seem like a neo.

He customised a ShadowShark and swam into dreamwelt through a Multi-User Carnival. It was a mixture of marketplace and playground, where the hustlers peddled surprise packages, containing either valuable gen or worthless tosh at the purchaser's risk, and the zap-heads conducted endless duels or orgies, getting in and out of the way.

Basically, it was a Dress-Up and Play Area.

To operate here, he not only needed to project a poseur's ident but also to intimate that there was a neo tosser at home, jacked into his parents' ports, belly bloated and limbs atrophied as he let the dreamwelt be more his home than the plush monad where he was meat-locked.

He morphed the ShadowShark from fishform to carform, and got out, wearing the distinctive cloak, mask, goggles and boots of Dr. Shade, the wholly-owned Leech International superhero. He had been fond of the Dr. Shade films as a kid, despite (or maybe because of) Mum's unaccountable loathing of them (and all other Leech efforts).

The Dr. Shade image was kiddie-cool enough to pass here. He had most of the heroes and heroines and gods and monsters who mingled in the carnival pegged as neo tossers. All womenshapes were Amazons with unfeasible breasts, and faces iconic of cool rebellion wandered by. Outlaws who coughed up registration fees and site subs. The Info-World welcomed phreaks and madpersons, but if you didn't pay your phone bill you were shut out, marooned forever in realwelt.

He was clever enough even to maintain a flimsy intermediate persona as "Jonathan Chambers", Dr. Shade's secret ident. If probed deeply, he'd pull out, leaving behind traces typical of a neo tosser.

As Dr. Shade, he slipped through the carnival.

The dreamwelt darkened. A pack of feral kids on armoured bikes wove in and out of the crowds, blasting each other and bystanders to fast-reforming pixel-clouds.

Fantasy figures exposed their assets in neon-lit windows, offering eighteen varieties of non-copyright sexual access. A lot of neos bankrupted their parents by letting their bar codes be read by the info-whores and compounding the fees to infinity.

As usual, this all seemed silly. But, as usual, it was a place to start.

He passed up all the offers of sex and slid into the darker streets where the snitches lurked. Info was air and water here, but could be bought and sold like anything else.

A news-blurt cut through the scene, shaking the overhanging eaves and the artfully strewn shadows. The dog story had escalated. Gunmints issued instructions for humane disposal of soon-to-be-dangerous companions or minions. Dreamwelt denizens were warned that if they were in a realwelt monad with a dog, they should jack out immediately and disable it. Horrorshow pics flashed: users yanked out of info jaunts by ripped-open throats.

The blurt finished. The alley scene settled.

There was a scuttle of snitches. Extending his shadowcloak, he netted the one he was after. She made a fluttering attempt to break free and graciously gave in, landing delicately on his palm.

"Hello, Tink," he said.

The cartoon fairy twinkled a greet.

Because J. M. Barrie had left the royalties on *Peter Pan* to Great Ormond Street Children's Hospital, and an Act of the Old Parliament extended that income in perpetuity, there was a copyright glitch. After the Mouse Wars, unlicensed McDisney avatars were purged from the Info-World, but the *Peter Pan* crew, with a few tiny alterations (the loss of the WMcD logo), were able to survive.

He had seen the loophole at the time and left it open. So Tinkerbelle owed him her dreamlife.

"What can you tell me about Seven Stars?"

The fairy buzzed and glowed like a tiny phosphor grenade and tried to get away.

"That tells me something," he said, in Dr. Shade's scary voice.

"It is foretold that the coming of the Seven Stars will bring about the Collapse," Tinkerbelle shrilled.

It was the Info-World's version of Armageddon. One big plug pulling, and global shrinkage to a dying white dot. Despite a million fail-safes, superstitions abounded, especially in the wake of the Vatican's Fall. There were always intimations of Collapse.

"Where can I find Seven Stars?"

"You can't," the fairy shrilled. "They find you. Then no one else does. Ever."

Tinkerbelle turned to a blip of light and vanished.

"But I believe in fairies," he declared.

Even here, removed from the actual, he heard the cacophony of dogs. The constant barking, breaking through all the mutes and muffles and soundproof shields, scraped his nerves.

* * *

"Mum," he said, "two names. Geneviève Dieudonné. Mimsy Mountmain."

Sally, his mother, looked distracted.

A lot of dog noise came over the comm-link. She lived in a country retirement site, where animals were a special feature.

But the names clicked.

Sally Rhodes stopped moving about the room and stood so the reader could fix her image. He adjusted the projection, so her three-dimensional bust—solid and flesh-tone, though with the telltale hologram sparkle—sat on his desk.

She had cut her hair and let it go grey. Her face was unlined, without the benefit of a skin-stretch.

She made a kiss-mouth and he touched his lips to the tridvid image. They both laughed.

Then his mother nodded him to sit back.

"I tried to find Mimsy Mountmain once, for her mother. And for someone else. Her mother was killed before I could get anywhere. I was paid off. Case closed. As far as I know, the blasted girl never did show up."

"And Geneviève?"

"She was part of it. She was also looking for Mimsy."

"She still is. At least, someone with her name. Actually, it can't be the same woman."

"Blonde, looks about sixteen, slightly French accent, stays out of the sun, old-fashioned girl outfits?"

"Sounds like her."

"If it is, give her my love. It's unfinished business. I'm sorry I'm out of it."

"So am I."

"Nonsense. You need to be on your own."

"How did you meet Geneviève?"

"She accosted me. In Pall Mall."

Mum pronounced it the old way.

"Snap," he said.

"I was looking for something called the Diogenes Club. They were out of business, but involved with whatever Mimsy Mountmain was up to. It went back years."

"The Diogenes Club?"

"That's right. Neil dug up some stuff on them. Nothing useful, as usual."

Jerome wondered about it. He said goodbye.

"Give yourself my love too," said Mum.

"I will. And mine to you."

They "kissed" again, and cut the link.

There was shooting outside. Not a running battle, as there had been briefly three years ago in the last of the Religious Wars. This time, it was a succession of single-shots.

Jerome turned the window on and scanned Upper Street. Men in armour dealt with dogs. They used jolt-guns, one charge to the back of the skull. A cleanup krewe followed, collecting the corpses. A lot of the dogs trailed leashes, and all had collar controls. Some unpersons harassed the pest officers. The dog story was stepping up, as if the unheard sound had become shriller, more maddening. Other species with canine levels of pitch were getting agitated.

Warnings were posted against approaching or sheltering affected animals. A raft of human interest stories offered cautionary tales of children ripped by loved family companions. Clinically blind people mind-linked to seeing-eye dogs reported that their skulls were ringing with sound, and censor blotches on the reports suggested not a few of them had become dangerous and were being treated like the street packs.

Over and over, news-streams emphasised that this was a global phenomenon. Global.

How many dogs were there in the world? Including wolves.

His teeth were on edge. He imagined he could sense the unheard sound. His eyeballs sang silently.

Did everybody feel this?

He didn't feel like comm-linking around his associates, and asking. There were thousands of mushroom sites on the dog story. Mediamass obscured any useful gen. It would take a while to purge the extremists and for a sensible centre position to coalesce. In the meantime, stay-at-homes were staying put, and get-abouts were accepting restrictions. Suggested codes of practice for travel in cities and designated country sites.

An across-bands newsblurt cut in. A major announcement was imminent on the dog story. He knew that meant a thirty-second deep-core ad probe was coming. He tore out his earpiece and hummed the Anvil Chorus with fingers stuck in both ears. He did not need to be infected with psycho-dependency on some new flavour of echt burger.

Then he tuned in again. Seven Stars was claiming responsibility. The ghost's message concluded with: "For the dogs, it will end soon."

A scramble of experts got on-stream and began pouring opinion and speculation onto the maelstrom. He jacked out of all access and tried to think.

When one of his deep-level search engines paid off, Jerome thought somebody must be extracting the urine.

He had an address for Mimsy Mountmain. She was supposed to be a terminal stay-at-home, a shut-in on life support. She was maintained in the Mall. His client had met him outside the building in which his quarry lived.

The dog story was a constant distraction. It was hard to hack through to info that concerned him. The dog story criss-crossed and trailed over every other pathway. It had been the same during the Religious Wars.

Emergency legislation was being passed, globally. Dog ownership was now illegal. There were painless extermination programs. Some of the more liberal sub-gunmints were merely interning the animals and working on a "cure".

Not having a dog, Jerome didn't care. The dog story just got in the way.

He was increasingly spooked.

He tried to get back in touch with Geneviève, but there was no back-up listing for the Brixton address she had given him as her piedater. The node they had used as a comm-link was discontinued and the charges for its creation and dissolution all laid to his account.

He had let her see his bar-code. She must have some sort of hidden reader, maybe an Eyeball.

It turned out that his client was the ghost.

He had seen her in the meat. She was real, not a projection of some unknown veg like Tinkerbelle.

And now she was gone.

As Dr. Shade, he was back in the carnival. The party seemed to be slowing down. Somehow, the dog story was throwing the Info-World into turmoil. It happened like that. Mammoth realwelt events made users jack out for once, depopulated the dataways. Fine. That made it easier.

Now, he was looking for Geneviève Dieudonné.

1893–1962 wasn't her. 1416–1432, though. There was something in that equation. That Geneviève didn't get to be older than his seemed to be.

What about 1902 and 1942?

He glided through archive sites, shadowcloak passing over icons and portals. Few came here but academic researchers. The neos were only interested in the now, the crashing wave of the present. And vastcorps employed balanced factions of muck-raking exposé merchants and raking-over cover-up krewes.

He moved into the past, down an almost-empty conduit. Similes of buildings lined the way, in regressing architectural styles, each with foundation stones giving away the year. The buildings housed the records.

Geneviève had yielded too few mentions. So he had to trawl wider. He had set up search engines to look for the Diogenes Club. Most of them crashed against security barriers, alerting all kinds of official warnings. He had received desist notices, but no enforcement operatives were coming at him, from inside or outside the Info-World. Regulation boards were too busy with the dog story.

During a crisis, there was a window of opportunity.

He fought against déjà vu, as he stood outside the simile of the building he had seen in realwelt yesterday morning. Then, he had just wondered why it hadn't been gutted for stores. Now, he knew it had significance.

There was even a simile of the bench where he had met his client. An information package lay on it, tied up with a big blue bow.

He looked at the gift. It could easily be a trap. He opened the package. Inside was a key-string. He ran the string through the swipe-slot, and the front door of the Diogenes Club opened.

Inside, the quality of the mimesis upgraded. As Dr. Shade, he entered a gentleman's club. He heard a rustle of newspapers, the discreet footsteps of servants. He smelled various types of tobacco smoke and the old leather of the clubroom chairs.

An attendant ushered him upstairs.

The Chambers of the Ruling Cabal were derelict. Cobwebs wound over everything, spun between chairs and tables and desks and map stands. He walked through the webs without breaking strands. Everything sparkled slightly.

The darkness dispelled as someone turned up a gas lamp. It was a well-wrapped mummy, androgynous in form, adept in movement. The mummy's eyes flickered. They were tiny screens. Red figures scrolled down.

There were others. A dog-headed man, in a broad Ancient Egyptian collar. The actor, John Barrymore. A swaddled invalid in a cocoon-like wheelchair, her head supported by a leather brace. And a red entity, a gemstone which shone with the light of stars.

Seven Stars.

Of course, all these were avatars of one person. One intelligence. He took off his goggles, and let his simile resemble himself.

"We understand you're out of pocket," Barrymore said. "You've been the victim of a prank."

"I was sent to find someone who seems not to be lost."

All the faces of Seven Stars smiled at once. Even the jewel.

"We're in a position to compensate you, and to prosecute your interests. To turn your commission around, we'd be willing to pay you well to find out the whereabouts of your former employer, the undead Mademoiselle Dieudonné."

"Interesting," he said.

He had a realwelt address. His mother's paper records were still in the firm's vault, and it had only taken an hour or so to find the notes Neil had deposited after the abandonment of the 1998 investigation. There, on headed notepaper, in a fine hand, was a personal thank you note, signed *Gené*. Without accessing the Info-World, he had

confirmed that the address—a suite at a private hotel in Kensington—
was still occupied. It was a throwback to his mother's type of
detective work. He didn't even allow himself to make comm-links,
for they contrailed through the InfoWorld, flagging themselves. He
used printed-out directories and walked across the city, avoiding
dogs and euthanasia krewes, to ask questions of a human desk clerk.

The hotel was off-record. Jerome worked out it had been
bought—for cash—around the turn of the century. A phantom
access signature implied it to be the property of a deceased lady
named Catriona Kaye, run by a permanent trust administered by a
firm of lawyers, kept open in accordance with Miss Kaye's will.

Actually, it was a hidey-hole.

Invisible to the Info-World, it was a vampire's coffin.

He couldn't even claim credit for brilliant analysis. Geneviève
had given him her address—the note, dated 1998, even mentioned
him—and all he had done was confirm it.

"For Mam'selle Dieudonné's location, we will pay a sum equivalent
to your aggregate earnings over the last five years."

This came from the mummy.

That flagged it. He was almost but not quite annoyed enough at
Geneviève to turn her over.

But the comm-link gave it away.

"I'll think about it," he told the Seven Stars. "It'll take time to get
and confirm the info you want."

"Very well, you have one hour."

Jerome jacked out and cut access.

The realwelt rung with the sounds of dying dogs.

He was shocked. The sudden withdrawal from the dreamwelt
was a heart-kicker, advised against by all help programs. But the
realisation had been jolt enough.

He had nearly been gulled.

Now, he had to get across realwelt London. There was a severe
curfew in force. All people-transport services, above and below
ground, were suspended. Groups of dog-lovers had banded together
to resist the extermination krewes, augmented by unpersons ready
to riot for any cause, and there were outbreaks of fighting in St.

James's Park and Oxford Street. He would have to get round that.

He could not drive, because he'd have to log a route plan in his auto's master program, and that would register in the Info-World. In the basement, he still had the last of the bikes he had pedalled through childhood. His dad, dead before he was born, had been a cycle messenger, and he'd felt that in pumping along tracks or out on the road he was sending out an "I Am Here" notice to the Beyond, paying tribute in his own way to the man he had never known.

In his mind, he mapped a route, zip-zagging around trouble spots, with a few tricky double-backs to throw off anyone who might be following.

Before he stepped onto Upper Street, he took out his earpiece and left it on the table beside the door. He checked himself for any other devices with Info-World signatures.

This was like being forced to walk after learning to fly. But doing without the wings made sense.

He cycled down the street. All the surviving dogs of London were howling. He recalled an early-century saying, one Neil had been fond of: Real is real.

She was waiting for him outside the hotel, hair shining with sun, unafraid of the rays. His heart sank and he searched himself. "Real is real," she said, almost apologising.

She wasn't wearing the hat, cloak and eyeshade today. That had almost been a Dr. Shade outfit, he realised.

"We had real people following you, not just search engines."

"Then you knew, when you asked for the address . . ."

"We just wanted to see if you fit the pattern. We've met a series of people like you. Almost a family tree. We've learned to appreciate you. You've fed into us."

"You're not Geneviève?"

She shook her head.

"No. Of course not. Though I do look like her. She wasn't my father or my mother, but she left something of herself in my mother, something that shaped me."

"You're talking in the singular."

"About Mimsy, yes. I am Mimsy."

He had been right. Too late.

"But *we* are Seven Stars."

"Is there a Geneviève?"

"Yes. She's inside. Upstairs."

He turned to go into the hotel.

"By the way," Mimsy said, "beware of the dogs."

The howling of all the dogs in London came from inside the hotel. A helmeted body lay jammed halfway out of the revolving door, protective clothing shredded.

Using a side-door, he got into the lobby and found the rest of a euthanasia krewe along with dogs alive and dead. He snatched up a jolt-gun and found it uncharged. Mimsy followed him. Indoors, she still shone. A red light, centred in her chest, radiated through transparent flesh and thin fabric. Star-points glinted, hard chips in the softer light. She was difficult to look at directly.

The dogs ignored her, but came for him.

They were too caught up in their own pain to concentrate on savaging him, but he still took too many nips and bites as he waded up the main stairs.

He threw dogs away.

On the first-floor landing, a giant Rottweiler, augmented as a guard minion, snarled at him. Its teeth were steel, probably envenomed. Veins stood out on its bulbous forehead. Its eyes were maddened red jelly.

He tensed, expecting a final attack.

Something burst inside the dog's skull. Grey gruel squeezed out of its eyesockets. It fell like an unstrung puppet.

He could almost hear the killing sound. His regrown front tooth ached. The plates of his skull ground against each other. Pressure built up inside his ears, producing pain in the drums and all the spaces of his head, throbbing under his cheekbones, around his eyes, at the base of his brain.

Dogs pawed towards him and fell. Skulls detonated like bombs, spraying blood and brain matter across faded floral wallpaper.

He took hold of the bannister and hauled himself up to the next landing. Mimsy skipped up beside him, unaffected. She had the mummy's red eyescreens. That avatar had been closest to her.

"This is just the first of them," she told him. "The new plagues. This is the curse of dogs."

The main door of the suite was open. A man lay dead in it. He wore a black single-piece suit and had the sign of the Seven Stars on his forehead. His throat had been torn out by some animal a little daintier than a dog. Neat slices opened his veins.

"One of mine," Mimsy admitted. "The old girl still has some bite."

He tried to equalise the pressure in his head, opening his mouth and forcing a desperate yawn. It helped momentarily.

"Don't worry," Mimsy said. "The plague will soon be over."

She picked up a frothing Pekingese and chucked its chin. The little dog's skull pulsed like a hatching egg. She pointed it away from her, and the dog's eyes shot out on geysers of liquid brain.

"Ugh," she said, dropping the dead thing.

He stepped over the man's body.

On a curtained four-poster bed was Mimsy's transformed twin. This was the real Geneviève, arced like a bow, clawed fingers and toes hooked into torn bedclothes. She lashed from side to side, whipping long hair. Her bloody mouth was full of swollen fang teeth. Her eyes were red, but not with an LED light.

Veins in her temples were swelling. "She's not human, poor love," Mimsy said. "She can hear things dogs can."

Jerome wanted to go over to the bed but Geneviève snarled at him to stay away. He minded she didn't trust herself not to strike out at him.

"If she isn't human, what are you?"

"Oh, I'm completely human," Mimsy said.

"You singular. What about you plural?"

"Seven Stars," she said, pulling down her neckline to show the red light burning under her ribs. It grew in intensity, as the unheard noise grew.

The cries of the dogs were cutting off, one by one.

Small objects on a bedside table rattled. Vibrations throbbed through Jerome, through the hotel, the city, the world.

Mimsy's flesh parted as the jewel rose to the surface. It climbed up into the base of her throat. It seemed to be talking.

"We are come from afar," it said. "We are the Plague Bringer."

For the last time, Mimsy spoke. "Just think," she said, "within a minute, dogs will be an extinct species. And vampires."

The howling had all but stopped.

The dogs were all dead. All over the world, dogs' brains burst in their heads.

Jerome ran to the bed and took Geneviève's hand. He was not surprised at the ferocity of her grip. He looked into her red eyes, hoping for an answer.

The thing that walked around in Mimsy Mountmain's body filled the room with red light.

Geneviève's eyes started from their sockets.

He *could* hear the maddening sub-audial whine now.

Cracks in Geneviève's forehead spread away from her temples, leaking thin blood, snaking up into her hair. Her mouth was open in a tooth-ringed circle.

"You're Jerome," she said, through agony. "You are all that's left."

Bloody tears the size of beetles crawled from her eyes, ears and nose. *1416–2025?*

She sat up in bed, a final jolt of killing current shot through her. Her head came apart with a crack. Bloody hair whipped him across the face and she was a limp doll.

The whine cut off, leaving a gaping silence.

In that silence, a world was left mad.

He turned, seeing red. Seven Stars walked out of the room.

Lawrence Talbot

BAY WOLF
by NEIL GAIMAN

Lawrence Talbot is, of course, the name of the character played by Lon Chaney, Jr. in the 1941 Universal movie The Wolf Man *and its sequels,* Frankenstein Meets the Wolf Man *(1943),* House of Frankenstein *(1944),* House of Dracula *(1945) and the Abbott and Costello spoof,* Meet Frankenstein *(1948).*

In the first film Talbot, the second son of a titled European family, returns to his ancestral estate situated in a distinctly Hollywood version of Wales. Mourning the death of his elder brother, Talbot is welcomed back by his father, Sir John (Claude Rains). However, when Larry attempts to save a local village girl from an attack by a gypsy werewolf, he is bitten by the beast before clubbing it to death with his silver-headed walking stick.

Now cursed himself, Larry soon realises that even a man who is pure in heart can become a wolf when the wolfbane blooms and the moon is full and bright . . .

Neil Gaiman's "Adjustor", Lawrence Talbot, was introduced in 'Only the End of the World Again' in the anthology Shadows Over Innsmouth *(1994). A Lovecraftian tale of detection and Deep Ones, only Talbot's lycanthropic private investigator could prevent the return of the Elder Gods. In the prose poem that follows, he once again confronts a modern mythological monster.*

Listen, Talbot. Somebody's killing my people,
said Roth, growling down the phone like the sea in a shell.
Find out who and why and stop them.

Stop them how? I asked.

Whatever it takes, he said. *But I don't want them walking away,*
after you stopped them, if you get me.
And I got him. So I was hired.

Now you listen: This was back in the twenty-twenties
in LaLaLand, down on Venice Beach.
Gar Roth owned the business in that part of world,
dealt in stims and pumps and steroids,
recreationals, built up quite a following:
all the buff kids, boys in thongs popping pumpers,
girls popping curves and fearmoans and whoremoans,
all of them loved Roth. He had the shit.
The force took his payoffs to look the other way
he owned the beach world, from Laguna Beach north to Malibu,
built a beach hall where the buff and the curvy hung and sucked
     and flaunted.

Oh, but that city worshipped the flesh: and theirs was the flesh.
They were partying. Everyone was partying:
dusted, shot up, cranked out,
the music was so loud you could hear it with your bones,
and that was when something took them, quietly,
whatever it was. It cracked their heads. It tore them,
     left them offal.
No one heard the screams over the boom of the oldies
     and the surf—
that was the year of the Death Metal revival—
It took maybe a dozen of them away, dragged them into the sea,
death in the early morning.
Roth said he thought it was a rival drug cartel,
posted more guards, had choppers circling, floaters watching for

440

when it came back. As it did: again, again.
But the cameras and the vids showed nothing at all.

They had no idea what it was, but still,
it ripped them limb from limb and head from neck,
tore saline bags out from ballooning breasts,
left steroid-shrunken testes on the beach,
like tiny world-shaped creatures in the sand.
Roth had been hurt: the beach was not the same,
and that was when he called me on the phone.

I stepped over several sleeping cuties of all sexes,
tapped Roth on the shoulder. Before I could blink
a dozen big guns were pointing at my chest and head,
so I said *Hey, I'm not a monster. Well, I'm not*
     your monster, anyway. Not yet.

I handed him my card. *Talbot*, he said.
You're the adjuster I spoke to?
That's right, I told him, tough-talking in the afternoon,
and you got stuff that needs adjusting.
This is the deal, I said,
I take your problem out. You pay and pay and pay.

Roth said *Sure, like we said. Whatever. Deal.*
Me? I'm thinking it's the Eurisraeli mafia,
or the Chinks. You scared of them?

No, I told him. *I'm not scared at all.*

I kind of wished I'd been there in the glory days:
Now Roth's pretty people were getting kind of thin on the ground,
none of them, close up,
were as plump and curvy as they'd seemed from up the beach.

At dusk the party starts.
I tell Roth that I had hated Death Metal the first time round.

He says I must be older than I look.
They play real loud. The speakers make the seashore
    pump and thrum.

I strip down then for action and I wait
on four legs, in the hollow of a dune.
And days and nights I wait. And wait. And wait.

Where the fuck are you and your people?
asked Roth on the third day. *What the fuck am I paying you for?*
Nothing on the beach last night but some big dog.
But I just smiled. *No sign of the problem so far,*
    whatever it is, I said.
And I've been here all the time.
I tell you it's the Israeli Mafia, he said.
I never trusted those Europeans.

Third night comes.
The moon is huge and a chemical red.
Two of them are playing in the surf
boy and girl play,
the hormones still a little ahead of the drugs. She's giggling,
and the surf crashes slowly.
It would be suicide, if the enemy came every night.
But the enemy does not come every night,
    so they run through the surf,
splashing, screaming with pleasure. I got sharp ears
(all the better to hear them with) and good eyes
(all the better to see them with)
and they're so fucking young and happy fucking I could spit.

The hardest thing, for such a one as me:
the gift of death should go to such as these.
She screamed first. The red moon was high
    and just a day past full.
I watched her tumble into the surf, as if
the water were twenty feet deep, not two,

as if she were being sucked under. The boy just ran,
a stream of clear piss splashing gold from the jut in his speedos,
stumbling he ran, and wailing and away.

It came out of the water slowly, like a man in
    bad monster-movie make-up.
It carried the bronzed girl in its arms. I yawned
like big dogs yawn and licked my flanks.

The creature bit the girl's face off,
dropped what was left upon the sand,
and I thought: *meat and chemicals, how quickly they become*
meat and chemicals just one bite and they're
meat and chemicals . . .

Roth's men came down then, with fear in their eyes,
automatic weapons in their hands. It picked them up
and ripped them open, dropped them on the moonlit sand.

The thing walked stiffly up the beach, white sand adhering
to its greengrey feet, webbed and clawed.
Top of the world, Ma, it howled.
What kind of mother, I wondered, gives birth to
    something like that?
And from high on the beach I could hear Roth
    screaming *Talbot,*
Talbot you asshole, where are you?

I got up and stretched, and loped naked down the beach.
Well, hi, I said.
Hey pooch, he said. *I'm gonna rip*
your hairy leg right off and push it down your throat.
That's no way to say hi I told him.
I'm Grand Al, said the monster. *And who are you?*
Jojo the yapping dogfaced boy?
I'm going to whip and rip and tear you into shit.

Avaunt, foul beast, I said.
He stared at me with eyes that glittered like two crackpipes
Avaunt? Shit, boy: Who's going to make me?
Me, I quipped. *I am.*
I'm one of the avaunt guard.
He just looked blank, and hurt, a bit confused, and
for a moment I almost felt sorry for him.

And then the moon comes out from behind a cloud,
and I begin to howl.

His skin was fish-skin pale
His teeth were sharp as sharks'
His fingers were webbed and clawed,
And, growling, he went for my throat.

And he said *what are you?*
he said *ow, no, ow*
he said, *Hey, shit, this isn't fair,*
then he said nothing at all, not words now,
no more words, because I had ripped off his arm,
left it, fingers spastically clutching nothing,
on the beach.

Grand Al ran for the waves, and I loped after him.
The waves were salt: his blood stank,
I could taste it, black in my mouth.

He swam, and I followed, down and down,
and when I felt my lungs bursting
the world crushing my throat and head and mind and chest,
dark monsters turning to suffocate me,
we came into the tumbled wreckage of an offshore oil-rig
and that was where Grand Al had gone to die.

This must have been the place that he was spawned
this rusting rig abandoned, half-in, half-out the sea.

He was three-quarters dead when I arrived. At first
I kept my distance: weird fishy food he would have been,
a dish of stray prions. Dangerous meat. And then,
I kicked him in the jaw, stole one shark-like tooth
that I'd knocked loose, to bring me luck.
She came upon me then, all fang and claw.

Why should it be so strange that the beast had a mother?
So many of us have mothers.
Go back fifty years and everyone had a mother.

She wailed for her son, she wailed and keened.
She asked me how I could be so unkind.
She squatted, stroked his face, and then she groaned.
After, we spoke, hunting for common ground.

What we did is no business of yours.
It was no more than you and I have done before,
And whether I loved her or I killed her,
her son was dead as the Gulf.

Rolling, pelt to scales,
her neck between my teeth,
my claws raking her back . . .

Lalalalalala. This is the oldest song.

Later, I walked out of the surf.
Roth was waiting in the dawn.
I dropped Grand Al's head down upon the beach,
fine white sand clung in clumps to the wet eyes.

This was your problem, I told him.
Yeah, he's dead, I said.
And now? he asked.

Danegeld, I told him.

You think he was working for the Chinks? he asked.
Or the Eurisraeli mafia? Or who?
He was a neighbour, I said. *Wanted you to keep the noise down.*
You think? he said.
I know, I told him, looking at the head.
Where did he come from? asked Roth.
I pulled my clothes on, tired from the change.
Meat and chemicals, I whispered.
He knew I lied, but wolves are born to lie.
I sat down on the beach to watch the bay,
stared at the sky as dawn turned into day.

And dreamed about the day I too should die.

Geneviève Dieudonné
SEVEN STARS EPISODE SEVEN

THE DUEL OF SEVEN STARS
by KIM NEWMAN

French-born Geneviève Dieudonné was the daughter of a physician during the Hundred Years War. Turned by the Dark Kiss of Gilles Chandagnac, she is now a vampire of a different breed.

The first version of the character, Geneviève Sandrine du Pointe du Lac Dieudonné, appeared in Kim Newman's Warhammer books Drachenfels *(1989)*, Beasts in Velvet *(1991)*, Genevieve Undead *(1993)*, Silver Nails *(2002) and the omnibus* The Vampire Genevieve *(2005).*

The second—and most realised—is Geneviève Sandrine d'Isle Dieudonné. She is a major character in Anno Dracula *(1992)*, Dracula Cha Cha Cha *(1999) and* Johnny Alucard *(2013).*

The Geneviève who appears in 'Seven Stars' is Genèvieve Sandrine Ysolde Dieudonné. She is also featured in the stories 'The Big Fish' (Interzone #76, 1993 and Shadows Over Innsmouth, *1994), 'Cold Snap' (The Secret Files of the Diogenes Club, 2007) and 'Sorcerer Conjuror Wizard Witch' (Mysteries of the Diogenes Club, 2010).*

If anyone is paying attention, they all have different middle names. There's also another one in 'In the Air', a story in Eugene Byrne and Newman's Back in the USSA *(1997).*

As the author readily admits, he is playing the old Michael

Moorcock multiverse game of examining the alternate lives of all his characters in vastly or subtly different worlds. The multi-part 'Seven Stars' is an attempt to thread as much of it together as possible, as is his multiple choice novel, Life's Lottery *(1998).*

THE SHOCK OF death. Is it greater for her, after so long? Despite what the records say, she didn't quite die in her sixteenth year. She just stopped being human. The young man holds her. She wants his blood.

The noise in her skull cuts off. A red fringe flops over her eyes. The pain ends.

Nothing.

A frozen moment. In a museum. Looking at a man looking at a mummy. His face reflected in the glass of the display case. Hers not. But he senses her, turns. Thinks about her. For a moment.

In another life . . .

Geneviève Sandrine Ysolde Dieudonné. Geneviève the Undying, daughter of the physician Benoit Dieudonné, daughter-in-darkness of Chandagnac, of the bloodline of Melissa d'Acques.

For her, it is over.

She is in darkness, unfeeling. She might be in woman-shape. Or something immobile, a sarsen stone, a tree. She sees nothing, but she senses.

There are others. Not waiting for her, but accepting her, recognising her.

Five others.

She knows they were once living too. And in that moment of knowing, she accepts her final death. The five are now six. They reach for her, not physically. She knows them, but their names do not come to mind.

Neither does her own.

Together, the six shine. At last, she knows perfect love.

Not yet complete, though. The Six must become Seven. Lucky Number Seven.

Then . . .

* * *

Red light.

Consciousness resumes, continues. She can think, remember, picture herself, imagine a world beyond. She has a sense of her body. There is still pain, and warmth.

She is not dead. Not any more. She is alone. Her five companions are gone. Bereft, her heart aches. A tear gathers in her eye.

Blood trickles into her mouth. Young blood, rich, peppery. It flows through her, bringing a jolt of wakefulness. Her teeth sharpen against her tongue. More blood is spilled onto her lips. She licks, red thirst alive, and feels strength growing.

Her night-senses come alive. She is acutely aware of the roughness of the cotton shift she is wearing, and of the scents that cling to it.

Hospital smells sting her.

She cannot sit. Her head is fixed in place by a contraption of steel clamps and plastic tubes. She swivels her eyes, and sees fluid flowing through the tubes, into her.

There is an alien object inside. Where the last pain was, she senses an inorganic plate, patching over the ruin of her burst skull.

She tries to raise a hand to her head. She is restrained, by a durable plastic cuff. She tries harder, and the plastic snaps.

Someone takes her hand.

"Getting your strength back, I see."

Alarms sound.

"You're in the Pyramid," the young man tells her. He is not a doctor. His face is familiar. "In London Docklands, what's left of it. The Derek Leech International Building. Some of the staff call it the Last Redoubt."

The young man is Jerome, Sally Rhodes's son.

He was there when she died.

Judging by the changes in his face, that must have been years ago.

"How long . . .?"

"Seven months."

She sits up in bed.

"You've missed a ton," he says. "The Plagues. The Wars. The Collapse."

She holds her head.

Her hair is close-cropped, for the first time in centuries.

"I think it's snazz," Jerome says. "You look like Joan of Arc."

"Good God, I hope not."

She remembers Jeanne d'Arc. It was during her war that Geneviève received the Dark Kiss, became a vampire. There was blood all around. She feels the back of her skull, fingertips pressing the skin over the plate.

"I don't understand what Leech's doctors did," Jerome says. "I've still not really scanned the info that there are such things as vampires."

"Sorry," she shrugs.

"Not your fault. Any rate, you're back from the dead. Leech says it's magic and medicine. You weren't properly alive, so it was easier to bring you back than it'd have been if you were . . . um?"

"A real live girl?"

"Yes, well, exactly. You were put back together months ago, but the hardest part was what Leech calls 'summoning you up'. Getting you to move back in, as it were. He's had a team of spooks—mediums, mages, nutters—working on it. In the end, I think he did it himself, reached out into the wherever and dragged you back. All this is new ground to me."

"Me too," she admits, again fingering her skull, gliding fingertips over her fur.

"Do you want a mirror? The scars on your head are healing. And you have none on your face."

"A mirror would be no good to me. They don't take."

Jerome goggles. She catches a little of his amazement, and sees herself through his eyes, alarmingly tiny in a big bed, face small and pretty on an egg of a head.

"I gave blood," he confesses, shyly.

"I know," she replies, taking his hand.

Things have changed while she was away. The boiling point of water is now 78°. That was the effect popularly known as the Plague of Fire. Around the world, spontaneous combustion is a general hazard, and this past summer has seen the uncontrolled burning of much surviving forested land and not a few townships and cities.

Monsters have come out of the sea, just as in the films of the 1950s, and devastated conurbations. That was the Plague of Dragons, though most called it the Plague of Godzillas. There are other natural catastrophes: insects have predictably run rampant again. Of course, with the interconnectedness of everything, it is hard to distinguish a genuine plague from a side-effect like war, famine, mass psychosis and post-millennial panic.

The Plague of Babel ended electronic communications. It did not shut down the Information World, as the Collapse Theorists prophesied, but habitually scrambles three out of every four transactions, providing convincing but fabricated images as well as texts and sound effects. Many of the scrambles are just garbage, but some are malicious. Economic and military wars have been triggered by caprice.

An Empire is falling. And the Emperor has busied himself not with shoring up the barricades but with engineering her resurrection.

She wonders why Derek Leech cares so much about her.

"You are familiar with the suppressed quatrains of Nostradamus?"

"Of course."

"In 1942, one of them led you to the Seven Stars."

"I didn't see it. The gumshoe did."

"Michel was sadly given to obscurity."

"I often wondered why he never predicted anything happy. Or world-changing in a trivial sense. Elvis's appearance on the *Ed Sullivan Show*. The discovery of penicillin."

Leech does not smile.

He is seeing her in his office at the apex of the Pyramid. Through the tinted screen-windows, the fires ravaging the city are crimson carpet patches. Black gargantuoids, lizard-tails whipping, sumo-wrestle in the burning ruins.

Banks of screens are grey and dead. This is the central node of a global net of information-flow, the heart of an electronic Yggdrasil that has bound together humanity and subjugated them to a man-shaped creature. It is just a room full of obsolete junk.

A few—Jerome's mother, for one—had protested that Leech's increasing dominion of the world reduced people to components in a global device, locked into cell-like monads, consuming garbage info, indentured spectators and consumers.

Under Derek Leech, history became soap.

When Edwin Winthrop allowed the Jewel of Seven Stars to be focused against the Axis Powers and their Ancient Masters, he smashed Empires but dipped his hands in blood. The trust handed down to him was subtly betrayed, a chink was opened in the world, and through that chink had squeezed Derek Leech.

Now, the Seven Stars rain plagues on Leech.

She should be happier.

The plagues come too late, when Leech's Pyramid is at the top of the world. They flow down the black glass sides of this building and spread out to the corners of the map.

This is the end, she thinks.

Leech takes a book from his desk. It is the only book she has seen in the Pyramid. Though access to electronic information is compromised, there is not a general falling-back to print or scribbled memos. Paper, its combustion point lowered from Bradbury's 451, is a hazard.

"During the late War, you were allowed access to only the quatrains relevant to the short term. Edwin Winthrop kept a lot from you, but a lot was kept from him. His ultimate part in all this, for instance. And yours."

He has her attention.

At a touch, he untints the glass. The fires leap up in vividity. Even the eyes of the battling beasts now burn like unhealthy neons.

In the sky, the moon is blood-red. And Ursa Major is missing.

"This is *wrong*," Leech says. "Whatever you think of the world you left, this is not an acceptable alternative."

She has to agree.

"The old world, things as they were before, can be bought back."

"Brought back?"

"No, *bought*. Everything is economics. Things can be as they were, according to Nostradamus, with seven lives twice-lost. Seven dead will return to the Earth, and die again. You are the first, and through

452

you the other six will be gathered. There is a death beyond death."

"I don't fear it."

Everyone asks her what it was like. She hasn't able to explain.

"I envy you, Geneviève. You know things I will never access. I must content myself with everything else."

"So, when it's over, you'll rule in Hell?"

"That, sadly, Nostradamus is silent on."

"Ain't it just the way?"

"Indeed."

In the heart of the Pyramid, she is ushered into an orrery, one of Leech's famous magical devices. A globe of interlocking brass and copper and steel partial spheres, gimballed like a giant gyroscope, it is a schematic of the solar system. It is an impressive bit of clockwork, but here is just a focus.

Leech has offered to dress the process up with ritual and chanting. Blood sacrifices, if necessary. But it is down to her to reach out, to travel back to the sphere from which he summoned her, to reach her companions. If they are brought to this world, they will be the Seven, who alone—according to Mad Michel—can check the unleashed plagues of the Seven Stars.

She has not told Leech that there are, by her reckoning, only Six Samurai. After all, de Nostre-Dame—whom she now regrets not visiting personally when she was a vigorous 150 and giving his throat a good wringing—is often only ball-park accurate.

One thing in the cards is that she alone will survive the coming Duel of the Seven Stars. She has already died twice—her change from human to vampire counts—and so she alone of the Merry Band has already paid her due and will live on, to see what Leech makes of the world and, unless she misses her guess, to do her best to see it isn't as dire as it might be.

The Seventh of her Circle bothers her. Does his or her absence invalidate the whole quatrain?

Damn all cloudy prophets and smug seers. Cassandra didn't get half the kicking she deserved.

She becomes the Sun, taking her seat in the centre of the orrery.

"I shall try to shine," she announces.

* * *

Leech isn't here, though she knows he must be watching over her from somewhere. He is a creature of the eaves, peering out of the darkness, a cosmic couch potato. Technicians of enchantment, plastic young women she thinks of as attendant demons, work the levers. And Jerome, another loose component in this clanking magical machine. If this is for anyone, it is for him. In honour of his mother.

She shuts herself down.

The orrery revolves.

Her five companions expect her. They have been incomplete. She is the pathway. Through her, they channel themselves. She senses more. Scraps of lives lost. Some familiar to her, some strange. As one, they dwindle into reality.

The orrery concludes its cycle.

She pulls herself out of the contraption, brain a-swarm with trace memories. The phenomenon is more acute than the mostly random mind-link she has with those living whose blood she has taken. It's like sharing skull-space with strangers.

"She's alone," a woman says. "It's over. We've failed."

"No," says Jerome. "Not yet."

Jerome helps her stand. He looks into her eyes.

Now, at last, the Circle is complete.

The red thirst comes upon her like a raging wave. Her fang teeth sprout like bone-knives. The strangers in her skull add to her need.

"Leech said a blood sacrifice would complete the forging of the Circle," Jerome whispers, popping his collar-seam. "Take me."

Her predator's lizard-like brainstem overrides all civilised restraint. In this state, she has no conscience, no personality, no qualms. She has only red thirst. She is a blood junkie, the worst sort of vampire bitch.

Her mouth fastens on Jerome's throat in urgent rape. She bites into his jugular vein, tearing through the skin and meat, and sucks in the great gouts of blood.

She feels his heartbeat under her hand.

His blood pours into her, along with much else. His mind is sucked entirely into hers, jostling with the other strangers. Chunks of stringy meat-stuff cram into her throat. She swallows and expands.

This is Geneviève, the Monster.

She sucks desperately until his heart is still and her body is bloated with blood.

She can not absorb all she has taken. Her mouth is full, her cheeks swollen.

This has happened before, three times in 600 years. These are her most shameful secrets, the unwilling sacrifices she has taken to ensure her continuance. She tells herself the red thirst is irresistible, like a possessing spirit, but that is a rationalisation. At bottom, she is convinced that she can will herself not to kill. She does not do so, through choice. She lets the lizard-stem take over.

Whether Jerome is a willing sacrifice or not, she has sinned again. She has lost something of herself. It is too late to give him the Dark Kiss, to bring him back as a vampire. He is dead, drained meat.

The attendant demons are appalled, and stay back, afraid she will turn on them. The strangers in her skull, blooded, are growing. They speak to her, like the voices that bothered Jeanne d'Arc.

"Soon, soon, soon," they whisper.

Four men, one woman.

No. Five men, one woman.

They are Seven. As predicted.

She is heavy, full to bursting, belly bloated, throat stretched like a snake's. The taste of blood is ecstasy on her tongue. At her feet lie Jerome's clothes. He is gone from them. Without his blood and his ghost, the meat has dissolved completely. His whole substance is in her.

"*Now,*" they cry, with one voice.

She opens her mouth, and a cloud of red matter explodes from her, pouring into the air.

Six shapes resolve in the cloud of bloody ectoplasm. The first is a thin, brown man with an open wound in his chest. He wears a classical garment and Ancient Egyptian court headdress. This, Geneviève knows, is Pai-net'em, who kept the Jewel of Seven Stars to himself for three thousand years.

Then comes a handsome man all in black. His clothes are Elizabethan in cut, but his sharp moustache is 1920s style. He carries a plaster skull in one hand and a duelling sword in the other.

"Time is out of joint," John Barrymore announces. "O curséd spite, that e'er I was born to set it right."

Next is Edwin.

He comes together as he was long before she knew him, in a muddy officer's uniform, young and haunted, ears ringing from bombardments.

"I died," he says. "In the trenches. The rest was just in my mind. No. Geneviève. You were part of it. The world after the War."

She takes his hand, feels him calm down.

"There were shadows like men," he says.

Now, a woman joins them. Maureen Mountmain, as full of life as when Geneviève fed off her. She is less bewildered than the others.

"It's the end of it," she says. "Mimsy must be stopped."

A young man Geneviève does not know has appeared. He wears cycling shorts and a baggy T-shirt. Very 1990s. His temples are shaved.

"Who are you?" she asks.

"Despatch, love."

He opens a shoulder-bag, and looks for a parcel.

The final member of the seven is Dr. Shade, the comic-strip avenger. He emerges from the last of the red mist, cloak trailing. His face is covered by a surgical mask and goggles.

A fictional character?

"That was a rush," says Dr. Shade. "Gené, you bit me. You really bit me." It is Jerome. He pulls down his mask, and presses his tongue to his teeth.

"But I'm not a vampire," he says. "What am I?"

"You look like Dr. Shade," she says.

"That makes sense."

"I'm glad it does to someone."

Death has made Jerome jauntier. He isn't the serious Information Analyst she remembers. He has inwardly taken on some of the aspects of the pulp hero whose uniform he wears.

"We're the old world's last hope," Pai-net'em says, not out loud but in their minds. "We are to check the plagues, and destroy the jewel."

The bike messenger, in particular, looks appalled.

Jerome's mind still races, dragging Geneviève who is still aware of the ties of blood between them along behind him.

"I know who you are," Jerome says to the messenger.

"I'm Connor," the cyclist says.

"You're my dad," Jerome says. "You died."

"We all died," Edwin says.

"And we will all die again," says Pai-net'em. "Our sacrifice will heal the world. Pharaoh can rule again, justly."

Pai-net'em had a lot to learn about Derek Leech.

"Why us?" Jerome asks. "Why us seven?"

"Because we're all responsible for it," Maureen says. "We touched it and it touched us. We died so that the Seven Stars might rise, in the body of my daughter. Some of us were destroyed long before our bodies were broken."

Barrymore nods, understanding.

"And now we're going to die again?" says Connor. "No, thank you very much. I didn't lay down my life to redeem the world. I was knocked over by a fucking van."

"Dad!" Jerome says, shocked. He is older than his father got to be.

"You lived on in him," Geneviève says.

"Big deal. He's dead too, right? What a mess. I wasn't going to ride a bike all my life. I was young. I could have made it. I had projects."

"Excuse me, Connor," begins Edwin. "Few of us are here by choice. We all resisted being part of this Circle. We didn't volunteer. Except for the first of us."

He looks at Pai-net'em, the Pharaoh's minister.

"And the last," Geneviève adds, remembering Jerome baring his throat.

"And who are you all?" Connor asked.

"We're the psychic detectives, Dad," Jerome says, sounding more like Dr. Shade than ever. "We're the Three Musketeers and the Four Just Men, the Seven Samurai and the Seven Sinners. We are the masked avengers and the spirits of justice, protectors of the innocent and defenders of the defenceless. We are the last hope of humankind. There are mysteries to be solved, wrongs to be righted, monsters to be vanquished. Now, are you with us? To death and glory, for love and life?"

Barrymore looks as if he wished he'd made that speech.

Maureen wants to make love with this masked man, *now*!

Edwin is quietly proud. Jerome Rhodes would have been Diogenes Club material.

"If you put it like that, *son*," Connor says, "include me in."

The Seven are whole.

Complete.

She feels their strength growing.

They stand together, in a circle. They link hands, and their strengths flow into each other.

"Pardon me for intruding in this inspirational moment," Leech says, through a loudspeaker, "but we are on a timetable."

Leech has made available to them a customised short-hop skimmer. Jerome recognises the lines, and realises it is a Rolls-Royce ShadowShark, melded with an assault helicopter and a space shuttle. It is sleek, black and radar-invisible.

Geneviève imagines Leech must be a little sad at parting with it. It is a wonderful toy.

Jerome, of course, knows how to fly the ShadowShark.

The flight is already keyed into the vehicle's manifest. She could have guessed where it is supposed to end. It is where it all started.

Egypt.

She is the last to board.

Leech is there to see them off. She knows that he wishes he were part of it.

Some would have traded with him if they could. From her, they knew what Nostre-Dame foresaw for them. To succeed in this, they would have to die. Again.

"I will see you when this is over," Leech says.

"If Michel wasn't playing a joke."

She climbs into the ShadowShark.

* * *

Continental Europe is mottled with fires. Rockets streak in from the Urals. Jerome easily bests the missiles. There are flying creatures, nesting among the cloud-shields. The skimmer takes evasive action.

The Seven no longer need to talk.

Geneviève, used to touching the minds of those she feeds on, is knotted emotionally by how much more complex, more vital this is.

For the first time, she is alive and aware. Going on alone afterwards will be a tragedy. She will be haunted forever by the loss of this companionship, this clarity, this love.

She senses the bindings growing. Between Connor and Jerome is a rope of blood kinship. She is strung between Maureen and Jerome, both of whom have given life to her. Pai-net'em and Barrymore and Winthrop fit into the circle, perfectly. Their similarities are bonds. Their differences are complements.

They drink of her memories, the many lives she has sampled. She lets Pai-net'em's ancient history and Barrymore's blazing talent flow into her. She knows their loves: Edwin's life-long irritated devotion to Catriona, Maureen's hot burst of generous desire with Jeperson, Connor's calculated but real attachment to Sally.

Throughout their times, the Seven have revolved around the Jewel of Seven Stars, closing in on a tiny constellation. Between them, they understand the bauble, a lump of red malice tossed at the Earth, and know its limitations.

As they close on the Nile, they become more aware of the pulsing thing at the end of their flight path. They are hooked, and being reeled in.

If she could stop time, this is the moment she would pick.

Before the holocaust.

By the bubbling waters of the Nile squats a clear ruby pyramid, in which burn the Seven Stars.

At first, Geneviève thinks the jewel has grown to giant size, dwarfing the sphinx and the old pyramids, but it is a solid projection.

The jewel is inside.

Multitudes gather on the shores of the great river. In the past months, cults have sprung up for the worship of the Seven Stars, or emerged from historic secrecy to declare themselves the Acolytes of the Plagues. Oblations are offered up to the Red Pyramid.

Occasionally, swathes of death are cut through the crowds. That merely encourages more to gather, pressing closer, praying and starving and burning and rotting. Robed priests ritually cast themselves into the boiling river.

Having been dead, twice, and begun to form a sense of what comes after, Geneviève at last knows the Jewel of Seven Stars is not a magical object. It offers only random cessation, cruel and needless.

It does not create anything.

Pai-net'em, who lay with the jewel in him, listening through the years to its insectile whisper, thinks it was a machine. Barrymore, who tore genius from himself as he was driven on by the jewel, feels it to be a malign imp. Maureen still believes it the catspaw of the Elder Gods for whom her uncles devoted their lives to blaspheming. To Edwin, it is a puzzle to be solved and put away. To Connor, it is unjust death, robbing him of the future. To Jerome, it is all misinformation, all garbage, all lies, all negatives, all deadtech.

And to her?

It is her enemy. And her salvation.

She knows now why the first curse—the Plague of Dogs—was aimed at her. Mimsy must have accessed the suppressed quatrains, probably when she took over the premises and archives of the Diogenes Club. Mimsy Mountmain had enough of a human mind to know that the vampire who had left traces of herself in her veins was the focus of the Circle of Seven, the only force which could break the weirdstone.

She's still my daughter, thinks Maureen.

Geneviève is infected with love for the girl in the Red Pyramid. The girl who looks so like her, as she was before the Dark Kiss, who has also been robbed of a life, of love and a world, by the Jewel of Seven Stars.

Mimsy is going to die too.

The ShadowShark settles by the Red Pyramid, on a stretch of sand blasted into glass. There are corpses set in the glass, staring up at the red sky.

They get out of the skimmer, and look at the Red Pyramid. The Seven Stars shine, trapped inside.

Geneviève feels assaulted in her mind, as when the whine that maddened dogs was killing her. The steel plate in her skull grows hot.

Pai-net'em wipes the sound from her mind.

She stands, propped up by Maureen. Her mind feels clean, invigorated. Together, they are strong. Barrymore and Pai-net'em open a portal in the side of the Pyramid, extending their hands and willing a door to appear. On the lintel, Barrymore creates masks of Tragedy and Comedy, which Pai-net'em equips with sphinx bodies.

Barrymore gives a theatrical bow.

A whip-like tendril shoots out of the portal and lashes the actor. His flesh explodes, bursting his doublet and hose. His skull, still moustached, looks surprised. He collapses. His voice dies in their mind.

It is a needle of pain. The loss is a devastation.

Pai-net'em grasps the tendril with both hands, and yanks hard, wrenching it loose. As he pulls, a grey wrinkling runs up his arms. His face withers to mummy-shape, and he crumbles again, coming apart as dust and dirt.

Coming hard on the first loss, this knocks the Circle back. Only Jerome is strong enough in himself to support the others.

They are all going to die. She had known that. But these first deaths are still deadly blows.

Her heart is stone.

Edwin takes the lead, and steps over the still-twitching tendril. She follows, and the others come after her.

Connor, she knows, wants to turn and flee, to go far from the Pyramid, to make a life here, in this world, to have all the things he missed. Only his tie to Jerome, which he doesn't understand, keeps him on course. To him, it is possible that this is some dying fantasy, as Edwin had thought his whole post-1917 life was, and that it doesn't matter.

A tunnel leads straight to the heart of the Red Pyramid.

Statues look down at them. Faces that mean something. Voices plead and threaten.

To Edwin, it is Catriona above all. Also Declan and Bennett Mountmain, Charles Beauregard and Mycroft Holmes.

To Maureen, it is Mimsy, Richard, Leech.

To Connor, it is the agents and producers who could have opened a life for him. Contracts are offered, cheques processed, projects green-lighted.

To Jerome, it is Mum, Neil, Sister Chantal, Roger Duroc.

To her, it is the Three.

Forgotten lives, taken in red fugues. Dafydd le Gallois, Sergei Bukharin, Annie Marriner.

And Jerome. Not Three any more, Four.

Her dead call to her, cajole, promise, abuse, fret.

There are others, a myriad bled and sampled and absorbed. They bother her like gnats. She is torn into by Chandagnac, the minstrel who had turned her and been destroyed when she might have saved him. And all those she had known and let die by not passing on the Dark Kiss, all she had let grow old and die by not succouring them with her blood.

She is a selfish parasite. She should not continue this charade of heroism.

The world is well lost, and her with it.

Jerome saves her, this time. The most recently dead, he has less time to brood, to adjust, less sense of business left unfinished. Bolstered by those aspects of Dr. Shade he has taken into himself, he fights off his temptations first, and is available to help her through.

He doesn't blame her. He is grateful to her.

In this adventure, he has finally come to know his father, to understand his mother, to get out of his monad and become a part of something greater than himself. At last, he has found a realwelt as vital to him as the Info-World.

She climbs along the thread of his love. She leaves her dead behind.

The silencing of the voices comes at a cost. Connor is empty and dry and old. Edwin riddled with bullet-wounds, choking on poison gas, caked with the filth of Flanders. They are not destroyed, but they can go no further.

"Go, for us, as for yourselves," Edwin says.

Jerome stands between Maureen and her. He takes their hands, and leads them into the centre of the Red Pyramid.

A final door opens.

The Jewel of Seven Stars is wearing Mimsy Mountmain. Geneviève feels, after 600 years, that she is looking into a broken mirror. Mimsy's hair is still long, and her face is a perfect thing of tiny jewel facets of red fire.

This is where the plagues came from.

"Mimsy," Maureen appeals.

The Jewel Woman turns, red-screen eyes noting their presence.

Jerome raises Dr. Shade's gas-gun and fires at the Jewel Woman. His pellet shatters against the gem-shields over her face. Once, there was a girl. Her tiny wishes and frustrations, nurtured by the jewel, powered the thing, pouring energy into it like a battery, subtly shaping the forms of the plagues it wreaks. Now, that girl is gone, a footnote. This is an alien. Geneviève isn't sure whether it is a creature or a machine, a god or a demon. If it has thoughts, they are beyond her understanding. If it has feelings, they are unearthly.

Maureen tries to love the jewel, to venerate it, to wake her daughter.

If it had fallen on another world, among other beings, would it have been different? Was it humanity that used this gift to unleash plagues? The first time, when Pharaoh gazed into its depths and wished to extend his rule beyond the known world, it was an accident, but man's character had let loose something that was somehow deserved.

Now, could Mimsy really be responsible? She had been shaped and robbed of choice as much as anyone else. Nostradamus had seen her fixed course too. The shadowmen that had taken Edwin were accumulating, in other forms, in this Red Pyramid. Mimsy was already wrapped in darkness.

Maureen touches Mimsy. The Jewel Woman thins.

"It's all right, love," Maureen says. "Let it end."

Mimsy's face, soft and bewildered, is clear. The jewel carapace is gone. Jerome shoots her in the head.

Geneviève feels the pellet passing into her own brain.

Eyes alive with betrayal, Mimsy falls, the Jewel of Seven Stars rolling from her chest. The years, held back by the spell, surge like a tide as Mimsy grows old and dies within seconds. She is a corpse before the discharge from Dr. Shade's gas-gun dissipates.

Maureen sobs. Geneviève hugs her, pulled close by their blood-bond. They are both ripped open by the death of the girl who had come from both of them.

The jewel is still active. It had been inside Maureen when Mimsy was conceived, when Geneviève tasted her blood. It is the dead girl's heart. The Seven Stars throb inside it, like drops of glowing blood.

The Red Pyramid is collapsing around them. Scarlet dust cascades.

Jerome picks up the Jewel of Seven Stars. Its lights reflect in his goggles. Through him, Geneviève feels its tug. It opens up possibilities. It is a source of great power. If they keep it, maybe it can be focused. For good. The world need not be left for Leech.

Jerome might *become* Dr. Shade, not just dress as him. No, says Pai-net'em. He is still part of them, freed if anything by his second death. Not yet. Perhaps never. The stone is at its weakest, emptied of plague, its host torn away, its influence overextended. It can be ended. Now.

Maureen is dead in Geneviève's embrace. She lays the woman down, brushing white hair away from her beautiful face. She has tried to do her best, to escape her family's past, to find something of worth in her inheritance. Of them all, she has loved the most.

There is night all around. The pyramid is thinned to a structure of fading light-lines. The jewel-worshippers wail at a sensed loss.

Jerome makes a fist around the jewel and squeezes. The red glow is wrapped in his black leather gauntlet.

She hears the first crack. Jerome squeezes harder.

"Get out of range, Gené," he says. "When this goes, I go with it. I have to die again, mind. You get to live forever. Tell Mum Connor was one of the good guys . . ."

The others are growing thin in her mind. Loneliness is gathering like a shadow.

Without the Seven Stars, how will humankind fare?

What is left for her?

"Go on, Gené. Run."

"No," she says. "It's not fair."

She takes the jewel from him. She is far stronger than him. Vampires have the grip of iron.

"You died for me last time," she says, kissing him. "Now, it's my turn. Give Sally your own message. And watch out for the world. Try not to let Derek Leech get back too much of what he had. And play outside sometimes."

She leaves him, faster than he can register, darting with vampire swiftness through the transparent ruins. She runs out into the desert, fleet enough to skim over the soft sands. The Jewel of Seven Stars screams in her mind as she squeezes it. The faults grind against each other, the starfires boil.

It is not too late to give in.

She could *use* the weirdstone.

Other voices give her strength.

There is a loophole in Nostre-Dame, as usual. If she dies a third time, the obligation is lifted from Jerome.

She is far from the Nile, far from water, lost in unchanging sandscape. This country has not changed since she was born. Not since the settling of the continents.

She falls to her knees and looks up at the sky. Twinkling in the night, she sees Ursa Major. It is back again. The plagues are over.

The world is set to rights.

And is on its own.

Dafydd, Sergei, Annie, Jerome.

She deserves this.

But at last she accepts forgiveness.

She crushes the jewel to red grit. Seven flames burst into fireballs, and she burns with love.

All find their moments.

Pai-net'em is honoured by Old Pharaoh, the great and wise king.

Edwin sees Catriona's smile for the first time.

John Barrymore is assaulted by applause.

Maureen Mountmain cradles Mimsy to her breast, and shares perfect love.

Connor gets the green-light on a life.

She is in the British Museum, snatching a glimpse of the reflection of a man's face, thinking of possibilities.

Jerome is free of them, journeying into the unknowable future. The thread that connects them to him stretches, and then breaks.

The sand drifts over her bones, burying them with a red scatter of jewel fragments. The Seven Stars pass from the skies, and the sun rises on the desert.

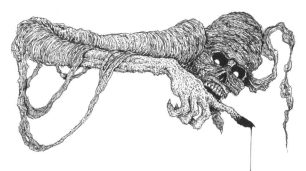

ACKNOWLEDGEMENTS

With special thanks to Dorothy Lumley, Steve Saffel, Natalie Laverick, Randy Broecker, Robert T. Garcia, Michael Marshall Smith, Mandy Slater, Jo Fletcher, Mike Ashley, Sara Broecker, Brian Lumley, Basil Copper, F. Paul Wilson, Steve Rasnic Tem, Douglas E. Winter, Stefan Dziemianowicz and, especially, Kim Newman. My gratitude as always to the late Philip J. Rahman for his kindness and support as a publisher.

ABOUT THE EDITOR

STEPHEN JONES is one of Britain's most acclaimed anthologists of horror and dark fantasy. He has more than 130 books to his credit, including Shadows Over Innsmouth, Weird Shadows Over Innsmouth *and* Weirder Shadows Over Innsmouth. *He has won numerous awards for his work, including three World Fantasy Awards, four Bram Stoker Awards and a Lifetime Achievement Award from the Horror Writers Association. You can visit his website at www.stephenjoneseditor.com.*

ABOUT THE ARTIST

RANDY BROECKER was born and lives in Chicago, Illinois. Inspired by the pulp magazines and EC comics he read as a child, his work has appeared in numerous books and magazines published on both sides of the Atlantic, including Weird Shadows Over Innsmouth *and* Weirder Shadows Over Innsmouth. *He was Artist Guest of Honour at the 2002 World Horror Convention and is the author of the World Fantasy Award-nominated study* Fantasy of the 20th Century: An Illustrated History *from Collector's Press.*